Queen of Cups: Part 2

James Durose-Rayner

Published by New Generation Publishing in 2017

Copyright © James Durose-Rayner 2017

First Edition

www.newgeneration-publishing.com

 New Generation Publishing

This is the second of the third part of a trilogy

I Am Sam
ITV 7
Queen of Cups: Part 1

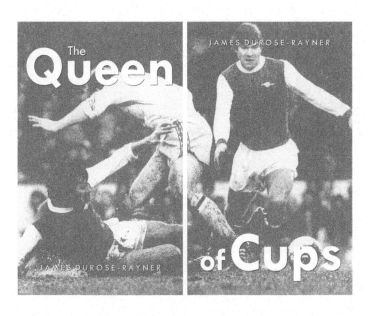

Cover Photograph. *Hunting in packs. Alan Hudson and Malcolm Macdonald win the ball in a game against Aston Villa at Highbury on 4th February, 1978.*
The foundations were being laid for something very special - however, history will tell you that these were never built on.

The Chapters. Queen of Cups: Part 2

*Questi giorni quando vieni, il bel Sole ...la la la la la-la-la-la, la la la
la. On days like these, when skies are blue, and fields are green.
I look around, and think about, what might have been.
And then I hear sweet music, float around my head.
As I recall, the many things, we left unsaid.
It's on days like these, that I, remember,
singing songs and drinking wine,
while your eyes played games with mine...*

*On days like these, I wonder, what became of you.
Maybe today, you are singing songs, with someone new.
I'd like to think, you're walking by, those willow trees.
Remembering, the lovely youth, on days like these.
And it's on days like these that I, remember.
Singing songs and drinking wine,
While your eyes play games with mine.*

*On days like these I wonder what became of you,
Maybe today, you are singing songs with someone new,
Questi giorni quando vieni, il bel Sole ...la la la la la-la-la-la, la la la la.*

On Days Like These, *Matt Monro 1969.*
From ***The Italian Job***

Chapter 27

On Days Like These

I woke up to two excited kids jumping on our bed.

"Dad, come on – the pool's great, are you getting up?" asked my daughter.

I looked at my watch, which told me that it was a quarter to eight.

"Come on dad," said my lad. "It's great."

"Where's M?" I asked.

"Making some breakfast," he said.

Just then, we were graced by her presence. "Are yer getting up?" she twanged.

"I've only just gone to bed," I told her.

I had. I'd been driving through the Alps, everyone chatting on whilst Matt Monro was in the CD player singing *On Days Like These* and geeing us all up for our *Italian Job* – and by the time we'd entered Northern Italy everyone was asleep, including my not-so trusty co-pilot who had been drooling against the window.

"Oi – you're supposed to be keeping me company," I'd told her.

That was while I was driving around Turin. By the time, I had hit the millionth Toll booth and just before we got to Genoa, she along with everyone else was bailing out zed's.

Tuscany had been our destination and now we were here. And I had to say it was lovely, but driving as opposed to flying – and on the wrong side of the road, was never something that I was ever going to look forward to. Emily on the other hand had got out the maps and itinerary and had made it sound great, and sold it to the kids, so much so, that they had been extremely excited.

"Dad can I take all my DVD's?" my lad had asked.

1

"No, I'll put them on a media box for you," I said.

"How can all my DVD's fit in one of those?"

"Easy," I'd told him.

Still, it made him ponder about it quite a bit – so much so, he'd asked Emily to confirm it to him. About a hundred times.

"It's like a little computer," she'd told him. "You can store loads of information in them."

"I've got some bacon and eggs on," smiled Emily, back in real time. "You want to have a look around – the house is absolutely gorgeous."

"Where's Herbert?" I asked.

"He was trying to ram the baby walker into the fridge about half an hour ago, which must have tired him out as he's now having forty winks."

"What time did you get up?" I asked.

"About seven."

"So, you've only had about nine hours sleep then?" I winked.

"Shurrup you," she twanged.

I went downstairs and into the kitchen to the smell of bacon and to see Herbert laid flat-out in his *hammock*.

"Doesn't he want any breakfast?" I asked.

"He's had it," said his mum. "He threw Weetabix all over the place. It took me ages to get it off the wall."

That made me laugh.

I picked up my bacon and egg sandwich and the kids took me outside to give me a guided tour of the pool area.

"Is looks deep," I said, whilst looking into the pool.

"Will you throw us in, after?" asked my lad.

"Sure," I said.

Emily slithered up to me and told me how nice everything was. Well that was until Herbert heard us talking then bawled out a few superlatives in baby talk, but seeing as though he could only say "Uh" for "Yes" – "Uh uh" for "No" – and "Bwaaaaaaah" for just about everything else. This was basically one of the latter.

"Stick a lifebelt on him and sling him in the pool," I said.

"The sun's not out yet," said my wife. "It'll be cold."

"Can we go in the pool?" asked my daughter.

"Yeh – do what you want," I said.

That was it and five minutes later there were two splashes followed by, "Crikey it's freezing" and then they were sat on the pool chairs with towel's draped around them and both chattering like a pair of Jackdaw's.

"We need to go shopping," said Emily. "As we didn't bring a great deal of food with us."

"I suppose *Tesco Online* isn't an option?" I asked.

"Highly doubtful," she smiled.

We patrolled the grounds and checked out the house before we jumped in the Mean Machine to do a recce on the town of San Gimignano.

"Have they got a football team, Dad?" asked my lad.

"No idea – although Florence isn't that far away," I told him.

"*Florence* like that girl on that *Magic Roundabout* programme that you used to watch when you were a little boy?" he asked.

"Exactly," I said.

That got him thinking.

"Is *Dougal* a place in Italy as well?"

"No, I think Dougal's a Scottish name."

"It is," said Emily. "It means black stranger."

"Shouldn't we talk to him then?" asked my lad.

"Who?" I asked.

"*Dougal* – that black stranger."

That set Emily off laughing.

"Mum says that Ross's dad brought a black stranger home."

"Really," I said.

"Yeh – he wasn't called Dougal though," said my lad.

"No, he was called Brian," added my daughter.

"Like the snail on *Magic Roundabout*, again," commented my lad. "He didn't wear a straw hat though."

By now Emily was in stitches.

Brian had actually been Ross's father's friend and was a Christian priest or pastor or whatever they call them – from

3

Namibia I think, and for the record he was an extremely amiable guy.

"He right got on my nerves," said my daughter. "Every time he said a word with an 'S' in it, he whistled."

"He'd make a good referee then?" I winked.

"He laughed like that giant black man off *Live and Let Die*," noted my lad, before giving us a booming "Ha, ha, ha, ha".

He did – he was right.

We drove through the countryside and into the town, parked up and slung Herbert in his buggy. Our remit being to procure some groceries and meat, whilst his elder brothers shopping list was somewhat different.

"I want some flippers for the pool," he had said.

"We're in the middle of the country – this isn't the seaside," I said.

Nevertheless, he still wanted a pair of flippers.

The town was lovely, with its narrow streets and stone houses, some of which had flowers hanging from window trays. It seemed a million miles from both London and Liverpool. That was until I copped sight of some man I thought I had seen before ride past on a scooter.

"I'm sure I've seen that guy before," I told Emily, who obviously hadn't, as at the time Herbert had slung his tippy cup full of orange.

"Oi, behave you," she smiled.

We bought about ten carrier bags full of groceries, before we hit the Macelleria and it was then I knew we were in Italy.

"M this is brilliant," I said, as we went inside and ordered different types of sausage, salami and such.

"I thought it might be," she winked.

I made a hole in what at one time would have been about a billion Lira and carted it back to the Mean Machine.

"What about my flippers," my lad had asked.

"Let's dump this lot first, and we'll go look," I said. "I've got arms like Stretch Armstrong."

"What the olden day's winger for Arsenal?" asked my lad.

"No, that's George Armstrong," I said.

4

We had another look around before we got plonked outside a tavern and I ordered a couple of coffees for us and some pop for the kids – much to the displeasure of Herbert, who immediately wanted to know why the wheels on his buggy had suddenly ceased turning – firstly by going rigid, then trying his utmost to escape from his hell.

"Oi Sammy – behave," I told him.

We had another wonder around – and actually did find a shop that sold snorkels, goggles and flippers, as well as a shoe shop that did a nice line in Italian designer shoes, which certainly aroused Emily's interest. "We should drive to Milan, while we are here," I told her. "There's some great shoe shops there."

"Could we go to the San Siro?" asked my lad.

"Sure," I told him.

"Have you been there before," M inquired.

I had. I was one of the few thousand present who saw Arsenal spank Inter Milan 5-1 – in one of the best performances by any English team abroad ever – and in a season where Arsenal should have won the lot.

"Did you go with Jeanette?" Emily asked.

I nodded, and suddenly saw a change of expression on my wife's face.

"M?" I shrugged.

"I'm sorry," she said. "Every now and then I think I've got you and we are doing something new together, then I find out you've done it before."

"I've never done any of this before," I said, as we walked around the piazza, watching both my eldest kids hop and skip a couple of yards in front of us. "I went to Milan to see a game of football."

I could understand where she was coming from, as I felt the same at times – however, with Emily there were no obvious reminders to stimulate any jealousy.

"I wish I'd met you first," she'd sometimes tell me.

The thing is, our life together is nothing like it was with me and Jeanette. M doesn't nag for one.

"So, these shoe shops, then?" she winked.

See?

We soaked up the sunny morning walking around and got back to the farmhouse to see a guy coming out of the gate, who we assumed must have been the caretaker.

What does he want? I wondered.

"How the hell are you?" he asked – albeit rather dramatically, as I dropped down my window.

"Good," I said.

"Lee and Emily," added my wife, as she got out the car and shook his hand. "We got here in the early hours."

John and his wife Hazel looked after the place and he assured us that everything in the house was *spot on.* "So, have you had a good look around?" he asked.

The last thing Emily nor I wanted was a long drawn out conversation about the property and both its history and surroundings, as we were here to enjoy the holiday – nevertheless, we certainly got it.

After M had eventually chucked him out, we put away the shopping and I nipped out onto the patio to catch up on some work.

Emily had done well – this place was about as good as it gets.

As my eldest two kids played over on one of the lawns, my wife made her entrance through the patio doors – both holding Sammy and wearing only a white bikini, and it was moments such as this that I really did wish that I had met her first. I have always said that she was perfection and I wasn't lying. Who could have ever mistreated her and had her leave? Only an idiot.

Just then.

"Someone's knocking at the door, somebody's ringing the bell – Someone's knocking at the door, somebody's ringing the bell – Do me a favour open the door and let me in ooo-yeah," sung a voice through the Tannoy at the other side of the gate that formed the entrance to the walled property. "Harmony Hairspray der-der-der – Brother Jam – Little Sammy der-der-der, Lee and M – so open the door and plea-ee-ese, let me i-i-i- i-i-i- i-i-i- in …Ooo-yeah."

I looked over at M, who just shrugged her shoulders.

6

I answered the voice at the other side of the gate and my worst fears were immediately realised. I had a Tottenham fan in my midst.

"The main man – Mr. Ars-e-naaaaal," he said, as he walked up to me and gave me a pretend shadow box, before focusing his attention on my daughter. "Harmony Hairspray give me a twirl."

He then picked up my daughter and threw her around eight foot up into the air and duly caught her on the way back down.

"Do me," insisted my lad, and fair play to him – he did.

"Sorry our Lee," said Stuart, as he trudged up the long path alongside me with his head down. "He made us fetch him."

A sorry looking Ginge followed on, "Yeh, sorry Lee."

Pedro had that effect on most people.

"Whoooof, M baby," he said, as he caught sight of my wife in her bikini. "What a figure – turnaround, bend over and touch your toes and let me see how much ya love me."

"Yeh right," she said. "What are you doing here?"

"We're planning a heist," he winked at my kids. "We are going to steal two billion tons of gold bullion from Juventus and drive it back to Tottenham in six Mini Coopers."

"Are you Pedro?" asked my lad.

"It's so Spurs can build their new stadium, employ an idiot manager and have ten years without a trophy," he lied. "But you can't tell anyone as it's a secret."

"But Tottenham haven't won anything in ages," stated my daughter.

"Yeh, they have," he argued. "We won the League Cup seven years ago, against Spartak Fulham, hammering Ars-e-nal in the Semi-Final on our way to total glory."

My lad quite rightly pointed out that there was no such club as Spartak Fulham.

"He means Chelsea," explained my daughter.

"Harmony Hairspray – not only totally beautiful, but also extremely clever," he winked, before he started cracking his knuckles and rubbing his hands together. "Just like her wicked stepmother, who if she needs any sun tan lotion

7

rubbing, in some of those hard to reach spots – then I'm her man."

"He's been like that for the last three hundred miles," whispered Ginge. "He's done both our heads in."

"The pool looks mega, M – any chance of borrowing those little ker-beeny bottoms that you're wearing so I can have a dip," asked our unwanted guest, whilst doing a bit of a cha-cha-charring with my daughter and having both kids laughing.

"I'll lend you some shorts," I told him.

"I'd prefer a pair of your M's bikini bottoms," he argued. "Preferably those that's she's wearing."

"Tough luck," she told him.

Pedro was supposedly on his European Tour which involved Paris, Stuttgart, Munich, Geneva, Milan and Rome – him obviously thinking that San Gimignano was some natural stopping off point.

"We're not in Rome until the fourth," he said, whilst stripping off his shirt and looking over at the pool, "so I thought I'd pop in and see how the Gooner jet-set live."

"Are you going in the pool?" asked my daughter.

A massive splash instantly answered her question, which was quickly followed by both kids joining him.

"We've checked into a hotel in the town," said Ginge. "*Dickhead* was adamant that he wanted to stay with you. I did tell him 'no', mate."

The paradox that was Pedro was at times totally unfathomable, but both my kids thought he was great. That however, may have been due to the fact, that he was indeed, completely brain dead – something which was made more than apparent whilst he played at *being a shark* in the pool for two solid hours, continually tipping them out of their dinghy and pretending to chew them up.

Herbert awoke from his afternoon slumber and pointed out the fact that there was indeed a stranger in our midst. He didn't say a deal – just pointed.

"A-Argh Sam lad," Pedro said, in his rather exaggerated Long John Silver-stroke-Mike Channon accent. "Are you coming to swab the deck with these two filthy landlubbers?"

As already stated, Sammy's vocabulary was fairly limited at this stage – however, and here's the thing, it only took him an hour to learn Pedro's name.

"Peedo" he pointed.

"No love," smiled his mum. "It's Pedro."

The Ladyboy that was Pedro had some unexplainable energy about him, and my kids couldn't get enough of it. Me and Emily certainly could, but the kids – they were mesmerised and in complete awe of the man.

To see him live on set, he was as is the name of his band – electric. He was an extremely aggressive individual, who always made sure that he smashed up the place and argued with anyone and everyone – however, watching him at the table with my three kids, was – well lovely, to be honest. He told them the story about him and his big brother caravanning in Southend and Clacton when they were kids and how excited they used to be when their dad had taken them fishing – and of course how much he loved his mum and dad.

"My mum's really nice," he told them. "A bit like M and your mum."

"What about your dad?" asked Harmony.

"He's nice too, but he's getting a bit forgetful in his old age," he winked. "He forgets to tell me that he loves me – not like your dad does with you."

That certainly got Emily's bottom lip wobbling.

That night we didn't get to bed until late and next morning we were flat out until…

"Who is this super hero?" yelled an exaggerated American Voice. "Jamie? Nope. Harmony the telephone operator? Nope. Pedro the mild-mannered janitor? Could be?"

This was followed by both Pedro and my daughter singing.

"Crikey –he's started early," smiled Emily, referring to *Hong Kong Phooey* – the number one super guy.

"Clean your teeth fellow anglers," boomed the voice of Pedro.

"What about our Sammy – does have to clean his teeth?" I heard my daughter say.

"Of course, he does," Pedro replied. "All five of them – go fetch the sweeping brush."

My lad came into the bedroom, whilst brushing his teeth. "Pedro's taking us down to that river at the bottom of the garden to catch some fish," he said.

"What – he's taking our Sammy as well?" I asked.

"Yeh," he replied, whilst spitting toothpaste everywhere, which was quickly followed by the unwanted visitor popping his head around the door. "Just going down to that stream with the young 'uns, Lee – that's unless M wants you to take them instead, while I stay here and keep her company."

Emily threw her pillow at the door.

"Thought as much," he grinned.

With the house empty, Emily gave me a cuddle and suggested a bit of yer-knowing. "I need to put the air-con on for a bit though," she said. "As it's definitely too warm for my stockings."

"Oh yeh?" I winked.

She sat up in bed, hit the remote for the air-con, pushed her hair back behind her ears, crossed her legs and deliberated for a bit. "Mr. Raybold" she nodded. "We should definitely do him."

"Who the hell is he?"

"I'm going to tell you, if yer shurrup for a minute," she winked.

I watched on as she proceeded to tell me the story about some guy who once lived near her mum and dads on Allerton Road – the infamous Mr. Raybold. "He looked a bit like that Arsenal football player from the olden days who Jamie was on about the other day – him with the long hair and no teeth," she said.

I was at a loss. "No teeth – who's that, Paul Merson?"

"No, not him," she said. "He had a right old looking face. He played in the same side as Sammy."

"Ian Ure?"

"Don't know him."

"George Armstrong?"

"Yeh that's him," she said.

"George Armstrong had teeth," I corrected her.

"Shurrup will yer and let me tell you the story?" she grinned, as she slipped into something a bit more comfortable – or in this case, uncomfortable, as the air-con hadn't yet had time to work its magic. "Mr. Raybold was much taller though – about six inches bigger than you."

"Six inches?" I inquired.

"Possibly seven," she winked. "Definitely much bigger than you."

I was hooked.

"My auntie had had this New Year's Eve party," she added.

"Which auntie?" I asked.

"Does it matter?" she shrugged.

"Course it matters – I like to know the scenery and the layout," I told her.

"Auntie Heather's," she nodded. "As I definitely remember Uncle Jimmy being *on one.*"

"On one, what?"

She shrugged her shoulders. "They were all out in the back garden – I think him and Uncle Stan were arguing with some revellers."

I could never keep track of M's thousands of aunties and uncles – none of who were actually aunties or uncles, but just cousins or second cousins of Mike and Sil'.

"I'd only be young – about fifteen or sixteen, when he sort of asked me for a New Year's kiss," she explained.

"Who your Uncle Stan?"

"No yer twit – Mr. Raybold."

Yeh – still hooked.

"So, as yer do, I gave him a peck on the cheek," she smiled. "And he gave me some money out of his pocket – fifty pence."

There was a short pause

"That it?"

"Yeh – did you like it?" she grinned.

"That's a right rubbish story," I told her.

"Oh right, so you wanted me to tell you what happened after that?" she shrugged. "The sort of whole story?"

"Why, isn't that it?"

No, it certainly wasn't it. It turned out that with no one being in the room, Mr. Raybold had pushed her up against the door and wanted a bit more for his money and had stuck his tongue down her throat. "It really shocked me," she said. "As he had a right nice wife and two children."

"What about your mum and dad?"

Emily shrugged. "What about them?"

"Where were they?"

"I can't remember off hand," she shrugged. "Probably outside."

"So, what happened?"

"That was it," she said. "Apart from him trying to get me over on to the settee."

Yeh – definitely hooked.

"I told him that I'd tell my dad if he didn't stop," she added.

"Did it stop him?"

"Uh sort of," she said.

"Sort of?"

"Yeh – he told me I had to kiss him back or he'd take the money back off me."

I was totally loving this story.

"And?" I inquired.

"Well I had to kiss him back, didn't I?" she said. "However, what happened after that really, really upset me."

"Why?" was always going to be my next question.

"It turned out that he had been giving one of my school friends who lived on Kelvin Road a pound a time just for her to show him her knickers," she said. "And I'd had to give him a long horrible kiss for just fifty pence."

"Didn't you offer to show him your knickers?" I inquired.

"No, because I didn't know about it until her dad had found sixty-three pounds under her bed and called the police."

That made me laugh.

"She wasn't all that good looking either," my wife informed me. "You definitely wouldn't have fancied her."

"Not my type?"

"Nope," she replied, whilst shaking her head.

"Who is my type, then?"

"Definitely me," she smiled.

"Are you sure about that?"

"Most definitely," she said, whilst playfully prodding me. "So Mr. Raybold, I think you and I have some unfinished business to attend to."

That was it. A deft header by M was followed by some tika-taka from me which had certain parties shouting from the terraces – and after nine minutes of pure unadulterated power-play the ball was in the net – one-nil to The Arsenal and everyone's a winner baby – yeah! As for Mr. Raybold? He was put back in the cupboard for another day, the dirty old fucking pervert.

After a shower, we descended for some breakfast and noticed that Pedro and all three kids had been in the kitchen before us, as there was stuff everywhere – and I mean everywhere. "It'll only take two ticks to clean it up," Emily told me.

Maybe so, if you're using a jet wash, I thought

"Have they been eating Prawns for breakfast?" I asked, looking at all the heads, legs and whiskers in the sink.

"It certainly looks like it," smiled Emily, before asking the question of did I fancy a bacon buttie?

"Most definitely," I replied.

In between tidying up all the mess, Emily made us up a plateful and we went out on to the huge patio, where we could hear all the kids – oh yeh, and Pedro's voice down at the river and where much to the disdain of my wife I got out my laptop.

"I thought you weren't going to do any work for a couple of weeks?" she said.

"I'm not," I lied. "I'm just going to check a few things.

"No, you're not," she replied. "I heard you talking to Tony Fisher and telling him that you were going to try and do some work on that documentary for Chris."

I did admit that the subject had been mentioned.

"You were also picking Brian Allan's brains about West Ham."

I gave her a bit of a shrug.

"That season where Arsenal lost to West Ham in the F.A Cup Final and where Liam Brady and Graham Rix missed penalties in that European final," she added. "At that stadium in Belgium where some Liverpool fans helped get all the English teams banned from Europe."

"Have you been bugging my mobile?" I asked.

"I don't have to bug your mobile to know that when you start talking to Tony – or Brian – or Martin Whittle or Gary Lawrence that there is some seventies documentary that you're on with," she winked. "Plus, I saw those two secret laptops you smuggled on board the Mean Machine that you definitely didn't want me to see."

"I just like football," I told her.

"I know you do," she smiled. "And you work so hard and I love you for it, but it's your eyes that I'm concerned about."

"If you were that concerned about my eyes you wouldn't have made me drive all the way to Italy," I said. "We would have flown."

"You enjoyed it," she lied.

No I didn't," I replied. "It was a really long way – and you went to sleep after you promised that you'd stay awake and keep me company."

"You still love me though?" she winked.

"Maybe?" I lied.

We ate our breakfast out in the sun, whilst I texted Chris to let him know that I had been rumbled – however, rumbled or nothing, I knew nothing would stop me researching both the 1977/78 and 1979/80 seasons as if Arsenal had invested properly, they could have won everything.

We cleaned up and I had a wander down to the river at the bottom of the garden to see Sammy with some water wings and a hat on and sat up in the dinghy in the middle of water, whilst the other three stood in the river with makeshift fishing rods.

"Hello dad," said my daughter. "This is great fun."

"It looks it," I replied, suddenly noticing that they were using our box of prawns as fish bait.

Emily followed me down sat on the grass, crossed her legs, took a few photographs and set off videoing from her phone and couldn't stop laughing at Sammy who was pointing at Pedro and shouting his mum – however, what was going to happen next nobody was expecting – and in all honesty, it was nothing short of brilliant.

"Shiver me timbers," yelled Pedro, in his Long John Silver-stroke-Mike Channon accent, whilst pulling at his makeshift rod, "A-arrgh, I think I may have got one, Jam Lad."

The way the makeshift rod was bending you would have thought he was landing a frigging whale.

"A-arrgh, I think I've got him," shouted the angler, whilst trying is utmost to stop himself being pulled into the stream.

He had indeed got one. A great frigging eel, which had all my kids and even Pedro screaming when they saw it out of the water, as it was nearly five-foot long.

"It's a snake," screamed my daughter.

"Is it dad?" asked my lad, as he dropped his rod to run for cover.

"Nah – it's only an eel."

"Do they bite?" asked my lad looking a bit worried.

Pedro answered that question for him, "Aaargh, the thing's biting me!"

It looked well-impressive as he juggled with it – in scenes reminiscent of Steve Irwin in the dusty Australian outback, trying his hardest not to get chomped by a Taipan during a night time recce out in some dirty great cornfield. "Lee, get it off me!" he screamed.

In the end, it released its vice-like grip on him and we all watched on as he tried his best to look like Alexis Sanchez, using some nifty footwork to try and get it unwrapped from around his legs.

"I hope you're getting all this on camera, M?" I said.

"Most definitely," she laughed.

In the end the eel must have got bored and just slithered off into some reeds.

"Can you catch one again, Pedro?" asked my lad. "That was mint."

I had to admit, I'd not seen anything like that before and it was well worth a €17 box of shrimps to see Pedro get attacked by some deadly eel – and Emily's video footage was top rank. "That'll definitely be going on their European Tour DVD," I laughed.

Pedro staying with us was short-lived and after a few days he was on his merry way to Rome, where they played two shows in front of packed audiences at both the Istituzione Universitaria Concerti and the Init, and where Pedro got involved in some after-gig brawl in some bar just off the Via della stazione tuscolana, split someone's forehead open with a Peroni bottle and ended up spending the night in the cells. Like I said, the paradox that was Peter La Greave was nothing short of unfathomable and the sight of him on stage viciously wrecking everything sight was the total opposite of the kind, caring and stupidly funny lad that had had my kids' total attention for three solid days.

"Nice one Cyril, nice one son, nice one Cyril let's have another one," Pedro had sung to the kids, as he let them know that this had been his No. 1 Tottenham Hotspur song, the night before he had left us to go and allegedly rob Juventus of their gold bullion.

"Do all clubs have songs, Pedro," my lad had asked.

"Sure, they do," he told him.

"My Granddad Bill supports Liverpool," my daughter said. "Their song is 'You'll Never Walk Alone'."

"No, it's not," argued Pedro, and he kicked off singing "We all live in a Robbie Fowler House, a Robbie Fowler house" to the music of *The Beatles' Yellow Submarine* and he had everyone joining in with the chorus – including me and Emily.

Both M and I knew that we were extremely fortunate to have such a beautiful life and be continually surrounded by some of the weirdest and wonderful people.

Chapter 28

Abi's Tales – *Take 4*

With ITV 7 off the air, Lee and M in Italy, Kirsty and Sinead on their holidays. Jeanette over in New York with Ross, Sooty excommunicated and half White Lion Street on tours, you would think that the place would be dead – however, it was anything but. Lee had kicked up a new company in White Lion Films, who both rented office and studio space off LMJ and who also employed Dean Monahan – or Dino rather, a well-heeled film director from Philadelphia, who was in charge of churning out a six-part series titled *The Invincibles* – and with it came a whole host of people. As for me, I had been temporary seconded as his assistant director and had the chance to learn how to put together a drama series from scratch, part of which included the casting.

I'd overseen screen tests and had helped shoot loads of documentaries – however, Dino had brought in a casting director from The States and it was the beginning of something that would be such great fun.

The series itself was loosely based around Lee and Sooty's past life and had been written up by two young screen writers from South London and I was the first to see the initial draft of the script.

"Is this true?" I'd asked Lee.

"Is what true?" he'd replied.

I passed him over the intended dialogue on what was around sixty sheets of paper, which had been bound together by two-piece filing clips.

"The time-line is wrong," he'd said on glancing over it. "But it certainly happened."

"And you are okay with this?" I'd asked.

"Sure," he'd replied. "Why?"

17

I had never been as excited in all my life. Was the script good? It was shit-hot to be honest, but that certainly wasn't the reason why. The main reason was that on Dino seeing M – he had become somewhat infatuated with her and had offered her the chance of being cast.

Did she take up the offer? She did, and out of all the characters that she could have picked, she possibly picked the most complex.

"I'd really love the chance to play Lee's mam," she'd said.

She could have quite easily been cast as one of the 16-year old girls, yet she had opted for a 35-year old widow.

Dino tended to cast the actors and actresses down at White Lion Street, but on several occasions, he had cast at ours – one of which had been M, and this would be something that none of us would have missed for the world.

"Read the words on – scene ten," Dino had told her. "And remember – it's the actor that makes the character."

She had been nothing short of amazing.

"What d'yer reckon?" she smiled, afterwards.

"You looked great Emily," he'd said, before he did no more and handed her a different scene and introduced a couple of props – one a settee, the other – a trainee cameraman, one Jono Greaves.

"You what?" a red-faced Jono had gasped.

"You don't have to act, just sit on the couch," Dino had told him, whilst marking some lines with an orange felt. "Follow Emily's lead and just read the highlighted lines on the script."

On glancing over the lines the look on M's face was a picture. "You have got to be joking?" she said.

"This is acting," he'd told her.

Me – I shot through to scene number 23 – and I couldn't frigging believe it. This was something that I had to see. In fact, this was something everyone had to see, so much so, a nice little crowd had gathered as the camera was set up close to where the action would be taking place.

"When you're ready, Emily," Dino had said.

M looked at her lines for what seemed like ages, did a bit of humming and erring and then walked over to young Jono, kicked off her shoes and knelt on the sofa at the side of him.

"I'm really glad you came 'round," she'd said, as she smooched up to the live prop.

"So, where… is the kid?" Jono had stuttered.

"At his gran's," Emily had whispered.

Jono went the colour of beetroot.

"So, what about Carole?" she'd further whispered.

"What …about …Carole?"

"What if she finds out?"

"She will …only find out if …if you tell her."

"I really do love you," she'd said.

"I …am sure …that you do?" a rather wooden Jono had stammered.

The next thing that happened was that Emily had said: "You can kiss me if you want."

Jono nearly died on the spot and just froze.

"I said you can kiss me if you want," Emily had nodded. "Really."

Jono looked over at Dino, who was looking into a monitor. You just had to be there – the suspense was unfriggingbelievable. Then he bottled it. "I can't," he said.

"What d'yer mean yer can't," Emily twanged, before standing up with her arms on her hips. "Am I that bad?"

Everybody in the studio was laughing their heads off.

"N-no, M," he'd said.

"It's okay, Jonathan," Dino had told him. "Just follow Emily's lead. And go back to 'she'll only find out if you tell her'."

The lad was as embarrassed as hell.

"There's nothing to be afraid of, you are only the prop," Dino had explained. "It's Emily doing the acting."

Jono nodded and under some duress and amidst all the laughter in the studio, he resumed being the live prop and fed her his line.

"I really do love you," Emily told him.

"Yes …I …am sure that …er, you do?" he mumbled.

"You can kiss me if you want."

To say Jono's face was a deep purple would have been an understatement, but I'll tell you this, it was possibly the best bit of life experience he would ever have as when he turned to face her she did no more than hit him with a right smoocher, so much so, you could have heard a frigging pin drop.

"Tell me you'll not leave me," she'd whispered in his ear.

"I …will not er …leave you," he'd stuttered.

Emily cupped her hands around his face and kissed him again.

"Scene," Dino had shouted.

We were all gobsmacked – not more so than young Jono, who after being patted like a dog and having his head rubbed by anyone and everyone was about to skulk away – however, M was nothing short of brilliant with the lad. "Thank you for doing that for me," she'd told him. "It can't have been easy with everyone watching."

Me? I could have cried.

What you have to understand is that we were like one big family, which is something that Jo over at White Lion had mentioned time and time again. Another part of the family had also been in the audience both laughing and applauding – and that was Becky Ivell. She was rising through the ranks like Bernard Cromwell's character *Richard Sharpe* and was not only in charge of LMJ's colourisation department, but also all the weekend's pitch side commentary team, with her clamouring after a spot in the studios – something, which strangely Lee had held off on, even though I knew it was only a matter of time before both her and Abigayle Gibbs would resurrect ITV 7's Fab Four. Had he told me? No. Nor had he told me that he had offered three guys he went to school with – and with no experience whatsoever, a chance of a career in TV. And more importantly, nor had he told me that something big was happening with ITV 7, and this particular morning I had six suits from its hierarchy descend on me – and without no prior knowledge.

"You do know Lee's not here," I told them, as I had Georgia Clayton bring them all a coffee.

They knew – and so did Lee.

"What the heck, Lee?" I said to him over the phone, once I'd finally got shut of them.

ITV 7 was to be a full-time 24-hour channel – not just football, but sports, and I suddenly realised that I was well out of my depth. "This will burn everyone out before we even start."

Him doing a live interview from Geneva for *News at Ten* had been nothing short of amazing and as that was the case ITV wanted him more than ever – and little did I know that he was currently putting ideas together on a laptop somewhere over in northwest Italy.

How did I know that? Pedro of all people told me. He had also told me over the phone that he'd had three days living with Lee and M out in Tuscany, prior to him doing a couple of shows in Rome.

"What were they like?" I inquired.

"Lovely," he told me.

"Did you know Pete La Greave has been staying with Lee and M?" I asked Jaime.

She told me she did, as she had GPS tracker systems on every camera and every vehicle.

"ITV Seven is going out twenty-four/seven," I told her.

She certainly didn't know that.

"So, will we all be in Manchester or what?" she asked.

I just didn't know. I really didn't know. What I was told however, was that one of LMJ's shows would be broadcast on ITV that night – 9.20 pm sharp, but for the life of me I didn't know what. Even Annie didn't know. "There's nothing that we have billed them for that tallies with anything going out tonight," she said.

As it transpired, Johanne over at White Lion was handling the billing on this one and as such it had us all scratching our heads.

I got in that night to Liza being a total bitch and a four and a half grand tax bill. Not mine – hers. And me telling her that I wasn't coughing up for it created a bit of a scene, and that being the case, she walked out. It was then I looked around at my life and put it into perspective. I needed more. I had seen how Pedro – with the help of Lee and M, had put together his home and how both Jody and Becky had prospered under their guidance. As for me, I was still living in this grotty flat with a partner who was as affluent as Alan Hudson – he's no relation of Jaime by the way. I threw a ready-made meal in the microwave, did some work and kicked up the TV, wondering what the hell LMJ had produced, that it had to have White Lion doing the billing.

I was soon to find out.

Lee had both filmed and produced it – a documentary that showed his wife – the real M.

I had obviously seen a few minutes of it, but I'd certainly never seen the finished article.

The camerawork was exceptional and it showed M in one of the studios over at White Lion Street sat playing violin with a seven-year old girl – Lee and Jeanette's daughter. The monochrome footage picked out every detail of their faces and each and every one of their actions. M was teaching Lee's daughter and the scene itself was not only beautiful, it was totally spell binding.

The camera blew out to see the rest of her class of four begin playing and people such as Jody Reeves, Pete La Greave and Joe Aitken were sat watching on in awe. Three of White Lion's biggest earners were watching on, as M taught her class of five the violin.

"I love teaching and I love music," M had said on screen. "The only feeling that could ever top it, is the love I have for my family."

I knew there and then, that this was the reason why M didn't want to do another series of *Live at The Warehouse*.

I watched on as scenes from their home came into view – M watching over Lee's son and daughter painting, her cooking in the kitchen and then watching over Lee's daughter as she played on the piano in their lovely white front room.

The camerawork was hypnotic, if not quite poignant.

"To learn a young child to read and write is a truly fantastic feeling, but it is something in life that they, as part of the curriculum, have to do. For a child to play an instrument and to this level without being urged to do it, is pure dedication, and the feeling I get from seeing them continually improve is quite something else," M had said.

She went on to explain that she firstly had three family members as pupils and taught them from home, with Lee being extremely supportive of her.

"He was continually working and with some of the noise that we were making, it must have really put him off," she added. "But never once did he ask me to stop, nor for me not to do it."

The film flicked back to the studio at White Lion Street, where a different five young girls were playing and where M was teaching them some music scales on a rolling blackboard, and again some big names from White Lion were watching on as she did – one of who was Ross Bain.

"I take small classes of five," she explained, "rather than do a *one on one*, as for some children it can be quite intimidating if not rather boring. This way, they can also make friends and from my perspective, I can still focus on each and every one of them."

The camera moved in on M playing, whilst encouraging her pupils to do the same, and the smile which she gave them was truly something else. Anyone would have put their heart and soul into something, to receive a smile such as that.

When the film flipped back to home it showed M in their big room talking to some parents and then talking to their child. Never had I seen anything such as this. This was teaching at a completely different level, and the way she conversed with them all was quite out of this world – and rather than the children call her Mrs Janes, she insisted that they call her M.

At the end of the 40-minute programme – which had been titled: *There's something in the way that she moves*, the credits played out with Electric Ladyboy's version of George Harrison's song of the same name and with muted footage of M playing the violin with Lee's daughter. That was the bit that I had already seen, which at the time had me wiping my eyes.

Lee and M were very private people, but by doing this, he had given the world a glimpse into their beautiful life.

My phone was red hot afterwards. Firstly, Jaime – then Jo – and then, rather surprisingly – M?

I can't ever recall M calling my phone – ever, so this was something of a shock, as was her inviting me over to Italy for Lee's birthday.

"Can I ask you a question?" I asked.

"If yer like," she replied.

"I love you both – Lee is like my big brother, but I always feel that I am being held at arms-length – so, why now?"

I think the three glasses of Casillero del Diablo that I'd just drank had something to do with that statement, and immediately after saying it, I regretted it.

"You're not, love," she said.

Yes, I was, I thought.

I then blabbed a little bit more than I should have, in that Jody, Becky and Pedro got open invites into their home, yet I did not.

"Jody stayed because she needed looking after," M told me. "And neither Becky nor Pedro have ever been to our home."

"Pedro has – he's just been at your place in Italy."

"It's not our place and he certainly didn't have an invite," she laughed. "Not that we minded however, as we both think a lot of him."

She then told me something, which I partly understood and partly didn't. "Lee is always working," she said. "I try to separate his home life and his everyday working life and as such, Sooty is the only one who has ever been a regular visitor."

"You know ITV seven is going twenty-four/seven?" I asked her.

There was a short silence.

"ITV had six suits from South Bank at *The Warehouse* earlier today," I added. "I really can't see how we can cover that kind of workload – especially if we get the deportation orders for Manchester."

She was more than well-aware of that and we spoke for a good twenty minutes, with my final words to her being, "I'd really like to be friends with you, M."

Chapter 29

The Sooty Show – *Episode 7*

The DNA test came back positive. It was therefore confirmed that I was father to a kid who went by the name of Donald Cook.

I currently had another two women pregnant, one of which was my wife and seeing how my luck was running, I was awaiting a phone call from Buzzy's missus – either that, or her arriving in Holland Park with a suitcase under her arm, which would have probably been just enough to tip me over the edge.

To say things were tense at home was a fucking understatement, and I needed some outlet – cue: Alan Hudson at my door. Yeh, and at 6.00 am in the morning.

"You are doing a documentary on me," he said.

"Am I?" I replied. "Says who?"

"Lee."

I rang the said Mr. Hudson's *agent* to have this little snippet of information confirmed and immediately got the international ring tone. He was out of the UK and no-one had told me. "'You abroad?" I asked.

"Italy," he replied.

"I've got some old bloke here who claims he's Alan Hudson telling me that I'm to do a documentary on him," I said.

"I know," he replied. "Look after him for the week and get him on camera talking about his career. I will email you over everything that you need to know."

"Yeh, but I don't work for you," I said.

"Earn your way back in then," I was told.

I rang Abi to ask for use of one of the studios and got passed to Jaime, which I wished I hadn't. In the meantime, I had the star of the show sat at my table drinking coffee as Libby wandered into the kitchen. "Who the hell is that?" she asked.

"My ticket back in," I told her, whilst at the other end of the phone, Jaime was giving me the bollocking of all bollockings.

"Do you speak to your mother like that?" I asked – and ended up getting more of the same. I pitied her fucking husband if he got the same treatment. I knew she was a bit bossy, but threatening to cut my balls off with a Stanley knife? I mean – come on!

"Do I get a fucking studio or what?" I asked.

"Yes," she replied.

"Good – I'll be up there at nine," I told her, before focusing my attention on my coffee-slurping guest. "You had any breakfast?"

He told me that he hadn't and mentioned this café on Wandsworth Bridge Road in Fulham that he went to – me thinking that it was some greasy spoon job that I'd get change out of a tenner from – however, this joker was ordering Bucks Fizz and eggs Florentine as soon as we got through the door.

"They do 'build-your-own' breakfasts, with avocado, sausages, bacon, salmon and banana bread," he told me.

"Really?" I said.

I knew there and then that if I had this guy in my shadows for a full week I'd be *boracic* and I told Lee exactly that when I finally got Chris Wainwright to release his Vulcan death-grip on me and let me into the studios. "This isn't Alan Hudson – more like the Earl of fucking Lucan," I told him. "I've just blown seventy-five quid on a breakfast."

"Just look after him," is all I got told.

Abi summoned make-up artist Chris Windley to polish him up a bit, and who on copping the *canvas* gave me a look as though I'd just taken a shit in his hat. "Just do your fucking best," I told him.

In the meantime, Abi let me know about the amount of footage we already had on him and exactly what of, and passed me a few sheets of paper as part of an email that Lee had sent over late last night, and after glancing through it I asked: "What's the actual subject here – a documentary on Huddy or an exposé on Terry Neill?"

"It's Lee's call," Abi replied. "Just do as he asks."

Meanwhile the make-up artist was totally pissing off our guest.

"And you can take that off him," I said.

"I'm trying to add some colour," he replied. "He looks a bit drawn."

I think coming off a 12-hour bender and having little or no sleep does that to you – and I mentioned that fact to both the said head of make-up and *Aunt fucking Sally*.

"I rarely drink before a game," the ageing maverick told us.

That figures? I thought. *His last game was thirty years ago.*

What is rarely mentioned, is that Huddy retired through a knee injury. The same troublesome knee that stopped Tommy Docherty from making top-flight soccer history by giving him his league debut at just 15 years of age – which would have been younger than Howard Kendall, John Sissons and Terry Venables.

"Docherty's part in Chelsea's success in the late-sixties and early seventies, should never be overlooked," Huddy told us. "The combination of him and Dave Sexton would have been as great as any in football, but as individuals they were flawed."

It sounded exactly like the Mee/Howe, Mercer/Allison and Clough/Taylor partnerships, with me immediately thinking that Sexton and Docherty seemed to follow each other in and out of the door at a few different clubs – Arsenal, Chelsea, Queens Park Rangers, Manchester United…

"Sexton was like Don Howe and were both great as everyday men on the training ground," Huddy added. "Put them in an office however, and they were like fish out of water."

"What would you prefer we call you?" asked Abi, on coming into the studio with someone to man the camera –

or *woman it* rather, as it was Becky Ivell – the Paul Madeley of LMJ.

"You can call me Al," quipped Huddy.

Obviously, he was expecting Chevy Chase to mime his lines for him!

"Where's Emmanuel Frimpong?" I asked, regarding the whereabouts of the pain in the arse that was Ginge.

"Him and the two lads are on tour with one of the bands over at White Lion," said Abi.

That was another thing I didn't know.

It was getting hard for me to look in the mirror as I got older, so god knows what it feels for the more famous – and I thought exactly that on Chris finishing Huddy's makeover.

Jon Sammels had been one of the beautiful *Faces* of 1960's football – like the cute Ian MacLachan or possibly the even cuter Kenny Jones – however, Huddy was much, much more. His halcyon years had ran parallel to the likes of the Rocket Man, Bolan and Ziggy – and as for Huddy himself – well he hadn't just been a *Face* – he was fucking 'Rod'.

'All I needed was a friend to lend a guiding hand – but you turned into a lover and mother what a lover, you wore me out – all you did was wreck my bed – and in the morning kicked me in the head..'

A truly brilliant player and watching Alan Hudson strut his stuff on the pitch in his pomp, was comparable to watching the The Faces main man, strut his on *Top of the Pops*. Saying that, neither Chelsea nor Stoke City had a pedantic Oddbod-like character that was John Peel, sat in the back four pretending to play with his mandolin!

Whilst Huddy had been having his make-over, I had been highlighting parts of Lee's email – which if I'm being frank, resembled one of Don Revie's legendary dossiers. I think Lee knew more about Alan Hudson than the maverick himself did!

I knew that Manchester United fancied him, but I never knew they had actually chucked in a bid of £200,000 for him. Leeds supposedly wanted him as well and all this was being picked up by Becky on camera – as was the next bit.

"I had been asking Dave Sexton for a move for months but was always told 'over my dead body'," Huddy explained.

"Then in January 'seventy-four I was told by him that I was trouble and that he had been trying to get me out of the club for ages. He then told me to *fack off.*"

That bit had both Abi and Becky looking at each other.

What was to follow was Alan Hudson's £240,000 transfer to Stoke City, which at the time broke the Record British Transfer Fee and which was swiftly usurped a month or so later when Everton paid £350,000 for Birmingham City's centre-forward, Bob Latchford.

"Me leaving could have been engineered. Chelsea were desperate for cash to pay for the East Stand, so what better way to raise funds than to sell me and Peter Osgood?" he added.

I had him in the camera until around lunchtime, when he started getting itchy feet.

I rang Lee to give him a bit of an update and he told me to just keep him out of the pub – however, whilst I was on the *dog* he decided to have a wander around the place and managed to find his way into Temporary Studio 5 where White Lion's sister company were shooting a steamy sex scene, which had to go for a retake after he, along with both actor and actress dropped their crutches – him hobbling through the door and giving it a "Jesus facking Christ!"

"It's not real," I told him.

"It looked facking real," he exclaimed.

I took Lee's advice and drove him down to the Coffee Shop where Fosis appeared quite pleased to see me. "Wanker Sooty," he said in his Anglo-Greek dialect. "I am surprised to see you in here after thing with Emi-l-ee."

"What thing with Emily?" inquired Huddy.

"He like that Francis Coquelin," Fosis told him. "Useless dirty bastard."

"Just a thing that happened at a school reunion," I told him – me obviously playing it down.

We sat down and I ordered an Espresso and Perrier, whilst LMJ's guest rubbed his hands together and ordered two pints of Magners cider along with a litre bottle of 12-year old Ouzo, two glasses and a bucket of ice. I vaguely remember having my teeth in the top of the table an hour or so later – however, the next thing I knew I was at some bookies down in Fulham. Apparently, Huddy had dropped £60 on one of Fosis' one-arm bandits and was going to invest it in a carefully planned five-horse accumulator, which to me, stood as much chance as winning as Massimo Cellino's three-legged pet project up at Elland Road did.

I had to give him his dues – he was very confident. I would have told him so, but the words wouldn't come out of my mouth at that particular moment in time. Maybe it was the liquorice in the Ouzo holding my teeth together – I don't know.

"I'll take you to this restaurant," he told me. "We won't have to pay for a thing."

As it turned out, one of the waiters at this place was an ex-Cypriot international who had played against him when he had won the second of his two England caps – and who had been something of an Alan Hudson fan.

"I told him," Huddy said. "There's one hundred thousand people in the stadium – why is it that you're continually following me around. Go follow one of them."

One thing that was bothering me was how we had got to Fulham from Grays Inn Road. Apparently, I'd parked my car at Lee's and we had caught the Tube. That was strange as I couldn't remember a thing, although M's dad rang me to tell me that some guy with crutches had been seen running away from it.

"Is it okay?" I asked him.

"I think so," he said.

I'd had around twenty-six missed phone calls from Abi as to our whereabouts. I don't know why she was asking me – I didn't have a clue where I was.

"I think I'm in Fulham," I told her.

"You think?" she inquired.

"The inside of bookies all tend to all look the same."

It was then I realised that Huddy was still your archetypal footballer in that he only worked for 90 minutes. Still – that was about 85 minutes more than Trevor Brooking ever did.

Huddy had been rubbing his hands together in expectation of his horse, which was running in the 3.30 at

Catterick – the *Wear A Yellow Jersey Handicap* – coming in. "It'll walk it," he told me.

Fully expecting it to walk it, I sat down – and fell asleep.

I remember calling in The Mitre and the Cock Tavern – but I can't remember anything at all about The Oyster Rooms ...or getting back to Maggie's and asking her to marry me.

"You were singing to her outside," said Huddy, who was laid on Maggie's settee and fiddling around with the remote control for the TV. "*Wimoweh.*"

"Wimoweh?" I asked. "What the hell's a 'Wimoweh'?"

"We were singing it in the Cock'," he said. "In the jungle, the mighty jungle, the lion sleeps tonight."

This Rod Stewart-stroke-Alan Hudson lifestyle didn't suit me at all. I had the hangover of all hangovers and it was only 7.00 pm.

I ambled out of Maggie's and down to the house in Holland Park to receive twenty-lashes from Libby's tongue – told her to "Bollocks" and then went to bed.

Groundhog Day commenced at 6.00 am next morning, when Mr. Benn appeared at the fucking door again.

"Look, I can't do this shit every day," I told him.

"Do what?" he inquired.

"Go frigging boozing," I told him. "I still feel drunk."

"It'll be the Ouzo," he told me.

I didn't need him to tell me that. I knew it was the Ouzo. A drink you should drink in moderation – and not by the half-gallon.

I got a shower and chucked on a suit before realising that my car was in North London.

"I've got a Taxi waiting outside," he told me. "Didn't I say? The meter's been running since I got here."

"You what?" I exclaimed.

This guy was absolutely brilliant at spending my money and rather than an over-elaborate and costly £300 taxi ride via Fulham – to be subjected to coughing for another fucking Bucks Fizz breakfast, I made sure we got to Frederick Street in King's Cross, only for me to find out that

I had copped a parking ticket as well as a frigging crutch mark down the side of the Jag'.

"That'll T-cut out," he told me.

The thing is – is that he sounded so fucking believable, as not even the best fucking panel beater in the world could take out an actual dint with a cloth full of jollop.

Take Two. Cue Huddy.

"When Docherty was manager of Chelsea," he started to explain, "he hated it when his players received international call-ups. He said that they started to save up their best form for that stage and their league form would suffer. Players would also mix and compare notes about salaries, bonus payments and other perks, which would inevitably lead to transfer requests when disparities came to light."

I was sick of hearing about fucking Tommy Docherty and the fact he brought three of the greatest British managers through in George Graham, Terry Venables and Eddie McCreadie, the latter of who never ever realised his potential. Again, this was down to what Huddy claimed was the "Duplicitous nature of the Chelsea board". He must have mentioned this about twenty-five times already. Or was I just imagining it?

I think he was spot on with monies being mentioned at international level however, as Terry Neill had said something similar on Graham Rix finding out what Manchester City's Kevin Reeves had been earning in comparison to him. "I'm a lot better player," he had told Neill.

As for the England international set-up, Ray Kennedy hit the nail on the head. "Players play for themselves," he'd said, "whereas at Liverpool, we played as a team."

Stan Bowles criticised the set-up too. "When we were playing against the decent teams, I got my fair share of the ball – however, against the weaker teams, I found that everybody wanted to be a superstar."

Don Revie – well it was said that he used international matches for his players to tap up their international team mates – Allan Clarke and Asa Hartford both spring to mind as possible successes – however, Alan Ball and Tony

Green possibly don't. Although it has been said that Revie thought the latter to be too inconsistent.

My head was still thumping from the hangover, when at around 11.00 am he finally got off the subject of Tommy Docherty, as Faranha brought us in some tea and biscuits. As for me, I brought Lee up to speed, and whilst I did, Huddy nipped out to reception to sign fifty Chelsea and Arsenal shirts for Basher and in return got £250 to invest at a Ladbrokes bookie's, and one which was conveniently located sort of hobbling distance around the corner on Bounds Green Road.

"He's been gone a long time," noted Abi, regarding the whereabouts of our geriatric maverick.

He had. Huddy had some penchant for wandering off everywhere – especially if there was a pub or bookmakers knocking about. Unfortunately, the Springfield Park Tavern was a short gallop from Ladbrookes and that's where he was – dinky pointing outwards, sipping at a pint and sat with his new best mate who had obviously bought him the frigging thing.

"I'm just having a quick one while I'm waiting for the results of the first race coming in," he said.

This guy was harder to control than George Best.

In the end, I thought *Fuck it* and asked Becky to fetch the camera around as I couldn't get him out of the place after he'd downed his fourth pint – his horse coming in, obviously giving him cause for celebration.

Lee went ape shit when he found out about his studios being *extended* half way up the street and in a pub. "You can't have him pissed whilst talking on camera," he moaned.

"Listen mate," I replied. "He could knock another fifteen of these back and still sound exactly the same."

At the end of day two, I was wrecked.

We had done the Chelsea and Stoke City bit – the fact that Ramsey had robbed both him and Colin Todd as well as England, of getting to the 1974 World Cup finals in Germany by freezing them out for three years after they refused to go on Under-23 duty – and the fact that he and Revie never hit it off. "He picked me to fail," he told me.

He had also given me his version of events at Arsenal, which totally intrigued my Italian-connection.

"He told me about the Rix-thing," I told Lee.

"Rix thing?" Lee asked. "What Rix thing?"

"I remember being on the treatment table when I got told that Terry had chinned Graham Rix in the gym over in the old red-ash car park," Huddy told us on camera. "When Terry came through I said to him 'That's about right for you, hitting a young kid – why didn't you chin Pat Jennings or Willie Young?' He just told me to 'Fack off'. That summed him up – hitting Rix, a skinny nineteen-year-old. I was the bad guy again for speaking up again."

In Neill's defence, some years later he did say that he had been wrong in retaliating, but the *speaking-up* part can be counter-productive – as it is a well-known fact that egos prefer to be massaged, as opposed to confronted.

Lee then mentioned the similarities of both Terry Neill and Billy Wright and the fact that they had both appeared, not only extremely dogmatic, but possessed a certain petulant nature about their personalities – and although between them they regularly invited confrontation, neither man really liked being challenged.

Neill had questioned both Alan Sunderland's languid attitude to the game along with his thoughtlessness stating: "With his ability, he could have done so much more. He had more technical skill than Kevin Keegan, but his attitude was not always right – and he was often extremely bitter."

"I found Alan Sunderland a terrific lad and player, who never caused any trouble," Huddy told us. "If a player has his say, it doesn't mean he's a problem."

Neill however, was somewhat cleverer than Wright and he realised after his first season, that he was lacking in technical nous and that his job was on the line and went out and did something about it. Wright however, did not.

Chapter 30

The Big Decision

We had been in Italy eight days and I loved it. I could certainly see why Liam Brady had left Arsenal for Juventus in the summer of 1980.

I loved the beauty of the place and of course the weather. If you have ever watched *A Year in Provence* - well, this was its Italian counterpart …just bigger …and better.

I also loved the fact that I was with the four people in my life that I loved so much. It was really something special. My headaches certainly weren't as intense and my eyes felt good – the easing up of the staring into my laptop or the monitor, obviously being the main reason why.

It also gave me and Emily a chance to talk, and it was here that we would plan our future.

ITV 7 was a juggernaut that was out of control. It was to metamorphosis from a weekend football channel into a weekly 24-hour sports channel, with football just being one of the many subjects it would cover. I had been running on empty into its final weeks. I couldn't really fault anyone for dropping out, as the hours were both long and unsociable, and the job took everyone out of London on a weekend. And I hated live broadcasting as it put you in one spot at a particular time, and that being the case it ruled our lives. Emily had been ruled before, and I hated having to see her do something that she didn't want to do. She, as I did, hated the fact that our special Friday's together had been kicked in the head and that my time with the kids had been cut short.

I had been the architect of this all-consuming vehicle, and ITV had offered me unbelievable terms as part of the renegotiation of my contract. This was my window of opportunity.

I remember sat out on the patio that balmy evening discussing it with Emily.

"Do you think that could really happen?" she shrugged.

"Anything is possible M."

A "Wow" was all I got back.

What I had suggested was exactly that – just a suggestion, but if it came off, a "Wow" would be a fair reaction.

Managing LMJ and White Lion was easy. I just delegated and they ran themselves. ITV 7 needed not only managing, but major technical input, live broadcasting, my starring role and its production.

Management is the easiest thing in the world if you have the right people behind you. I had been blessed by having Abi, Jaime, Annie and Johanne. These were my Don Howe, Dave Sexton, Malcolm Allison and Peter Taylor who all made my job so easy.

I knew ITV were toying around with the idea of a weekly channel around the time me and M had taken the kids to Blackpool and the grilling I got via *News at Ten* had firmly reinforced their belief. I looked at the overall picture and saw a few things, one of which was that if I wasn't careful, they would run me into the ground until I was wasted. I had other ideas and firstly requested an increased financial package more in tune with the workload.

ITV played hardball – they always did. The money I was getting wasn't really a problem – however, I certainly made it one, well not so much me, but my legal people. I just listened to what they had to say.

A few days before we drove over to Italy I had gone into ITV's head office and signed on the dotted line, more than doubled my salary and in effect got handed a longer contract. However, there was much more to it than that, especially as they wanted *The Sooty Show* to continue as part of ITV 7's infrastructure and with LMJ to handle the contracts – as I was told that Sooty himself, had become quite problematic in his demands.

They also wanted me to come up with a business plan to show how I could actually make it all work.

Emily was made aware of everything – however, one person who was not, was Sooty.

One of the things I had chosen to do was to try and look after an ex-football player who had fallen on hard times and who both Emily and myself liked immensely. It was the first time ever that I had ever thought about using an ex-pro.

I knew Alan Hudson to be intelligent and have a vast knowledge of the game and of that there was no doubt. He had a forthright opinion on anything from the failings of a 4-2-3-1 system to how a bottle of Chilean white is best served. If you needed an honest answer, he was certainly the man to give it. His social life however, was quite something else and I needed an insight into what made my flawed genius actually tick, and I had therefore delegated – and put Sooty on *Huddy-sitting* duty.

This particular evening, I sat on the bank of the stream that ran at the bottom of the garden deep in thought whilst trying to put everything I was doing into perspective. The fish were dipping as the midges hovered above in small swarms, whilst just over the hills the sun was setting.

"Have you seen that eel, dad?" asked my lad.

"I haven't mate," I replied, as he sat down next to me.

"Mum phoned."

"Is she okay?" I asked, whilst at the same time giving his head a rub.

"She said she has been in Macey's – that big shop where the real Father Christmas goes, and bought me something."

"Oh yeh."

"Mum says that you and her once went there."

"Yeh, we did," I said. "It was a long time ago, though."

"Didn't you have me and our Harm' then?" he asked.

"No, neither of you had been born."

There was a slight pause as his brain ticked away in the background.

"When the new baby is born will you stop seeing us?" he asked.

"No, of course I won't," I told him. "What makes you think that?"

He just shrugged his shoulders.

"I love both you and your sister a lot," I said. "Nothing will ever stop me from doing that."

"Did you love mum, when I was born?"

"Yeh, of course I did – I still love your mum now."

"Why, when you live with M?" he asked.

"Your mum is a beautiful lady who gave me two beautiful kids," I told him.

He gave me a smile – however, I could still *hear* his brain ticking away in the background.

"I'll not be able to play in the football team with Erv' if we go to New York, will I dad?" he asked.

"No, mate." I replied.

"Will you watch them?" he asked me.

"I will – and I'll try and pretend that you are there when I do."

His mind had obviously been working overtime.

Emily then came walking down the lawn and complained about the turnyroundything on the barbecue not working and mentioned that my flawed genius had tried checking in.

The turnyroundything was the rotisserie, the flawed genius obviously being Huddy.

I walked up to the farmhouse to see Herbert in his baby walker trying to ram raid the garage doors with his big sister giggling at him. "He knows there's something inside," she said.

He did, as it had been his big sister who had picked him up to show him through the window.

"Can we look inside?" my lad had also asked on us getting here.

We could have, but there hadn't been any keys, and I certainly wasn't going to ask the caretakers of the property if they had any, as it had taken M nearly an hour to get rid of them that particular morning.

"Right boring, she is," Emily had said. "She was talking at me for god knows how long and I still haven't got a clue what she was on about."

Her husband had been the same, and had been totally convinced that Muhammed Ali had actually fought Frank Bruno, and that Bruno had nearly 'done him'.

"You're thinking of Mike Tyson, mate," I had told him.

"Tyson never fought Ali," he had replied.

Sometimes, and with certain people it's just best not to get involved in any conversation whatsoever.

"Did she mention their Derek?" I'd winked at my wife.

"Their Derek?" she'd chuntered. "I was sick of hearing about their Derek."

Just for the record, her brother Derek was a 56-year old Manchester United fan that had never had a girlfriend.

"Oooh – he's not bothered about girls," Hazel had told us on the first day of our holiday. And on the second and third, if I rightly recall.

"He sounds right gay," M had whispered.

A gay Manchester United fan – who would have thought?

I rang up the flawed genius to see what he had to say.

"He's got a bit of an attitude," Huddy said, in regard to Sooty. "And his wife's a right moaning cow."

That made me laugh.

Apparently, they'd had a spot of lunch at an Italian restaurant around the corner from The Barbican Tube station – on Long Lane, I think.

"The place did really nice food, and all he did was moan about the price of things," Huddy added. "He said 'I aren't paying nine-bar for a piece of melon'."

He then explained that he never the ordered the melon and went with the Mediterranean garlic prawn starters and a nice piece of fillet steak, which had been washed down with a few bottles of Sicilian red – a rather subtle Nerello Mascalese followed by three bottles of Frappato.

"A bit of surf and turf," Huddy informed me.

"Where is he now?" I inquired.

It turned out they had both gone back to Sooty's and that Libby had kicked him out. Not her husband – but the flawed genius.

"Did she have much to say?" I inquired.

"She called him a piss-head and threatened to wrap one of my crutches around my neck for knocking over some great flowery pot in the hall, but that's about it."

Mmm. Huddy had apparently broken one of her beloved antique Jardinières.

I rung off after ten-minutes chit-chat and attempted to kick up one of my laptops to access Sooty's interviews with Huddy, which Abi had slung up on Dropbox – however, that definitely wasn't happening as I had made a promise to Emily of keeping away from work – and just sending and answering email's. The fact was, that at times it was extremely hard for me to keep away from a subject that I loved.

"Your eyes, love," Emily had said. "You need to look after them."

The intensity of setting up that colourisation department did have a lot to answer for.

"So, your turnyrondything?" I inquired.

"It won't work," she said, sort of scratching her head.

I pillocked about with it for a bit, but I didn't really have the tools, even though my lad had subtly suggested looking in the garage – him totally knowing that there was a Kayak or canoe in there along with loads of boxes.

"You just want me to go in the garage."

"Too right," he said, as he followed me over to the door to the place.

"I'd ask for the keys, but we'd never get rid of the caretaker," I said.

"Just smash the door in then," he said. "Like they do on telly."

The doors were similar to those on the farmhouse itself – only bigger, and even those on the house were around three-inches thick.

"Erv' said his real dad used to boot the doors of their house in, all the time," he said.

"Yeh, that's why he's doing eight-months in Durham jail," I replied, whilst still weighing up my options.

Emily suggested chopping the padlock off with an axe.

I just gave her a glare.

"It was only a suggestion," she grinned.

"There is an axe, dad," my daughter added.

There was. It was in with all the wood and kindle that was used to fire up the log burner and if I'm being honest, it was a fairly big one – a bit like Jack used to fell the beanstalk, and as such it was certainly big enough to lop someone's limbs off.

"Dad should do it, shouldn't he, M?" said my lad.

"Your dad's definitely not strong enough to lift that big axe," she winked.

Maybe not, but a bare-chested dad was – and I took the lock clean off with the greatest hatchet-swing of all time. Not even Huddy could have done the lock on Tony Waddington's drinks cabinet as clean and efficiently as that.

I slung what was left of the padlock and opened the doors to reveal two cars – both of which had been covered with tarpaulin sheets, the said Kayak, along with boxes upon boxes of toys – the exact same boxes that Sammy had caught sight of through the window – and that being the case, he hurtled past me in the baby walker and went straight for them.

"Can we play with them, M?" asked my lad.

"Of course, you can," she replied.

And dad was tasked with carrying out all the boxes of toys and emptying them on the lawn.

Cue: the turnyroundything.

Piece of piss – the fuse had gone in it.

"So, what are you wanting to barbecue?" I inquired.

"I'm not," she smiled. "Well not just yet, anyway."

The next thing I knew there was a car *beep-beeping* at the gates.

"I wonder who that is?" I said.

The answer was soon upon us when a voice shouted through the Tannoy, "Awight, mate?"

My lad was elated to see a black Volvo trundle up the long drive, dragging a caravan behind it and his best mate waving to him through one of the rear windows.

"It's Erv'!" he shouted.

It certainly was.

"Now you can fire the barbecue up," smiled my wife, as she came up to me and gave me a hug.

Emily's power-play was well and truly hard at work.

Chapter 31
Les Èchangistes

I had been having some weird dreams over the past few weeks, which wasn't anything new as such, as I always had an active mind – which was something that Emily had helped more than stimulate time after time, but just recently any psychiatrist would have had a field day, such was their intensity.

"I wonder why you dreamt of that?" Emily had said on one particular occasion.

In the short time since we had been together, we had gone through quite a lot and as that was the case, we had tried to stay honest and very much in touch with each other's inner self.

That possibly sounded really fucking pathetic, so perhaps I could have worded that slightly better!

I'd never done the wholehearted pouring my heart out honesty-thing, as with my life it was nothing short of a minefield – however, M had been carefully navigating her way through it since *Day 1*.

"I dreamed of that *thing* at Wortley Hall again," I told her.

"You've got a right dirty mind," she grinned.

"Yeh I know," I replied. "And it's you who's on it."

She quite liked that and so did I – however, after the first few times, I'd started having variations of the dream – and each and every time the events surrounding it, had gotten worse and worse, not at least its conclusion.

The Sooty Show with his really special guest star M, had gone from being just exactly that, through the motions to something so brutal and macabre, that I was not only waking up terrified, I was also getting worried about actually going to bed – which was most unlike me.

At first it was a case of never being able to get back to the room in time as someone was there on the staircase or landing stopping me – someone in a grey shroud, either in the way, making excuses or even worse – pulling me back. And I could never make eye-contact with it, but I certainly knew the voice. "Don't go in there – stay here," it had said on one occasion.

I woke up in a cold sweat, with Emily looking over at me.

"Are you okay, love?" she asked.

"No," I told her.

She cuddled up to me and as I started to drop off she asked me, "Was it your mam again?"

"That *thing* in Wortley Hall," I nodded.

"Perhaps we ought to go back and exorcise your demons," she whispered. "You can give me a right proper *yer knowing*."

I didn't particularly like mentioning it, but every time I went back there in my dream, the scenery changed. The building got more decrepit and downtrodden and the scenes more macabre – the last time of which, some of the windows had been broken, the curtains were hanging off the wall and there was a big fire blazing up the chimney back – and I could actually smell the dampness all around. Upstairs I could hear my wife in pain and more than likely being hurt, whilst I was downstairs in the cellar burying a child's body in a shallow grave – and with that thing that often spoke and which sounded like my mum, standing in some corner peering over at me.

"Perhaps you're thinking of your baby that died and your mam not going to the funeral," Emily said.

"It's just a really horrible dream, M."

This had been the worst of the lot and I had got up with a splitting headache.

Apart from being a bit *touchy-feely* with each other, Tony and Sally had been quite good company and the night before both me and M had done-in a few bottles of wine with them – not in the Huddy or George Best class, but all the same, a bit more than we would normally have had, so I put the headache down to that.

Watching M and Sally cooking breakfast in the big kitchen was quite strange as there was no regiment or structure in what they were doing and they both did things differently – not like with M and her mum or gran, who worked in some form of telekinetic unison – however, the banter between them was something else, so much so, I had to shake my head at times surrounding Sally's brutal honesty about Tony's alleged shortcomings. I just hoped that M never talked about me like that.

Tony, was possibly the most laid back person I had ever met – any more laid back and he'd be in a coma, but the one thing that I had seen over the months was how he loved both Sally and her son.

"He really dotes on them," Emily had told me.

"You really dote on us," I'd replied.

"Yeh, I do a bit, don't I?" she'd winked.

What was a bit special between us, was the similar relationship all four of us had.

Sally had left her nutter husband with Irving and sought solace with an old-school mate in the Hemingford Road area of Barnsbury, before she had met Tony – whilst M had left hers to bunk up with me. The only real difference was that it was me who had the kids and not Emily.

"I met him through my friends' husband," Sally once explained in regard to Tony. "He was so nervous that he never shut up talking."

Again – another similarity to M!

"I thought she was *bladdy* gorgeous," he had told us.

If that was really the case, I wondered why he didn't have a photo of his *wife* pinned up in his office at work and had one of mine – a promotional shot courtesy of Gossard, with Emily dressed in only her underwear.

"Why would he want some poster of me?" my wife had asked one night, whilst sat on the bed. "I certainly wouldn't want one of him."

"It's a man-thing," I'd told her.

"You've got no pin-ups on your office wall," she said.

"Yeh, I have," I'd said. "You."

That got her mind ticking.

"Morocco," I said.

"What – the photo of me six months on, in a bikini – that's your pin up?"

"That's my pin up," I winked.

"All the photo's you have of me and that's the one you have pinned up in your office?" she smiled.

I thought it was a bit special and therefore I told her so.

Once all the kids were out around the pool area it had been more of the same as the night before, with Tony tipping me the wink that this had been arranged for quite a while – them caravanning in the south of France and nipping over into Italy to spend a day or two with us. I obviously knew that to be the case, but M had not really said anything – however, she did mention my night terrors to them and it was then, Sally had become extremely interested.

"Subconsciously, I reckon it's because you don't want to lose your children," she said.

"Why would I bury them?" I shrugged.

"I don't think you are," she said. "I think the decrepit house-thing is a sign of your fear – your house becoming empty if-you-like. M's crying is probably of her being upset and you trying to bury your memory or guilt."

I gave a shrug and said nothing, although I had to be honest – it did freak me out a bit.

"You're a really good dad, Lee," she said. "All the parents at school think so – and Ted thinks the world of you."

"He just fancies M," I said.

"Behave," winked Emily.

Tony had given me a brief tour around the caravan when they had arrived – which, I have to say was his pride and joy, and as such I'd been given a more thorough guided tour next day – HM Customs style, where he showed me all the little nooks and crannies where he stashed all his cigarettes and booze to flog to his mates at the market.

"I can generally make the petrol and camp site money with the gear I fetch back," he smiled. "I was going to come down in the fish van so I could take more back, but the clutch went on it."

Thank god for that, I thought.

We had a natter about football and I told him that M had barred me from doing any serious work.

"She's concerned about my eyes," I told him. "That colourisation department I set up last year has really bollocksed them up."

"So, you're not doing anything?" he inquired.

"Yeh and no," I said.

I then told him about this *Terry Neill-thing* I was on with and the fact that I had Alan Hudson in the studios on a two hours a day scenario.

"I've supposedly got Sooty looking after him," I said. "I should imagine he'll be checking himself into rehab soon and declaring himself bankrupt."

"Who the footballer?"

"No Sooty," I said. "Huddy's a bit of a hell-raiser."

"How old is he – he's got to be knocking on?"

"Age has nothing to do with it," I said. "Back then and outside of football it was birds, booze and the bookies."

"What about now?"

"Nowadays he takes a keener interest in football."

I told him about the quantity of footage I had of him along with the feedback he'd been giving me that had given me a totally different viewpoint of Terry Neill.

It was assumed that at the start of the 1977/78 season that certain problems had been ironed out and that Arsenal meant business.

£500,000 for Trevor Francis.

£400,000 for Butch Wilkins

or £350,000 for Graeme Souness.

and £300,000 for Derek Statham.

Francis was class, scoring a hat-trick against Arsenal in the previous season and so as not to be outdone Malcolm Macdonald hit one as well – however, Francis had made his point and Birmingham would welcome the money, as would Chelsea. 'Come in Master Wilkins, your time is up'.

As for the 24-year old Souness – he was an interesting player, who had been with Tottenham, but had reportedly been homesick. They had therefore sold him to Middlesbrough for £30,000 in 1972, which just goes to show that a manager with as much savvy as Bill Nicholson does make the odd mistake. He had played his part in both Middlesbrough's 3-0 and 4-1 demolitions of Arsenal the season prior, but Arsenal as a club had been all over the place at that time, with Neill and Wilf Dixon trying to conjure up some form of system that didn't ship in goals – and barring shoring-up the goal with sections of ply board and four-by-two, it seemed as if they had tried everything.

Buying Tottenham Hotspur's transfer-listed Willie Young for £80,000 had seemed to plug the gap, but as Arsenal would find, it was only a temporary solution.

Neill said that he had wanted a tall dominating centre-half when he had signed him for Spurs, so one could assume that he had wanted the same for Arsenal, describing it as a seven-year relationship which was sometimes turbulent, but never dull. "People have often expressed my surprise at being able to get on with Willie Young," Neill had said. "However, I always admired his will to win and felt that he was a far better player than he was ever given credit for."

"Young will always need astute players alongside him, for while his height gives him a natural command in straightforward aerial situations the ball is apt to bounce unpredictably off various parts of his anatomy below," said David Lacey of the *Guardian* post-Young's Arsenal debut. "Furthermore, his slowness on the turn and into the tackles sometimes leads to him conceding free kicks in dangerous positions."

The purchase of Young along with his partnership with O'Leary had stopped the rot and eventually put a halt to Arsenal's savage losing streak. Neill had a lot to thank him for, but nevertheless, the Arsenal manager would be looking for an upgrade and a player to replace him come September 1978.

What of Derek Statham as Arsenal had a Northern Ireland international left-back in Sammy Nelson?

Neill had said of Nelson in how he could behave irrationally and it sometimes showed in both his play and actions. He was a crowd favourite, but football is a serious game – and you need winners, not jokers. I had mentioned before that Nelson had gone AWOL for a few days after being sent off after 56 minutes in a friendly match against Racing Club Paris in November 1972 – and then there would be that career defining incident on 4th April 1979, where he dropped his shorts and stuck out his backside at Highbury's North Bank after he scored Arsenal's equaliser, having been barracked by the self-same section of the crowd after turning the ball into his own net earlier-on in the 1-1 draw against Coventry City.

If you want to see another side of Nelson – watch him in Leeds United's 3-0 win over Arsenal up at Elland Road on 25th March 1972.

"Arsenal definitely needed a top class left-back," Huddy had told me. "I liked Statham as he was very good player, but it was Kenny Sansom who was tailor made for Arsenal. Now he was a terrific footballer."

With Arsenal supporters expecting big names through Highbury's revolving door it came as something as a let-down when none came.

In came Northern Ireland's 1976/77 Young Player of the Year, 19-year old Jim Harvey – a £20,000 signing from Glenavon and 19-year old Steve Walford, a £25,000 signing from Tottenham Hotspur.

The newspapers were talking up a summer of investment in the hundreds of thousands – maybe a million – and all Arsenal had laid out was £45,000 for a couple of kids. And if you consider the deals for Rimmer, Howard, Rostron and Armstrong, there had been no real outlay. Arsenal hadn't actually spent anything. In fact, they had made money.

You had to love Arsenal – if they could do things without spending money, they would.

I sat jotting things down and imagining what could have been, whilst over on the drive Tony had the hood up on his car, and was topping up the radiator and windscreen wash before checking the oil. My lad and young Irving were booting a ball around on the main lawn, whilst his wicked step mum and Erv's mum were sat over on the patio with Herbert being fed from a silver spoon by his big sister – and to the sound of music in the background. It was how a summer should be spent ...or so I thought.

I'd never really described Sally – nor Tony for that matter. She was a rather buxom 27-year old – around 5'6, slim – and had blonde hair, which she more often than not, had tied up. I am sure it was dyed, as at times I thought I noticed dark roots in her crown – although, I couldn't be positive on that. Was she pretty? Yeh, not bad – but she was certainly no-one that I would go for – but as I've often said, I tend to be fairly picky. She also had a Geordie-dialect, possessed that strange sense of humour and dressed quite well. Certainly not in the Emily or Jeanette sense, but all the same, she was always fairly-well turned-out.

I walked over to the Volvo, sipped at my coffee and watched Tony under the hood meticulously checking that everything was in order. '"You getting ready for the drive back up into France?" I asked.

"I think Sally was wanting another day here," he said. "She thinks the world of you both."

She had made that point a little more than quite obvious last night, I thought.

I may have thought it, but I never actually said it.

When people have had a drink, one of a few things can happen. In this instance, Tony had fallen asleep – and as the consumption of alcohol also has a tendency to lower ones' guard, honesty rears its head, and as such Sally had been extremely complimentary to Emily. "You're so slight," she had said. "And so, flipping pretty, I just want to cuddle you."

And she did.

Drink also brings out the bullshit as well.

As for me, I had my thigh rubbed a couple of times and got told how lucky Emily was to have me. "I can only imagine how happy you make her feel," she winked.

Drink also tends to help overcome any inhibitions –
that is of course if there was any to start with.

Emily had sat on the bed crossed-legged that night – even though merry from the drink, scratching her head in thought. "I can't make out if it's me she fancies, or you," she whispered.

"Both," I told her.

I wasn't wrong either. If it had been up to Sally she would have been climbing in bed with us – as all she wanted to do was kiss Emily – and on Tony finally managing to release her grasp on my wife, she threw herself on me. Drink eh?

From what Tony told me, they as a couple were having certain problems. If I was being honest, as a couple I thought they got on fine – in fact, more than fine, and there was certainly nothing that I could see, that I could put my finger on. Then again, if you're not looking for it, I suppose you never see it.

"I'm trying my best to hold on to her," he told me. "I love her that much I'd do anything for her."

We spoke at length and I had to admit – I just thought they were quite nice people. And my lad thought the word of Erv' and his *new* dad – however, his new dad wasn't too fond of the old one.

"Her ex-husband is a right evil manipulating bastard," he said.

I had been told and I let him know.

Both Emily and Jeanette had relayed the story of him following her down to London and giving her a good hiding after he had finally found her – and then trying to drag her back up home, so much so, she had resided in a safe house for a while. Tony had been her salvation.

"Just get a restraining order put on him when he gets out (of prison)," I said.

There's a bit more to it than that," he said.

There was. Sally still loved him.

I looked over at the patio to where both our wives were sat – Emily and my daughter were encouraging our Sammy to stand up and walk – yeh, and that definitely wasn't happening, whilst Sally had been laid back on a sun lounger and who suddenly lifted up her sunglasses to peer over at me.

Something didn't fit here, and it wasn't just her bikini top.

That afternoon we decided to have a run into San Gimignano. There was a fishmonger in the marketplace who sold fresh Lobster – I mean really fresh in the still being alive and attacking you sense – and Emily had been on about doing some as soon as we arrived.

"What, you boil them alive, M?" my lad had asked.

"Yeh love," she told him.

"You can hear them screaming," I told him. "The sound is unbelievable."

"That's a total fib," Emily said. "That's just the air that gets trapped in the shell."

My lad and Erv' were well into the thought of watching M sling a few live lobsters into a boiling *vat of oil*, so much so, the fishmongers had been our first port of call, with both lads infatuated by the creatures.

Being in the trade, Tony gave them the inside track on the life of a lobster, whilst Emily spewed out some broken Italian, and ordered ten of the things, some langoustines and a couple of kilos of what were huge tiger prawns, paid the man and told him that we would be back to pick up the order in an hour.

"Sarò di nuovo in un'ora," she had said – repeatedly.

"Silly man," she chuntered. "I'm hardly likely to be dragging that lot around with us in the shops."

You had to hand it to her, if she wanted something, she generally got it.

Walking around the town, with M linking me and watching my daughter push her younger brother in his buggy was nothing short of *wonderful*, as was watching the sight of my lad and his mate talking of things such as football, play stations …oh, yeh and New York – the one thing that I had tried to put to the back of my mind.

Tony and Sally lagged behind us and Emily whispered something, which sort of rang true in that she was always pulling him down – tongue in cheek more than not, although some of it could be construed as being quite cruel – yet now they were acting like a pair of love sick fourteen-year olds, holding hands, kissing and now chasing one another and tip-tapping. If I'm being honest, I found it a bit embarrassing. My thinking being that you can do whatever you want in your own home – but I certainly wasn't one for being overly affectionate in public.

I suppose *wonderful* could have been stretching it a bit!

The more we were in their company the more I noticed different things springing up. I suppose every one of us are different, but there's a certain etiquette about how you act when kids are present – especially mine, and the full-on kissing sat at a bar in the piazza was the moment I nipped it all in the bud.

"Tony – come on mate – pack it in," I said.

What was happening was that they had been advertising their affection for each other. Not to the public in general, but to us. I had seen this try and play out on me before and I was therefore no stranger to it. The building of a great friendship with the similar situations (us and them) – having the same avid interests (football, kids, films and music) – the indulging in great conversations (family and work) – the so-called deep honesty (Love and sex) – and the ever so well thought out conclusion.

These two idiots were fucking swingers.

All the previous night they had been nothing but fun – the bouncing around of nice healthy dialogue and the odd curt comment, followed by a wink. He had been great company, but his girlfriend I had to say had been rather over-complimentary and a bit *touchy-feely*. Nothing out of the ordinary – but all the same, I was quite certain that I knew where this was heading.

Three easy steps to ruin a friendship: My wife wants you to shag her. I want to shag your wife. Let's shag.

Emily had done a great job on the lobsters, even though Sally did a bit of prodding and poking about with hers and after the kids had gone to bed it was then that they made their *big play*. It's generally always up to the female to pave the way. I know it's off topic – but think of the Moors Murderers and Myra Hindley. Someone had to get the trust of the kids to get them in the car, as Brady was someone who could have never done that. It's always the woman and in these cases, it is putting the wife completely at ease, before she goes to work on the husband. As soon as the husband drops his guard, then the other party moves in. It's how these so-called liberated people work. They hunt their pray.

Since arriving, I had been in her sights. I hardly acted like some deer in her headlights as she had gibbered her *sweet nuthin's* at me over the table, whilst at the same time rubbing the inside of my thigh. Our life was Premier League and we were at the summit. This duo were struggling in the Championship and still trying to work out their strategy. How they had acted in the piazza had indicated their one-dimensional tactics – her giving me they eye, whilst pretending to straighten up her cleavage. They had one play and one play only and that was easily counteracted by the woman at my side. I had Emily and Emily blew every other woman away. She was exactly what a woman should be.

Sally kicked off her shoes and went into the pool – almost fully clothed and the play was set. "Are you coming in, Lee?" she asked.

This was followed by both her top and her bra coming off as she splashed around.

"Come on in, the water's lovely."

Tony looked over at me in anticipation, hoping that I would.

"What time are you on about going tomorrow?" I asked him.

And there you had it. In a totally different league.

Early very next day I was out on the patio sharing a bowl of Weetabix with Herbert, whilst the sun came up. Well I wasn't really, I was on the laptop – working and researching a piece of information about Tony Currie of all people – and him wanting to leave Leeds United and hook up with a London club, with Arsenal supposedly interested in him as a possible replacement for Alan Hudson.

Herbert was in his baby chair insisting that I try some of his cereal, so much so, he slung a dollop of it onto my keyboard.

"Eat it like a good lad or I'll chuck you in the pool," I told him.

"Water," he said.

"Yeh – good boy – water."

That was a new word, as was "Erv'."

There was movement over at the caravan. It appeared that the Gypo's were leaving.

"Morning Lee," said Tony

I gave him a nod, but that was as far as I was prepared to go.

I sought solace in my Tony Currie story and noted that on the 2nd April 1979, that the *Daily Express* had run a piece saying that Currie's wife, Linda, wanted to move back to her *native* London and that Leeds may be reluctantly forced to sell their 28-year-old England midfielder.

"I will be seeing my manager again as soon as possible to discuss the situation, but I do not want to leave Leeds," Currie had said, before answering questions of his wife's wish to go back down south. "Questions like that are very personal. It is certainly not something that I am prepared to talk about."

There had been suggestions that they were swingers – something that Currie had acknowledged in later life.

Stupid parents can ruin it for their children and I felt sorry for young Irving as he hadn't a clue what was going on. "Why are we going mam?" he asked.

Emily came down, just as they were ready for leaving and my lad was a bit downhearted to say the least. "Can't they stay a bit longer?" he asked. "We were going to go fishing for that eel later."

I just rubbed his head and told him that if they didn't go today that they would miss their ferry.

"See you Erv'," he shouted – my lad knowing that with New York on the horizon, that he would possibly never see his mate again.

Sally's little lad just waved through the rear car window and they were gone.

"You handled everything brilliantly," Emily told me afterwards.

I had known the minute we had sat down at the bar in the piazza what their game had been and they both knew that I knew and as such, it was either hold back and try again at some later date, or go all out and see how it played.

"It's a game," I told her. "And the chase is all part of it."

"She kept on going on about how nice looking you were …and some other things," she said, before adding. "But they seem so close – touching each other and holding hands and all that."

"It's how they do it," I said.

"You seem to know a lot about it," said my wife. "Did you and Jeanette ever – yer know."

"Never," I told her. "But it wasn't for the lack of Libby trying."

That bit certainly shocked her.

Chapter 32

Rose Garden

The thing that had happened with Tony and Sally had really pissed me off, especially as there had been no consideration for their lad. With people like those, sex is the be all and end all. And where do you go after you've done that – you kick up to the next level and so on and so on – so much so, that the reality is sucked from your life.

Both Emily and myself love a *yer know* – I mean, really love it. That is with each other and the only things that get in the way of us *yer-knowing* are the things in your head. I didn't need to take things to a new level. I had all on dealing with the level I was at.

I thought no more about it and decided to crack on with Basher's *Terry Neill Years* and rather than look at his management I thought I'd nip back into the archives to try and find out more of what actually made the guy tick, as back in mid-August 1962, Bill Holden of the *Daily Mirror* had made comparisons with the-then 20-year old Arsenal captain and 21-year old Bobby Moore of West Ham United – referring to them as the "Boom Boys" of British football: "These are the Young Commanders – players who have the determination to take a grip on the game."

"There's a touch of the Danny Blanchflower about him – the clear blue eyes, the lilt of the voice, the whimsical aside in conversation," wrote John Bromley of the *Daily Mirror* on 21st September 1962. "And there's the confidence, too. The sort of confidence you find in men who are natural leaders. I'm impressed by his maturity, his dedicated approach to the job of being a professional footballer and the fluent way he discusses the captaincy without any self-heroics."

What was strange is that even though Neill played for the bigger club, he went on to win absolutely nothing, whilst Moore – well, he won almost every honour in the game, including the World Cup.

Fast-forward five years and Neill was presented with the best chance that he would ever get of winning honours as a player. Being an almost ever present in Arsenal's 1967/68 season – missing only half a dozen games – the club made their return to Wembley for the first time in 16 years after a 6-3 aggregate win over Huddersfield Town (3-2 at Highbury; 3-1 at Leeds Road) and were pitted against Leeds United in the 1968 League Cup Final.

However, Bertie Mee did the unthinkable and dropped him. Neill was made substitute and the petulant side of the player reared its head, so much so, he was accused of deliberately missing the line-up when the two teams were introduced to Princess Alexandra.

"During the manager's team talk before the game I just sat at the back of the dressing room reading letters and at the end of the game I walked straight into the dressing room, not even bothering to pick up my loser's medal (tankard)," Neill had said in later life.

Norman Giller of the *Daily Express* however, was treat to the two sides of Neill straight after the game. "This whole sickening business has set question marks flying around in my head about the future – perhaps a change of clubs will be best all around," he had told the journalist.

About missing the *mingling with royalty* bit, Neill back-tracked, before introducing his own bit of blarney: "I was just pulling a track suit on when the call came for us to leave the dressing room. I was fumbling around like a blind mouse in a cage and simply couldn't catch up with the rest of the lads."

The signs were there: Neill and Mee would never see eye-to-eye again.

Regarding his relationship with his manager, Neill indicated that Mee suffered from 'Small Man Syndrome' stating that he could be too officious at times and that they often went head to head – with his manager publicly threatening to fine him for comments he had made in the press about the manager dropping him – this time for another game, against Manchester United.

"There were times when I felt like dropping him," Neill said in later life.

Like he did with Graham Rix – the player Neill himself dropped for the 1978 F.A Cup Final?

This was all good stuff and I wondered what Bertie Mee would have thought of Neill being given his job.

Billy Wright was convinced that his protégée-cum-incarnation was destined for greatness, with the-then Arsenal manager telling Bill Holden, "I believe he has the gift of leadership – possesses the drive and the understanding of the game and the ambition that does not allow him to accept a set-back."

Wright's comments came after on the club's 1962/63 pre-season tour of Sweden, where Arsenal had beaten Gothenburg 5-1, with inside-forward John Barnwell hitting one of the goals for The Gunners.

It would be strange how both Gothenburg and John Barnwell would figure in Arsenal's attempted resurrection of its glory years and Terry Neill's greatest period of management – Gothenburg again being battered 5-1 by Arsenal in the 1980 European Cup Winners Cup Quarter-Final and the fact that Barnwell would go head-to-head with Neill as manager of Wolverhampton Wanderers in the 1979 F.A Cup Semi-Final. What is also strange is that the other inside-forward for Arsenal during the clubs best-ever season between the two Championship winning seasons of 1953 and 1971, Jimmy Bloomfield – would be manager of Orient, the team Arsenal would play in the 1978 F.A Cup Final.

I loved parallels, coincidences – call them what you will.

What is also strange is that whilst with Wolves and Orient, both managers would undergo life-saving operations – Barnwell after sustaining a serious head injury after fracturing his skull and Bloomfield as he'd been diagnosed with stomach cancer.

The last game they ever played together for Arsenal was on 30th August 1960, in a 2-0 defeat up at Preston North

End, which got me thinking about doing some form of documentary on the two.

Who could not love football history?

This was all getting extremely interesting – however, Emily asked me to knock off for a few hours as she had a picnic on her itinerary and as such, we spent the morning – and half the afternoon in some nearby albeit rather dense woodland – with both eldest kids being able to ride their bikes along its tracks in search of grey wolves, weasels, stoats and what have you – and with their youngest brother tugging away at a tippy cup of orange, whilst sat in his buggy and being chauffeured by his chatterbox of a mum.

As for me I had been ladled down with a picnic hamper and a cooler box with enough grub in them to sink a ship, and on finding a clearing M laid out a huge red checked tablecloth, put the radio on and gave Sammy the chance to try and do a bit of standing up. Unfortunately, however, he enjoyed crawling much better and as that was the case I had the thankless task of continually retrieving him. "Can't we just tie him to a tree?" I said, after the fifth or sixth time of fetching him.

"Aw – he just wants to play with his brother and sister," Emily chuckled, as she put some food out.

When I wasn't *fetching and carrying* Herbert, I was being attacked by loads of midges.

"Why don't they attack you?" I said, whilst swatting them. "You taste loads better."

"Stop moaning and try this," smiled my wife, as she fork-fed me some crayfish and prawn in what was a pinky taramosalata-type sauce.

"Mmm, that's well-nice," I said.

Emily shouted the kids over and we all tucked in, with my lad becoming quite the epicurean aficionado. "I quite like that cayenne pepper on my new potatoes, M," he'd said, whilst wolfing one down, before suddenly going off point. "I love it here – don't you dad?"

"I do mate," I told him.

"I wish Erv' could have stayed though."

I looked over at Emily, who just gave a shrug of her tiny shoulders.

Whilst we ate, I recalled a conversation with Huddy about average players – *Yes-men* and the like, and I found myself reading something that our flawed genius had recently told Rex Graham of the *Daily Express* in that sometimes winning is the worst thing that can happen, citing England's winning of the World Cup in 1966 as being a prime example.

"England had the best inside forward in George Eastham and the best striker in the world in Jimmy Greaves watching from the bench," Huddy had told him. "It was a case of winning with lesser players such as Roger Hunt, Jack Charlton, Nobby Stiles and George Cohen. They were very average players, but they fitted into the system Alf Ramsey wanted. That was a bad thing for English football because all club managers went out and did the same."

It is exactly what I'd been saying for ages and had been a blueprint for success at several clubs – Arsenal's 1970/71 season included.

"We in England don't embrace the Glenn Hoddles, the Tony Curries, the Matt Le Tissiers or, dare I say it, the Alan Hudsons," added Huddy. "For years England have been using midfield players who just run around. These types of players are just like robots."

Regarding sheer averageness – if that's even a word, Huddy had told me, "When you look at Carlton Palmer, I think it tells the story in a nutshell – if he was an England player then we might as well let the ball down and all go home."

That then got me thinking about Arsenal trying to sign Calvin Palmer (no relation) on 18th September 1963, with Billy Wright telling Nottingham Forest manager Johnny Carey at the time, "Don't do anything until I get there."

Don Revie of Leeds United and Stan Cullis of Wolverhampton Wanderers both wanted the 22-year old, Skegness-born, tough tackling box-to-box, albeit extremely confrontational midfielder – however, who should steam in there and buy him for £35,000? Huddy's mate and mentor,

Tony Waddington. And who was the player that he would replace? Eddie Clamp.

My head was all over the shop with this, which was something that had been mentioned to me by Emily only a few weeks ago, when I'd forgot to pick up the kids from their mum's.

"Aren't we forgetting something, father?" asked my wife, on me getting home, post-peck on the lips and her looking around for a couple of missing persons.

I shrugged my shoulders.

"It's Friday, it's five o'clock and it's Crackerjack," she winked.

"Shit," had been my reply.

I told her that I'd pick the kids up as she had taken Herbert to the vets for yet more inoculations and when I eventually got down to Clerkenwell I had two angry offspring sporting coats and backpacks, both growling at me.

"I can't believe you forgot about us," my daughter had said. "M must have mentioned it about a million times the other day."

As for Sammy and his jabs – it had been his mum's idea to make sure that he would never contract any contagious disease – ever, and the intensity of her research made sure that our offspring had seen nearly as many syringes as Pete Docherty. That's the hat wearing musician who played with The Libertines and certainly not the pipe smoking ex-Manchester City and Derby County inside-forward with the baffling body swerve and explosive shot.

I laid back on the grass deep in thought and fell asleep only to be awoken by a wife rolling an ice-cold cherry around my lips. "Yer dropped off," she whispered, before biting into the fruit.

"How long have I been out?" I asked.

"Maybe forty minutes," she said, as she took another piece of fruit from a bowl. "D'yer want one?"

"Nah – I'm good," I said.

"Come over here and put your head on my lap and talk to me," she garbled.

I did, and she played with my hair whilst rattling on about one thing and another.

My lad was right – it was lovely here.

"Are yer sure you don't want one?" she asked.

"Go on then," I said, prior to her popping one in my mouth.

"I could quite easily live here," she said. "Could you?"

You had to hand it to her – she was rarely negative about anything and I glanced over to see Sammy laid flat out in his buggy and both kids scrambling on their bikes.

"I like the nice weather and the fresh air," I told her.

"Me too," she garbled, whilst merrily chomping away on piece of fruit.

"Maybe if you still love me when I'm say forty-five or fifty – we could maybe plan to retire somewhere like this," I told her.

"What really?" she smiled.

"Why not? It worked for John Thaw …and his wife was another whiny-faced cow."

"Who – Lindsay Duncan?"

"Yeh – imagine waking up next to her."

That had her giggling.

"Thinking about it, we should watch that one night," I said.

"We should," she replied, whilst still multi-tasking by eating cherries and twiddling with my hair, before suddenly going off-point. "Can I ask you a question?"

"About football – certainly," I said.

"No, it's not about football."

"So, long as it's not about ex-wives, girlfriends or kids who I caught nits off, then."

"No – it's about Libby," she said.

"What about her?"

"Did you and her – well, yer know?"

"You must be frigging joking," I said.

"You said that she *hit* on you, though."

"What – and that means I have to have given her one?" I said. "I'd rather stick *it* in a thirty-two-amp socket."

That made her smile.

I then told her exactly what happened – nothing.

"Did yer tell Jeanette," she inquired.

Jeanette hadn't been stupid and the last thing she had wanted was Sooty's sticky little fingers prodding and poking about with her as part of some cheap and dirty swapsy. She hadn't been all that fussed in me doing it after she'd had the kids, so he had absolutely no chance. Nevertheless, I doubt if she would have gone to the pains of CS gassing him prior to wrapping a vase full of flowers around his head.

I looked at my watch, which told me it was five minutes off 3.00 pm. It also made Emily assume that her line of questioning had pissed me off.

"I'm sorry," she said. "I shouldn't really ask questions like that."

"Why not – you're only being inquisitive."

"You just tend to look at your watch when you're bored," she said.

I had no idea why she thought that as I never could never have been bored with her and I said as much.

"I just remember that time in the *Garden*," she said.

"What – our garden?"

"No, great yer nit – Covent Garden."

I then knew exactly what she meant.

"Lee – I'm pregnant," she had told me over the phone.

I'd met her in some restaurant a few days later and all I remembered doing was looking at my watch and wanting it all to go away.

"I'm really sorry, M," I told her. "I was a bit selfish back then."

That made her smile.

"If I could go back and change a few things, then that would certainly be one of them," I said.

"Mine would be turning up at your mum's house when I was sixteen and demanding that you marry me," she said.

"Really," I laughed.

"No, not really," she mumbled. "That's also me just being a bit selfish."

"Selfish?" I shrugged. "How's that being selfish?"

"It is a bit," she said. "As I'd never want to rob us of the children."

"Our life's perfect, M."

"I wish you were right, Lee," she said.

"I am."

"It's quite perfect now," she mumbled, "but I'm really dreading going home."

My kids and the New York-thing had been playing on her mind.

"Things can change," I said. "Trust me."

She just gave me a smile, whilst still playing with my hair. "I really hope you're right, love."

They can. Donna Harding and her husband never came down to London, when I'd thought it was a nailed-on certainty that they would. I'm not really sure what happened – however, it was M's call if she wanted to tell me.

"You never really asked me about Donna," she said, whilst at the same time obviously reading my mind – again.

"Probably because it's none of my business and if you wanted to tell me, you would."

"I went off her a bit when I read the script for the series," she said.

"Oh yeh?"

"She also implied a lot of things – the one that stood out was that it should be **her** living in London with you and not me."

"She implied or said?" I inquired.

"Implied is definitely the right word," she nodded. "When you really read into what she's written, you start to see lots of double-meaning's hidden beneath the surface and some of it's really not very nice."

"It's called being a *bitch*, M."

"I'd really hate it if you ever called me that, Lee."

"M – that's the last thing that I'd ever want to call you."

I got another smile aimed my way.

I had read up on the meaning of the word 'blarney' a few times, whilst I had been on with the Terry Neill documentary. It basically means underhanded lies and bullshit, which are used to both deflect and manipulate –

basically the ability to tell a man to go to hell, in such a way that he will look forward to the trip.

"Terry Neill had been the ideal figurehead for the club," said Frank McLintock. "The way he spoke, dressed and conducted himself with charm, perfectly reflected the board's image of the club and themselves."

That was until he stuck two fingers up them after being made twelfth man at Wembley and refused to go out for the royal handshakes and national anthem and as such was relieved of being club captain thereafter. However, even then he tried his "blind mouse in a cage" blarney to cover-up his actions.

I remember Emily being nothing but honest about our honeymoon destination, with Donna Harding immediately seeing it as something to usurp and subtly giving it the "We went to Paris" dialogue.

I was to also find out that it had been the same with a wedding present that I'd bought her.

We had never really decided on a honeymoon beforehand as we'd been that pre-occupied with the wedding and life itself, therefore we spent our actual wedding night at home. On awaking next day, I said, "Come on M – let's shoot off somewhere for a couple of days."

Emily had been ecstatic. "Can we go to Bridlington?" she asked.

"Brid' – what really?"

"Mmm," she nodded.

"I thought you'd fancy going somewhere a bit warmer," I told her. "That's why I bought you these."

It was then I handed her a present.

Emily opened the small parcel and pulled out a pair of sunglasses and I got an "Aaagh – I love you so much".

"So, you don't fancy shooting off to Barcelona, Madrid or Rome …or somewhere like that," I'd asked, as she carefully examined them.

"No, I just want you to take me to Bridlington."

Even now, those sunglasses are one of Emily's most prized possessions.

Donna had copped them straight away, but had never said anything – however, during the latter letters of her correspondence she certainly had – with the school reunion being the catalyst for bringing them up.

"I would have thought that Lee wouldn't have fallen for going to something (school reunion) as fake as that," she had written. "The teacher will ring the bell and all those silly little girls will go running to him like bunnies with their tails on fire. There they will be – swaying their fake blonde hair from side to side and talking up their little plastic lives through their fake Colgate smiles, whilst all the time trying to hold firm the façade, with nothing more than a few millimetres of Louis Vuitton.

"I think that was a barbed comment aimed at me," said Emily.

There was nothing about her which was fake – and that included the £500 pair of *bins*, which were currently attached to her head.

It had taken Emily nearly five months, over a dozen letters and a few texts to rumble her.

"She disguises it very well," she told me.

"Not when you know what you're looking for, she doesn't."

"What was she wanting?" Emily asked.

"Who knows?" I shrugged. "Trouble, probably."

We got back to the farmhouse sometime later and I found myself trawling through Sooty's interviews with Huddy, some of which were quite enlightening – especially when he was asked about Arsenal trying to sign Gordon McQueen.

"I think Arsenal have had their fair share of average number fives," he had said – one of which was -yes, you've guessed it – Terry Neill.

I'd never thought of McQueen being an average player though, but he had a point, especially when he mentioned how West Germany had moved Franz Beckenbauer back from midfield in a bid to create the play out of defence.

"That was who I learned my game from, moving deeper in my role at Stoke and getting the ball from the goalkeeper, which back then had the opposition shaking their heads, as the centre-forward certainly didn't want to pick you up. Just ask Malcolm Macdonald!"

Don Howe had done a similar thing with Frank McLintock, even though his short ball to Peter Simpson during the March 1973 game against Derby County at Highbury had kick-started a catalogue of mistakes that would eventually have Arsenal throw away a second League and Cup Double.

I then looked at something that Robert Armstrong of the *Guardian* had noted about Arsenal. "One of the reasons for Arsenal's dismal lack of consistency almost certainly lies in defence," he wrote. "Rice, Nelson and O'Leary generally give a good account of themselves going forward, but in their primary role in the back four they are often caught out by the swift raid down the wings and the accurate pass pulled back from the bye-line. Square organisation allied to slowness on the turn have opened the way to Arsenal conceding goals."

He also mentioned the tactical danger in trying to seal off the evident gaps in the back by using Brady in a more defensive role – in that it would stifle the supply line to Macdonald and Stapleton. A double-edged sword? Hardly. Neill had found the option in Hudson, but his failure to successfully man-manage the player caused immediate problems, with the journalist adding, "Neill is not noted for his cool logical analysis of his team's tactics and this lack of detachment may prove a drawback in handling internal complications."

Getting Don Howe back to the club had been part of the solution, but Neill's lack of detachment and parsimony at director level couldn't have helped.

I was all over the place with this, which was down to me getting continually side-tracked and none more than my wife, after all the kids were in bed.

"Emily se sent un peu négligé et doit être donné une certaine attention," seductively pouted my heavily made-up wife, as she clippety-clopped into the kitchen. "Et Emily veut sa chatte chaude et humide montrant certains trop."

"Wow – you look good," I told her.

I wasn't lying. She did.

She came over and closed my laptop, pushed me back in the chair, hitched up her dress and climbed over me, before cupping my face with both her hands and planting one on me.

"Chatte?" I garbled through the kiss. "Is that a cat?"

"Presque," she winked.

"I love you," I told her.

"Je connais," she whispered. "Et je t'aime aussi."

It was all very cinematic in a *La chasse à l'homme* kind of way and as always, nothing short of brilliant.

"What did yer reckon?" she beamed, straight after the really dirty deed had been done.

What did I reckon? Same as I always reckoned – there was certainly no way that any other kids were going to play with my toys! And that included both Sooty and the live prop that just a few minutes earlier I'd seen her audition with, courtesy of both Dropbox and my shit-stirring assistant – namely one Miss Abigail Tyson.

"Anyway, I need a little word with you, missus" I said, as I beckoned my finger.

"That sounds ominous," she smiled.

"Have you seen this?" I said on kicking up the media file in question.

"Oops," she giggled.

Post-ten minutes of soft core porn, which included a retake, I then asked the question, "Who's idea was this?"

"Uh, uh," she shrugged.

"Eighteen months earlier and you'd have been on a frigging sex charge," I said.

"He's dead good kisser for his age," she winked.

"Really."

"Mmm," she nodded. "I was really surprised when he put his tongue in my mouth."

"What really?" I gasped.

"No," she smiled, as she sat on my lap and gave me a cuddle. "I'm only kidding."

"Thank god for that," I said.

"I put mine in his though."

I just shook my head.

"Two or three times," she mumbled, whilst in thought. "Yeh, three."

I couldn't believe her at times.

"I hope him that they cast as Donna's dad is good looking," she said. "I'd hate to kiss anyone that's – yer know, really ugly."

Like I said – I couldn't believe her at times.

The person who this little audition had hit the most however – and according to Ginge, had been Stuart, as he and Jonathan were now 'not talking'.

"So, are there any more hot scenes like this?" I tentatively inquired.

"I only did that one in the audition," she said. "But out of the twelve scenes that I'm in, there are three that I sort of do that in – yer know, the big one where you walk in on ...yer know, yer mam."

"Oh right," I said.

"I'll not do it, if you don't want me to," she smiled.

"Don't be daft," I told her.

"You don't mind then?"

"I think you look awesome M – and I know that you'll blow everyone away."

I got yet another smile that I could have framed – however, the problem wasn't the professional way in which my wife had dispatched her kisses or indeed her canoodling prowess, but the fact that she was playing the part of a woman loosely based on my mum and it had got certain thoughts running through my head. I then told her about the time when all this was all going on – not when I was sixteen like in the series they were making, but in *real time* when I was eight.

"Deep inside I used to know," I told her. "I used to get sent to my Auntie Margaret's."

For some reason my auntie and my mum never really hit it off and on her having to look after me, she had made that point known. I had been beaten – you know, badly beaten. "Stand still," she had screamed, one particular time whilst propping me up with one of her hands around my throat. Then I got a fist in the face. Not once – numerous times, and I told Emily exactly that. "I didn't know what I'd done wrong M," I said.

Emily was aghast.

"It happened a lot – I tried to tell my mum, but she was always preoccupied," I said. "Watching her prune herself up for a date with him – and for me to be left with her."

"That's awful, love," she said.

"I remember a song playing on the radio at the time," I said. "I can't recall what exactly, but it has been present in those horrible dreams I've been having. You know, when all the bad stuff is happening."

"What song?" she shrugged.

"Not sure," I said.

I then gave her some words that I remembered.

"'Smile for a while'," I said. "But the tune in my head is a lot different to the one I heard as a kid – I used to pray for my mum to come and pick me up, but sometimes she never did."

Just then there was a knock at the door.

"I'll get it love," Emily said, as she jumped off my knee to answer it.

It was the boring caretaker.

"Whey, hey, hey," he said in his Eric Morecambe-voice, on M opening the door. "You look smashing – are you both going out?"

"Not that I know of," Emily shrugged. "Is everything alright?"

"The lock has been broken on the garage," he said. "You've not had anything taken, have you?"

Emily explained that it was me who had done it as the kids had been curious as to what was inside, and that she would pay for a new lock.

"You didn't need to break it, the keys are in the cupboard," he said, pointing over to the place where the bin bags were kept. "I never had the chance to tell you as you are both always busy."

There was a bit of a white lie in that lot – and us *being busy* was definitely it. We just wanted quality time together, and having some boring caretaker prattling on about irrelevancies such as him being a one-time champion pool player back home in Manchester, winning singing competitions whilst dressed up in his Elvis garb and *Kojak* being in *The Magnificent Seven* wasn't really my idea of quality time – even though my lad did quite like him. "Do Elvis for us again, John?" my lad had asked.

"One for the money," he Elvised. "Two for the show…"

And that is one of the sixteen reasons why I didn't want him around. Any excuse to sing in your face and he would.

"'Smile for a while'," Emily said to him. "What song is that from?"

"Smile for a while and let's be jolly – love shouldn't be so melancholy, come along and share the good times, while you ca-a-an," he sang.

I suddenly felt a scurry of rats running up my spine.

"It's *Rose Garden*," said Emily. "The song was Rose Garden."

"Lynn Anderson," said John, before breaking out into song and gyrating his shoulders, "…I can promise you things like big diamond rings…"

However, Emily stopped him dead and slung him out. "I can't be doing with that all night," she said.

I then spoke for ages about things that had happened, with one of the things being – me pissing the bed at six-years old and having to see someone about it, which had really been embarrassing.

"Rotherham social services were as crap back then, as they are now," I told her.

"Didn't your mam know what was going on?" was a question that Emily quite rightly asked, and which was a question I didn't really know the answer to.

"It was Sooty who stopped it all," I said.

"Sooty?" she shrugged.

"He told his dad."

And that was one of the many reasons why I had clung on to him all my life, why I thought so much of him and why I had so much guilt floating around in my head about taking everything from him. I spewed everything out. Everything.

"He told his dad what was happening and he went around and ended up hitting them both," I said.

"Both?" Emily shrugged.

"My uncle was there as well," I said. "He was as bad as her. Sooty's dad leathered them and went scatty with my mum. He even brought my gran to the house."

That was it – my gran had been mentioned – I couldn't say anymore and Emily just gave me a massive hug.

"The thing with Sooty," I said, shaking my head. "Sooty, along with my gran and granddad helped me get to where I am, so to speak."

"Yeh, sat in a kitchen a thousand miles away from home, absolutely heartbroken," she said, whilst still giving me a cuddle.

I felt guilty in not fighting for the kids and ruining Sooty. In my mind, I appeared a coward for the first and nothing short of a bastard for the second. The kids had kept me from doing something stupid after Jeanette had thrown me out and Sooty had indirectly stopped all the violence and brought my grandparents back into my life. As for M – she was my cog in the middle that made everything work and I can't emphasise enough how much I loved her. But how I just wished that Sooty hadn't done what he had.

"Rose Garden," Emily said. "Your mam's *Rose* and you are digging the *Garden* ...yer know, in your dreams."

"It is hardly a garden, M," I told her. "I am hiding the bodies of two kids."

"It makes sense what Sally said," she replied. "Hiding your guilt at not fighting for them – the big empty house – the upset – your mam."

I woke up early the next morning and went and checked on all three kids. "Did you sleep okay," Emily asked, on me coming back into the bedroom.

The dreams were still there, but I had to admit after several times of hearing Lynn Anderson explain her *Rose*

Garden theory, courtesy of both Emily and YouTube, the haunting music hadn't been there – however, my dad had. With me as a little kid on a motor boat at the Children's Pleasure Ground in Bridlington – however, when I looked up it wasn't my dad – it was Frank Stapleton.

"I slept fine," I lied.

Emily grilled some bacon and made some coffee and told me that she was glad that I had told her.

Not the fact that Frank Stapleton was really my dad, but about all the other stuff. I certainly wasn't glad that Sooty's mitts had been where they shouldn't have been and I told him as much when he rang in at lunchtime.

"I've told you I'm sorry," he said. "About fifty fucking times. I was pissed. I'm sorry."

"How's Huddy doing?"

"The same," he said. "He knocked the house up a six o'clock, sat in front of the camera for a couple of hours, nipped out to see Basher and then went for a pint. I'm just driving down to Heckfield Place in Fulham to bail him."

"What – the police?"

"Yip," said Sooty.

I knew he'd had brushes with the law in the past – drink driving, being the main thing and on 24th February 1975, he'd even had them pursuing him during a game – a 0-0 draw at Kenilworth Road, where he had been spat at by a section of the Luton Town support following a controversial decision by referee Tommy Reynolds in not acknowledging a legitimate goal.

"We were playing superbly and heading for the title, and that was why it was so heated," Huddy had told me. "We totally outplayed them and it was only a matter of time before we scored, and then I played a one-two with Geoff Salmons, went around their goalkeeper before rolling it into an empty net. The next thing I know a defender had rushed back and scooped it out and just as it was going to touch the netting. I thought the referee was joking when he waved play-on. That led to furious scenes and at half-time as I was walking off this chap spat in my face so I wiped it off and replied by giving him the same. A copper stepped in and as I was so mad, I also gave him a piece of my mind."

James Lawton of the *Daily Express* had expressed worries that Hudson's passion and outright honesty could lead to something more sinister as only a couple of weeks' prior, referee Gordon Hill had pulled up the player at White Hart Lane during his team's 2-0 win against Terry Neill's floundering Spurs, and told him that he was getting far too big for his boots – partly because the player often referred to the official who took charge of the F.A Cup Semi-Final he played in between Chelsea and Watford at White Hart Lane in 1970, as 'Benny'.

"The remarkably candid Hudson, whose brilliant midfield play this season has been the most consistent reason for Stoke City's Championship leadership and which has made him a front runner in the players' own footballer of the year poll, was extremely lucky not to be sent off," Lawton added. "Hudson himself regrets losing his head and spitting at those fans, but says he was badly provoked and it was a piece of retaliation – which he did admit later-on, is no excuse."

"He was allegedly passing dodgy twenty's in some shop down Fulham Broadway," Sooty had explained.

This had Basher Enterprises Inc. written all over it.

"Abi got in touch with your legal people and they are down on site now trying to make it go away," he added.

"Just tell Abi that we passed them him and that we've been subject of copping for a few," I said.

"That's exactly what she did say," he replied. "Unfortunately, he had a wad of notes that could have choked a fucking donkey."

"He didn't spit at them, did he?" I inquired.

"Huddy? I don't think so – why?"

I then told him about the spitting incident pre-Arsenal.

"He's sometimes too fucking honest for his own good," said Sooty. "He told Libby that she'd do well to drop a few pounds and smile a bit more – she went berserk."

The candidness of Alan Hudson. Every time I thought of him, it raised a smile.

I kept asking myself the question of why Neill hadn't looked at the bigger picture. All players are different and therefore each one requires a different approach. He didn't get on with Ball – he got shut; he didn't get on with Hudson – he got shut.

On Jimmy Harvey's brief stay at Arsenal he'd had this to say: "The midfield was very competitive and it was tough trying to get into the squad. At that time, Liam Brady was recognised as the best midfield player in the country and, in my opinion, Alan Hudson was every bit as good – a marvellous player."

It was a hard one to fathom.

"What did you talk about on camera?" I asked Sooty.

"Terry Neill."

"The only thing in Terry Neill's favour when it comes to him not buying players, was that Arsenal did have a very tight wage structure, and I was led to believe that they wouldn't break it for anyone," Huddy had said. "My problem when signing was that money was secondary, which is partly why I haven't got any."

Again, the candidness of Alan Hudson!

"I only ever asked about money after my first season at Chelsea and after being picked for the World Cup squad," Huddy added. "I wanted a raise from seventy-five quid a week – and you have to remember that Johnny Haynes was getting hundred quid a week ten years prior – but Sexton said, 'Come back when you can put six England caps on my desk', which when I worked it out fifteen years later, that if that was the case, I would still be on the exact same wage."

Johnny Haynes was on £110 per week in 1964, which is the equivalent of £2,050 in today's money.

Huddy's wages would have been the equivalent of just over £1,100 a week.

Just for the record, Terry Neill was in Arsenal's reserves at the time Hudson had his first full season and was earning exactly twice as much.

"So, what else have you been up to?" I asked him.

"Apart from chaperoning Huddy – trying to de-woodenise the three fucking stooges," he said, obviously referring to our three school chums. "Not much – what are you up to?"

I told him that we'd had some visitors *swing* by, but as they had pissed me off, they had left.

"The fishmonger and his wife?" he inquired.

"The same," I said.

Whilst I was on the dog and bone to Sooty, Emily was speaking to Jeanette, and telling her of her concerns for me, which totally went against the grain as the last thing I neither needed nor wanted was Ross Bain knowing any of my business. The big news was however, that Jeanette had failed to land the job and Emily passed me her phone ...whilst I gave her Sooty to talk to.

"I'm sorry Jeanette," I told her.

I had been under the impression that her getting the job was a formality – a done-deal, so much so, there had been contracts flying backwards and forwards – with Annie and our law firm going through amendment after amendment and I told her as much.

"I fluffed the final screen tests," she told me. "I possibly had a bit too much on my mind."

I listened to her talking about the kids – us – me and Emily – her mum and dad, but not Ross.

"The kids have been great," I said.

"M says you've had Tony and Sally over?"

"Tell me about it," I replied, before giving her the edited highlights.

"I told you, didn't I?" she gasped.

Jeanette had been in their company whilst at our house and had noticed a few things. "They just want to shag you both," she had said.

The strange thing was, was that she hadn't said anything to M about it.

"So, what happens now," I asked.

There was a short silence.

"I have a load of work for you if you want it," I told her. "ITV Seven is going out twenty-four/seven and ITV's new head of programming wants you to host some reality show."

She didn't say a deal, but I knew that something was afoot, and it was Emily who told me – well she did eventually.

Cue: the Sooty conversation.

Emily hadn't seen nor spoken to Sooty since the *thing* at Wortley Hall. What he did was very wrong and that was that. It was up to me if I spoke to him, but that was my choice, as it was M's if she didn't. Again, and as with Jeanette, she didn't really relay the contents of her conversation and would just give it me in dribs and drabs over the next few weeks. She was rather happy about something however.

"So, it sounds like the children aren't going to New York?" she said, as she put her arms out before giving me a "Yah-ooo". And whilst I swung her around I got told that she really loved me.

The idea of that lifted a huge weight off my shoulders, so much so, after breakfast we all went down to the stream to look for that big eel – my lad with his makeshift fishing rod in his hand and me with a couple of great football nets that I'd found in the garage.

"Yer'll not catch it in those," Emily said.

She was right, but the pike I trapped in them a few hours later was truly something else.

"Dad, do they bite?" my daughter had asked.

My lad didn't. He was paddling in the stream trying to get it in a bucket of water. I had to say that it was a tidy size – easily a good couple of feet, and I got reprimanded for saying as much.

"We measure properly," Emily said. "In millimetres, centimetres and metres."

"If we catch it M, are you going to kill and cook it for us?" asked my lad.

"I am certainly not," she said.

"You killed those lobsters," he noted.

She certainly didn't have an answer to that.

It was me who finally got it into the bucket – and yes, the things do bite and I had to shake it off my hand. I was just thankful, being the wise old angler that I am, that I'd been wearing some gardening gloves, otherwise Emily may have well been sewing a couple of digits back on.

"Can we throw it in the swimming pool, dad?" asked my lad.

"It'll die if you chuck it in there you divvy," his sister, rather eloquently explained.

"I suppose you could put it in the bath," Emily said. "That way we will be able to see how it acts and maybe you could write to Mrs Peters and your Granny Kate about it."

I knew exactly how it acted. The thing attacked anything that got in its way.

We ran a bath for it, with my lad trying to feed it frozen prawns and salami. I must admit, to say it was a predator, it didn't appear very hungry and just laid on the bottom of the bath looking a bit pissed off.

As M had banned me from working on my laptop I had been in the garage most of the afternoon going on into the evening trying to get this old Alfa Romeo to start. When I say old – I mean old. Apart from a bit of bubbling around the wheel arches it was a really nice car and I couldn't understand why someone would just cover it over with a sheet of tarpaulin and leave it.

Nowadays, I wasn't your archetypal motoring enthusiast. I put petrol in and fill up the windscreen wash and that's about it. I did however, have a play about with this for a few hours, so much so, when Emily came looking for me she was surprised to see Mr. Top Gear himself, both covered in oil and with a twin-carburettor in his mitts. "I didn't know you knew anything about cars?" she smiled.

Both Sooty and myself had been mad about them – Sooty adamant that once he passed his test that he would get a Ferrari Berlinetta Boxer, therefore it was something of a let-down when he came around to our house in some shitty gold Capri.

Once I passed mine, I studiously chose which car I would get and it certainly wouldn't be some rubbish Ford. My granddad had said to me that owning a car was a privilege and something that he and my gran could only have ever dreamed about, and I remember driving to my gran's as pleased as punch when I'd finally bought mine. "By heck lad, that's one hell of a motor," he had said.

I had just bought a Datsun 240Z – something, which was to be the start of my love affair with fast cars.

My granddad told me that a driver needed to look after his car and as such he had bought me a Haynes manual for it – which was something that I had retrieved from my mums before the new owners moved into her bungalow.

Sooty never ever looked under the hood of his car – ever, and just used to complain to his dad about any problem that he had with it – so much so, Pete used to end up spending half-a-day under the thing to fix whatever was wrong with it.

I used to spend hours under the bonnet with my granddad, with my gran continually bringing us out cups of tea.

My granddad may have never had a car, but being a fitter he was very mechanically minded and whilst cleaning out the carburettor on the table, I told M and my daughter the exact same tale. As for Herbert – he was kicking out zed's over on the couch, whilst my lad was upstairs with his pike. "She used to have me drive her everywhere," I said.

"You speak of your gran with so much affection," Emily said.

I did. It was strange where your mind takes you and I often wondered how my life would have been if my dad hadn't had died so young.

"My first car was a mini," Emily excitedly told my daughter. "I thought it was really great. It was red with a white roof."

"Did it break down when it rained?" I winked.

"Yeh – how did yer know that?" she shrugged.

Chapter 33
Abi's Tales – *Take 5*

A taxi-ride to London City Airport and a two hour-plus flight into the former Amerigo Vespucci Airport in Florence was just what the doctor ordered. What a feeling you get when you board a plane and leave all the work and the stress behind you.

"Would you like anything from the drinks trolley," asked the British Airways stewardess.

I certainly would my dear, I thought.

Three days in Tuscany and reading a good book by the pool kicked off by a chilled glass of wine on an outbound flight. As Lee would say – 'You can't whack it'.

I hadn't been abroad since I was fifteen – and then it had only been a miserable week in Lloret-De-Mar – the main highlight of which was being touched-up on the beach by some lad from Swansea and then having something a panic attack after he coaxed me into reciprocating the deed. That had been the first time that had happened, which was embarrassing enough, but after the fourth time of my longstanding boyfriend of six months trying it on and me having a seizure, post-throwing-up I sought some advice at some family planning place in the Margaret Pyke Centre on Wicklow Street – only for me to come away ten-times more confused than before I went – which is a story that I certainly don't want to share.

Now however, I was bound for the grandeur of Tuscany and the walled town of San Gimignano.

M had sorted the flights and the transfer and I was to spend my time in some stone built farmhouse up in the hills as part of their family. I couldn't believe it, and as I sipped at my wine and tapped away at my notepad, the feeling I had was one of pure happiness.

The last few weeks had been strange, especially as I had terminated my relationship and was currently searching for my own place. I wanted something like what Pedro had – three storeys high and everything in it being my own.

Liza had kicked off big style, which was more to do with the fact that one of Lee's old mates from school had asked me out a couple of times. Zak Carr or Z-cars if you're talking to Lee or Sooty, had gone through a messy divorce when he was in his mid-twenties and had been living with some girl up until three weeks ago. I think the London-thing had been a bit too much for her. Well – that and me, as on the third time he asked me out I thought – *Yeh, why not*. He was absolutely nothing at all like I imagined and I had to say that I had a lovely time. A nice play at the theatre and an even better meal at an Italian restaurant – and with him picking up the bill. The thing that made it more special is that he is really good looking – you know, not just good looking – *but drop your pants* good looking. Not that I did however, as he never even tried anything. I know I am a bit out of practice but I thought I would have at least got a kiss. I mentioned it to Jaime, who mentioned it to Johanne, who the big mouth that she is, mentioned it to Jody. That was a big mistake.

"She's a lesbian," she told Zak.

"What exactly are you doing around here?" I asked her.

"I always come around here," she replied.

"I know – and you frigging do my box in," I told her. "Why don't you go down White Lion Street and bother Jo."

"Because Jo told me to come here and bother you."

There was no answer to that.

All men think that because you are gay – or in my case gay-ish, that you have some warped ideas when it comes to sex, and that you are into this, that and the other. In my case, *that and the other* were something that I certainly wasn't interested in.

"You're gay?" Zak had asked.

"I'm finding myself," I told him.

And four nights later, I did – knocking on the door of one of the flats at White Lion Street, to find out why his interest in me had suddenly ceased.

"Do you actually fancy me?" I asked him.

I had to ask that question, as I was never really sure of how I looked to the opposite sex.

"Sure, I fancy you," Zak told me. "It's just that Lee was pretty clear about the *no office relationships* part of the contract."

That was rich coming from him. He's married to M who's the presenter of *ITV Sessions* and who does all the majority of all the A & R over at White Lion and who has recently been cast as his mum in *The Invincibles*. He's been married to the other presenter of *ITV Sessions* and who's tied to a three-year contract. To my knowledge, he's took Faranha home at least half a dozen times and has also had Johanne's bra off, so I can assume that he either doesn't mean it or that he wants everyone to himself, so much so, I told Zak exactly that.

Mmm, glad I got that one out of the way, I thought.

It still made no difference as in Zak's words, he didn't want to mess it all up.

I was never overly confident about my appearance, but I certainly wasn't insecure either ...I think?

"Do you reckon I'm pretty," I asked Johanne.

"I'm not gay Abi," she replied.

"I'm not saying you are – you, cheeky cow," I told her.

To say how good Johanne looked, she never seemed to be in a relationship either, which in all honesty, I've always found strange. She lives in Ramsgate, which means the 6.30 am train into St. Pancras each morning and one stop on the Northern Line over to Angel. On Monday's and Friday's however, we tend to have a breakfast meeting up at T*he Warehouse*, which means her getting on the Piccadilly Line – and dependant on which shoes she's wearing, getting off at either Bounds Green or Arnos Grove. Now here's where there's a story. On her return journey on the Piccadilly Line – especially on a Friday, she often complained about getting crowded, and in some cases – groped.

"What do you mean *groped?*" I asked.

"Touched up," she said.

I'd been on the Tube billions of times and never come across anything such as that – but saying that, I never wore high heels and a skirt up my arse – and nor was I blessed with Jo's other physical attributes – the self-same ones that allegedly had Lee chasing her around in his car.

She explained that it tended to be the Tube between 11.30 and 11.45 am.

"Finsbury Park is the worst," she whispered.

"Which carriage?" I inquired.

"It doesn't really matter," she said. "They always find you."

It sounded rather eerie when she said it like that, nevertheless, this fair young maiden jumped at the chance of taking some paperwork down to White Lion Street this particular Friday. Mmm …and three days the following week. What happened? Zilch.

This got to be a bit of an obsession and left me scratching my head. Maybe I did have B.O.

"I'm getting sick of the lousy tube ride back into King's Cross," Jo had snapped, some weeks later in the wine bar after work.

Apparently, she had been really crowded and really – you know, touched up.

It was doing my head in, especially when she revealed the intricate details. I must have done that tube journey another dozen times, so much so, I was beginning to feel like Vincent Schiavelli's frigging subway apparition in Jerry Zucker's *Ghost* – You know the one? "Get off my train!"

"So, you've not been groped yet?" Kirsty eventually inquired.

I hadn't – so much so, I was starting to get a bit of an inferiority complex – especially when Jen from the contract cleaning company had complained about it four days on the trot the week before.

It got to the stage where I even had my hair and nails done, put on a really tight dress and wore my best heels.

"Going somewhere nice?" Lee inquired.

"I'm just dropping some stuff in at White Lion Street and calling for some lunch with Jo," I'd told him.

"I thought you'd got a date," he'd winked.

Again – nothing. I was depressed as hell.

Back in real time: "Are you going to Florence?" inquired the Italian man sat in the seat next to me.

That was an absolutely stupid question, seeing as that's where the frigging plane was going.

"I am from Pratolino," he said.

That figured, I thought.

"I'm going to San Gimignano," I replied, whilst eloquently knocking back my wine.

"It is quite a beautiful place," he said.

Forty-five minutes and three small bottles of wine later the conversation was still flowing and so as not to be a party-pooper, I ordered another drink.

I rarely used to drink – it must have been either meeting Kirsty or since ITV 7 had kicked up, that I had acquired quite a taste for the stuff, so much so, I had got to be quite the connoisseur. I'd gone from the standard half-gallon bottles of Lambrini and on to the really dry stuff at eight quid a bottle. Like I said – quite the connoisseur.

"Have you been drinking, again?" Liza often asked.

"I just called at the wine bar after work," I told her, sort of totally underplaying it.

"So, do you have a boyfriend?" asked the guy next to me.

Mmm, this was interesting, I thought. *Could it be that I'm being chatted up?*

"I've being seeing someone," I told him.

It wasn't really a lie. Zak had taken me out.

"Is it serious," he asked.

"Er... not really," I sort of said.

"I am divorced," he said, whilst putting his hand on my leg.

Yes, finally, I thought. *A grope.*

"Didn't you like her?" I asked, which I knew as soon as I said it, was a really stupid question.

He then proceeded to tell me of the breakdown of his seventeen-year marriage …and his eleven-year one before that.

"How old are you?" I inquired. "I mean, exactly?"

Mmm, he was 49 years old. Still he appeared to have all his own teeth and was quite nicely dressed. Oh yeh, and his hand was still on my leg.

"I think you have a similarity to the actress Demi Moore," he said.

"She's got to be well over fifty," I told him. "I'm only twenty-five."

"I meant when she was younger," he said, as his hand moved a bit further up my thigh.

This being chatted up and groped was quite thirsty work, so much so, I ordered another couple of bottles of wine.

The guy was nice enough, but there was certainly no way he was getting my phone number and that being the **case** I made sure that I dragged mine through customs a lot quicker than he did his – and to find my carriage awaiting directly outside Arrivals.

"Chuck yer case in the back and jump in," smiled M.

"I've just had some old Italian guy angling for my phone number," I told her. "He thought I looked like Demi Moore."

"She's got to be over fifty years old," said M. "Anyway – you're much prettier."

That made me smile, as did the sight of Tuscany – the rolling green hills with the stone farmhouses dotted around its landscape.

"There's some water in the back," M told me. "It should still be cool."

The landscape reminded me quite a bit of Kent, was it not for the roadside cafes with tables lined up outside and covered with their red checked table cloths.

"What's Lee been on with?" I asked.

"In between me trying to keep him off both laptops he's spending his time either playing with the children or trying to get some old Alfa Romeo to start," she laughed. "He's had half the engine out of the thing."

"He doesn't strike me as your typical mechanic," I said.

"Apparently, he's brilliant," she winked.

That had us both laughing.

The phone then rang.

"Speak of the devil," she said.

"Hiya M," said Lee over the 'hands-free'. "Did you pick Abi up okay?"

"No, she wasn't there."

"Good – I didn't want her to come anyway," he lied.

"I heard that," I told him.

"Hiya kidda – 'you have a nice flight?" he asked.

"Not bad," I told him.

M then explained that we were about ten minutes away and would he open the gates.

On getting there, you just had to see it – the place they had got was absolutely massive. A stone built farmhouse set in its own grounds bordered by a river and which comprised a series of huge sprawling lawns, several stone patios and an unbelievably big pool. Oh yeh – and Clémence Poésy's idiot twin sat sunning herself at the side of the thing.

"You want to come see the swimming pool," shouted Jody. "It's full of water."

I knew there had to be a downside.

I got two "Hello Abi"s from Lee's children and handed them a couple of toys that I'd picked up from the airport. "I'm sorry, but there wasn't much choice," I told them. "It's only a small airport."

Mmm, they don't seem too enthusiastic, I thought.

"Don't you like Thomas Tank?" I asked.

"Yeh – when I was two," said Jamie.

"Thank you, Abi," said M. "They are both very nice."

"Yeh, thank you Abi," Harmony said, whilst nudging her brother. "Say thank you then, you divvy."

Lee appeared pleased to see me. He kissed my cheek, carried my case upstairs and showed me to my room, before opening the patio doors onto the stone balcony. I had to admit – it was all brilliant.

"M – 'you got a shirt or something I can borrow?'" I shouted out onto the patio. "I don't want to be traipsing through the house wearing just a bikini."

"Go in our bedroom and borrow one of Lee's," she replied – and therefore I did.

As I have said already, I had known Lee for over eight years, but I had never stayed over and that being the case I had certainly never ever gone into his bedroom. There were M's shoes all boxed up in one corner, her make-up and perfume on an oak chest of drawers, which housed a huge mirror and a king-sized oak four-poster with some French maid's costume hung on a coat hanger.

Fancy dress? I thought. *Nobody had told me that his birthday party was fancy dress.*

I came down into the huge kitchen and noticed that M had already poured me a wine, which I took out onto the patio along with my book – however, the next thing I knew it was 4.30 pm. I must have dropped off. I looked around to see M at a table over on the other patio and under a big Cinzano Bianco umbrella chatting and playing with all three children, whilst Jody was over at the other side of the pool putting sun tan lotion on – or trying to.

It'd probably help, if she took the lid of the thing, I thought.

Just then, Lee came walking over from what must have been the garage and wiped his hands down and straddled one of the other sunbeds. "Give it here and get your arse plonked," he told her, whilst patting the end of the sunbed.

She then sat on the end of the sunbed whilst he rubbed lotion all around her neck, shoulders and lower back. I couldn't believe it. Was M actually watching any of this? Then Jody turned around and sat opposite him cross legged on the bed. Me? I couldn't frigging believe it.

Jesus Chrst! He's never going to do her front, is he? I thought.

He didn't – he just rubbed some lotion around her face and eyes, slapped her arse and sent her on her merry way, before walking over to M and the kids.

I looked over at Jody, who was straightening up her sunglasses and then over at Lee and M.

Did that just really happen? I thought.

I gulped at my warm white wine and dropped off again only to awake around 6.00 pm with the bottom of my legs burning like hell. So much for the all-over tan!

"You've been flat out all afternoon," M smiled, on me walking into the kitchen. "Lee's firing up the barbecue in a bit, so I hope you've got an appetite?"

Me – I could have eaten a horse, and as such, I rather stupidly mentioned it.

"We're not having horse are we, M?" asked the idiot with the all-over tan, who was now sat at the kitchen table cutting up some salad – mmm, and still in her skimpy bikini.

"No, love," M smiled. "It's just a figure of speech."

"I'm going to freshen up," I told them.

I could never understand how they put up with her, as she did my head in. She was another one who never seemed to have a boyfriend. Mind you, I think if Lee had rubbed me down like he'd just rubbed her down, then I'd not be half as agitated as I was now. Was it Jody annoying me or both my lobster-red and very sore shins. A cold shower is what the doctor ordered and I on getting to the bedroom I turned it on, stripped off and climbed in the bath only to nearly break my neck on some great fucking fish.

My screams, I am sure could have been heard from miles and miles around.

"Oops, I forgot about Frank," giggled M, on arriving in the bedroom at speed to see me both bare-arsed and petrified, along with ...bits of salami on my shins?

Frank, it turned out, was some ferocious albeit extremely pissed off man-eating frigging pike that Lee had caught in the river at the bottom of the garden. The thing must have been a yard long. Although his eldest son was very much against it, Mr frigging Pike got carted out of the bedroom in a great bucket by his dad and rehoused back in the river.

I finally got my shower and put on a dress and went down for some dinner, where M handed me a cold glass of dry white wine and where the idiot would once again test my patience.

"Your legs are red," noted Jody.

"Tell me something I don't know?" I replied.

"Do you know who Trevor Womble is?"

"Possibly a big mouse-thing that picks up litter on Wimbledon Common?"

"No," she frowned. "He played for Rotherham United – didn't he Lee?"

Lee just gave me a wink.

M did us an extremely nice meal and watching her with Lee was ...well, quite something else. They were always affectionately chatting and interacting with each other, which I more than saw after Jody and the children had gone to bed as we ended up sat on some really comfy outdoor three-piece suite, or whatever it was, around the southern part of the pool, with M both sat across her husband and sipping her wine, whilst he dutifully multi-tasked, by both speaking with me and rubbing her feet.

As for M, she just listened on while we chatted and it was then I brought up the $1,000 question. That of Zak Carr and the *no office relationships*.

"I put that in place for Sooty," Lee winked. "You're your own person, Abi – you do what want."

"Do you like him, M?" I asked.

"He seems nice enough, Abi love," she replied. "Just be careful that you don't get hurt."

"Hurt?" I shrugged. "Why would I get hurt?"

"Zak, Dean and Jarv are all northern lads," Lee added.

"Once they get wind of how the *London-thing* works, it's quite possible that they'll be all over the place."

"You are a really pretty young girl with everything going for you," M told me. "You're a great catch for someone."

That made me smile.

"What M's saying is that you are too nice a girl to be getting used," Lee added. "Just be careful."

Thinking about it, it was a bit like listening to my parents, but whereas my parents made their exact feelings known by stamping their authority, Lee and M just offered advice, which was something that Pedro had said when I'd gone back to his place. "They are just really nice people, Abi."

I then told Lee and M exactly what he – Pedro, had said as regards them both.

"Pedro is a really caring lad," Lee told me. "The way he acts is just a front."

"He loves your children," I told them.

"And they love him," said M.

"He'd make a really good dad," Lee nodded.

We sat outside chatting until around midnight and on one minute past, M gave her husband a peck on the lips and wished him a "Happy birthday". I had seen them together loads of times, but never ever like this. I must have had quite a bit to drink as I couldn't remember getting to bed and I awoke in the middle of the night only to see what I thought was some grey shrouded woman in the corner of the bedroom sat on the chair – and as such I remember freezing on the spot, before falling back to sleep and then being awoken by what seemed like loads of footsteps across the landing. Thinking about it, the dream I had was as though I had been pinned to the bed with traffic all around me.

I eventually plucked up courage to get out of bed and peek through the door and onto the landing, only to get the shock of my life, as I saw Jody – dressed only in a scanty little nightie, going into Lee and M's bedroom, which on the closing of the door, was followed by voices and laughter.

Lee, M and Jody? I thought. *What the...?*

I then thought back to the X-certificate lathering down of Jody by the pool, and her sat crossed-legged on the sunbed directly in front of him. I mean who sits cross-legged in a bikini?

Mmm, only an idiot I suppose.

All the same, things between the three of them were strange. Why would a couple in their thirties want some dippy twenty-year old bit off skirt with them all the time?

I walked up to the bedroom door and knocked, before opening it. Being nosey? Nah – I would just ask if they minded me going downstairs and making myself a coffee. However, on opening the door, I got a right shock. Jody was certainly under the duvet with M ...but so were all three children.

"Hiya Abi," M whispered. "You may as well jump in with us – we've got a house full."

As it transpired, part of M's family had flown into Pisa from Luton late last night – their Ryanair flight being delayed three hours, along with some other faces that I certainly knew. That being the case they had all turned up at the house.

"M told me to get in bed with you," said Jody, "but there was definitely no way I was ever doing that."

"You're talking like I'm some flipping molester," I said.

"All the same, I slept in the chair half the night."

Mmm, that explained the woman in the chair, I thought. *But where was Lee?*

Out poolside, having a cup of coffee with Alan Hudson …and Basher …and Stevie Kell.

"So, are you getting in with us then?" winked M.

"Yeh, why not," I said.

And I did.

Chapter 34

That Damned Cat

Both Emily and I loved company – however, we had got more than we bargained for last night and therefore my birthday surprise was lost. M had sorted the hotel accommodation and flights – however, the airline being delayed threw a major spanner in the works and seven taxis were in the courtyard around 3.00 am this morning, one of which contained Mr and Mrs Basher, Mr and Mrs Kell and *There's only one Alan Hudson.*

Over the short period of time since Chris had been with me on this Basher Productions caper he had turned into something of a bit of a Michelangelo Antonioni character. It was hardly a case of him grandiloquently miming camera angles, offering pompous debate with his inferiors or indeed wearing a kerchief around his neck and calling everyone "luvvie" – however, telling Ryanair that he made films and then asking them if he could upgrade to First Class was a bit daft. As was rolling up to the house in a white stretch limousine.

"I'm not getting in that thing," Stevie Kell had told him.

"What are you on about? There's loads of room inside."

He was right. The first offer of a lift was taken up by Huddy who duly dove inside and requested the key to the drinks cabinet.

"I think this film making stuff has gone to your head," Stevie added.

One of the said *daft* bits about the limo was the fact that the driver had to do a 72-point turn to get the frigging thing back down the drive as all the other taxis behind had hemmed him in.

"Is that Badger-man famous?" Sil' had asked a few days ago, with regards to Basher – which was something that had Stevie grinning.

"Only in Staines and West Drayton," I told her.

It also transpired that Basher fancied coming directly to the house as opposed to the hotel and therefore all the taxis ended up following the limo and hence chucked a spanner in our sleeping arrangements. We managed to get all three kids in with us along with Jody after she'd told us that there was no way that she was getting in with Abi. This was the cue for me getting kicked out of bed just two hours later and making a full English breakfast for N5's dynamic duo and one third of the triangle which took apart West Germany in 1975.

"Do you have any avocado pears?" inquired Huddy.

"Not off hand," I said. "Why do you?"

Sooty had tipped me the wink on Huddy's so-called exquisite tastes in *breakfastry* and there was no way on earth that I was scrumming up a tree for any pears at five in the morning – avocado or otherwise.

"Where's your champagne?" asked Alan.

"Champagne?" I asked.

"I was going to make us some Bucks Fizzes," he told me.

"These two were on it last night," exclaimed Stevie. "They were both pissed as farts signing autograph's in Luton Airport. It was right embarrassing. Anybody would think he was Stephen Speilberg."

"Who me?" asked Huddy.

"No, fucking *Badger*," said Stevie.

Basher's idiosyncrasies aside, The Alan Hudson – Terry Neill thing had been a brilliant idea, and would possibly have never happened was it not for him. However, the Huddy-*thing* carried more weight for me and I knew if I could man-manage him properly, I could get the best out of him. Not so much for the documentary – as that was relatively straightforward. The reality is that I was considering Alan for ITV. We already had *The Sooty Show* – so, why not have *The Huddy Show*.

We had 168 hours a week to fill – therefore why not have Huddy having a weekly spot talking 1970's football and so on. He was extremely honest and forthright – he knew his football inside out and back to front, so why not? Emily also liked him, and saw him as someone who needed a break, especially after the events surrounding his *so-called* accident and his life falling apart thereon afterwards. I was certainly up for it – however, I really needed to know the best way to handle him, so I could get the very best from him.

Sooty had had him for a few weeks and Huddy had run him ragged. Sooty was definitely Terry Neill. I was hoping that I could be more his Tony Waddington.

"Arsenal never saw the real me and I loved Highbury more than anywhere else," Huddy had told me. "Those heated floors and the walk down the Marble Hall – irreplaceable."

He appeared to beat himself up quite a bit over his time at Arsenal. Okay, the 1976/77 season wasn't a great season as there was no rigidity about the team's formation nor its tactics. Huddy had made his debut in a 1-1 draw with Leeds United on 4th January 1977, describing himself of being quite innocuous and his performance being totally overshadowed by United's Tony Currie. The reality of it however, wasn't quite like that.

"Crowds love good players. That is one reason why Highbury was packed to watch Alan Hudson unveil his elegant, expensive talents for Arsenal," wrote Frank McGhee of the *Daily Mirror.*

Arsenal had continually battered at the door, with Hudson going close early on and in front of the Clock End with Ross, Stapleton and Brady all rattling the woodwork

"Currie consistently hit more telling passes than Hudson, though they both played more than reasonably well, even though they had been out of action for more than a month," added McGhee. "Hudson and Currie were the biggest names among the creative artists, but the presence of so many other good players such as Brady and Macdonald guaranteed that it was an unusually enjoyable game."

Terry Neill told Steve Curry of the *Daily Express* after the game, "I was pleased with Hudson's debut, but it will be a month before he is really fully match fit."

"I didn't enjoy the game against Leeds too much, because I was frightened that the stomach muscles would give way again and that I'd be out for a long time," Hudson had told Curry. "But the longer the game went on the more confident I was that I'm on the mend. I feel that I am just coming into my own again after a very depressing period of my career and Arsenal are just the club to help me re-establish myself."

Five days later Hudson had teed-up Trevor Ross to strike Arsenal's winning goal in the F.A Cup Third Round – a 1-0 win away at Notts County and a match where Macdonald missed a penalty after 85 minutes.

The following Saturday a dreary 1-0 win at Highbury against Norwich City sent them up to fourth place in the table – seven points behind leaders Liverpool, but with three games in hand. Pat Rice hit a well struck goal from an acute angle from the right, which went in off the woodwork and which was enough to win the game – however, Frank McGhee of the *Daily Mirror* wasn't all that impressed.

"Half a million pounds is a lot of money. And when a football club spend that plus a bit more – on just two players, we are entitled to expect something special – however, something special is what we didn't get from Malcolm Macdonald and Alan Hudson at Highbury against Norwich," he wrote. "There are excuses for Hudson, a shop-soiled snip at £200,000. He hasn't been at Highbury long – though the month Arsenal manager Terry Neill felt he would need to settle into the team now has only one more week to run, with no real sign of it happening. Perhaps that is because Hudson – so extravagantly gifted with talent, became too accustomed to running the whole show with Stoke and Chelsea as he was the equivalent of producer, director, scriptwriter and star. He may need much longer to learn to live with other Arsenal players, who don't – and apparently won't – accept that every move has to go through him, flow through him and come from him. Perhaps it is because Hudson persists in operating from a position too deep that his passes seldom hit where it hurts – inside scoring range. Perhaps he was hampered on this particular day, by shins which in the morning, will offer painful testimony that the most effective kicks aren't always landed on the ball."

McGhee wasn't wrong either – Hudson had been picked out and badly clattered by Norwich City's pacey midfielder Colin Suggett on a few occasions.

"When at my peak, a player such as him wouldn't have got near me," Huddy told me.

"Arsenal's new £200,000 signing Alan Hudson has a slim chance of being fit for the game at Birmingham tonight after clashes with Norwich City's Colin Suggett," wrote Malcolm Folley of the *Daily Express*. "Worse than the physical damage he has suffered is the fact that after just three games for Arsenal, the critics have begun to make themselves heard."

Someone sitting near Folley at Highbury on seeing Hudson hit the ground, supposedly said, "A light ale bottle must have fallen out of his shorts and hit him on the ankle", causing the journalist to cite the fact that his reputation as a "King's Road reveller" hadn't died.

Hudson at Arsenal was a very square peg in a very round hole. He was at Arsenal back then, what the supporters at the club have been complaining about the clubs' *lack of* for years. A world class deep lying midfielder.

"Alan Hudson was an acquired taste – yet he was also a player who was ahead of his time and such savants often suffer as a consequence," said ex-Derby County winger Alan Hinton. "Few had witnessed anyone quite like him. Initially, fans may have experienced some culture shock as he carved defences to pieces – not with pick axe, but with a paring knife. Short passes to keep possession at first, then a ball dissecting the defence into bits. Hudson was very much the orchestrator – his approach of short passing being the forerunner to tika-taka."

So, how exactly would that solve Arsenal's problems now?

"His touch on the ball, his vision, his energy and the the fact that he didn't give the ball away," added Hinton. "Far from being solely a finesse player, Hudson could tackle and run and run and run. His feints and close control enabled him to beat defenders on the dribble. He was also ahead of the game in terms of his knowledge and neither fans nor players were used to a player playing all these triangles, give-and-goes, flicks and supporting players."

"Alan is nowhere near his best yet, but once we get the team sorted out, he will open up so many new dimensions for us. He knows how we feel and what is the best way for him to play," said Terry Neill after the Norwich City match. "We probably played a little more directly than he's accustomed to, which is why it seemed that he was being by-passed in midfield at times."

Neill had hit the nail on the head. The 1976/77 Arsenal approach was in most parts a one-dimensional one, and one which used Macdonald's blistering pace and power – sometimes to great effect, but sometimes not. And there was more to the problem than just replacing one older world class player with a younger one. The fact was, is that Ball and Hudson both had hugely contrasting styles, which is one of the many reasons that they could play so well together.

"After playing together with Alan Ball for such a long time it's a bit weird playing with Alan Hudson," said Liam Brady post-Norwich. "They are vastly different players, but I'm looking forward to establishing a new partnership. We all know that Alan Hudson is a good player. If we keep plugging away it shouldn't take too long for him to slot in."

The problem was an obvious one. Ball's departure had created a void. Ball was a marvellous albeit vociferous one-touch footballer player, Hudson was a deep lying schemer who liked to carry the ball out of defence, before building up play.

Suggett, the player who had clattered Hudson, had been no stranger to controversy, and was at the centre of the storm during the Leeds United versus West Bromwich Albion game on 17th of April 1971, after referee Ray Tinkler played advantage by insisting that The Baggies' record £100,000 purchase wasn't interfering with play when Jeff Astle put Albion 2-0 up, something which not only helped give Arsenal the title, but also the events thereon afterwards would play their part in robbing Leeds of the 1971/72

League and F.A Cup Double. Fans invaded the pitch, which ultimately forced Leeds to play their first four home games of the following season away from Elland Road. Even though at the seasons end they had both a superior goal average and goal difference to Champions Derby County – they also had one less point. The two results that would come back to haunt them were: a 0-0 draw against Wolverhampton Wanderers at Leeds Road, Huddersfield and 1-1 draw with Tottenham at Boothferry Park, Hull – both games they would normally have won.

Arsenal's next game was away to Birmingham City and it was a match where Arsenal's defensive frailties were exposed, even though following the 3-3 draw, the club were now unbeaten in ten games with Chris James of the *Daily Mirror* stating that Arsenal were "Dark horses for the League Championship".

A Malcolm Macdonald hat-trick claimed the point, with goals after 44, 74 and 83 minutes – responding to a similar feat by Birmingham's 22-year old Trevor Francis, who had hit his goals somewhat earlier after 30, 35 and 51 minutes, with his last one being a penalty after O'Leary had handled. Even then, Arsenal should have won the game as Trevor Ross had a shot come back off the woodwork.

Terry Neill told Alan Williams of the *Daily Express*, "I feel this is the best Arsenal side since they won the double in 1971."

He was very much mistaken as a nightmare sequence of results was to unfold and their season implode.

All this discussion happened over the breakfast table out on the patio, the midges from the river finding out that Alan Hudson wasn't just a tasty footballer.

"They must like the alcohol," noted Chris.

"Then why aren't they circling you," argued Stevie.

The camaraderie between the two had always been lively.

Emily came out on to the patio armed with Herbert, who she passed over to Huddy, while she got him his breakfast. He had more or less got through his miserable crying stage and now just did it at intervals on a seven day a week basis.

"Has he learned to walk yet?" Huddy inquired.

"Yeh, about as good as you," I winked.

"Maybe we should build him a baby walker," Stevie said with regards to Huddy. "I'm sick of keep falling over those stupid crutches."

Alan took it in good humour and tried to get Sammy to stand up on his own. "He's getting there," he said, as he dangled my youngest by the arms.

Huddy and the football player Emily had named our Sammy after, may well have been as different as chalk and cheese personality-wise, but as football players they had huge similarities.

"I think we were very much of the same opinion as to how we wanted to play our football," Jon Sammels said of Alan. "It wasn't always easy in those days."

Ex- *Daily Express* journalist Norman Giller had told me the exact same.

I knew that Alan needed something – a responsibility, something which he didn't really get at Arsenal. That was until well after the fallout, post pre-season tour of Australia.

Arsenal's 1977/78 season was a season on par with 1972/73, whereby but for a few dodgy decisions by the management, a few bum results and some lousy luck with injuries, Arsenal could have well taken everything, the team was beginning to become that good.

On 27th December 1977, Arsenal were third in the League and three points behind leaders Nottingham Forest and awaiting a League Cup Quarter-Final showdown with Manchester City at Maine Road and looking towards a good run in the F.A Cup – their Third Round opponents being Sheffield United at Bramall Lane.

Hudson had been in and out of the side – but more out than in. He had a fractious relationship with Terry Neill, of that there was no doubt, the fallout from Australia still in both the player and managers' minds. Newly re-appointed Don Howe tried healing the rift, but maybe things had gone a bit too far – who knows. The player had been transfer listed and still wanted out – however, he still wanted the opportunity to play.

"Alan Hudson becomes the reluctant substitute in Arsenal's match at Wolves today," wrote Kevin Moseley of the *Daily Mirror* on 27th August 1977. "Acknowledged as one of the most gifted midfield players in the country, Hudson sits on the bench – despite a plea for the reserves."

Hudson told Moseley, "I was sub on Tuesday against Everton and didn't get on. I picked up the win bonus, but I'd rather lose the money and play. Everyone needs matches, especially at this early stage of the season to reach peak fitness and I enjoyed my game in the reserves last week. I certainly don't want to be in the position that if I'm called into the team, I'm not able to give my best."

Hudson never got on the field and wouldn't do so until 10th September 1977, when he was included in the side to play up at Villa Park.

"What has passed over, is done with," said Terry Neill, which was quite the dignified statement.

Did he actually mean it? was quite another question entirely and one which only he knew the answer to.

Nevertheless, strangely wearing the No. 4 shirt, the still-transfer-listed Hudson went out and put on an impressive display that had John Pyke of the *Sunday Express* purring at his performance. "The introduction back to Division One football of Alan Hudson showed what a waste of talent there would be if he left Highbury. Hudson may lack match practice, but his supreme skill showed through."

Arsenal had battered Villa, only with ex-Arsenal players doing what ex-Arsenal players generally do – performing well against their old club. Jimmer Rimmer was in outstanding form and Alex Cropley stole the winner in injury time. It was quite a come down, but certainly nowhere near the doom and gloom the result suggested. "On the evidence of Saturday's piece of robbery by Aston Villa," wrote David Miller of the *Daily Express*. "It is Arsenal, not Villa who are shaping for a League title bid."

During the game, Hudson had put Brady through for a one-on-one but he had blasted over – Willie Young had hit the woodwork – and Rimmer had denied certain goals from both Stapleton and Macdonald. During the course of the season, Villa would *rob* Arsenal of four valuable points, but there was another downside to this match – Hudson had to have X-rays on a suspected broken ankle and it was an injury that would keep him out for five games – two of which they lost 1-0 and 2-1 away at Norwich City and Manchester City respectively, along with a 0-0 draw at home to Liverpool in front of 47,110. Five points dropped from a possible ten – hardly title winning form.

Manchester City's manager Tony Book looked beyond the result and told Derek Wallis of the *Daily Mirror* that they were the most balanced Arsenal side that he had seen in years. They would have possibly looked even more balanced if Peter Simpson who had been standing in for Willie Young – who had been out with a knee injury, hadn't been sent off for two bookable fouls on Peter Barnes.

The other four points during those five games came courtesy of 3-0 and 2-1 wins at Highbury against both West Ham United and Leicester City respectively, who were not only out of form, but by the end of the season would be staring relegation in the face – not at least Leicester.

"Arsenal could have hammered ten past them," wrote Malcolm Folley of the *Daily Express*. "If there is a more impotent team than Leicester in the First Division, then I haven't seen them. Arsenal didn't just beat them – they demoralised them in a one-sided match too embarrassing to watch."

"Under Don Howe, we're getting the same spirit and the same togetherness we had when we won the Double when he was here the first time," Arsenal captain Pat Rice told Folley. "We never argue with one another anymore, and we are all prepared to work for each other."

The fact that Sammy Nelson had had to step in and break up an argument between both Rice and Trevor Ross during the match, made that statement seem rather strange.

Both Hudson and Willie Young were back from injury to face Queens Park Rangers on 15th October, with Hudson telling Malcolm Folley of the *Daily Express* of how understanding the Arsenal support had been, which was made all the stranger, when Hudson was on the back page of

Monday mornings *Daily Mirror* telling Kevin Mosely, that he must quit the club.

"For someone who cost so much money and who always appears to be in trouble of some sort, the crowd would have been entitled to jump on my back," he had told Folley. "Unbelievably, I've never taken any stick and the people here have been different class. It makes me wonder what sort of reception they would give me if I played like I can."

Arsenal beat a resilient Queens Park Rangers by a bizarre goal from Malcolm Macdonald after 80 minutes. "On paper Arsenal fielded one of the most skilled and technically sophisticated line ups in the League", wrote Alan Hoby of the *Sunday Express*. "There were those teasing tormentors of opposing defenders in Liam Brady and young England prodigy, Graham Rix. Returning too after a long injury was Alan Hudson. He played well. He ran, worked and covered with exemplary diligence. He did not waste one of those single short passes, but where was the early ball, which could split defences?"

A valuable two points in the bag and a decent game, yet Hudson still wasn't happy.

I firstly remembered what he had told me after I put my point over, that he actually did play quite well for Arsenal.

"We set ourselves standards," Huddy had said. "Whilst at Stoke City my aim was to be the best player ever and had I been a manager, I would expect exactly the same. Even when we were winning, if I was not a *nine out of ten*, I was extremely disappointed."

I thought back to the words of Tony Morley after he'd knocked back Arsenal in January 1976 – in that he had to be certain that he would enjoy his football. A decent winger can fit into most sides – however, the engine room of central midfield is much more intricate, and Hudson still found himself as that very square peg, telling Moseley, "I'm not saying anything against anyone at Arsenal, it's just that Arsenal are not for me and I am not for Arsenal."

Whereas before it had been Terry Neill and Wilf Smith forcing the reshape of the midfield, now it was Don Howe –

the highly knowledgeable intermediary that had carefully reintroduced Hudson back into the side.

There were continual mutterings in the press that Ray Wilkins was to be Hudson's replacement and according to Harry Miller of the *Daily Mirror* on 11th October 1977, that Arsenal were pursuing Gerry Francis.

It made sense as Hércules de Alicante Club de Fútbol, who had finished thirteenth position in La Liga the previous season, wanted Hudson and had made inquiries with a view to purchasing him. And rather strangely with a view to loaning him to the current Dutch Champions, Ajax for the rest of the season – a team who were currently stuttering their way through to the Quarter-Finals of the European Cup, as Hércules already had their quota of non-Spanish players – all of who were South American and two of which were Paraguay international goalkeeper Humberto Núñez and Argentinian international midfielder Gerónimo Saccardi, the latter of who won both the Copa Interamericana and Intercontinental Cup with Independiente in 1972 and 1973 respectively. However, when you looked closely at the others – they were hardly *Angels with Dirty Faces* and represented nothing more than a band of brigands that would have even had Huddy scratching his head, if not checking his pockets.

The contingent was made up of several Argentinian's – defender Carmelo Giuliano and strikers Horacio Abel Moyano, Alfonso Troisi and Pedro Verde, the latter of who was the uncle of Juan Sebastian Veron and who would figure in the euphoria following the 1978 World Cup and a player who would follow Alex Sabella into Sheffield United before, and according to United's commercial manager Peter Garrett, stealing the Sheffield & Hallamshire County Cup on his way back out in 1981 – and straight after beating Sheffield Wednesday at Bramall Lane, 3-2. Really!

Not to be usurped by a minor crime of the theft of a Friendly trophy, they also had Argentinian and ex-Penarol striker Raúl Castronovo in their ranks. He was banned for two years for helping fix a match in late-April 1980, between the already-relegated CD Málaga and UD Salamanca – a team that hovered three points above the drop and where the home side went down 3-0 after a fee of around £22,500 was said to have exchanged hands.

There were also a couple of Uruguayans in the squad. Montevideo-born striker Piero Lattuada, who was at one time on Liverpool's books and the ex-Sevilla midfielder Carlos Nelson Lasanta Morales who was transferred to Austrian side FC Admira Wacker Mödling, before returning to Alicante and doing time in prison after his involvement in two armed robberies at savings offices in the town.

Like I said – nothing more than a band of brigands.

However, what would unfold would come as a shock to most Arsenal supporters.

Arsenal travelled to Ashton Gate to play Alan Dicks' Bristol City, a team who had taken all four points off Terry Neill's new-look Arsenal the season prior and who had more recently, just been labelled 'Butchers' by Hibernian chairman Tom Hart following a feisty 1-1 draw at Easter Road in the first leg of their Anglo-Italian Cup Semi-Final – a game where City's Norman Hunter and Peter Cormack had both received their marching orders. What is also rarely mentioned is that during the last days of Bertie Mee's tenure, Arsenal had offered the promotion chasing Bristol club £250,000 for the services of their talented centre-back Geoff Merrick and striker Tom Ritchie.

On hearing that his clubs first game in the big time 14 months' prior would be at Highbury, Dicks had told Jack Steggles of the *Daily Mirror*, "You can bet they will be going flat out to prove they are worth the money that Arsenal offered, by helping us to win."

They did. Tom Ritchie set up Paul Cheesley to score the only goal in what was a much-deserved win.

As for Cheesley – he had just been selected by Don Revie for the Under-23's and was being tipped to play for the senior team – and just three days after the victory at Arsenal and in a game at home to Alan Hudson's Stoke City, a cross had been sent into the box and as he challenged Peter Shilton for the ball he fell badly. It was an innocuous looking clash but Cheesley ripped his cartilage, tore ligaments and chipped a bone in his knee. At the age of 23 and with a blossoming career ahead of him, he would never play again.

This season however, Arsenal were a totally different proposition and came away with a 2-0 win, courtesy of goals by Graham Rix after 44 minutes and Malcolm Macdonald another 44 minutes later and where James Mossop of the *Sunday Express* said, "In only his second full game of the season and in a commanding Arsenal performance, Hudson showed those touches of class that have frequently decorated his career."

The reality of the situation was however, was that the player had the proposed move to Spain at the back of his mind. "Hudson is the £200,000 star in a personal vacuum. A forlorn figure who stood in the corridor under the stands asking for someone to help him unravel the mystery surrounding his proposed transfer to Hércules de Alicante Club de Fútbol."

A rather paranoid Hudson told Mossop, "For the second match in succession I have heard that they are watching me and that the clubs have agreed terms."

"We have been interested in Hudson for some time and nothing has cropped up yet to make us think that he'll not play for us next season," Hércules secretary Vincente Companie had told Kevin Moseley of the *Daily Mirror*. "There is no hurry, as under Spanish regulations Hudson cannot play for us until next season."

Arsenal were active in the transfer market and there was going to be a departure in midfield, but a lot of what was happening depended up on events at Goodison Park and in particular, Bruce Rioch – the player that had broken Hudson's leg whilst he was at the peak of his powers with Stoke City.

Meanwhile Arsenal had pressing business in the Third Round of the League Cup, which meant that Alan Ball was back in town with something of a point to prove.

"Southampton freewheel into Highbury for tonight's League Cup match intending to take it nice 'n' easy," wrote David Miller of the *Daily Express*. "The effect could be a nasty shock for Alan Ball's former colleagues on his first return to Highbury since his £60,000 transfer 10 months ago."

"Arsenal will tonight find themselves used as no more than a stepping stone when Alan Ball leads Southampton into Highbury for what should have been an emotive return for the little midfield maestro," added Nigel Clarke of the *Daily Mirror*.

"I don't have to prove anything to anybody because I'm in a team and one that believes it is good enough to get back into the First Division," Ball told Clarke. "This match will show us just how good we are. Personally, I can't get very enthusiastic about the match. We did speak about Arsenal after training yesterday ...for just fifteen minutes. We are not really bothered about them, because we have no fear."

You had to love Alan Ball.

A crowd of 40,749 turned up to watch Ball be sent home with his tail between his legs. A penalty from Liam Brady after 78 minutes and a deft header by Frank Stapleton from a cross by Graham Rix four minutes later put paid to a rather resilient Southampton side, who in truth should have been put to the sword much earlier, with both Macdonald and Stapleton going close in the first few minutes and a diving header from David Price grazing the woodwork.

"The result was the proper one, if only because in Brady, Rix and Alan Hudson, The Gunners possessed the men to break the dominating pattern of rhino-like physical challenges," wrote David Miller of the *Daily Express*. "Hudson gave perhaps his best display since arriving at Highbury – swift, alert and creative."

It was all starting to click and next up were Birmingham City – the club who had just recently appointed Alf Ramsey as caretaker manager – with a Pat Rice header five minutes from time sparing Arsenal's blushes in what was an exasperating 1-1 draw. What was worse, was that Malcolm Macdonald had twisted his knee, which forced Arsenal to show their hand, with recent £30,000 signing from Peterborough Mark Heeley having to play the whole of the second half.

"Thirty-one thousand supporters echoed their team's frustration as nothing went right," wrote Alan Hoby of the *Sunday Express*. "And in midfield, Liam Brady spoilt a lot of moves through over-elaboration."

Hudson didn't do over-elaboration, but then again, he hadn't played – he had been out with flu.

Continual abdominal and ankle injuries not only blighted his run in the team, but pissed off Neill. Now out with flu? Neill would do his damnedest to get shut or freeze him out – however, somewhere in between, Bruce Rioch re-joining Derby County kicked off a merry-go-round of transfers. Arsenal's other out of favour midfielder Trevor Ross signed for Everton for £170,000 and Arsenal bought Alan Sunderland from Wolverhampton Wanderers for £240,000.

"Bruce Rioch's return to Derby is as unexpected as was his departure," wrote Dave Horridge of the *Daily Mirror*.

Rioch was an extremely capable and feisty Scottish international midfielder, who when he was a 20-year old with Luton Town, was being tracked by eventual League Champions, Leeds United.

"Great footballer, but not a very nice person," Huddy had told me.

Rioch's about-turn was all about his family. "I want to move back to the Midlands because my wife can't settle on Merseyside," Rioch had told Horridge. "Everton are a super club, but my family's happiness must come first."

Trevor Ross didn't get on with Terry Neill – possibly down to the fact of how the player had looked up to and had admired Alan Ball, or possibly not. "I was lucky enough to have the pleasure of playing with Alan Ball in the Arsenal midfield," he had told the *Manchester Evening News*. "He was both an unbelievable professional and a fantastic person."

The Ross-to-Everton transfer had been in the pipeline a couple of weeks prior, which was fueled further by Neill's attitude towards the player, so much so, that midway through a reserve match Ross had taken his shirt off and was said to have thrown it in the managers face.

"I got on with him although I found him a little naïve," Huddy had said of Trevor Ross. "I was certainly shocked to see him move for so much money though, which was similar to a young lad at Chelsea – Gary Stanley, who Everton paid well over the odds for."

As for Alan Sunderland, the player himself couldn't believe the move. The England Under-23 international had been on the transfer list at his own request since September.

"He's a good player and I fancy him in an attacking role, although we have the added bonus that he can play anywhere," Neill had said. "He's a young player, who has still to reach his best."

Whilst all this was going on, and according to John Lloyd of the *Daily Express*, Hudson's move to Hércules de Alicante Club de Fútbol was back on and officials from the club were due at Highbury the day after the Sunderland / Ross transfers, to continue transfer talks.

"They would have been here already but were delayed due to *flight difficulties*," Arsenal secretary Ken Friar explained to the journalist.

Flight difficulties? Benidorm to Gatwick? How the hell could that be difficult?

What history will tell you is that the Hudson transfer to Spain, never happened and that Neill would be livid as come early December he would fine the player, whilst at the same time joining a five-horse race to sign Queens Park Rangers' 26-year old midfielder Gerry Francis for £400,000 – with Kevin Moseley of the *Daily Mirror* saying on 8th December 1977, that the west London club would be interested in a deal that involved a player exchange – Hudson?

Moseley had described Francis as one of the few potentially world-class players in the country and a day later ran with the story of Terry Neill fining Alan Hudson.

"Hudson will appeal against Arsenal's decision to suspend him for two weeks for a breach of club discipline," wrote Moseley. "Manager Terry Neill slapped the ban on, after Hudson had publicly claimed that Neill didn't believe that he was injured."

"My left leg has been put in plaster for at least two weeks, so I couldn't play," Hudson had said. "Yet I read that the boss said it was a case of either resting me or playing me. I was only putting over my point of view."

Neill was getting irater by the minute.

Hudson had been out with flu and missed the game with Birmingham City. He had been left out during the subject of a failed transfer and a minor nose operation during his teams impressive 2-1 *smash and grab* against Manchester United at Old Trafford with Macdonald and Stapleton scoring. He had been left out of the rather thrilling 1-1 draw at home to second-place Coventry City, where Arsenal had been 1-0 down after three minutes only to see Macdonald sent off some four minutes later for belting Terry Yorath around the ear.

A possible loan move to Fulham was also being mooted, where it was said that he would play the rest of the season, before his protracted move to Spain.

What happened? He returned in the No. 10 shirt for the game up at Newcastle United – only to get clattered on the shins again …and then be out injured.

"Talk of Arsenal winning the title may not be so premature," wrote Tony Hardisty of the *Sunday Express* after their 2-1 win at St James' Park. "There is no doubt that their blend of skill, steel, youth and experience makes them an impressive squad just now."

Gordon Milne, manager of Coventry City echoed similar sentiments the week before. "Arsenal are easily the best side we've played."

Yorath however, wasn't all that fussed about Arsenal nor Highbury. He had been continually jostled and harangued by the Arsenal players, who claimed that he had tried to get Macdonald sent off and was continually jeered by the North Bank, so much so, that he had to have a police escort out of the ground. Macdonald was facing the possibility of three games out – one for the sending off and another two for bringing the game into disrepute by either giving linesman *the bird* or for calling him a wanker – not sure which one!

What made the win at Newcastle more inspiring, was that they had done it without the suspended centre-forward who said, "We're the best side in the country right now but Newcastle fans are something special and they certainly don't deserve the rubbish they are getting."

Stapleton and Sunderland hit the goals in Macdonald's absence, whilst David Price hit a 30-yard shot against the upright – however, The Magpies were in turmoil. They had recently sacked their manager, Richard Dinnis and were initially looking to appoint Eddie McCreadie. Not appointing the world-class and ex-Scottish international and Chelsea left-back and appointing Bill McGarry instead, would turn out to be a huge mistake and was another story for another day, but what was being said about Arsenal in the press was absolutely spot-on. They were looking a great side.

In the meantime, Ray Bradley of the *Sunday Express* was putting Nigel Moseley of the *Daily Mirror's* two and two's together and suggesting that Hudson could move to Queens Park Rangers, as Arsenal had given Hércules de Alicante Club de Fútbol the weekend to think over what was to be a £190,000 transfer.

This was the very same weekend that 31-year old Peter Storey, would sadly quit the game.

Come Tuesday, a few things became clear: Newcastle United had made a verbal offer to bring Malcolm Macdonald back to Tyneside; and the player himself had been slapped with a £100 fine by the F.A for bringing the game into disrepute. What was still unclear is what was happening with Alan Hudson. Nothing much really. Manager of Hércules, Viktor Gartner had been in London trying to tie up the deal – however, Arsenal's maverick told Malcolm Folley of the *Daily Express*, albeit with an air of aloofness, "It is still far from settled. I am having dinner with Viktor and I will tell him that I want to see his club before I sign."

You just had to love Huddy. What a fucking guy

Nevertheless, Arsenal were still looking for his replacement and Neill approached Manchester City about the possibility of buying their 24-year old midfielder, Paul Power, which was confirmed by the *Daily Mirror's* John Bean on the Friday – however, Neill was also keeping tabs on Bolton Wanderers midfielder and England Under-21 captain,

Peter Reid, who had just told his manager that he wanted out.

What would happen the very next day could be considered forerunner to the construction of The Emirates – a major sports complex at Alexandra Palace and a shared ground for both Arsenal and Tottenham Hotspur.

"This visionary move by the directors of the famous North London rivals aims also to provide England with an alternative international home, in place of Wembley," wrote David Miller of the *Daily Express*. "Discussions between the clubs and the far-sighted G.L.C. have taken place over the past two months, and a feasibility study is likely to begin during the next few weeks."

On the football front, Alan Hudson would be frozen out for what would be 14 games, although half of that period was through injury and an internal suspension by the club. Macdonald took his place for the visit of Derby County, who's new manager, the industrious and vociferous ex-Arsenal captain Tommy Docherty, was giving them new hope. False in the long term, but new all the same.

Without Hudson, Arsenal reverted to a 4-3-3 system, and Derby's four-man midfield, which included both Scottish internationals Bruce Rioch and Don Masson, overran them. Steve Powell, the player that helped blow a hole in Arsenal's title hopes in March 1973, was given the spoiler job on Brady, whilst Derby's recent signing from Bohemians, Gerry Ryan continually dragged David Price out of position. On the one-time Brady did manage to shake off Powell, he put Macdonald through for a one-on-one with the goalkeeper and the forward fluffed it. Sunderland also missed a gilt-edged chance before Ryan seized on to weak header back to his goalkeeper by Stapleton and poked it home after 49 minutes. Sammy Nelson replied with a shot from an acute angle to get Arsenal on level terms after 55 minutes. Then out of nowhere, a 35-yard *googly* from new signing Bruce Rioch stunned both Jennings and the crowd, with Macdonald stating that the ball must have swerved seven or eight foot whilst in the air before creeping under the bar. Arsenal tried to press but as with the Derby home game in the 1987/88 season, they got caught on the break, with Steve Powell spectacularly connecting on to a Terry Curran cross and sending his diving header into the bottom corner. Arsenal 1, Derby 3.

Post-Derby, Neill stated that his team hadn't done their talent justice and according to Ray Bradley of the *Sunday Express*, they could be going to make a rather underwhelming raid on Neill's former club, to sign Hull City's Northern Ireland international winger, 19-year old Dave Stewart – a player who was taken on as an apprentice from Bangor by the Arsenal manager in the summer of 1974.

Whether it was *kosha* info or just Bradley putting his two and two's together, who knows?

Stewart had huge similarities to Neill's signing on 3rd October – the 19-year old Mark Heeley. Both were of a similar age, both naturally gifted wingers, both quick and talented and both very lightweight. The Stewart to Arsenal move never happened and Chelsea bought him May 1979 only to release the player six months later and without him ever playing a game.

Heeley was described as some 'teenage wonderkid', coming through Peterborough United's youth system. He made his debut at just 16 years of age, and who, according to *Daily Mail* columnist, Adrian Durham, had all sorts of disciplinary issues off the pitch, with some of his former team-mates mentioning big drinking sessions and mixing with the wrong people, which was possibly one of the main reasons why his talent was never realised. Alarm bells should have been raised when the player had been so pissed off with The Posh's then-manager John Barnwell, about failing to win a place in the starting line-up, that he even refused to sit on the bench.

Neill admitted later-on, that sometimes you can drop on a great player from the lower leagues – however, he also stated that this wasn't one of them, citing that the player did have a problem with his attitude.

After 20 appearances including seven as substitute for Arsenal, he was offloaded to Northampton Town, before dropping into non-League ignominy and eventually retiring from professional football aged just 23. As for Stewart, he was transferred to Scunthorpe United, and had three seasons there, before following the exact same path as Heeley. He retired from the game aged just 25.

As Durham had inferred – what a criminal waste of talent?

Emily arranged both couples a taxi to their hotel and they left shortly after 10.30 am, although trying to get Chris to leave was a tall order, especially as the house was becoming quite a vibrant place, not least after Jaime and her two kids had arrived in town courtesy of the 6.25 am flight from Gatwick …oh yeh, and Johanne.

These were to be staying with us – however, Emily certainly wasn't all that fussed about the idea of the latter, even more so, when she came poolside in her bathing costume. "This was a right rubbish idea," she told me.

"Don't mind Jaime's kids," I winked.

"I don't mean Jaime and the children," she nudged. "Yer know exactly what I mean."

"Well, I wonder whose bright idea it was to ask her?"

"Mine," she mumbled.

"Well, there you go then."

M's brainwave was the old exorcising of one's demon's train of thought – you know – to confront the problem. "We are having a few people over for Lee's birthday party," she had told Jo. "I'd really like it if you could come."

There was nothing like loading up a shotgun and shooting oneself in the foot.

"I just didn't want to look insecure," she told me.

And here she was now, whittling like hell and looking out the kitchen window at her sat poolside.

"Wow!" exclaimed Abi, as she came into the kitchen and saw the head of White Lion rubbing herself down with oil.

"Exactly," sniped Emily.

"Just think if she'd have worn a bikini," said Abi.

"Yer wouldn't get a bikini top that could hold that lot up," grumbled Emily.

Huddy – who had just copped some beauty sleep had missed all the new arrivals and was in the exact the same mind-set as both Emily and Abi. "Good god, I wish I was ten years younger," he said, as he looked out the window.

"Yeh – you'd be fifty-four," I told him.

"Who is she?" he asked.

"Head of White Lion," I told him.

"White Lion?" he inquired. "I keep hearing that mentioned – what is it?"

"A record label."

"So, how do you know her?" he drooled.

"She works for me," I said.

"I thought you said she was head of a record label?" he said.

"She is – I own it?"

"You own a record label?" he asked.

Huddy was extremely inquisitive – as was I about him having frigging *dinner with Viktor*.

"Why don't you slip into a pair of Speedo's and go tell her about all them *doggies* that Ron Suart used to make you do," I told him.

"Doggies?" Emily grinned.

"Don't get too excited," I told her. "It's not what you think."

Emily just shrugged her shoulders.

"A 'doggie's' what I gave you a few months ago, when your new shoes were rubbing you after we'd seen that band."

"Right," said Huddy. "A cold shower it is then."

Two minutes later came a loud shriek from upstairs. He'd only gone and frigging walked in on Jody in the bathroom.

"There's birds everywhere," he innocently shrugged.

"Who the hell is he?" shrieked Jody.

"Alan Hudson," I told her.

"Who?"

"He's an ex-footballer," I told her.

"He probably knew Trevor Womble," a hot on my heels and extremely inquisitive Abi had grinned.

"Did I?" he asked.

"Played for Rotherham United – apparently," she told him.

115

"I told her that," argued a rather heavily lathered-up Jody. "She thought that he played for Wimbledon."

"That rings a bit of a bell," duly nodded Huddy. "Womble of Wimbledon?"

As it was, I ended up showing Huddy to a bathroom where there was an actual shower in and with no female soaping herself down underneath it.

"Who was she?" he asked.

"She works for me as well," I replied.

Just then he caught sight of my effervescent mother-in-law walking along the landing.

"Wow she's fit," Huddy whispered. "Does she work for you as well?"

"No, it's M's mum," I told him.

"Hello Alan, love," she twanged. "Did you have a nice sleep?"

"Is she from Liverpool?" he whispered.

"Yeh, she lives near Tranmere Rovers' ground," I told him.

"Is she married?"

"Yeh, to M's dad," I said.

Mike and Sil' had come in on a later flight from Manchester and were to spend seven days with us as they were both adamant that they wanted time with all their grandkids – especially the two that were supposedly bound for New York.

My idea was to have a shower, do a bit of work and then have another crack at trying to get that old Alfa Romeo to start – however, on getting out of the en-suite I found that Emily had other plans.

"Jesus Christ, M," I gasped. "You can't being doing that – the house is full of people."

She'd only gone and slipped into French Maid-mode and handcuffed herself to the bed.

"Les enfants sont avec mon mam et je besoin de tu pour me montrer un peu d'attention," she whispered. "Surtout ma chatte."

"What's that mean?" I inquired, as I dried myself off.

"Layman's terms – my mams got the children and I want yer-knowing," she said.

"I thought you said that chat was a *cat*," I said, as I did a casual recce through the patio doors and peered over the balcony to make sure that all the house guests were where they should be.

"Considérez cela comme une partie de votre cadeau d'anniversaire," she whispered.

"Birthday present?" I inquired.

"Exactement," she winked.

"You didn't have to do all this," I told her, as I climbed on to the bed. "I was happy with it being just us here."

It transpired that Emily had had this in her head since the day of booking the holiday. "I want to give Lee a massive party," she had told Jaime, and between them they had sorted everything out on the quiet – Mr Basher esq, being the one who totally bollocksed up her surprise – and just 15 hours before kick-off.

Did she mind? I don't really think she did, as to M it just made things a hundred times more interesting.

"Tant pis," she had shrugged. "Le chat est outta le sac maintenant."

"What's that mean?" I'd asked.

"Never mind – the cat is out of the bag," she smiled.

"Ah, so chat is *cat*?" I'd said.

"Sort of," she smiled.

We were due to have around fifty or sixty people over, for drinks, food and some music. It was a mix of friends, family and colleagues – however, two of the people I loved certainly wouldn't be there – that being Sooty and Jeanette, the latter of who was currently trying to get M up on Facetime.

Brrrrr – brrrrr it vibrated. And that was just the phone!

Emily slithered out of her steel shackles and answered it.

"Jin," she smiled. "How are you?"

"I'm at Heathrow trying to get a connection," she said. "I really could do with a friend."

Emily immediately picked up the phone and took it out of the bedroom and on to the landing and by the time she had come back in, she was left scratching her head.

"Dead embarrassing that," she told me. "Abi's just asked me if its fancy dress tonight and Alan's asked if I could make his bed and lay a couple of fresh towels out."

"That's what you get, parading around on the landing like one of the cast from a French porn flick," I told her.

That made her laugh.

"So?" I inquired. "What's up?"

"You have to be in Milan at around three o'clock," she said. "You're picking Jeanette up."

"Why am I picking her up?"

"Me and Jaime need you out, while we sort everything," she said, sort of hands on hips.

"Milan? It's got to be four hours away – why didn't she fly into Pisa or Florence like the rest of them?"

"Je ne sais pas et ne se soucient pas," she winked, whilst at the same time climbing on the bed and waggling her arse. "Now are you going to show me the attention that I deserve or what?"

Half an hour later after what was a rather violent yer-knowing session, I was both on my way up country to Milan – and on my own. Still, it gave me time to do some thinking.

After the defeat to Derby County, questions were being asked about Arsenal's credibility as potential League Champions and next up were Hull City in the Fourth Round of the League Cup at Highbury, with Alan Sunderland cup-tied and John Matthews filling a role in midfield.

Matthews had joined Arsenal as an apprentice in 1971 but didn't make his league debut until three years later, in a 1-0 win against Leicester City up at Filbert Street on the opening day of the 1974/75 season.

Initially a defender, Matthews moved into midfield but struggled to secure a regular first-team place and a broken ankle he sustained in December 1975, put him out of the game for 11 months.

"Matthews was a beautiful striker of the ball with good feet, but Terry Neill didn't know where his best position was," Huddy had told me. "And neither did he …I think?"

It was a game at the back end of the 1976/77 season up at St. James' Park, where Matthews possibly had his most notable game for the club and where Arsenal, in front of a crowd of 44,677, gave Newcastle United their first home defeat for 12 months. Arsenal came away with a 2-0 win, courtesy of a Macdonald header after 42 minutes, with Matthews putting the game out of reach with a goal nearly quarter of an hour later, after he had dispossessed right-back Ray Blackhall. Not only did he score the decisive goal, he had also hit the woodwork.

"I remember him hitting this ball from the halfway line, and I thought as he struck it 'What the hell is he doing?'" Huddy added. "The ball shaved the bar with the goalkeeper Mick Mahoney well-beaten, and I thought 'Christ!'"

As for the Hull City game, Neill had told Steve Curry of the *Daily Express*, "Under these kinds of circumstances you are always grateful for a quick game to try to get a poor performance out of the system."

"Supermac was not so super against Derby on Saturday when he was closely courted by Colin Todd and Roy McFarland," wrote Curry. "But he will know that he missed two chances, which he would have tucked away without any fuss two years ago."

"No player is more conscious of his duty," Neill added, regarding Macdonald. "He doesn't need Don Howe or myself to remind him when he's below par. He sets his own standards."

Hull City came to London and were duly hammered 5-1, with Matthews nicking a couple of goals in the process.

"Liam Brady last night devastated Hull City with his deadly left foot. The Arsenal midfield man carved gaping holes in the heart of the Yorkshire team's defence," wrote Steve Curry. "Billy Bremner, one-time master of the same art, could only stand back and admire the footwork."

A curling Brady free-kick had opened the scoring after 16 minutes, and he had a part in three other goals, even seeing one of his shots come back off the bar on 38 minutes.

Macdonald latched on to a pass by Brady to tee Stapleton up after 21 minutes, whilst Macdonald himself headed home a corner after 40. After 64 minutes Brady floated in a free kick which Stapleton knocked down and Matthews finished off and then four minutes later he sent Matthews through to make it 5-0. Willie Young conceding a penalty in the last minute of the game was the only blight on what was a perfect performance. Next up, an away game at Ayresome Park, where last season Arsenal had well and truly been slaughtered – twice, 3-0 and 4-1, with Neill adamant that his side "couldn't beat a team of dustbins", as he so eloquently put it.

The background to the Middlesbrough game is that Liverpool had unsettled Graeme Souness, by launching a £250,000 bid for the player a couple of days before the match, which was the Anfield club's first attempt to get the player. What is also rarely mentioned is that Middlesbrough manager John Neal would sound out Arsenal about the purchase of Macdonald immediately after the game.

This was a strange one – why would the likes of Newcastle United and Middlesbrough be sounding out Arsenal about their record signing and all-action centre-forward? A player who had only been at the club 16 months. Straight after the fallout from the tour of Australia, Macdonald was available for transfer and according to Neill, there had been no takers. So why now?

Arsenal played a Souness-less Middlesbrough off the park, but had to wait until late in the game to seize the initiative, even though David Price had had a legitimate goal ruled out early on in the second half. The continual harrying paid off and pressure by Macdonald forced Terry Cooper to put through his own goal after 88 minutes. 1-0 to The Arsenal.

"We were full value for our win and were ahead of Middlesbrough in method and individual skills – in a different class in fact," Neill told Jack Heather of the *Sunday*

Express. "Do not be surprised if we go on to win the Championship."

Macdonald showed the same contempt for Middlesbrough has he had done with his former club, labelling them nothing but a "Third Division club".

"Neal caused a stir after this game when he insisted he would be making an enquiry for Supermac," wrote Peter Cooper of the *Daily Mirror*. "But Arsenal manager Terry Neill, who turned down an approach from Newcastle a fortnight ago, insisted last night: 'We have made our position clear – Malcolm is not for sale.'"

This wasn't entirely true.

Meanwhile the news was also out that day that Arsenal were looking at Gerry Francis – "The Half Million Man" as Moseley put it; and a day later two £300,000 bids from Liverpool and Manchester United had done their bit to unsettle Scottish international and Leeds United centre-forward Joe Jordan – and just as the Yorkshire club were due down to North London.

Twice in one week? Good old Liverpool!

"Jordan remains noncommittal after talks with Leeds manager Jimmy Armfield yesterday, that were supposed to clinch his future with Leeds," wrote John Bean of the *Daily Mirror*.

"I didn't discuss a new contract. I wanted to establish my transfer situation with the manager," Jordan had told the journalist. "I'm sick and tired with the whole business. I wish something could be resolved."

Leeds had offered the best contract any player had ever received at the club, but player power was at work and Jordan wanted out – as did Gordon McQueen, who would be the subject of a bid by Arsenal on 31st January 1978. The bait? Malcolm Macdonald.

"Arsenal manager Terry Neill is ready to offer striker Malcolm Macdonald plus cash to Leeds, for Gordon McQueen," wrote Bill Elliot of the *Daily Express*. "The Leeds board meet to discuss the McQueen situation and I believe Arsenal will have made a firm offer by then."

Draw your own conclusions, but this all smarted of secret handshakes and double-dealing. "Macdonald is not for sale," Neill had just recently bellowed in the press. And then this?

Make no bones about it and as I've already stated – the elephant never forgets, and the fallout from Australia was possibly still at the back of Neill's mind.

So, troubled and Jordan-less, Leeds rolled into town on 10th December 1977, with Arsenal intent on giving them, what they generally gave Arsenal, and after 58 minutes the deadlock was broken. Willie Young had put this *all-new* Arsenal 1-0 up. However, it was the *all-new* Leeds, that the press were drooling over. With Jordan unsettled, he had been dropped from the side and Armfield had played five across midfield, which included three wingers and which had thrown the North London side somewhat – and unlike the seasons preceding fixture where Arsenal had given them a 1-1 battering, Leeds had totally outplayed their hosts.

McQueen – the subject of the Arsenal Supermac swap, hit an equaliser one minute from time forcing a 1-1 draw. Leeds were still Arsenal's bogey side.

My pain in the arse that was my ex-wife had given me a right ball ache of a journey, which was a near on 500-mile and eight-hour round-trip and any fight against M's decision was immediately knocked back. "Be a good lad and do as your told," she said, as she pecked my lips. "Jeanette needs picking up."

I did done a bit of chuntering, whilst looking for my mobile phone, wallet and car keys.

"Je vais tu faire une promesse - Allez chercher Jeanette et quand tu reviens, vous pouvez venir dans ma chatte humide," she whispered in my ear.

"You mentioned that *cat* again," I said.

Seeing as Jeanette would be in Milan about an hour before me, I gave her call – and just as she was boarding, whilst totally leaving out the fact, that I was more than pissed off about wasting eight hours of my life having to pick her up.

"What made you want to fly into Milan?" I asked. "Florence and Pisa are only an hour away."

"Sorry," she said.

Uh, I definitely couldn't be mad with her now that she'd apologised.

"Look I'm not going to get to you until about four o'clock," I told her. "Can you remember Piacenza?"

"Vaguely," she said. "Is that where we went after Arsenal lost against Roma and you had your wallet stolen."

Jeanette's memory was still spot on. Arsenal had played in Rome and we had missed the flight home the next day – again, so we thought we would see some sights and stayed in the city for a couple of days and had a drive up to Milan, stopping for something to eat in Piacenza – which let me tell you now, was a dead crap stop off point. I'd only been there ten minutes before I'd been pickpocketed.

"You remember that church on Via Pace?" I asked.

"Sort of," she said.

"Well, I'll text you the exact location and then you can jump in a taxi outside arrivals and get it to take you there and I'll meet you," I said.

"Thank-you, Lee."

I looked up to see Emily looking at me. "You've been to Rome before as well?" she asked.

"Yeh, we lost one-nil," I told her. "We beat them on penalties, though."

"No, I mean with Jeanette?"

I just shrugged my shoulders.

"So, you've been to Italy twice before?" she asked. "And with Jeanette."

Mmm, I'd seen Arsenal win against Udinese as well, I thought.

I may have thought it, but I certainly never said it. Well not at that precise moment, anyway. I had also been with Jeanette in Turin to see us scrape a 0-0 draw with Juventus, but the worst time ever was the 2-0 defeat against Napoli – the Christmas when Jeanette had kicked me out.

"I'm not lying to you, M – I have been here another twice – Udine in the north-east near the Slovenian border and Turin. I've also been to Naples, but Jeanette had kicked me out by then."

"I'm sorry," she said. "It just really upsets me finding out that you've done loads of other stuff – and without me."

"Who do I love?" I asked.

"Me," she said.

"And who do I fancy more than anything in the world?"

"Me, again," she smiled.

"And who am I going to be with for the rest of my life?" I winked.

"Definitely me."

"Well there you go then," I told her. "We'll be able to do all the things that you've ever wanted to do."

That bit pleased her. "Je vais garder ma chatte, chaud pour tu," she winked.

Rather than go through Florence and Bologna, I did the scenic route along the coast road, but all I had on my mind was that damned *cat*.

Chapter 35

The Sooty Show– *Episode 8*

I'd got back in by the skin of my teeth, however I had another problem awaiting me. The Bounds Green Studios were very much down to the bare bones, with Annie in charge of what was a skeleton crew and some American film director shooting scenes of what would be *The Invincibles* – a series loosely based on us when we were kids. My task was to get Jarv, Zak and Carter up to speed with how we rolled, my remit being to put three documentaries together: Blackpool's Anglo-Italian Cup successes of 1971 and 1972; the Old Firm: 50 years – The events surrounding 5th September 1931, where a goalkeeper died on the pitch and the Ibrox disaster on 2nd January 1971; along with Jimmy Adamson's ill-fated reign at Leeds United, the latter of which interested me immensely.

I've never really described the set up at the studios, but there are quite a few offices and rooms upstairs – all glazed, probably so *Numb nuts* can see what's going on inside, and one of which had been given to me by Jaime, so I could get the three lads up to speed. I even had a black plaque with my name on it – however, Jaime had refused point-blank to have it put on my door until I had completed what I understood to be my 10,000-day probationary period.

"We research the tabloids, we get the film footage, then we interview some people," I told the lads – all of who seemed really keen.

"What – from nineteen-thirty-one?" asked Jarv.

"No, that's where we have to be a bit more imaginative."

Whilst all this was going on, Annie Dixon, was looking a bit perturbed, but that was nothing new as she had some medical condition that no fucker knew about and which made her a miserable cow. Thinking about it, I wonder if that's what Libby had?

"The only thing that makes me fucking miserable is you," she'd snapped – Libby that is and not Annie.

She had worn me out ragging on about both pregnancies – including hers, along with the kid I'd sired called Donald Cook – oh yeh, and me tapping up M's damp spot, the latter of which was beginning to drive her insane. I was hoping for a quick suicide, so we could all live happily ever after, but all I got was a load of verbal and a smack in the mouth.

Cue: Mizz Dixon.

"I need you to come with me," she said.

I didn't really speak to her that much as she wasn't that talkative, and all she ever seemed to do was snarl and grunt.

"Why – what's up?" I inquired.

I followed her down into the foyer and then out in the car park and towards Bounds Green Road and its Tube station. I was just glad I had my jacket on as it started spotting with rain. All the way there she never spoke one single word – even when we boarded the train for a nine-minute journey to Cockfosters. It was intriguing though, I'll give her that.

All the office reckoned that she looked like that actress – Rosamund Pike – which she did, but I think it was more to do with the actress's characterisation of the psychotic Amy Dunne. Her hair was blonde, although I'm not sure if it was real, and she tended to have it in a bun – you know, like some school mistress, and wore very little make-up.

The destination? Bondy's old flat.

"I didn't know you lived here," I told her.

I didn't – nobody told me anything. As for Bondy – I'd not seen him in ages.

She gave her standard grunt and put the key in the door only for me to cop sight of ...yeh, none other than Bondy.

"I thought you were on *Crimestoppers'* 'ten most wanted'," I said, shaking his hand. "What are you doing here?"

"I need Lee," he told me. "And I can't get hold of him."

"Yeh, he's changed his phone number," I said.

It turned out that Bondy had returned from Thailand in need of money – and a lot of it.

"You can't get Lee involved in any shit," I told him. "It's different now. He's one of ITV's movers and shakers."

"It's a short-term loan," he told me. "I'll have it back to him by the end of next month."

He needed Lee to loan him £90,000.

I looked over at Annie, who just shrugged her shoulders.

Bondy had been sailing close to the wind since this *thing* that happened in South London a few years ago. I liked the kid, but he was trouble.

The upshot was that if it hadn't been for Bondy, it is quite possible that none of us would be where we are now, as it was he who made us a lot of money in the beginning. He never went into specifics, but I assumed it was for some *deal*.

"There's a few thousand in the office," Annie told me, "you know – Basher's money."

"He can't go using that," I told her. "The people he deals with use money counters – you know – note counting machines, and it'll show up straight away. The last thing he wants, is to end up face-down in the river."

I then got Lee on the phone and explained the situation.

"Are you driving?" I asked.

"Yeh – to Piacenza," he told me. "Jeanette's dumped Ross Bain and is now in Milan."

"Well that's good news," I said. "So, what about Bondy?"

"Get Annie to sort the money and I'll cover it."

And that was it – just like that.

I wonder if he'd lend me ninety-grand? I thought

Bondy was always Lee's mate more than mine, and he got on with Jeanette like a house on fire. As for how Annie was going to give it him the money in cash, I had no idea, but I suppose that was her problem.

Later that evening when I was ready for knocking off, Annie popped her head in. "Do you fancy doing something tonight?" she asked.

It was either the fact that she fancied me, or some underhanded ploy to get shut of the witness. As a woman, she had all the right physical attributes that someone *such as me* would look for – you know, two legs and a pair of top bollocks, but mentally, she was someone that you'd generally steer clear of?

"Sure," I said.

Drat! Women had always been my downfall, with part of my problem being that I couldn't say no – or in M's case, that I couldn't take no for an answer.

"Meet me outside Turnpike Lane Station at eight o'clock," was the last she said of the matter.

I was under the impression that it was for a swift half around the corner and I certainly had no idea why the hell she would want to meet me in somewhere like Ducketts Green. Nevertheless, it all sounded rather intriguing and as such I told Libby that I'd be home late as I had rather a lot of work to catch up on.

"I thought you were staying at Maggie's tonight?" she said.

Idiot, I thought. *I was under the impression it was Friday.*

As 8.00 pm drew near, I drove the short distance to Turnpike Lane and parked up around the corner on Carlingford Road, only to get bollocked by some resident for stealing his space. "I'll only be ten minutes," I told him.

I walked around to the station entrance to see Annie coming out, both smartly dressed and with a carrier bag in her hand.

"Hiya," I said.

"Follow me," was all she could grunt.

We walked a few short strides until we came to a pawnbroker-stroke-cheque cashing place and cagily looking around, she rattled on the door, so much so, it had me quite agitated. We heard locks being unlocked at the other side of the door before some geezer with a bald head opened it and invited us inside. It was interesting, I'll give Annie that much. The place itself was full of second hand shite – you know, rubbish jewellery and the odd musical instrument and certainly nothing to write home about. Annie handed the guy what looked like a bankers' draft and the man put a box on the counter and proceeded to count money – and a lot of it, and with a note counting machine that Annie passed him out of the carrier bag. "I don't want any duds," she snarled.

That was quite a good move as there was about £350 worth of 'Basher-money' in it.

"Where are, you parked?" she asked me.

"Just around the corner," I told her.

"Well go get your car and ring me when you're outside."

The transaction was relatively straightforward and we set off on our way to Cockfosters, but not before some car tried running me off the road on the junction of Hedge Lane and Taplow Road. "Put your foot down!" Annie shrieked.

I was doing nearly 80 mph all the way up Hedge Lane dodging in and out of cars. I had to admit, the thought of being robbed at gunpoint along with my imminent death through dangerous driving was giving me a right buzz, so much so Annie looked over at me and actually ...smiled.

A vehicle pulled out of New River Crescent causing me to mount the island to get by it, only for the car chasing us to hit the vehicle head on. It was a right crash, made all the more scenic by it turning on to its roof and a car on the other side of the road running in to it. My white high-performance sports car that was the alleged cause of the three-vehicle pile-up was the subject of a few column inches in the *London Evening Standard* a day later, as was Annie when I finally got her back to the flat and leant over the settee. Not that she appreciated it however.

"Is that it?" she asked.

Thank you very fucking much, I thought.

"Why what was up with it? I inquired.

I had a right to know. I'd done hundreds of women and never had any complaints. I mean, I even half-lived with a porn star, so to some extent I must know what I'm doing. This had really pissed me off, so much so, that I went home to Libby, who seemed quite pleased to see me until I told her about my adventure with Annie – obviously leaving out the facts surrounding its poor ending.

"So, she just wanted you there as some sort of back up?" she asked.

"That's about the long and short of it."

"It all smells a bit fishy to me," she said.

Did it – I mean does it? I thought.

The very next day I let Lee know the runners and riders so to speak, and all he wanted to know was had I got all three lads on with the three documentaries that he'd requested.

"We have plenty of footage and are to interview some of the people that were at Ibrox," I told him. "One of who missed the bus, so he wasn't able to stand where he generally stood. His best mate did however and died."

He seemed pleased enough with that.

"So how did your party go?" I inquired.

"'Interesting' is how I'd probably describe it," he replied.

Chapter 36

The Tale of Two Wives

I woke up that Sunday morning with Emily both awake and cuddled up to me and rubbing her fingers through my hair. More strangely however, was the fact that Jeanette was in bed too.

Shit, I thought.

"Morning love," Emily whispered, whilst at the same time, planting a peck on my lips. "Are you feeling any better? We were all a bit worried."

"Why are we all in bed together?" I asked – rather apprehensively, if I'm being honest.

"It was like you blacked out," whispered Emily.

"Blacked out?" I asked. "I can't have had that much to drink."

"You were complaining of a migraine and couldn't pronounce your vowels," she said. "We gave you a couple of Anadin's and took you to bed and that's when you zonked-out."

I couldn't for the life of me remember anything about actually going to bed, although that would soon change as the *dream* I had was of Emily and Jeanette sat on the bed ... and with Jeanette crying.

"That wasn't a dream," whispered my wife.

I totally remembered Pedro and loads of music and dancing. In particularly, getting marched onto a stage beneath a temporary marquee by Chris and Stevie Kell before copping a face full of cake from a sexually charged wife dressed in a sparkly cream dress.

"I definitely remember you singing," I said. "And you pushing a Black Forest gateau in my face."

That bit had her giggling.

Emily's idea was to feed me my birthday cake with a big wooden spoon whilst she sang me her version of a very much pre-arranged "Cos, Baby I Don't Care" in her rather exaggerated spoilt bitch-mode, that would have put Wendy James's original to shame.

"Yer definitely liked my shoes," she whispered.

I definitely did – especially the ribbons around the ankles and I told her so.

"We made a great night of it," she smiled. "It was the best party ever – totally brilliant."

"So, when did you both decide to climb under the duvet?" I inquired.

"About five-ish – after me an Jin had put the world to rights," she whispered.

Then Jeanette awoke, which put paid to our conversation.

As I've said, at times I couldn't for the life of me, fathom Emily out. Was it some kind of raw innocence or was she just stone bonkers. The thought of me with Johanne drove her to despair, even though nothing ever happened – yet with the woman I had been the closest to, she didn't mind sharing her bed with her. Once I got shut of my first wife, I had to take this up with my second – and I did whilst she was cleaning her teeth.

"We both love you," she garbled, "and we don't want anything bad to happen to you."

"So that's why we had a three-in-the-bed?" I asked.

"It wasn't a three-in-a-bed," she laughed, whilst at the same time gargling.

"There were three of us in the thing," I said.

"We just wanted to make sure that you were going to be okay," she added, whilst spitting toothpaste all over the sink.

"And that's why you both got in bed with me?" I inquired.

"And that's why we both got in bed with you," she replied.

I just shook my head and went downstairs to find the kitchen like a bomb site and Alan Hudson helping his namesake Jaime, with the pots. "I've bagged all that rubbish up," he said.

I told you he thrived on responsibility!

Life's all about timing and me stumbling across Huddy had been exactly that, as was him missing out on the Stoke City manager's job in 1985. He had applied for the vacant job, just as me and Sooty had all those years ago, but whereas we were kids and had done it for a laugh, Huddy had not.

"I was at some function in the Royal Lancaster Hotel in London when I was approached by the Stoke City chairman – Frank Edwards, and he asked if he could have a word in private," Huddy had explained. "We went into the corner of this room where he asked if my letter of interest in the vacant managerial position was serious."

It is easy to understand that being a manager comes with a huge responsibility. Stoke had just had their worst ever season and had bombed out of the top flight. The club had only recorded 17 points – two of them coming on 30th March 1985, in a 2-0 win against Arsenal – a game where an ageing Alan Hudson on loan from Chelsea and an ageing Sammy McIlroy had bossed Arsenal's £1 million midfield and what was both their third and final win of the season. What was worse, was that that Stoke's supporters had stopped attending matches – the very thing that had prompted the Arsenal board to sack Billy Wright in 1966. The match against Arsenal had only managed to draw in a paltry crowd of 7,371 – however, 25 days later that would nearly halve, as only 4,597 turned up at the Victoria Ground to see them lose 3-2 against Norwich.

Stoke City needed to consolidate and bounce back quickly – but Alan Hudson as being the man to oversee this?

There were pluses in that he had played under the management of Tommy Docherty, Dave Sexton, Sir Alf Ramsey, Terry Neill and Don Revie, but there was also the fact that between 1970 and 1978 he had been making headlines in the tabloids most weeks, and some of it for all the wrong reasons.

"Mr Edwards I think, was impressed with my honesty and he asked me to phone him on my return to Stoke on the following Monday morning to discuss it further," Huddy had added. "However, he had sadly died in the early hours of that morning."

How does a chairman or a board of directors go about appointing a manager? What attributes do they look for? I mean, Frank Edwards had given the job to Bill Asprey, a player who had played in the same Stoke City side as Eddie Clamp during the time that the club had been Champions of the Second Division in 1962/63 and had managed to pick up a League Cup runners-up medal, the following season. However, from a managerial perspective, it had to be said that he was a bit of a *Jonah*.

He joined Sheffield Wednesday's coaching staff in 1968 – they got relegated in 1970. He jumped ship to become Noel Cantwell's assistant at Coventry City, before becoming Don Howe's assistant at West Bromwich Albion in 1972. They got relegated in 1973. He then went abroad to coach in Rhodesia and saw Robert Mugabe seize power and had to return to the UK. He was then appointed manager of Third Division Oxford United in July 1979, where under his stewardship the club narrowly avoided relegation by two points before finally getting sacked just before Christmas 1980. This followed just seven wins in 25 League games with the club looking relegation certainties, along with plummeting attendances – including a record low of 2,526 and regular chants at the Manor Ground of "Asprey Out, Asprey Out". He then went to coach in Syria, which was another job he got the sack from. In fact, the only thing of any note he achieved whilst in management was coming up with the idea of the famous donkey-kick free-kick routine, that was executed by Willie Carr and scored by Ernie Hunt in a League game against Everton on 3rd October 1970 – and even that was banned.

Even though Roger Taverner of the *Daily Express* had broken the news reporting that 60 councillors from Stoke City Council had all been regularly praying in hope of some divine intervention as Stoke City's only hope of salvation, their prayers had been only half-answered. Asprey was suspended by the club on 14th April 1985, only for Tony Lacey to take over as caretaker manager.

Asprey, who had suffered a heart-attack during the season, told John Bean of the *Daily Express* that Lacey had been undermining him and claimed a lack of assistance from his assistant. "The Board have put the club in the hands of a man who actually refused to help me with first team training when I was struggling and knew my health was cracking up," he said. "It is indicative of the Board's lack of realism that Tony Lacey has been appointed caretaker. A lot of things have been going on behind my back."

According to Huddy, Lacey was even worse than Asprey – possessing all the charisma of an undertaker and the tactical nous of a prat. Played eight – lost eight. If the club thought Alan Hudson to be a gamble as manager – what exactly were these two jokers?

"This was possibly the lowest point of my playing career, being in a club with two people like this," Huddy told me. "They hadn't an ounce of ability between them and I used to try to work out just how they actually got their jobs."

Jaime made me a coffee and took it outside on the patio, only to see another caretaker mowing the lawns. "How the hell are yer?" he shouted. "Great party, last night."

I couldn't be doing with a rather thick-skinned Elvis in my face – me vividly remembering him trying to sneak into my birthday-bash wearing some white sequinned jacket and matching Lionel Blair's and Basher forcibly removing the gate-crasher via a trip head first into the pool, therefore, I went back inside only for Johanne to come prancing into the kitchen in a bikini. "Great party, Lee," she said as she pecked my cheek, before pouring herself a coffee and going poolside.

"I saw that," winked Emily, as she came into the kitchen with all three kids, plus Jaime's two.

"Dad is Patrick Thistle a good player?" asked my lad.

"Shit hot," I lied. "Nearly as good as Clyde Banks."

"Is he related to Gordon?" he asked.

"They are both football teams, you numpty," I told him. "And it's Partick, not Patrick."

Then it was the bikini clad Jody's turn to come into the kitchen and kiss my cheek. "You okay Hun?" she inquired.

"I'm good," I told her.

Then it was Abi's turn, "Hiya Lee," she said, giving me a kiss. "Thanks for last night – it was lovely."

I couldn't remember that much about last night, least of all the going to bed bit – however that would soon change as Ginge, Stuart and a rather cagey Jono had dropped by and had videoed everything – the footage of which was now being uploaded onto my laptop – some of which would form part of the behind the scenes bit of Electric Ladyboy's European Tour …and unbeknown to us at the time and more importantly, some of which would dictate the direction of all our lives.

That aside, my thoughts on the Jeanette-*thing* were two-fold: Jeanette and Ross were no longer an item, which pleased me in as much as he had become a problem – yet on the other hand it didn't as Jeanette was now unattached – therefore, she would be in my face again.

"She needed to talk to someone," Emily had whispered to me earlier. "And as the house was rammed – we talked in the bedroom after we'd put you to bed."

On picking her up in Piacenza I got the hug of all hugs – however, I'm missing out something here. Ross had given her a backhander, which was something that I had noticed as soon as she'd lifted her sunglasses. "I don't really want to talk about it, Lee," she had told me.

It was Emily who had told me – with both my game-plan and M's carefully constructed power-play obviously helping to create the division.

"I wanted Lee to dig his heels in," Jeanette had cried. "The fact that he didn't tore me to pieces. I couldn't believe that he wouldn't fight for the kids. It broke my heart."

"I went crackers with him," Emily had told her. "Just ask my mam."

"Harmony told me what he'd said to them, about me being a brilliant mum and him telling them that I deserved the chance," Jeanette had added.

On threatening to go back to the UK, Ross had slapped her face, which was something that certainly needed rectifying. Emily knew how I would feel after being told, but she told me all the same. "Lee, you definitely need to know this, love," she had said.

I needed to take control of the situation and everything around me. This was one of the reason's I must have blanked. I rarely got stressed, but this had done me. Jeanette used to shout and scream and shout and scream and I just took it. She had tried that approach with Ross. It was bad man management *à la Terry Neill* and he'd given her a slap.

"Udge up a bit," Emily smiled, as she squeezed onto my chair to watch what I was doing on the laptop. "Are you still thinking about us all going back home?"

"I'll do whatever you want, M," I said. "The problem isn't there anymore."

She cuddled up to me and whilst deep in thought she rubbed her fingers through my hair. "We need to tell the children and ask what they want," she said.

Watching both kids hug their mum on her arrival at the house was fairly cinematic, especially as both me and Emily stood back to take it all in – however, one thing their mum didn't tell them was that the New York-thing was off. Emily on the other hand, certainly did.

"So, we're not going to live in New York?" asked Harmony.

"No love," smiled Emily. "I'm hoping that we can all have our beautiful life back and that our Sammy can see his big brother score his first goal for the football team and watch his big sister – who he loves so much, play her violin in front of all the school."

I had to hand it to Emily, she never ceased to amaze me.

"I never wanted to go to New York," said my lad.

"I didn't either," added my daughter.

"I did," I winked. "But you all stopped me."

That afternoon was brilliant and seeing as now the kids weren't going Stateside, I could have some time on the *Basher-project*. "Okay," said Emily. "Just a couple of hours."

Amidst kids the noise of kids splashing and female voices chattering, I nipped back into the surreal world of Alan Hudson, only to see the man himself being pushed around the pool on a big blow up crocodile, with what looked like a gin and tonic in his hand.

"Crunch week for Arsenal midfield star Alan Hudson," wrote James Connolly of the *Sunday Express* on 18th December 1977. "He finishes a two-week disciplinary suspension tomorrow and hopes to have the plaster off his leg on Thursday. Then comes further talks with Terry Neill on his future."

Arsenal had set a fee of £200,000, which Huddy had always maintained was unrealistic as he had missed five months of last year through injury.

The day prior, an Arsenal team suffering from the side-effects of a midweek jolly over in the Middle East, had visited a rather stuttering and spluttering Coventry City up at Highfield Road – a team who had suffered both a massive loss of form and who had just recently been on the wrong end of 6-0 battering by Everton. Arsenal claimed their fifth away win on the bounce with Frank Stapleton being denied his hat-trick after having a goal ruled out – however, his two headed goals after 31 and 50 minutes made sure that his club came out 2-1 winners.

"There are three reasons why Arsenal can bring the League Championship back to London for the first time since they did the Double in 1971 – Liam Brady, Frank Stapleton and Alan Sunderland," wrote David Miller of the *Daily Express*. "Their fifth consecutive away win leaves Arsenal perfectly poised for a New Year thrust for the title – built around the skill of these men. I believe that the present team, which is reacting keenly to Don Howe's coaching, is already more flexible than that of the Double team."

Come Boxing Day, Tony Stenson of the *Daily Mirror* was purring about Arsenal saying that the club had underlined their Championship potential further with a 3-0 win at Highbury over a rudderless Chelsea, with goals from O'Leary, Rix and Price and which was further underlined two days later when they travelled up to The Hawthorns to rip apart an extremely capable West Bromwich Albion, beating them 3-1.

"Arsenal had the look of League Champions yesterday. This sixth away win in a row was a club record – beating the total set up in the Double year of 1971," wrote Nigel Clarke of the *Daily Mirror* after their second three-goal performance of the Christmas holiday, where Macdonald had seen his shot crash against the bar before Alan Sunderland opened the scoring with a tidy volley after 12 minutes. Macdonald headed them further ahead two minutes later and after 78 minutes of what was an extremely heated game, where fouls were continually going unchecked, the striker raced into the penalty area only to be brought down by John Wile, with Liam Brady converting to make it 3-0. The only blight on the performance was a 20-yard shot from Laurie Cunningham two minutes later, which gave a certain respectability to the result.

"We are only three points off the top and that's a nice position to be in at this stage," said Terry Neill. "This was a difficult game in unpleasant conditions, but if you are to win anything you have to adjust to an English winter."

The downside of that result was that Macdonald, who scored once and who might have had two others, had to have six stitches in a shin wound and left the ground on crutches.

"I took a hefty tackle that jarred every bone," the Arsenal striker told Steve Curry of the Daily Express, "But it would take more than that to keep me out of the side at Goodison Park. If we can win up there, and defeat Ipswich on Monday, I'm sure we will win the title."

All eyes were now on Arsenal...

"They came to parade their talents as challengers to the First Division runaway leaders Nottingham Forest and Goodison Park was alive with expectancy," wrote James Mossop of the *Sunday Express* on New Year's Day, 1978. "But if Brian Clough, the bold and adventurous Forest manager had seen this stuttering misshapen game, he would have laughed all the way back to his city on the Trent."

On 50 minutes and at 1-0 down, Malcolm Macdonald had raced through for a one-on-one with the Everton keeper George Wood – and had fluffed his lines – again, the leg injury he received at The Hawthorns forcing him off the field one minute later. Arsenal had caught a touch of the Jekyll and Hyde's and went down 2-0.

Ray Bradley's column in the *Sunday Express* suggested that Memphis in the United States – a club now managed by Malcolm Allison, could put in a bid for Alan Hudson prior to the Ipswich game – something that would be backed up by Steve Curry of the *Daily Express* later in the week.

The big news however, was that amid Manchester United's interest in Leeds United's £350,000 valued Joe Jordan, his club had offered him a £400 a week contract plus £80 a point along with a £25,000 tax-free testimonial in three years' time. What history would tell you, is that Leeds would suffer as Arsenal would in 1981 with Frank Stapleton, in that both the wages paid and the ambition shown by the Manchester club, would rob both clubs of two great centre-forward's.

Neill was assessing the situation closely. In Leeds losing Jordan they would need a striker. Neill's blarney had put Macdonald in the frame of two potential suiters in Newcastle United and Middlesbrough – however, there was a bigger picture in that he was hoping that the crocked and often-misfiring striker could be the bait to lure McQueen to Arsenal.

"Terry Neill will spend again and spend big if it means consolidating Arsenal's Championship challenge in the New Year," wrote Harry Miller of the *Daily Mirror*. "While Nottingham Forest are the success story of 1977, no-one should doubt that Arsenal are ready and able to steal their glory."

Neill had told the journalist, "I haven't bid for any players this past week but I've certainly inquired about several. I would definitely spend again, if I was convinced the money was for the right man."

Ray Bradley of the *Sunday Express* had inferred that Leeds United's 21-year old Welsh international Carl Harris, was

Neill's primary target, after his brilliant showing at Highbury on 10th December.

"Neill knows he has the full backing of his board to strengthen his squad, but emphasises that he is prepared to only buy at realistic prices."

What is true is that Neill had inquired about Harris – the player who Ipswich's Mick Mills had described as his most awkward ever opponent and that Leeds had mentioned a fee that was not only unrealistic – it would have also smashed the current Record British Transfer Fee.

At the same time as the Harris to Arsenal story was confirmed has having *wings*, the 'manager's spy' had been over at Ewood Park on a scouting mission. The player? Blackburn Rovers' 19-year old defender John Bailey.

"If anything, this team has got more skill, but like the 1971 team – the spirit at the club is what we had that year," explained captain Pat Rice. "David Price should get more credit. He covers so much ground. He does an unbelievable amount of work, so much so, I'm glad he is playing for us and not against us."

On 2nd January 1978, Ipswich Town rolled into N5 and after 36 minutes Brady swept the ball down the middle and Macdonald cleverly dummied to let the ball run through for Price to carry it forward and fire past Paul Cooper. 1-0 to The Arsenal.

"David Price is emerging as a most important man in Arsenal's bid to keep pace with the Nottingham Forest League Championship gallop," wrote Harry Miller of the *Daily Mirror*. "The 22-year-old midfielder has been pushed into the shadows for much of this season as Liam Brady and Graham Rix have grabbed the Highbury headlines."

"David Price came to the help of Arsenal's depleted strike force yesterday to keep The Gunners in the thick of the First Division title chase," wrote Steve Curry of the *Daily Express*. "Arsenal were emphatically superior to Ipswich."

Arsenal would have won by a bigger margin if the referee hadn't disallowed Macdonald's strike after 10 minutes and Alan Sunderland's volley hadn't come back off the post.

Ipswich boss Robson poured cold water on Arsenal's so-called superiority and told Trevor Stenson of the *Daily Mirror* afterwards, "If that's the best Arsenal can do, I don't think they have much chance of the Championship."

On 7th January 1978, Bramall Lane would set the scene for Arsenal's F.A Cup Third Round fixture against an in-form Sheffield United – a steady Second Division outfit and the team that had unceremoniously dumped them club out of the cup some 19-years earlier after United's Billy Russell had taken goalkeeper Jack Kelsey out of the Fifth Round tie with just five minutes on the clock. The right-back for Sheffield United that day? Cec Coldwell – the man who was currently caretaker manager of The Blades.

Arsenal didn't just beat them however, they destroyed them.

"Arsenal had the match won after 20 minutes of artistry, arrogance, precision and power – everything admirable in the game," wrote Alan Thompson of the *Daily Express*.

A header by David O'Leary after seven minutes kicked off the rout, with Pat Rice laying it on a plate for a trade mark left foot strike by Malcolm Macdonald, which hit the goalkeepers bottom left hand corner two minutes later. After 14 minutes a poor header by 32-year old ex-Scottish international Eddie Colquhoun was seized upon by Frank Stapleton, only for the referee two minutes later to penalise David O'Leary for handball and award United a soft penalty. Jennings saved it with his legs and after 18 minutes Macdonald powered in a header which hit the back of the net courtesy of the underside of the bar. Arsenal were on fire and Stapleton wrapped things up after 53 minutes after latching onto a cross from Macdonald on the right and aiming a diving header past the United goalkeeper. 5-0.

"Arsenal were superb in every department," said Cec Coldwell. "We could not mark them and if we had played from now until next Monday we would not have won enough of the ball to have made any difference to the result."

"The raw and undiluted power of a side standing on the threshold of greatness sent Arsenal striding joyously along the stern and testing road to glory. For the five-goal thrashing they handed out to poor Sheffield United emphasised, this unswerving declaration of intent that they are not going to fall easily by the wayside on the way to Wembley," wrote Peter Welbourn of the *Sunday Express*. "Few teams could have lived with Arsenal as they assembled a performance based on discipline, arrogance and adventure. The Gunners were four up after an amazing 10-minute goal burst that had United mesmerised like rabbits in the glare of a speeding car's headlights."

I'd had enough of the laptop as that splitting headache had started to come back, therefore I popped a couple of firefighters and went into the kitchen to grab a cold drink, only to see Huddy still laid in the middle of the swimming pool on the blow-up crocodile.

"He's not dead, is he?" I asked, whilst shouting out through the window to the seven sun-tanned beauties laid out by the pool that were M, Sil', Abi and the four J's – Jeanette, Jaime, Johanne and Jody – and all in that order.

"Nah, he fell off about ten minutes ago and had to be rescued by Jo," shouted Emily.

That was most definitely a set-up and had the words "deep lying schemer" written all over it, as our geriatric maverick had been drooling over Jo and her *twins* since the moment he had laid eyes on her.

"Come out and have five minutes with me," added my wife.

I did, and the first thing she inquired about was my headache.

"I'm fine," I said, on sitting on the edge of her sunbed.

"My dad has taken Sammy for a walk in the buggy," she smiled. "'Dead peaceful isn't it."

"I thought there was a kid missing," I said.

"The rest of them are trying to catch fish in the stream," she told me. "Jamie's adamant that he's seen *Frank* and the *Cuban*."

"The Cuban?" I asked.

"Yeh – the deadly eel that Pedro caught the other week," she laughed, as she sat up on the sunbed and lifted her glasses. "D'yer fancy a trip into town tonight – just me and you?"

"I could do that," I replied.

"Are you two on about going out?" asked our earwigging *Rebel without a Crocodile* – seeing as he'd just fell off the thing – again.

"Possibly," I told him.

"Yeh, it's couples only, so you're barred," winked Emily.

He swam over to me and asked how far I'd got on the Arsenal-documentary.

"I'm in January 1978, you've got your plaster off your leg and are back in training," I told him. "It's looking good."

"M says you might be going back to the UK a bit early?" he asked.

"Maybe," I replied, before hitting him with the big one. "Are you up for your own show?"

The smile I got wasn't quite like Emily's, but nevertheless – it was one you could have framed.

"1970's football – have a think about it and toss me a few ideas."

He did. He wanted to toss them at me there and then – and with immediate effect.

"Just have a think about it," I told him. "You're starting to look good in the camera and you're coming over as quite *not so* aggressive."

"I've never been aggressive," he said.

"Really? The other week when you were talking about Mick Mills, Sammy Chung and Tony Lacey you were doing a bit of twitching," I told him. "If you'd have had a gun and a wheel man handy you'd have gone looking for them."

"You watch far too many gangster films, Alan," added Emily.

"No, I don't," he argued.

"Yeh, you do," I said. "We had a great party last night and you were inside watching *Donnie Brasco* with Mike."

"Forget about it," he said.

"Yeh, exactly," I told him. "Now go and have a think about what I've said and toss me some ideas."

Huddy was beginning to be like one of the family. You know – the old uncle that comes and stays at Christmas, sits in your best chair watching telly and telling you all his tales, whilst at the same time emptying the drinks cabinet.

"I'm going inside to make a White Russian and finish watching that film," he said, on climbing out of the pool. "Do you fancy one?"

What did I tell you?

That night it gave my very tanned wife the chance to slip into a posh frock and put on some rather striking sandals, which had no backs in them.

"What d'yer reckon?" she smiled, whilst standing for inspection.

"The same as I always reckon," I told her. "You look lovely."

"You always say right nice things," she smiled. "It's one of the millions of reasons why I love yer so much."

"Anyway – what's the menu for tonight – seafood or pasta?" I asked.

"I certainly don't want any pasta," she said. "Italian restaurants are rubbish when it comes to pasta."

I had to agree – she was right.

"There's never any meat in them," she winked. "And you know how much I like my meat."

I certainly did.

We drove into the town and had a walk around. It was a bit strange, as for the past few weeks we'd not really spent much time on our own together – apart from bed that is, and even then, we'd recently had both Jeanette and Jody dossing with us. We talked and talked and talked. Well M did. I just listened and listened and listened.

"What are yer saying?" she chuckled. "That I talk too much?"

"I've never said that," I replied.

"Good job," she winked.

As we sat at some table outside a bar in the Piazza a scooter pulled up opposite, with its rider dismounting. I never really took a deal of notice until he began taking photographs of us. It was the person that I recall seeing on us first arriving.

"I think you've been noticed," I said.

"Well hold me hand and say nice things to me then," she twanged, whilst passing me her mitts. "I don't want any rubbish photos appearing anywhere."

"Is that dress torn?" I inquired.

"Where?" she asked flummoxing around and standing up.

I could wind her up all day long.

The bar man came over and I had M order us both a dry white wine. "I fancy picking at a load of different starters," she told me. "Like we did in the Sushi bar near Albert Dock."

"That sounds good," I said.

It was – it was great.

It was around 11.30 pm when we got back in – only to find Huddy with our Sammy sat on his lap and both of them engrossed in watching *Godfather II*.

"Hello love," his mum said to her delightful offspring. "How long have you been up?"

"Since nine," Huddy told her. "We watched some old Stoke City matches and I talked him through England versus West Germany game."

"What really?" she asked.

"No – I put him the *Clangers* on and he thought it was rubbish – so, we're watching this."

"Where's everyone else?" I inquired.

"That boring caretaker bloke came over and asked if Mike and Sil' fancied going over for a drink," Huddy told us. "They ended up taking Trevor Womble with them as if they hadn't I'd have strangled her."

For the record, Trevor Womble was how Huddy referred to Jody.

"Why – what's she done?" M laughed.

"Me and your lad's trying to watch the *Clangers* and she wouldn't shut up talking – mainly about them looking like baby pink elephants and the fact that they lived in dustbins."

"Where are the others?"

"They went out on the lash somewhere."

"'You fancy a drink, Al?" I asked him.

"Nah – I'm good, Lee."

Again – what did I say about responsibility?

That night in bed I had my customary chat with Emily, her happy in the knowledge that we had got what she termed as our *beautiful life* back. She was right, apart from the heavy workload and the odd obstacle that had been slung in front of us our life was beautiful – as was she. For some strange reason however, we got into a conversation about walking on the beach over on The Wirral and me throwing stones for a dog.

"We're definitely not getting a dog, M," I told her. "We've got enough on with the ferrets."

That much was true. If it hadn't been for Edie and Bill currently sitting them, they'd have ended up over here with us.

"I'm not asking for one," she said.

"Well, where's this conversation actually heading then?" I inquired.

"Nowhere," she said. "I asked you to walk with me and yer did."

That made me smile, as did the next bit.

"We've had some really fantastic times, haven't we?"

"The best," I replied.

That would soon change as around 2.30 am we had a knock on the bedroom door. It was Jeanette.

"You're definitely not getting in with us again," I told her.

"What's up Jin?" Emily asked.

"I'm going back with Jaime and her two, in the morning," she said. "And I'm taking Harmony and Jamie with me."

"Okay," I said, "if that is what you want."

She never said anything and just nodded.

I may not have been able fathom out M at times – however, it was the exact opposite with Jeanette.

I'd never said anything as such to Emily – but being that they were supposedly the best of friends, why hadn't they been sat talking to each other on the sunbeds? She hadn't even laid near her. In fact, after leaving our bedroom I couldn't recall one conversation that had taken place between the two. I'll make no bones about it, Jeanette was doing this to spite us. Her personal life was up in the air and she had walked into ours at a most inopportune time – firstly, by flying into an airport 250 miles away, and secondly, just a few hours before a party where lots of people were due to turn up. She expected to upset the apple cart or put a spanner in the works, so to speak. The crying and getting in bed with us – what was all that about? She was trying to push every available button to create lots of different problems, but all she found on walking into our life in Italy, was that nothing changes. Our life in Italy is exactly the same as it is in Frederick Street and the same as it is in Hamilton Square. So, long as the main cast are the same, your life is where you take it, hence why she intended to remove two of the main players – our kids.

"That's not really very nice, is it?" Emily said.

"It isn't M – no."

"She's been a bit stand-offish with me all day," she said, as the penny could be heard dropping. "I offered to lend her some swimming clothes, but she just sat at the other side of the pool talking with the others."

"Her life's a bit of a mess," I said. "The upshot is, is that if she's pissed-off, so should I."

"And are you – yer know, thingied-off?"

"I have you," I said. "What have I got to be pissed off about?"

I got a cuddle for saying that as well as a peck on the lips and a rather wandering hand. "Je t'aime tellement?"

"I love you too," I told her.

"Tu êtes seulement avec moi parce que vous aimez ma chatte," she pouted.

It was that damned *cat* again.

Chapter 37

The Prince of the Road

Us leaving Italy was inevitable after Jeanette had taken the kids. It was what she wanted and it's what she had achieved. What I got had been a long drive back, a ferry delay at Dover and on walking into the house, a splitting headache like you wouldn't believe. I popped a couple of Anadin's, put the kettle on and commenced emptying the Mean Machine, whilst M appeased a travel-weary Herbert and went through the mail.

Neither of the kids had been best-pleased with their mum's decision, Harmony kicking off good style. "Just because your life's rubbish – don't go spoiling ours."

Even her eight-year old daughter had read it right.

"Harmony – don't talk to your mam like that, love," Emily had said. "It's not nice."

"Sorry M," she said, before looking up at her mum. "Sorry."

"Why do we have to go?" my lad had asked. "It's great here – can't we just go back with dad and M?"

It was what it was and it was their mum that had called the shots.

"You have to read this," said Emily, passing me some letter.

Mmm, one of the directors of the company that had bought both me and Sooty out almost a year ago was attempting to sue me for breach of contract – the fact that I couldn't produce sports documentaries for three years through any company of my own. They had obviously got wind of Basher Productions Inc. and M as one of its directors.

"Is it serious?" she inquired.

"Not at all," I replied. "I work for ITV and they produce. At the moment, the *Terry Neill-thing* with Chris is nowhere near completed – and my name certainly won't be going on it."

"So, where are they coming from?" she asked.

"An out of court settlement, probably," I winked. "I'll play along with them for a while and then wipe the floor with them."

Another obstacle? No, not really.

"Good grief!" she gasped, on seeing a copy of some magazine that had been pushed through our letterbox. "Yer have to see this, Lee."

I was on its front page – both bare-chested and lathering down Jody with sun oil.

"The King of the Swingers" the front cover read, whilst inside there was around a dozen photos with captions and some editorial. Looking through it, the publication made out that we were having some wild orgy – with bikini clad females everywhere. There was even a photograph of Sally Nattrass in the pool … and minus a bra.

This was anything but how it had been. We'd had a lovely time.

"I can't believe how cruel people can be," mumbled Emily, whilst looking at a photo of her outside the bar in the piazza. "I've never argue with you – ever."

"All the booze and the birds – it's all got a bit hot under the collar for Emily Janes," the caption read.

There was also a photograph of Abi giving me a peck on the lips in the bedroom that she'd slept in.

This was wrong – really wrong.

The photographer must have been using some mega-long lens and had just caught me carrying her case up to the room and opening the patio doors. This was utter madness. There was even a photo of Johanne trying to get Alan Hudson back on his crocodile. "One-time maverick footballer Alan Hudson also joins in all the fun," it read.

"It's a good job your mum and dad were actually there," I said.

There was not one photo of the kids anywhere. It was constructed to look exactly like it was – some sex party. The guy who had put all this together was the face that I had noticed on the scooter the day I'd arrived in San Gimignano. The man who last autumn had tried to run some exposé on the breakup of M's marriage and the man I had threatened to finish.

Fortunately, the one person that had suffered at the hands of the press had been something of shoulder to lean on whilst all this was going on – Huddy. "The press are never interested in the truth, M," he told her. "They just want headlines."

He was spot on.

"I was with you from the morning of Lee's birthday and all I saw was a lovely family with lovely friends," he'd added. "You're much better than them – let it go and move on."

ITV also were extremely unhappy with what had been printed and even more so after I'd told them that it was all made-up, and as that was indeed the case, they made their move to commence legal action.

"And what – give them more publicity?" I told one of their paralegals. "I'm with Huddy on this one – let it go and let's move on."

Another problem arose – and one heavily linked to ITV's new head of programming.

Cue: Stacey Tirford – the well-stacked albeit rather obsessive wife of the Tall Dwarf.

"Lee," she shouted whilst getting out of a vehicle in the car park. "I really need to speak with you."

Jesus Christ, I thought

"This is a really bad idea," I told her.

"I need to talk to you," she said, on her coming over.

"If your husband gets wind of you here, he'll do is damnedest to make my life a living hell."

"He already is," she said. "Who do you think sent the newspapers the press release about your new wife and Tim Sutton and who do you think tipped the journalist off about Italy?"

"Who – him?" I shrugged.

However, that was only the start.

I was then let know that although *The Invincibles* would be made, it certainly wouldn't be going out on ITV, nor would Jeanette be getting to host a show. The Tall Dwarf was not only trying to hurt us, he was also inviting me to invest both my time and money for false promises and a zero return.

"And he told you all this?" I asked.

She gave me a nod, before touting her body as part of some quid pro quo arrangement.

"What – me and you?" I shrugged.

"I'll not tell him, this time though," she said.

"Yeh, and you said you'd not tell him last time and you did," I told her.

"I was a bit depressed."

Although I listened, that was as much as I did do.

"Your wife's nice," she said.

"Yeh, I know – that's why I married her."

However, that's where the conversation would end as I then went inside and let ITV's CEO know exactly what was happening. I then told him that I'd give Sky Atlantic the option on *The Invincibles*. On hearing that, he went crackers – not so much with me, but with the Tall Dwarf, who thought that as I was beneath him in the *food chain*, that he could come around to the studios later that day and do the same to me. Fortunately, Basher assisted in helping him leave – head first, which impressed Jody no end, so much so, that she asked him if he'd do it again.

"It's Tai Kwan Do," Chris told her, before putting over an exaggerated Japanese accent. "It is a style of fig-hhting that combines elements of Kar-hhate with Chinese and Korean mahh-rtial arts."

"That wasn't Tai Kwan Do," Kirsty argued. "You just slung him in some hedges."

The Tall Dwarf was anything but happy and after doing a bit of pointing at Chris – he left.

I then let ITV know that he was now barred from the building, which created a problem in that the *ITV Sessions* were filmed here.

"Come on Lee," said one of the suits that had a couple of points in the business that was our White Lion label. "The programme falls under his jurisdiction."

"Then fucking sack him," I said.

Both businesses ran without any problems, so the last thing I needed was for some overgrown midget sticking his oar in – however, the fact that I had already invested a few hundred thousand pounds in *The Invincibles* had really, really pissed me off.

Both Abi and Jaime were in the same mind-set – do what I had told ITV, make it and offer it to Sky Atlantic.

It was okay them saying it – but my potential outlay was in the *millions* and for one full week I would be continually hassled by ITV's hierarchy. If it wasn't one thing it was another, so much so, that I blew a fuse – and blacked out again.

"It's stress," the doctor told me on taking my blood pressure and having a look in my eyes with some little telescope-thingy. "You just need to take it easy."

M had told me the same. Since we had got back from Italy I had been working 12, 13 and 14 hours a day – and that was just in the office. Even at home, I was working. "Lee, I'll not tell you again, switch off your laptop," she said.

The whole ITV 7 thing was an extremely big workload, made a million times worse with the insistence that we use their studios in Manchester.

I'd brought more people into the setup and I was due to have a meeting with a guy from New York called Josh Sippie about anchoring some of the weekends football, who when ITV heard I was planning on using an American, went absolutely berserk.

"He's not only a nice-looking face that knows his football inside-out and back to front, he's also an accredited sports writer and journalist," I told them. "Whether you like it or not, it is going to happen."

Every time I appeared to make a move – they tried not so much blocking it, but appeared as if they were trying to control me.

Cricket, Rugby, Tennis, Athletics, Boxing, Formula One, Horse Racing – you name it, ITV 7 would be running with it. My head was a fucking shed and it hadn't even started. "I'm struggling here, M," I told my wife one particular night. "I'm sure these are out to break me."

She sat on the bed cross-legged with her knees up to her chin as I gave her the brief on what was happening.

"Pack it all in," she said. "We've got plenty of money – let's leave and fly back out to Italy."

M's solution just meant running away. I had too many people dependent on me to do that. What I would do is put my case over to ITV and try and force the issue – however, what I had done by firstly undermining the Tall Dwarf and then going head-to-head with its hierarchy, was that I had made enemies – them thinking that I'd just become a little bit too big for my boots.

Sooty had worked his way back in and the stuff that he'd both got from Alan Hudson and of course how he'd groomed Jarv, Zak and Dean – if groomed is indeed the right word, with the Ibrox Disaster in 1971 making extremely compelling viewing, had been spot on. As for Huddy himself, he had given me an array of ideas, one of which was extremely good – if not extremely plagiarised – however, I needed his show or shows to be a professional set up with him in the chair and not just some old maverick and boozer's reunion.

I gave him a cameraman – Stuart, and sent him on his merry way. As with *The Sooty Show* I wanted *The Huddy Show* to be compelling viewing.

"Are you sure about him?" Kirsty asked.

"Why not? I was sure about you," I told her.

I then had Annie Dixon in my face. "I need a few days off," she said.

"Okay," I said.

And that was that, I thought, until I saw her go over to Sooty ...and what followed, nobody was expecting – least of all Sooty. She gave him a right smack in the mouth, booted both his shins and then turned his desk over.

"Enlighten me?" I asked him. "What the hell was all that about?"

"She's pregnant," he told me.

"What – she's actually had sex with you?" I asked.

"What's that supposed to mean?" he snapped.

For all her foibles, peculiarities, idiosyncrasies and what have you, Annie was quite a tidy looking woman and certainly not someone who would fall for someone as transparent as Sooty.

"It all got a bit heated after the car chase," he said.

Huddy couldn't believe any of this. "So, you've currently got three women pregnant and have recently found out you've got another kid somewhere?" he asked.

"Possibly four," he said. "Buzzy's missus rang me up while you were in Italy."

"Why don't you just bag up, you dickhead?" was what I initially said.

He was getting as bad as Vince Vaughn's character in *The Delivery Man*, which was some film Jody had brought around to watch a few nights ago. I'm just glad he'd not got what he wanted from Emily, otherwise his fertilised egg would have probably cuckooed mine – and rather strangely I said it.

"That doesn't even make any fucking sense," Sooty said, whilst straightening up his desk.

He was right – it didn't.

I went in to see Annie and told her that I was here if she needed me – however, the glare I got back from her was extremely intimidating. What I couldn't understand however, was that if their brief encounter had supposedly only happened a few weeks ago, how did she know she was pregnant? Like I said – very strange!

That lunchtime I met Emily and Herbert in the Coffee Shop, the latter of who was now both walking and bumping into thing's, as was Fosis cumbersome offspring who had just tripped over his limp.

"I've been watching him for the last ten minutes," Emily whispered. "He limps on different legs."

"So, does Sooty," I told her. "Annie Dixon has just given him a right clout."

"What was that for?" she asked.

"He managed to put in her what he intended to put in you," I said. "Mainly a couple of shots of his highly volatile, albeit extremely fertile liquid gold."

"What she's pregnant?"

"Apparently," I grinned. "I wish I could be a fly on the wall when he tells Libby."

That had her smiling.

"Anyway, what have you two been up to?" I asked.

"Tell daddy that 'we've been down to Borough Market'," she said, as she passed me my second son.

There was absolutely no chance of that and instead he tried sticking a squashed-up quaver in my mouth, which he insisted that I eat.

"Da-dad," he said.

There you go – he had finally said it.

"Good boy," his mum told him.

"Have you seen anything of Jeanette?" I asked.

"No – nothing," she replied.

Ah well, nothing like a bit of peace and quiet, I thought

I got served an Espresso and a Perrier water and we spoke about a few things, one of which was that we needed to go up to The Wirral as there was some engagement-do for one of Emily's cousins.

"Sound," I told her.

"And I'm on telly tonight," she smiled. "Come Dine with Me."

Oh dear.

I got back in work to find Basher in my office. "I'm glad I've got you in here," I said as I removed him from my chair. "Have you been putting it about that we are doing a documentary? I'm only asking as I've got some corporate law firm poking about in my affairs about breach of contract."

"No," he lied.

"Well I'm glad that's sorted then," I said, before inquiring. "So, what do you want?"

Mmm, he wanted to know when he'd be getting a return on his fifteen-grand investment.

"Soon," I told him. "That's unless you want me to just quash the deal and give you back the money."

To be honest, I hadn't done much on the documentary as we'd been all over the place and I wasn't sure on how I figured on going about the phase of the 1977/78 season following the annihilation of Sheffield United in the cup, as it was here where the wheels would come loose and several stupid points would be dropped.

On the 14th January 1978, Wolverhampton Wanderers were due at Highbury, but the mutterings in the press suggested that Arsenal were after another central defender, with Ray Bradley of the *Sunday Express* stating that the club were keeping tabs on Tony Gale – not the swinging fish man with the buxom wife, but the 18-year old defender from Fulham – however, the most interesting thing was that an unhappy Gordon McQueen had created massive problems for his club the weekend before, when Manchester City went over to Elland Road and duly dumped them out of the F.A Cup. It wasn't so much the defeat that emphasised his unhappiness, but the fact that he had punched his own goalkeeper in the face – the said incident being picked up by the BBC's cameras and shown to millions of viewers later that evening on *Match of the Day*.

What had also happened is that Joe Jordan had finally been sold to Manchester United.

"What a funny-peculiar week it has been for Gordon McQueen," wrote Alan Thompson of the *Daily Express* the day of Arsenal's League match with Wolves. "On Saturday, he dots his own goalkeeper and gets knocked out of the F.A. Cup; on Sunday he apologises and says he is happy at Leeds; on Tuesday he is substantially fined for ungentlemanly conduct; on Thursday he asks for a transfer; and on Friday the request is granted, and he is dropped. And today managers are contemplating spending £500,000 on signing him. Does anyone else find it sickening and sordid?"

Neill was certainly interested, but certainly not at that fucking price.

"Arsenal skipper Pat Rice reckons the time is ripe for Malcolm Macdonald to begin the goal blitz that could launch

The Gunners to the League title," wrote Nigel Clarke of the *Daily Mirror.* "Macdonald has collected only 11 goals so far this season and has failed to score in a League match at Highbury for three months. This time last January he had scored 15 goals – 14 of them in the First Division and finished with an overall total of 29. It would be a great moment for Macdonald to start getting among the goals again as Arsenal enter a vital four-match run that will be a searching test of their pedigree to win honours."

Liverpool's hard-man of defence had recently added to that by telling Nigel Clarke, that Arsenal were average – and that they would win nothing, as long as Macdonald was in the side.

As I had already said, a misfiring and often-crocked Macdonald would be the bait for McQueen to Arsenal, but would Neill be able to sell it?

What was happening at the time was that Manchester United had been wanting to show more ambition than just signing Joe Jordan and had an agreement in place with Queens Park Rangers for a £445,000 deal that would take Gerry Francis to Old Trafford. Again – Arsenal had inquired, but that was as far as it had gone.

Arsenal easily dispatched Wolves in a 3-1 win, although James Mossop of the *Sunday Express* criticised their finishing. "One vital quality was missing as Arsenal continued their bid to bring this season's silverware to Highbury – the killer instinct, the remorseless hounding that has opponents keeling over in submission, the ruthless clawing at the quarry until the very last gasp," he wrote. "Against a timid, toothless Wolves side they sprang into a two-goal lead and then fell into the same slipshod ways of their half-hearted rivals."

Brady had cracked a free kick through a wall of Wolves defenders and into the bottom corner after only four minutes, and Macdonald headed a second from an in-swinging corner from Graham Rix on 18, only for the game to peter out. In between, Stapleton had missed a gilt-edged opportunity to score as had Macdonald when he was put clear after 32 minutes, only to be foiled by goalkeeper Paul Bradshaw. Just to make things interesting, Willie Young who was just back from a knee injury headed an own goal after 68 minutes, which had let Wolves back in.

"So slovenly did Arsenal become, that Young rammed the ball into his own goal when, there was no Wolves player within a dozen yards," added Mossop.

Stapleton finally put the match beyond doubt towards the back end of the game when he seized on to a pass from Macdonald to fire past the goalkeeper and make it 3-1. It had been a good result – but in truth, Arsenal ought to have had the match wrapped up early-on and put half a dozen past their visitors.

"What surprised me was the way they seemed to be niggling at each other right the way through the game," Wolves' Kenny Hibbitt told Steve Curry of the *Daily Express* after the game. "When a team is up at the top of the table like they are, you don't expect them to be having goes at each other. They should be encouraging one another."

The togetherness that Pat Rice was talking about the month before was always a myth – Arsenal were misfiring and two culprits had been publicly named: Macdonald and Young.

Still in the news had been Arsenal-target Gordon McQueen, who had again been dropped from the side to face Everton in the Quarter-Final of the League Cup, with his club Leeds United looking to reinvest any money from the sale – possibly by making a £500,000 bid for Trevor Francis – and as Arsenal prepared for a trip up to Maine Road to play their League Cup match, things were becoming extremely interesting.

"Five incredible saves by Pat Jennings last night kept Arsenal in the League Cup. Jennings saved twice from both Dennis Tueart and Peter Barnes and once from Asa Hartford as City's assault grew to a crescendo," wrote David Miller of the *Daily Express*. "Arsenal had first slammed a studded iron door in City's face, then winger Barnes ripped it off its hinges. This confrontation of two fine teams, who now replay for a Semi-Final place on Tuesday ultimately assumed memorable stature because Barnes unleashed the skills, which give England supporters optimism for the future. He switched late in the first half from left flank to right and reduced Arsenal's previously impregnable fortress to crumbling rubble as he turned Sammy Nelson inside-out."

The truth was though, that Arsenal again, ought to have been well out of sight by half-time and well before Jennings had to make two world class saves from Barnes after 64 and 70 minutes and from Tueart two minutes from time. 0-0 and to be continued.

In between the League Cup performance and Arsenal's next match up at the City Ground against runaway League leaders Nottingham Forest, it was confirmed that Manchester United had pulled the plug on the Gerry Francis deal and had set their sights on another target and prepared to make a bid for Gordon McQueen. Their manager put it over as the deal had been "suspended" rather than their interest ending, with Dave Sexton telling Nigel Clarke of the *Daily Mirror*, "We have to do the McQueen deal first. We will then try for Francis later. I realise that this means we could lose him, but the signing of McQueen will be our priority."

Arsenal travelled to Nottingham Forest and got soundly beaten 2-0, with goals from David Needham after 33 minutes and Archie Gemmill after 64 – the latter coming after one of several sloppy passes in the match by Liam Brady.

The match could have been a whole different affair had Alan Sunderland netted what was an easy chance after Rix and Brady had set him up on goal after 28 minutes. Even at 1-0 Arsenal were not dead and buried.

Brian Clough said after the match, "Arsenal staggered us for 15 minutes after half-time when they poured forward, playing two men wide and two centre forwards."

This was a strategy which would be deliberated in depth by David Miller of the *Daily Express* just prior to Arsenal's extremely high profile and penultimate game of the season.

"Forest knew Liam Brady is one of the most effective and ambitious passers of the ball in British Soccer," wrote Frank McGhee of the *Daily Mirror*. "But rather than cutting him off at the knees by clogging him – which Clough insists he detests, they shut down the most menacing men Brady wanted to feed – Malcolm Macdonald and Frank Stapleton. In this match, they both became the Soccer equivalent of eunuchs. The lazy, irritating Macdonald managed one dangerous shot, Stapleton one less."

The reality was a defeat and a change was needed. Would Arsenal join in the action and go head-to-head with Manchester United and smash the British Transfer record by bidding for either McQueen or Gerry Francis, or even with Leeds United for Trevor Francis – a player who Denis Hill-Wood had already approached Birmingham City for and who had explained that the directors at St. Andrews had appeared "cool" on Arsenal's offer?

"He's not for sale at any price," chairman Ken Coombs had told Joe Melling of the *Daily Mirror.*

That wasn't entirely true.

The latest player Arsenal had reportedly inquired about, according to the *Sunday Express*, had been Bristol Rovers' promising 19-year old striker Paul Randall, who would go on to hit 22 goals in 36 appearances for The Pirates that season.

Next up was the League Cup Quarter-Final replay against a vastly improving Manchester City side, with manager Tony Book stating, "Our performances over the last seven or eight games have been the best I have seen from any City team I have known as both player or manager."

That was indeed some statement and that being the case, Arsenal were expected to have another huge game on their hands – however, what City hadn't expected was that Arsenal would have Alan Hudson back and sitting on the bench. Enter *The Prince of the Road* playing before a crowd of 57,748 – which according to some of supporters, didn't tell the whole story.

"They were doubling up at the turnstiles all around the ground – there must have been well over sixty thousand in that night," said Nat Young – an old-school Arsenal supporter and one-time teenage soccer prodigy over at Tottenham Hotspur – that was until he had his career cut short after a sever bout of glandular fever. "It was heaving and I was in the middle of the North Bank, and of course, being just twelve years old, you got caught up in every emotion of the crowd."

"Alan Hudson, out of Arsenal's first-team for more than two months last night fired a second half surge towards victory in the Football League Cup," wrote David Miller of the *Daily Express*.

It was Hudson's first game since last November and the combination of his elegance and vision seemed to have a galvanising effect with Liam Brady," wrote Frank McGhee of the *Daily Mirror*. "Having someone else to share the midfield load, Arsenal started to flow relentlessly and if any team deserved to win it was Arsenal."

Hudson had given Arsenal more variety and ideas and his introduction was explosive as almost immediately he fired a fierce shot just wide from a return pass from Macdonald, before making his presence known as he intelligently switched the play to either flank, bringing both Arsenal full-backs through on overlaps.

With half an hour to go Corrigan emulated Pat Jennings in the first encounter with a stupendous one-handed save from Stapleton, before a contentious penalty was awarded when Manchester City's Dave Watson was adjudged to have brought down Macdonald on 76 minutes.

Despite City's pleas, referee Alf Grey pointed to the spot and Liam Brady duly sent Corrigan the wrong way celebrating the deadlock being broken by swinging on the crossbar. 1-0 to The Arsenal.

Hudson told Harry Miller of the *Daily Mirror* afterwards, "I had a feeling it was going to be my night. I'd only been on the pitch five minutes when the crowd started chanting my name. That gave me a wonderful feeling. They are marvellous people, these Arsenal fans and they deserve the best."

"Alan Hudson has opened the door on his last chance to be an important player with an important club," wrote David Miller of the *Daily Express*. "His finely measured performance in Tuesday's League Cup Quarter-Final replay gave Arsenal, who are aiming for three trophies, a new tactical dimension."

"Alan is a class player," Don Howe had told Miller. "He made all the difference. Not only does he conceal his intention until the last moment, he is wanting to combine with everyone in the team. He is always available and he's so good at playing out of tight situations."

"It was my stomach injury – the pain used to come on after an hour," Huddy told me. "I was having to hold back the whole time, but I knew playing for forty-five minutes, that I could give it my all."

There was certainly a lot more to that story, however.

"The funniest moment I had with Terry Neill, was perhaps when in the early stages of the Manchester City League Cup match," Huddy had told us. "Don Howe knew that we were getting outplayed in midfield and started telling Terry to make a change, which kept falling on deaf ears. I was sitting behind Don and Terry, along with Tony Donnelly when Terry finally said, 'Huddy your coming on'. There was about fifteen minutes to go to half-time. I nudged Tony and said, 'I'm not coming on now, my feet are facking freezing'. When we got inside the dressing room I said to Tony, 'Clean my boots mate, I'm going to warm my feet up and win us the match', and as I sat on the edge of the bath running hot water on my feet the doors swung open and in came the players, with Terry saying, 'Right, I'm making a change – John (Matthews) you're coming off and Huddy you're going on'. The rest is history. But the following day the *London Evening Standard's* headlines read, 'Masterstroke by Arsenal manager', which had me howling. He certainly didn't want to bring me on. It was only Don who kept on at him that swung it. But he told the *Standard* that **he** saw that we needed to change things."

I got home around 6.30 pm, just in time to kiss Sammy goodnight and wave him off to bed – however, on seeing me he wanted a *stopping-up ticket*. "Okay then," said his mum. "Ten minutes and then it's na-night time."

Emily watched on smiling, as I juggled with my son. He was coming on great – walking at just under 12-months old and saying "dad, dad". It was just a pity that he hadn't really mastered the art of knowing when he actually needed the potty, as at that said moment his face, I had to say, smarted of constipation. "It's got to be as uncomfortable as hell shitting in a nappy," I said.

All I got from his mum was a bit of a growl and an "I can't believe it – I've just put that on him."

He had something of a penchant for soiling freshly applied Pampers just before bedtime – generally about ten minutes after they'd been put on. "I'm sure he does it on purpose," chuntered his mum.

"It's better he does it now, rather than him have to lay in it all through the night," I told her.

"I suppose so," his mum replied, before directing those exact words at Herbert. "I suppose me having to change your bum is better than having you looking uncomfortable and being miserable, eh?"

"I wonder if Diane Abbott wears a nappy?" I said.

That certainly had M giggling.

The *Come Dine with Me* at our house had obviously had to be rescheduled, with Ms Abbott being less than complimentary about M, in every way, shape or form, so much so, she had just stopped short of labelling her 'Scouse white trash'.

"I've never done or said anything wrong to her at all," Emily had told me post-Ms Abbott's first poisonous barb about her in the papers. Then bang, bang, bang, more of the same had followed, which had M chewing glass – and a gnat's bollock away from sitting in the rocking chair and polishing her shotgun.

She had given M a four out of ten, for her Lobster Thermador.

"I worked really hard on that and I was nothing but nice with her," Emily had said. The others had given her nine's.

Cue: The return visit to Hackney and M's well thought out review. "I can certainly see why she's so obnoxious, miserable and grossly overweight, having to eat what could only ever be described as absolute pig swill," Emily had said. "If I could give it less than none, I would."

"We can't run with that," claimed the show's director.

"Yeh, yer can," she had twanged. "Run it."

"That must have been the best *Come Dine with Me* ever," I told my wife after watching it later that evening.

Emily's phone was red hot straight after, with fellow-gooner Ian Smith the first one to congratulate her. "That was shit hot, M," he said. "You were brilliant."

Emily had gritted her teeth and waited for the moment and bang! She'd done her.

According to the rumours circulating around Channel 4's HQ, Ms. Abbot had gone berserk and threatened to strangle the show's producer, Martin Dance with her bare hands and rip off David Lamb's head and shit down his neck. I don't know how true these rumours actually were, but she certainly seemed more than capable of doing it and I had visions of her clumping down Horseferry Road turning over cars, ripping out parking meters and kicking over phone and letter boxes.

I was considering doing a bit more on Basher's documentary, seeing as he had been nagging me for its completion – however, Emily had different ideas. "I'll be mad if yer start doing work at this time of night," she told me.

I looked at my watch, which told me that it was 10:40 pm.

"What are you wanting to do?" I shrugged. "Watch a film?"

"Uh uh," she replied.

"Oh, right," I said.

"How do you mean – oh, right," she said, with both hands on her hips. "Either I get yer-knowed or there'll be mega bother."

Servicing M was getting to be a full-time job. Only the other week I'd been in the shower wincing at the bruising that her teeth had made.

"You get far too carried away," I'd told her, as I limped out of the shower.

"Why, don't you like it?" she'd winked.

"Yeh of course I do," I'd told her. "But if you do it any harder you'll end up frigging breaking it."

She was like some sex-bomb.

"I'll put some of our Sammy's Sudocream on you," she grinned.

"No, you won't," I'd told her. "You piss about with it, so it never gets put on the right place."

Back in real time I had a wife slither up to me and crunch my fingers in the lap top. "I promise I'll be gentle with you."

Yeh, that train of thought was immediately debunked as soon as she'd nearly bit off my ear.

"Ouch," I said. "That really hurts, M."

"I just love you so much," she said.

I knew that.

Early next day I came into the house smelling of coffee and Emily sat at the kitchen table doing a *Tesco's* shop online, whilst Sammy was sat in his high chair slinging Weetabix all over the place. "Hiya love," she said. "There's coffee in the pot and I've got some bacon under the grill."

Perfection, eh?

I kicked up my laptop and listened to Huddy talking of his thoughts at that particular time, whilst Emily stopped what she was doing, passed me a coffee, sat on my knee and twiddled with my hair.

Just after the win over Manchester City, Huddy had stopped at a pub that he had never been in before with his mate and driver, Tony Davis and had sat in thought over his future, thinking that if only he could get over that abdominal injury and get back to playing at his best for an entire 90 minutes – however, that was never going to happen without complete rest.

"Had it been the last match of the season, I would have come back one hundred percent and shown the rest of the lads that I was fully committed," Huddy had told us, whilst speaking into the camera. "I'm sure with all the stuff that was being written about me in the papers, that they certainly doubted that."

Don Howe was integral to everything surrounding Alan Hudson's role with Arsenal.

"With Don at the club and feeling how he did about me, I truly thought that I would have become a big part of the team instead of a bit part," Huddy had added. "Don was magnificent, in fact, the best coach I have ever come across. Don brought some sanity back into the club, who actually could have been relegated under Terry such was his absolute inability to man-manage – however, saying that, and as I've said already, Don was certainly no manager himself."

Arsenal's next game was a F.A Cup Fourth Road tie at home to Wolverhampton Wanderers, with it being widely assumed by the press that an out of form Malcolm Macdonald would be making way for Alan Hudson, as the previously League Cup-tied Alan Sunderland was legible for this game. However, that wouldn't happen as Frank Stapleton was now out injured – he had twisted his knee.

"The boys are very chirpy at the moment," Wolves manager Sammy Chung said. "We were very disappointed about the way we played at Highbury a fortnight ago and the players want to prove to themselves and everybody else that they are good enough to live with the best."

"Sammy Chung – another clown," Huddy had told me.

Prior to the game, Manchester United were trying to negotiate with Leeds over McQueen – their initial bid falling £100,000 short of the British Transfer record – however, Derby County manager Tommy Docherty had steamed in with a bid and smashed it, with Leeds manager Jimmy Armfield immediately accepting their offer. Derby had bid £500,000. However, what would happen is that McQueen would turn it down flat stating that he wanted a bigger club than Derby and that he did quite fancy Manchester United.

"Our interest in McQueen is finished," snapped Docherty. "Jimmy Armfield told me that the player had refused to even consider joining Derby."

Manchester United must have been loving it.

Then Tottenham Hotspur showed an interest, reportedly bidding £500,000, which according to Robert Armstrong of the *Guardian*, was again swiftly accepted by Jimmy Armfield and then countered by the *Daily Express'* back page headlines: "Arsenal go for McQueen".

In between all that, Arsenal had dispatched Wolves with a goal in the last minute coming from the supposed makeweight in the McQueen deal – Malcolm Macdonald.

"An incredible, last minute of pure melodrama, won this frantic Cup tie for Arsenal. In those blazing seconds of over spilling emotion, tragedy struck this brave Wolves side when Bob Hazell, their 18-year-old centre-half, was sent off after a clash with The Gunners' Graham Rix," wrote Alan Hoby of the *Sunday Express*. "With time running out, Rix wanted to get on with a corner. But the hefty Hazell, who up to then had been magnificent at the heart of the Wolves defence, was slow to release the ball. There was a scuffle and Hazell struck the Arsenal man. Amid a deafening uproar from the 49,373 crowd, referee Clive Thomas ordered off the heartbroken Hazell. Liam Brady took the corner and the ball arched into the crowded goalmouth where Willie Young nodded it over to Malcolm Macdonald – who coolly headed home."

The two players whose careers with Arsenal were under threat by the clubs' *interest* in Leeds United's Scottish international central defender had combined for the winning goal.

Prior to that Kenny Hibbitt had hit a wonderful goal from 25-yards to equalise Alan Sunderland's headed goal after 15 minutes. Arsenal's win had been undeserved, yet Price had forced a great save from Bradshaw; and Hudson who's neat passing had again provided some rhythm to the attack, had had a fine lobbed shot cleared off the line, with Hoby adding, "Who would have thought that after Macdonald's disappointing play, he would snatch the winner and salvage a few shreds of his own waning reputation?"

Come Tuesday morning Terry Neill's intentions were made clear.

"Manchester United will be shocked to find London's title chasers are a real rival for McQueen's signature," wrote Bill Elliot of the *Daily Express*. "Jimmy Armfield says he expects a further call from Arsenal this morning and I expect that will come from the Bournemouth hotel where Neill and his players are relaxing this week. The offer of Macdonald may well tip the balance Arsenal's way and is not entirely unexpected, for Supermac has had a less than happy season following his £333,333 move from Newcastle United."

History will tell you that it didn't happen and on 2nd February 1978, McQueen signed for Manchester United for a fee of £495,000 – a deal which had been £5,000-plus short of beating the fee paid by SV Hamburg to Liverpool for Kevin Keegan.

In other news, the draw for the Fifth Round of the F.A Cup had been kind and a home tie against Third Division Walsall was on the agenda – with a chance for Arsenal to exorcise the 45-year old ghost that had haunted the club since its 2-0 defeat at the hands of The Saddlers back in 1933.

However, next up was a match at Highbury against Aston Villa, with Alan Hudson telling Malcolm Folley of the *Daily Express* about a team meeting Don Howe had held, stating that some Arsenal players may be sub-consciously thinking about Tuesday's League Cup Semi-Final first leg match with Liverpool and that they would kick themselves if Forest fall away and they have been concentrating solely on Cup ties. Howe had spoken from the memory of Arsenal's run-in to the Championship on the way to their League and Cup Double in 1971 when they overhauled Leeds, who once held a seven-point lead, just as Forest were doing at the moment.

"We had a good meeting. Don stressed it is today that counts. We must win everything – League and Cup while we can, because, the chance may not arise again," Hudson added. "People like Pat Jennings, Pat Rice, Malcolm Macdonald and I know what it is like to play in a Cup Final and the younger players like Liam Brady, Graham Rix and David O'Leary may believe that they have years ahead to fulfil their ambitions, but it is worth remembering that for all the years Johnny Haynes played the game, he never appeared in a cup final nor won a Championship medal and if we lose to Villa tomorrow, our rivals will be rubbing their hands."

Losing to Aston Villa was exactly what happened. An own-goal by Malcolm Macdonald after 23 minutes – however, there was much, much more to the story. It was a game that should have never been played at all, with referee Lester Shapter in two minds, whether to call it off or not.

Villa manager Ron Saunders said, "I wanted him to inspect the pitch again – just half an hour before the kick off – just to see if it was still there – it wasn't – it was completely under water."

"It might have been huge fun for the spectators, though I doubt it, because they too were getting soaked by the driving curtains of rain," wrote Frank McGhee of the *Daily Mirror*. "Sometimes the ball stuck leaving players skidding comically after passes which hadn't arrived; sometimes it slid and made them look idiots when they couldn't control it; sometimes the ball fooled everyone and hit a firm patch and went bouncing out of play. In short, the customers didn't get what they paid for – a game of skill."

The goal came after Jennings had punched a corner out, only for it to strike Macdonald's shoulder and rebound into the net.

"Despite the terrible conditions," added McGhee, "there were other occasional aspects to admire. Hudson in Arsenal's midfield, fetched and carried like his namesake, the butler, in television's *Upstairs Downstairs* and Jimmy Rimmer in Villa's goal had a personal they-shall-not-pass vendetta against his former club, with a series of death defying saves."

There was also a bit more to the game as Don Howe waded into both Brady and Macdonald after the match – with him telling Brady to mix up his game a bit more, rather than continually telegraph his intentions. As for Macdonald, he took some stick for continually *playing* to the crowd, and leaving his team a man light when a move up front broke down. As a coach, Howe spoke a lot of sense and after Brady initially telling Howe to "Fuck off", they worked on those shortcomings – and a tasty patch of form occurred. However, after two League defeats on the bounce, Nottingham Forest were now nine points in front of Arsenal and looking at the reality of the situation, there was no way back and the title was now out of Arsenal's hands – as bar a Forest implosion, the cups were all they could look to.

Chapter 38

Abi's Tales – *Take 6*

Italy was now just a distant memory. I'd had a great time – in fact, I think we all had and it was now a case of being back to the grindstone. Lee had restructured everything beneath me, whilst to the side of me Dino had been attempting to run Jaime Hudson ragged, duly getting his backside kicked in the process as there had been constant studio overruns, with some shooting having to be undertaken well after hours, so much so, Lee and M had been working extremely long hours.

As expected, Becky Ivell and Abygaile Gibbs got their promotion to join Sinead and Kirsty as part of Lee's *Foxy Fab Four* and along with Sooty headed up five various departments that split every sport into categories and at 22-years old Becky would become head of football on £150,000 a year. It was a move, which had everyone looking at each other, as we expected that job to be a shoe-in fit for Sooty.

The *Three Amigo's*, as Lee called them – Jarv, Zak and the Unstoppable Sex Machine got installed under Becky, whose colourisation department was now in the capable hands of Cat Ulchenkö and which had a backlog of work like you wouldn't believe.

Lee had rewarded his one hundred percenters and everything was changing.

After the reshuffle, me and Kirsty met up with Jo and Jet from over at White Lion and we went to a wine bar, and Kirsty let them know exactly what was going on. "A new sexy title and a twenty-five grand a year raise," she said, whilst knocking back her first Jack Daniels and Coke of the night.

"Yeh, but don't you have to know a bit about boxing and stuff?" Johanne had inquired.

"They wear gloves and batter hell out of each other," she replied, "what else is there to know?"

Sinead knew absolutely Jack-Shit about Formula 1, so that one would definitely be interesting.

That night I got absolutely hammered and found myself at Lee and M's, with the latter sobering me up with a black coffee. "You shouldn't drink so much," she told me.

She was right, I'd had a right skin-full, so much so, even Oliver Reed would have been impressed. I woke up after hearing footsteps on the stairs and found myself both bollock naked and in a bedroom that I didn't know. I think Lee carried me to bed, but I couldn't be sure. I also had absolutely no idea who had undressed me.

I mooched downstairs with the headache of all headaches to find Lee in their basement kitchen just going out for a jog. "You okay Abi?" he inquired. "You were pissed as a fart last night."

"Big, big headache," I told him.

"Anadin's – top drawer – left hand side," he said, before going outside.

"Morning Abi," said M, as she came into the kitchen wearing an old Arsenal shirt that absolutely buried her. "Do you want a coffee?"

"I could murder one," I told her.

She flicked on the TV, put it on mute and then turned on the Radio, before going into the fridge and taking out some bacon. This was the life I wanted – a nice home, with a nice husband – and yeh, I wanted a nice baby too. Their life was perfect. Everyone said it, even Jody – and she was thick.

The Zak-thing didn't go very far – however, Pedro had been keeping in touch – by text message mainly, as he was on tour. Liza had bailed and hooked up with some fake friends and was now out clubbing every night. As for me, I felt really out of sorts and was going nowhere.

"You're a really pretty girl and you have the world at your feet," said M. "You need to realise just exactly who you are."

That certainly put a lump in my throat, as did something else.

"You told me about your old boyfriend last night," she said. "And the *thing*."

Fucking shit, I thought.

M must have seen the expression on my face change.

"Don't worry, love – it won't go any further."

"Was Lee there when I said it?" I asked.

"He was," she said.

Double fucking triple, quadruple fucking shit, shit, I thought.

"Lee loves you and he certainly would never ever say anything," she said.

Apparently, I'd poured my heart out to them and told them everything …oh yeah, and about me wanting to have a proper heterosexual relationship and the reasons surrounding why I never really had. My phallaphobia.

"Have you heard anything from Pedro?" she asked.

"I get the odd text," I mumbled.

"It's a busy couple of weeks for me," she said. "I've got to be Lee's mam in four different scenes this week – I'll be just glad to get it over with."

"You can't be nervous?" I said.

"It's not that," she smiled. "If I hang about any longer it'll start showing – that I'm pregnant that is."

"I didn't know that you were."

"Yeh – a few months," she said. "We've kept it a bit low key."

"I just thought you were putting on weight," I lied.

"Yer cheeky cow," she laughed.

"You can't tell, M – honestly."

I couldn't tell – even when we were all poolside in Italy.

"So, how's Lee been with these steamy sex scenes everyone's on about," I grinned.

"They're hardly that," she replied. "A bit of a kiss and a cuddle is about as far as it goes – and that's only in a couple of scenes."

"Yeh – I saw your last kiss and a cuddle," I laughed. "Young Jono fell to pieces, got hooked on Calpol and started writing to *Dear Deidre* and now your Stu won't talk to him."

That had her laughing.

I got into work a bit earlier than I normally would, as for some reason Lee and M get up in the middle of the night and the first person I saw was Huddy. "How long have you been in?" I asked.

"Since about five, five-thirty," he replied, as young Jono set up a camera in front of him.

"By the way," I winked at Jono. "Your girlfriend's due in today."

I thought I'd get some feedback, but all he did was go the colour of beetroot.

"So, what exactly are you doing?" I asked them.

"Watch and learn," smiled Huddy, before Jono gave him the heads-up that they were ready.

I nipped and got a coffee and heard Huddy yapping in the background. "On the right wing was the player who'd been in the England side who had beaten Brazil in the Maracanã Stadium in Rio de Janeiro and who was one of the biggest waste of talents probably ever seen in this country," Huddy said. "When he put his mind to it Chamberlain could skin any full-back at any given time, but it was his head that was the problem."

Chamberlain ...Brazil, I thought

"Instead of rolling up his sleeves and getting stuck in, he ambled around the pitch as if 'tomorrow would do'."

He certainly had a point.

"Maybe he would have been okay in today's game with clubs having big squads and players having to fight for their places, but he was the big fish in a tiny bowl and at the time he was in the England side while his club were firmly rooted to the bottom of the League."

"Sorry, Alan," I interrupted. "Who is it that you're actually on about – Alex Oxlade-Chamberlain?"

"No – his dad," he said.

An "Oh right", was all I could muster.

The next thing I knew, was that Jaime was in the house and that temporary studios were being put together with

174

carpenters and what have you, clobbering away. I took refuge in my office and cleared a load of work off my desk only to be told by Faranha, that M was in the studios.

Wow – this I had to see, I thought – however, what would happen is that I would be commandeered by Lee to download a ton of football footage from the archives. "It's for Basher's *Terry Neill Years*," he said.

"Can't it wait?" I asked.

All I got was a shrug, so needless to say, I put it on the backburner and made my way into Temporary Studio 5, which had been made to look like the front room of some rubbish council house and where M was getting dolled-up by Chris Windley. As for Dino, he nodded over whilst checking over three monitors, which ran from three different cameras. "You okay Ab's?" he asked.

"Great," I replied. "It's all dead exciting."

I had to hand it to M, she looked nothing short of amazing, even though they had made her dress down for the part. The actor then came in wearing a pair of glasses and reading his lines. This was supposedly a guy called Vic or Victor – I can't remember which, although Dino pointed to a monitor, which had all the actual lines on it.

M eventually saw me and gave me a wave. "I'm dead nervous," she whispered, on coming over.

"So, this gadgy is supposed to be the guy Lee's mam had an affair with?" I said, pointing at the bloke wearing the bins and chuntering to himself.

"No, I don't think so," she said. "I think he's supposed to be Sooty's dad."

"I don't think he is, M," I replied. "The kid cast as Sooty is black – I know that as Sooty went berserk when he found out."

That bit I certainly did know as Lee had been pissing himself.

"No, that was re-cast," M whispered.

Uh, I didn't know that, I thought.

Just then Jaime came in to the studio and told Dino that the lights were going on for silence in two minutes.

"Emily," said Dino. "You need to take up your position."

Although it was interesting, I couldn't make head nor tale of what was happening as it was just dialogue and a bit of pointing with no music nor anything. It was a bit like watching some amateur dramatic production then *whack* – the bloke slapped her around the face and she hit the deck to shouts of "cut".

"Was I okay?" smiled M, as she knelt up and looked over. Me? I thought he'd really lamped her.

This was dead interesting, so much so, I pulled up a chair to watch. This was definitely a billion times better than what I did.

"We'll try the doing the same scene again," Dino said.

And they did, this time the man kicked M while she was on the floor. I couldn't believe it – it was nothing short of brilliant. Next up however, were some scenes without M, so I nipped back upstairs to do what I was originally asked to do and asked her to text me when her next scene was ready.

A few hours later and after the mind-numbing task of downloading and categorising film footage whilst having to do my own job, Lee came into my office to find me faithfully obeying his orders and dutifully multi-tasking.

"How's M doing downstairs?" he asked.

"She's brilliant," I said. "I can't believe how good she is."

He then pulled up a chair.

"'You okay?" I asked him, as I did this, that and the other.

"Sure," he said.

Uh – okay then, I thought, as I continued what I was doing.

"I just wanted five minutes with you and to just thank you for everything that you do for me."

That certainly took me aback, so much so, my bottom lip went and I burst out crying – me, having absolutely no frigging idea why. "What did you say that for you rotten sod?" I eventually managed to sniffle.

"It needed saying," he said.

"Well, you've never said it before," I told him, whilst wiping my eyes.

"I know – and that's why I've said it now."

"Well thank-you very much for frigging upsetting me," I told him.

"So, you're looking for a house?" he winked.

I am but the prices are too high and to get somewhere I could afford means loads of travelling," I blubbered. "That's why… that's why I'm out half the time …as I get as depressed as hell thinking about it."

"You have me and M," he said.

They knew that from the inebriated conversation that I'd had with them both last night, that apart from the fact I couldn't stomach the sight of *all things pink and erect* – that I lived in semi-squalor and even though I earned a nice income, the rent and bills had been crippling me – especially, as Liza had dumped her tax bill on me and which through my own sheer stupidity had been my fault entirely. I had left my Pin numbers and passwords lying around and she had transferred a lump of money that I'd been saving up for a deposit for a house directly out of my HSBC account and into hers – and without my knowledge, and had paid off her debt. Lee and M weren't stupid, hence why they had been trying to pull me closer to them.

"You are a really pretty young girl with everything going for you and you're a great catch for someone," M had told me over in Italy. And just this morning she'd added to that. "You have the world at your feet. You just need to realise who you really are."

"You knew about the Liza-thing?" I asked him.

"I get to hear a lot of things, Abi, but I can't help you if you don't tell me."

My bottom lip went again. "She took over four thousand pounds," I further blubbered.

Christ, I was a right whiny cow, I thought and I couldn't believe how utterly pathetic I'd been.

"Pull yourself together Miss Tyson," had been the words of my sixth-form tutor as I cried after being told that my grades weren't anywhere near good enough – and that I needed to pull my socks up.

Back in real time Lee had left my office after dropping me off another load of paperwork, some of which was

Huddy-related, therefore whilst I had about a hundred downloads going and signed off on a few things, I shouted him into my office.

"Is everything okay," he asked.

"Fine," I said, as I invited him to sit in the chair opposite – the exact one which Lee had been in some 40 minutes earlier.

"Lee's not spoke with you about money, has he?" I asked.

He just shook his head.

"Well it's my job to make sure that we do," I said.

I then gave him a schedule as regarding the proposed late night showing of *The Huddy Show* or shows, rather, along with details of his team.

"My team?" he inquired.

"Yeh – you have to have a frigging team to help you research, write it and request all the footage and whatnot that you need," I told him. "And if what we get after the first couple of months comes up to scratch, Lee wants you on the shop floor of ITV Seven on a Saturday afternoon.

He just looked at me. A bit blank if I'm being honest.

"It's a huge responsibility – and looking at what you've both got planned, you will need to put your teams of fives together – you know, ex-football players from teams that relate to a certain era."

It was extremely rare that Huddy was ever stuck for words, but there you go.

"Lee says to leave it with you – but he says you can't have anyone who will make your show or ITV Seven look bad – again, his words not mine."

He just sat there both smiling and nodding.

"It works out at around two thousand a week," I said, as I signed it off. "Any problems – let Lee know and he'll sort it."

I then handed him the chitty to give to Annie Dixon. If he embraced the job he'd be taking home £100,000 a year …and all that was down to him being honest with Lee. "What was the reason behind the big fall-out between

George Armstrong and Terry Neill," Lee had supposedly asked him one night.

Lee had been gearing him up for this for months. "Huddy deserves a chance," he had told me. "It's now up to him how far he wants to go."

Alan Hudson – another of Lee's so-called one-hundred percenters!

Around 5.40 pm and just when I was ready for knocking off I received a text from M. "I'm on in 10 mins xx," it read.

"Don't start without me x," I texted back.

Dino had had things moved into a completely different studio and for the life of me I still couldn't work out was happening as the acting, without music looked – well a bit rubbish if I'm being honest and certainly not like TV.

"It's all about the editing and the effects," Dino winked, as he showed me exactly what he was doing.

Cue: M.

At first, they'd got her talking to this kid who I'm assuming was the lad loosely based on Lee, but if that was the case she must have given birth to him when she was about four – as in my eyes that's what the age difference looked like. She had an aura about her when acting as she did on *The Warehouse* – however, here she was being serious and at times shouting.

"Cut," shouted Dino, before ordering a re-take along with another and another and another.

Around 8.45 pm we finally got to the last scene of the day and the nitty gritty – and I have to say it was well worth the wait, as it was a brilliant scene made all the better by the seventeen re-takes, Dino ordered. I'm sure he was some kind of pervert, as he had that actor kissing and rubbing up M's legs and inner thigh every which way and from every angle possible.

"It's a bit raunchier than I'd imagined," I whispered to M, prior to the re-takes.

"Yer telling me – he keeps on adding bits," she said, with regards to the pervert director.

"So, do you really like – yer know, kiss properly and that," I inquired. "I'm just asking as it looks a bit on the real side."

"A bit too real for my liking," she whispered. "And he hasn't undone his trousers yet."

"He undoes his trousers?" I gasped.

"Apparently," she said.

Yes, apparently, he frigging did, and I am telling you now, that when this show actually goes on air it will have thirty million viewers such was the scene. It was hardly *Basic Instinct*, but boy – it looked real. And M? To say she'd never acted before, she was unfriggingbelievable and I was now her number one fan.

"I just pretended I'm with Lee," she told me in the toilets afterwards, as she washed off all the make-up and cleaned her teeth.

Again – lucky frigging Lee.

Chapter 39

Barbie

"Never, ever call me that," Emily had snapped. "Ever."

One of the actors on *The Invincibles* set had called her Barbie – and she hated it.

"What?" he shrugged. "Barbie?"

"Yes," she said.

"Why what's wrong with Barbie?" he grinned.

He soon found out as she had summoned Chris from the door and he gave him the finger in the face along with the accompanying death threat. "Her name is Emily or M – it's that simple."

Chris looked at everyone in the studio to make sure that this would never happen again and I'll give him his due – it didn't.

"That's what *he* used to call me," she had told me one particular time, after I had mentioned the dreaded B-word. "All the time."

"All the time?" I'd shrugged.

"It's how I used to have to answer him," she'd mumbled, regarding her ex-husband. "I hated it."

Sleeping with the Enemy wasn't in it – her ex-husband was a total control freak, and he'd not only had M erase her northern identity, she'd also had her name taken from her too.

"He never called me my name – just that word," she'd told me.

"No problem M," I'd replied. "It'll never get mentioned again."

And it hadn't, until now.

I had been dropping Arsenal's League Cup Semi-Final match with Liverpool into Basher's documentary, when the main man himself popped his head in.

"Hiya Chris – what's up?" I asked.

"Your M's a bit upset," he said. "I've just had to have a word with one of the actors."

I walked downstairs and on to the set and it was that quiet, you could have heard a pin drop.

Dean shrugged his shoulders and mentioned what had happened and I looked over at Emily reading through her lines and then over at the kid who'd mentioned the B-word – and who, if I am being honest, looked a bit edgy. I suppose meeting a full-on Basher does that to you – but it wasn't so much that, more to do with the fact that I was both M's husband and the series' Executive Producer – and as such, the guy at the top of the *food chain*.

"Lee – I'm really sorry," he said. "I don't really know what I've done wrong but whatever you think it is – I'm sorry."

"It's okay mate," I told him. "It is really personal and goes deep."

I then walked over to Emily who wasn't upset as such – just mad. "Honestly Lee, I feel like screaming," she said.

"Channel your anger," I nodded. "Use it in your acting – that's how my mum was – really intense and angry. Come on kidda – stick with the plan."

I managed to get a smile and I did no more than walk her over to the kid, who immediately apologised to her. "I'm really, really sorry Emily," he said.

And believe me – the lad meant it.

Fast forward a couple of days and I managed to get some spare time to work on the Arsenal documentary and I couldn't believe how good they had played at times, especially over the two legs against Liverpool in the Semi-Final of the League Cup. They really ought to have hammered them, with Macdonald and Stapleton spurning several great chances during the home leg.

The days running up to the first leg at Anfield, Arsenal were again being linked with Trevor Francis with

Birmingham's chairman again telling Nigel Clarke of the *Daily Mirror* that neither 24-year old Francis nor 23-year old centre-half Joe Gallagher would be allowed to leave St. Andrews, even though both had submitted recent transfer requests, so much so, Francis must have had writers' cramp, as this was his fifth one. This had come after he had been fined by his club for remarks that he had made in the *Sunday People*, only for the *Guardian* to run a piece straight after titled 'Francis: The One Million Pound Prisoner'.

"League Cup Semi-Finals tend to be free of the almost unbearable tensions of their F.A Cup counterparts," wrote David Lacey of the *Guardian*. "Strategically they are often more interesting and from time to time they produce a classic encounter. Arsenal have lost only once in five visits to Anfield, but that was last season and the two players who did more than most to tweak the Kop's pride – Alan Ball and John Radford, have long since left Highbury. Nevertheless, and even though they will be without cup-tied Alan Sunderland, Arsenal should be capable of producing the sort of performance, which will give them the edge in the return game. Clearly Alan Hudson, in sight of his second League Cup Final, has regained his taste for English football and his influence, so important in their Quarter-Final replay against Manchester City, could be crucial and with Hudson, Brady, Rix and Stapleton they should be able to worry an uncommonly fragile Liverpool defence."

Game on and Arsenal hammered them – unfortunately, it was the result that counted and not the performance. Liverpool won 2-1 with a goal from former Arsenal striker, Ray Kennedy after 81 minutes, but that didn't tell the whole story – as the downloaded footage showed.

Arsenal went ahead on 12 minutes, Macdonald ghosting between Emlyn Hughes and his goalkeeper Ray Clemence and volleying home a Frank Stapleton knock-on. Arsenal were on fire and minutes later, Clemence was beaten again – this time as Stapleton rounded the goalkeeper after he had received a well-weighted knock down by Macdonald and had raced between Phil Thompson and Tommy Smith –

however, his shot had lacked power, with the latter able to desperately scoop the ball off the line.

"We were actually the better side, but we had no luck," Huddy told me. "I played okay but was still nowhere near my best and I remember when we were one-nil up that we were on the attack and I broke down the left and Sammy Nelson came running up on my outside and just inside their half. I rolled the ball to him, but instead of simply staying behind the ball and taking it into his stride he got too far in front of me. The ball hit his heel and bounced to a red shirt – Ray Kennedy, and he smashed it fifty yards up field to David Fairclough who squared it to Kenny Dalglish, who basically slid in the equaliser out of nothing."

Therefore, after 25 minutes the scores were level. Liverpool 1, Arsenal 1.

"We should have had the ball in their half, been one-nil up and in control – instead we were level," Huddy added. "I could have shot Sammy, as from there on it was backs against the wall. You cannot give goals away against teams like that. Anfield was tough enough without gifting them both possession and goals."

In the second half Arsenal went at them again with Harry Miller of the *Daily Mirror* saying, "There was an anxiety about Liverpool's play in the second half as Graham Rix defied the intimidating atmosphere and in one marvellous run beat both Terry McDermott and Tommy Smith before hitting a low cross that Stapleton just failed to meet."

"Hudson, as he had done against Manchester City in the Quarter-Final replay, gave Arsenal extra variety and better balance in midfield," wrote David Lacey of the *Guardian*. "Both he and Brady consistently eased themselves into telling spaces behind McDermott and Case and with Rix taking positions wide, Arsenal were appreciably better than Liverpool in mounting movements of width and penetration from the edge of their own penalty area."

Arsenal were on fire, and after 69 minutes there was an eerie silence from the 44,764 crowd as Willie Young powerfully headed home a corner from Graham Rix. Arsenal were 2-1 up. Or were they? Whilst the Arsenal players celebrated the goal, a crowd of red shirts swarmed around referee George Courtney, who after some deliberation disallowed the *goal* for some marginal infringement – of what, neither the Arsenal players nor the press had any idea.

Jimmy Case had a fierce shot saved by Pat Jennings before the winning goal came – Phil Neal taking a quick free kick to Fairclough on the right, who in turn hoofed in a high centre which Kennedy chested-down, partly being dispossessed by Young before firing his second attempt past Jennings.

Liverpool 2, Arsenal 1 and to be continued.

A couple of days later – Arsenal were in the news, they had gone out and bought a 41-cap international centre-forward, who possessed a rather impressive goal per game ratio – hitting the net every two games. "I want to become the best player in the world and England is the place where I can improve my game," the 21-year old blonde-haired striker, had told awaiting reporters from the *Daily Express* after his flight had landed in London. That striker was John Kosmina – a player who was signed from Adelaide City for £20,000, scoring a goal in his country's 3-1 win against Arsenal on 20th July 1977, which formed part of the club's much publicised and ill-fated pre-season tour of Australia.

This *Wizard of Oz* however, would make only one league appearance – coming on as a substitute in a 2-2 draw with Leeds United on the opening day of the following season, before being shipped back to where he came from.

"Thinking back, it was probably an opportunity lost," Kosmina recently told James Maasdorp from *ABC News*. "At the time, I just wasn't ready for the huge gulf in difference between English and Australian football. It was an eye-opener, and I certainly learned or benefited more after I came back than I did when I was there."

Next up was a league match up at Filbert Street against bottom-placed and the mixed bag of washing that was Leicester City – a team had gone three months without a win and where George Armstrong and Eddie Kelly were ready to gun down their loquacious ex-*boss* as he rode into town.

"I understand Frank McLintock's position as I have been through difficult times in my own managerial career," a rather pontificating Neill had told Steve Curry of the *Daily Express*. "It is important for Frank to carry on doing his own thing at Leicester – to keep a belief in himself and his ability to manage. Now is the time that stamina and courage are needed in abundance."

I bet big Frank really appreciated the advice from a guy who was not only two years younger than him, but a player who he had firstly taken over the captaincy of Arsenal from; and secondly had helped firmly displace out of the team and into the reserves.

Neill had quite *wrongly* stated in later life that it was Peter Simpson establishing himself alongside McLintock that had forced him out of Mee's preferred first eleven. It wasn't like that at all. Simpson had been first choice centre-back whilst playing alongside Neill, ever since a 3-1 win against Fulham at Craven Cottage on 23rd March 1968. As for McLintock – he had only ever played in central defence a handful of times as emergency cover prior to his permanent move there in the first leg of the Fairs Cup Quarter-Final over in Romania against Dinamo Bacau in March 1970, where he both partnered up with Simpson and where Don Howe would form the catalyst for the back-line of what would become the Double team.

Make no bones about it – Neill saw Don Howe moving McLintock into central defence as the straw that broke the camel's back and at 28-years old saw his future elsewhere – and that being the case he took up Hull City's offer of player-manager and was transferred.

Strangely and after a great performance up at Anfield, Terry Neill opted to leave out Alan Hudson – his place being taken by Alan Sunderland, who the manager was utilising on the right side of a four-man midfield, even though the Mexborough-born player openly admitted that he preferred playing up top.

"Hudson has been playing well and still has an important part to play in our season," Neill told the press. "With Alan Sunderland ineligible, he will be back in the side for the return League Cup game against Liverpool and if we win he could be playing at Wembley."

"The high point of this abysmal match came when Leicester City managed to score their first goal in two months and which was greeted by the long-suffering crowd with a roar more of incredulous relief than delight," wrote Ronald Atkin of the *Observer*.

"It would have been better perhaps for all concerned if this game had gone the way of the majority and been called off," added Charles Burgess of the *Guardian*. "Better for Arsenal because their rather uninspired display will have done nothing for their confidence, prior to their imminent League Cup battle with Liverpool."

Arsenal could only manage a 1-1 draw – and their goal had come after a handball in the box, with Brady converting – putting the penalty past Mark Wallington by tucking it into the goalkeepers right-hand corner.

Brady's initiative had been praised – however, the Arsenal performance had been lacking and although Macdonald had rattled the Leicester crossbar from 30 yards with a minute left on the clock, it was a point dropped with David Lacey of the *Guardian* citing that the exclusion of Hudson had somewhat upset the rhythm of the side. "Hudson has an ability to make space in crowded areas and thread passes through the narrowest of gaps, which enables Arsenal to put pressure on their opponent's uncertain defence," he said.

"I suppose that, ideally, a midfield man should be able to win the ball, beat people and pass accurately," Liam Brady told James Mossop of the *Sunday Express*. "If you ask me to define the perfect midfield player I would say Alan Hudson."

Liverpool were due down at Highbury on Tuesday night and a crowd of 49,561 turned out to witness Frank Stapleton hit a volley from point blank range and over the bar after just 15 minutes – Macdonald race on to a pin-point pass by Graham Rix after 32 minutes only to lob over Liverpool's onrushing goalkeeper and past the far post – along with a snapshot 11 minutes later, which forced Clemence into a world class save. David Price then hit a cracking shot from the edge of the box only for it to again be equalled by the goalkeeper – however, as the game wore on, Arsenal became stifled by Liverpool's experienced spoiling tactics and chances then became far and few between. Arsenal had been shut out.

Arsenal 0, Liverpool 0. (1-2 on aggregate)

"I have nothing but praise for the lads," Terry Neill told David Miller of the *Daily Express*. "Clemence made some fine saves and Malcolm Macdonald was terribly unlucky."

"We were the much better side over the two legs," Brady told James Mossop of the *Sunday Express*, before pointing to the Anfield club's vast experience at playing both home and away in Europe. "It was their experience that won them the tie."

Arsenal were indeed the better side. I knew that more than anyone as I had watched both games, jotting down timelines and what have you. I was just about to add some further action replay into the mix – however my pleasure was short-lived as I was rudely interrupted by some suits from ITV – one of which included the deputy CEO. Apparently, they had in part, been persuaded by the 25% shareholders of White Lion into altering their stance somewhat and wanted to see some footage – or a taster, of our multi-million investment that was *The Invincibles*. I hadn't even seen any footage myself as yet – however, I had let on that Sky Atlantic were extremely interested and that being the case, my minor partners must have insisted that ITV move quickly or lose the series. I wasn't really lying, but I wasn't telling the truth either, and that being the case it could have been construed as being nothing more than brinkmanship. The fact was, that we were in dialogue with Sky Atlantic – and ITV knew this – however, what they did not know, was just how far the actual dialogue had gone. And the truth was – not very far.

I then let them know that if they fancied it, we would be talking at £15 million down and 25% royalties.

"We initially got offered it at cost-plus," said a suit.

"I know – and then I got told that ITV weren't interested," I told them. "So, blame your fucking head of programming."

My plan was working – I'd got them!

All the other week I'd had Abi and Jaime looking at me rather cagily as they had been the only ones allowed on the set of *The Invincibles* and I had to admit, I was more than a bit intrigued to see how it was all panning out. I would have asked Dean, but he had been shooting on location the past couple of days and had even dragged Huddy over to a field on Hackney Marshes, for our flawed genius to give him some tactical choreography. Therefore, I held off the suits for a few days by arranging a meeting – and one which would include the said director, before nipping over to the editing suite and copying a few scenes on to a hub so I could have a shufti at them. Unfortunately, I then got side-tracked by Johanne over at White Lion. "The Queen and Pistol are in," she said.

Ross had been testing my patience for months and had come back into the studio after a few tour dates – therefore, I commandeered Basher and drove down into Angel to meet the front man – and what followed was a case of me directing my anger and leaving my head of security to pick up the pieces. "Any come back and you'll not be dealing with him," Chris told him. "You'll be dealing with me."

The easiest thing would have been to have delegated the smack in the mouth – however, this one had been just a bit too personal, for me to let it go.

It had been a strange few days and that night I got in to quite a surprise.

"Emily?" I gasped.

"I'm having a go at trying to exorcise me demons," she twanged, on slithering up to me.

I had a wife dressed in some pink and white striped mini skater dress and shiny tights along with some pink stilettoes and a matching pink handbag with a diamante clasp. I certainly couldn't forget the clasp as it matched the thing in her hair. "I like the diamante tiara," I winked, as she tried her best at straightening it.

"It's a bit wonky," she grumbled. "I think it's for someone with a much bigger head."

"So, who am I then – Ken?"

189

"No, yer Lee," she twanged. "Yer always Lee."

"So, where did you get this little lot from," I inquired.

"The shoes and handbag were from *Modatoi* – the shoes were nearly twenty-one euros and the bag thirty-two," she said.

"What about the dress?"
"Just over a tenner from *New Look*," she said, looking down at it. "'About all it's worth, really."

"What about your crown?" I winked.

"Uh – that was from some rubbish bags and bangles place off Oxford Street," she said, before noticing something different about my appearance. "What have you done to your hand?"

"I gave Ross Bain a slap," I told her.

"What really?" she smiled.

"Yeh, for trying to tap you up," I lied.

"You did not," she laughed.

"Anyway – so, how does this little charade go about exorcising your so-called demons?" I asked, changing the subject somewhat.

"You have to be mean to me and keep calling me that word."

"What word," I asked.

"Yer know what word," she said.

"What – Barbie?"

"Yes," she chuntered.

How the hell that would exorcise anyone's demons I hadn't a frigging clue, but there you go.

"Look M…." I said

"I'm not M – I'm that word."

"Emily, pack it in," I said. "You are who you are."

"You've got to do it Lee," she said. "I really need you to be mean and say that word."

"It's not happening M," I told her. "I love you to dress up and whatever, and yeh – you look great – well really great, but I married you because you are Emily."

"If you say it, then in my head it won't seem so bad when anybody else does," she said. "Please, Lee – just do it for me, love."

190

In the end, I succumbed to her wishes and I let her cook my dinner, wash and dry the pots and I chose the film. It had been a great idea by M as I'd not seen *The Good, The Bad and The Ugly* in ages. I also got to bang the iconic doll on the sofa after I'd done being really mean to her. I had to admit, bar having to call her Barbie every ten minutes – and M grating her teeth at it, it had been a cracking night.

"So, are your demons well and truly exorcised?" I asked on her coming into the kitchen, early next morning.

"I enjoyed being yer-knowed, but everything else was dead rubbish," she chuntered.

"I thought it was a great film," I winked.

"I'm not on about that," she smiled. "Yer know what I'm on about."

I knew exactly what she was on about – mainly the great pile of ironing I'd made her shift while I'd watched it!

I loved a good film and I certainly knew I'd got one come 11.20 am the next morning, so much so, I had to lock my office door and close the blinds. I just didn't have the words to describe it and it was around two hours later when I plucked up the courage to phone Emily.

"Are yer whispering?" asked my wife. "'Cos' I can't hear you very good."

"I've just seen about twenty retakes of that scene you did with Vic Harding," I murmured.

"He's not Vic Harding," she said. "His real name's Greg Davies and we only did seventeen."

"Seventeen?"

"Yeh, seventeen retakes," she said. "Dino wanted to get it spot on."

"Well I think he succeeded."

"By the time, we'd done the last one I was aching like heck," she told me. "Anyway – why are yer still whispering?"

I didn't know – and all I wanted to do was watch them again – and again – er, and again. In fact, I had Georgia Clayton knock on my door twice to see if I was still alive. "You okay in there, Lee?"

I was – even though I was walking like Herr Otto Flick when I eventually did answer the door.

I'll be honest – I couldn't wait to get home that night – unfortunately however, I had a problem thrust into my lap by Abi. Stuart and Jono had just had a big fall-out and had regrettably had a go at each other. Obviously, I knew what the problem was – mainly my sex bomb of a wife.

"I'm ragging it in if he stays," Stuart snapped at me.

Apparently, his fellow college graduate, colleague and mate had been winding him up about him being his sisters live prop, hence why I had them both in my office, before showing his mate a side of me that he'd never seen before, but one which Stuart certainly had.

I told them both to sit down and threw Jono a colour supplement from the *Sunday Times* and I told him to open it at a certain page and read the piece that I had highlighted. He did and then he looked up at me before I told him to pass the magazine over to Stu.

"So, you've both read it?" I asked.

They both nodded to say that they had – however, Stuart was looking at the floor.

"Emily wanted to be cast as a character that over twenty other actresses went for, all of who did their casting not here, but down at the studios on White Lion Street," I said. "All those women had to do the exact same as Emily. And these were professional actresses, which is something that Emily is not."

Stuart finally looked up at me.

"Emily wanted the part more than anything because it is loosely based on my mum and she didn't want anyone else getting it. Therefore, she worked extremely hard and learned all her lines and tried to get into character," I told them. "And not wanting to cock it up she followed the direction that had been given to her by Dean, who is one of the best directors on the east coast of America and she followed it to the dot. If she hadn't done as he'd asked she wouldn't have got the part – it is that simple. The director told her to do it and she did it – and by Emily getting the part and being cast as my mum she not only got a part that she wanted more than anything – she has also saved us a lot of money by me not having to employ some actress."

I then directed my gaze at young Jono.

"Kid – you are not only taking the piss out of me, but my wife," I told him. "Neither of us deserve any of this shit as we have been nothing but great with you. But here is the thing and I hope you are adult enough to take it. You ever say anything about my fucking wife again and I will not only sack you – I will wipe the fucking floor with you."

He went rigid.

"If you think I'm fucking kidding – then try me."

I then turned to Stuart.

"As for you – I love your sister more than anything in the world and no-one more than you fucking knows that. So, anymore whining and bitching and the same goes for you – You will be out."

I looked at them both – hard.

"Don't ever test my fucking patience again," I snapped. "Now get out and both grow the fuck up."

Mmm, that seemed to work, I thought.

As for the piece in the colour supplement, it read: "Emily Janes is the consummate professional and from a director's point of view she is one of the easiest people I have ever had the privilege directing," explained Dean Monahan. "You ask and she does."

Yip – she certainly did.

Chapter 40

Pulp Fiction

The football season was upon us and Emily had gone up to Birkenhead with our beloved offspring on the Friday morning as there was some family *do* over at some Village Hall off Teehey Lane in Bebington, which was about a ten-minute drive from Hamilton Square.

"Are yer sure you don't want me to wait until the children get out of school and then we can all travel up together?" she asked.

"You are wanting to go help your mum," I said. "Anyway, it'll save you having to drop me off at the studios early tomorrow morning."

"It's a pity you couldn't have got that cute old Alfa Romeo working," she grinned. "We could have had that as our spare, so could always travel up together."

"I did get it working," I told her.

I did. I just didn't envisage having to drive a car which had the rear brake pads welded to the callipers. To be honest I'd never seen anything like it before – slave cylinders mounted on the axle tubes, which sort of operated the callipers by a system of levers and cranks? Weird – but hey-ho, there you go.

"Anyway, we could have had a spare car, but you turned your nose up at it," I said.

"What car?" she shrugged.

"My mum's."

That made her laugh – especially when I reminded her of her stubbornness to accept it.

"We've had some really great times, haven't we?" she beamed.

We had, and exactly 11 minutes after I'd waved Emily and Herbert off around 7.30 am I had my orders via the phone to pick up my kids from Clerkenwell at 4.00 pm-sharp. "And don't be late," my daughter had stressed. "I have to get ready for Auntie Joy's party."

Emily had sorted it with Jeanette that both my kids could have what they always termed as a "stopping up ticket" and that being the case Cinderella could go to the ball – and as such M had taken my daughter into the city and had bought her a really posh frock and some new shoes.

As for my lad?

"I don't want no posh frock," he'd said, whilst multi-tasking – half-watching his sister doing twirls in her dress and him playing F.I.F.A 2015 and eating toast and marmalade and getting it all over his face. "I'll just wear my Arsenal kit."

"You can't wear a football kit for a party," Emily had told him.

"Can't I?"

"I bet we could get you a really nice sports shirt," she'd winked. "Like the one's Cristiano Ronaldo wears."

That had certainly appeased him and as such I knocked off a few hours early only to get stuck in North London traffic and undertake the torturous drive up the M6 and have my lad continually questioning me after I'd finished having a conversation over hands-free with Jaime who had mentioned having loads of problems with the *rosters*.

"Rosters?" he inquired. "Like that Bob Marley – him who Arsène Wenger likes?"

"No, you twit," his sister eloquently exclaimed. "A roster is a list – you are thinking of a Rasta."

"Am I?" he asked.

"It's short for Rastafarian," Emily told him when we finally got to Hamilton Square. "It's supposedly a type of religion, but I think Bob Marley probably saw it more as a way of life."

I thanked god that she'd finally explained it to him as we'd had him yacking about it for the last forty miles of our journey.

Cue: the party.

My daughter was always fascinated watching Emily put on her make-up and my wife often gave her a running commentary about different shadings and what goes best with what, so much so, she couldn't wait to start wearing the stuff.

"When you get to our Lucy's age I think you can start putting a bit on," Emily told her.

"Can't I put a bit on now?" she inquired.

"Not really," she replied. "You've got loads of time to grow up and you don't want to go ruining that lovely complexion by covering it up, do you?"

M received a bit of a sulk in reply.

"That's not the beautiful little girl that I know," my wife told her, before breaking her stance. "Go on then – a bit of lippy should be okay."

And she took a glittery lipstick out of her handbag and carefully put it on her.

My daughter was elated and had spent the next ten minutes looking at herself in the long mirror in the hallway – which I must admit, quite reminded me of her mum. The self-same mum that would bollock me come Monday evening, for letting the wicked step-mum do the dreadful deed, which in her mind and eyes – and without actually seeing the result, had supposedly made her daughter look like paedo-bait.

Her tirade had upset Emily, in that she was about to apologise – however, I derailed that train of thought straightaway.

"Jesus Christ Jeanette, it was only a bit of glitter?" I'd told her. "Get real."

However, that would be three days in the future and this was now, and as such we had dropped Herbert off with Bill and Edie as that is where he would be lodging for the night – and that being the case, he received the same treatment as he did when he visited Mike and Sil's, in that he immediately had his nappy removed and was planted on the potty. And in this instance by his *not so* great granny. And that being the case, he bawled like hell.

"Good grief," laughed Bill. "It's our M."

"You're right there," added Edie.

"Thank-you very much," said the woman standing next to me with the hands on her hips – namely their granddaughter.

Although my lad really wanted to go to the party, he had done a bit of humming and erring about altering his plans – and him also staying at Bill and Edie's, as the former had been promised by the latter – his great gran, who he thought was equally as lovely as his Granny Sil', of a homemade fish and chip supper, along with the main feature of the night – *War of the Worlds*.

"It's a bit scary," Bill had told him, after he had explained the plot and described the dreaded tripods.

"Is it really scary, M?" he asked, wanting it confirmed.

"Mmm, it is a bit," she said.

"Is it as scary as *Day of the Triffids* or that *Time Machine* film with them horrible Morlocks?" he further inquired.

"Ten times scarier," she told him.

He debated with himself and eventually decided against having a night in and hiding behind the settee, with M promising him that she would procure the exact film from the purveyor of dead scary films – namely the Internet, as soon as we got home.

Trivialities aside – a family party in a house or what have you, is fine as you feel comfortable, tending to know all the faces – however, what we would be entering would be a bit different. As the place was much bigger, a whole host of neighbours, near-neighbours and friends of friends had been invited. The party itself was at some village hall opposite a bit of a shopping centre and a pub and like with the school reunion we were immediately made the centre of the attention with anybody and everybody honing in on us. However, later-on in the evening and after people had knocked back a few drinks, it would become rather annoying – for me especially.

Mike and Sil' picked up on this early on, and along with a couple of M's pretend aunties and uncles became quite protective, and as such and with a little help from a few tables and chairs formed a bit of a human blockade. My kids on the other hand, quite liked it, especially as our Lucy was chaperoning them and introducing them to loads of pretend cousins, one of which was a kid sporting a set of National Health rims held together by a plaster, who was soon to be introduced to me.

"Oh yeh, and who are you," I inquired. "One of *The Proclaimers*?"

"Dad, this is Specky," said my lad.

"Specky?" I shrugged. "You can't call him that – what's his real name."

"Prenton," the lad told me.

Poor sod, I thought – especially after I'd been informed by Emily, that both Pat and Gary Park were his parents.

Patricia Park, was from the Storeton area of The Wirral and had been one of Emily's old friends from school. Sil' and Mike had also been good friends with her parents as well – a bit like mine and Donna's if you like, but without the added bonus of Mike shagging her mum. I'd met her a couple of times – once over at M's Auntie Elsie's and another whilst I had been painting the steel steps that formed the fire escape behind the house on Hamilton Square – and to be honest she seemed okay. However, around 9.40 pm she came over and caught my wife's attention. "Guess who's in?" she grinned.

I never thought anything of it until I saw M's demeanour suddenly change some two minutes later.

"You fancy a dance, M?" came a voice from behind me.

She just shook her head as I turned around to see who was asking her the question. It was some sun-tanned guy around 5'8 with longish mousy brown hair who was dressed in a white shirt that hung over some designer ripped denims.

"'You alright, pal?" he asked me in his scouse accent.

Years of meeting and dealing with people is never ever wasted and I immediately disliked what I saw, so much so, I stood up to face him and put out my hand.

"What – yer want me to hold your hand?" he scoused, whilst making both his Jimmy Tarbuck impersonation and joke known to the table – or tables rather.

The fact that I never took on the quip nor laughed at his joke and just said nothing certainly put him on the back foot.

"Andy Gardener," he said, as he cagily shook my hand.

He had no need to tell me who he was as I'd seen him before – stood on a beach in Rhyl with a sixteen-year old girl in a bikini that some sixteen years later would become my wife, and who in between would try and worm his way into her life several times.

I was just about to sit down before he re asked his question. "Come on M, have a dance with us?"

This had been the first time that I'd ever seen Emily mute as she was seldom lost for words.

I turned to the guy and looked down at him, but I was being bypassed. He wasn't looking at me but straight at my wife. This was possibly the most thick-skinned and ignorant guy that I'd ever met – and believe me when I say it, I'd met a few.

"Come on M," he scoused. "Have a dance."

Just then, Mike – along with two of M's uncle's – Jimmy and Rob, dutifully removed him, which saved me the task of doing the job.

This is what I didn't want and all Emily could do afterwards was apologise. "I'm really, really sorry Lee," she said.

I told her it was okay, but it wasn't and rather than go to bed, I went into the study and fired up both laptops and went through all the weekend's schedules and sent a few emails, so much so, I had a wife come downstairs around 4.00 am to find me crashed out over my desk. I'd blacked out again ...Not that I told her that, however.

"Come to bed love," she said.

I looked up at her – her lovely blonde hair, her long eyelashes and perfect lips, and all I could think of was the reality of the night before, in that she had been left dumbstruck by some overbearing Scouser in a ripped pair of jeans.

Why didn't she just tell him to fuck off? I thought.

"Come on love," she said. "Come to bed."

I had been thinking of crying off going to the party as late as yesterday morning and all I could think of was: *I wonder what would have happened, if I hadn't gone?* And I had this vision of them smooching on an empty dancefloor, her looking up into his eyes and both smiling and laughing as he spat his *sweet nuthin's* in her ear – and while Pulp's *A Little Soul* had played in the background – the exact same song that had been playing at the very time he had come over.

I rarely got jealous-jealous, more pissed off than anything, but this? This had done me.

I'd seen her do loads of retakes of some soft-core TV porn with some big bloke from a *Channel 4* sit-com along with her successfully being cast after sticking her tongue in some 17-year old live prop's mouth and ear and telling him that she loved him, and all that had done was make me want to bang the arse off her ten times more than I did already. But this? This had given me a hollow kind of emptiness inside – possibly, because this hadn't been fiction, it had been real.

"Do what you told me," she mumbled. "Direct your anger."

"What – on you?" I said.

"If it'll make you love me again," she said. "Yeh, if you want."

"I'll always love you, M – I think that's the problem."

"What?" she shrugged. "That you love me?"

I nodded. "I think I love you too much."

I wasn't lying either.

She came over and sat on my knee and put one arm around me and put the hand from her other through my hair and kissed my forehead. "All I've ever wanted is you," she said. "I want to grow old with you and live in that old stone farmhouse that you promised us."

"In Italy?" I asked.

"No, you've been there too many times with Jeanette," she smiled. "I want yer-knowing somewhere where you've never yer-knowed anyone before."

"Really?"

"Yeh – 'cos I get dead jealous," she twanged.

"Me too," I admitted.

I did go to bed and as Herbert the human alarm clock hadn't been in the house, we ended up oversleeping, much to the amusement of my wife who refused to have me rushing around, telling me that ITV 7 wouldn't fall apart because I was running a few minutes late.

"It's the first day of the new season," I told her.

It was, and after a great day at the office, my other unfaithful wife decided to rear her head the very next day: Arsenal 0, West Ham 2.

"Totally unexpected, but totally pleased," Brian Allan had told me on our way back into London.

As for West Ham? Terry Neill should have learned from them and I jotted a few things down to remind me of exactly that.

Chapter 41

The Return of Monty Python: *And now for something completely different*

There was nothing like wrestling with a computer, monitor, keyboard and mouse after you've had to park your car half the way down the street because somebody has taken your parking space and then having to knock at my own front door to get in as the wife had double-locked it.

"M?" I shrugged, on the door being slightly pulled ajar.

"Wrong house," she lied.

"No, it's not," I told her, before totally noticing her appearance. "Anyway – what's with the glasses …and the blouse?"

"I'm a teacher," she said. "And a dead strict one – yer late."

"No, I'm not," I argued. "Huddy asked if I could sort his computer out and I've had to park half way down the street."

"Why what's up with it?" she asked, as she took the keyboard and mouse off me.

"He says that it's not reading his memory stick with all his books on," I told her. "He says it's converting to some form of Japanese or Hebrew."

"Yeh – he'll probably be using the old Microsoft Word," she said.

I really ought to have thought of that and I said as much.

"You weren't to know," she smiled, before suddenly realising that she was quickly slipping out of character. "So, why are you late?"

"I'm not," I shrugged.

"Sixteen minutes," she snapped.

"Your hair looks nice – a bit like when you do the British Airways stewardess."

That brought a smile.

"Er – um," she coughed, as she prowled around me. "You've still not explained why you're late."

We had certainly done the dirty French schoolteacher before but never the dead strict English one wearing glasses …and crap clothes …mmm and holding a cane.

Then – thwack!

"Jesus Christ, M," I said, post getting walloped around the back of my legs. "That frigging hurt."

"It meant to," she said, as I got shoved up against the dining table.

"M – behave," I said, as she bit my bottom lip.

There were times when I wished my wife had the same phobia as Abi …mmm, and rather stupidly I mentioned it.

"That's a really hurtful thing to say," she said as she stopped what she was doing and pulled out one of the chairs from beneath the dining room table to sit down and sulk.

Then what followed was a sharp pain at the back of my eyes – and one like you wouldn't flipping believe.

"Are you okay, Lee?" Emily asked. "Lee – Lee?"

I blacked out again, only to awake a few minutes later, with M both upset and panicking as I had fallen against the dining table and split my right eyebrow open. "I'm really, really, really sorry, love," she said, as she held me whilst at the same time trying to tend to the cut.

"It's okay M," I said.

"I'm getting really worried now, Lee," she said. "This is anything but normal."

And not even M kneeling over me in her seamed stockings could dull the blistering migraine that I now had tearing away at the back of my eyes.

"I'm sorry for being a bit thoughtless," I said, on getting to my feet.

"I know I sometimes go a bit over the top," Emily nodded. "It's just that I love yer so much."

I loved her too – however, I didn't go beating her with a big stick – and when I said as much it created a bit of levity and I saw that beautiful smile return to her face.

I went down into the kitchen to wash the blood from my face and popped a couple of Anadin Ultra's.

"It looks like a fairly deep cut, Lee," she said. "You should really get it looked at. Do you want me to run you to the A and E?"

It wasn't that bad really. I think the amount of blood had made it look much worse than it actually was, so much so, I offered myself up for some home schooling as soon as the tablets had got stuck into the thumping headache. Yeh – and after the school mistress had cleaned up a couple of pints of my blood off the floor – or in Emily's case, 1.13 litres.

"We don't have to if you don't want," she lied.

"Really?" I winked.

"Yeh we do," she smiled, as she clambered over me. "And I promise I'll not nip, scratch or bite yer."

"It's the being whacked with the big stick-bit, that I'm concerned about."

However, there was a knock on the door.

"Saved by the bell, eh?" I said.

"You'll have to answer it," she said. "They'll think I'm going bonkers if I go to the door dressed like this."

"Why, what's up with it?"

She looked down at herself and then over at me. "Yer definitely can't be serious?" she twanged.

Her *summer collection* courtesy of eBay comprised some black bodycon tube skirt, which cost about five quid and which tomorrow would be a duster, along with some white sleeveless chiffon blouse which cost about half as much. No idea where the glasses came from – but then again, M was always full of surprises.

I did as I was asked and answered the door. It was Mrs Sosk. Apparently, Ray Parlour had just been seen rifling through our bins again.

"It's only Madge, M," I shouted down.

"What's the matter with your eye?" inquired Mrs Sosk.

"Emily hit me with that big stick," I lied – sort of.

Just then my wife appeared at the top of the kitchen stairs. "Hello Madge," she said. "Take no notice, as I certainly did not whack him in the eye."

"Ooh, that's a lovely blouse," noted our neighbour. "I really like that."

"Three pounds ninety-six off eBay," said Emily, before totally telling a white lie. "I only wear it for teaching."

"That street cleaner has just been through our bins again," I told her.

"He was hanging about the other day," said M.

That much was true as Huddy had chased him off.

"Was that Ray Parlour?" he'd asked post-slinging a crutch at him.

"He told Lee that his name was Derek," Emily had told him.

"It's a strange how these ex-players all go to pieces," Sooty had apparently said after my lad had relayed that snippet of information to him. "Sol Campbell's just signed on as a lollipop man down at the Burlington Danes Academy on Wood Lane."

"Has he Uncle Sooty?" my lad had asked.

"Yeh, he likes parading around in front of the mirror wearing the big reflective jacket."

Jeanette told Sooty off for that.

My lad had been so insistent about what his Uncle Sooty had told him, that I'd called in at Clerkenwell on the way home from work one night to sort of try and dispel the rumours. Well not really, Basher had got him a few Play Station games courtesy of his underworld connections – mainly one his mates down at the Wheatsheaf and Pigeon on Penton Road – and on dropping them in, I ended up getting quite the surprise as there was a Brentford fan was in our midst.

"Paul," I said, putting out my hand. "It's really nice to see you, mate."

It was. Ross Bain had made me appreciate him a thousand times more than I ever had before.

"I was going to tell you," explained my rather secretive ex-wife.

Mrs Sosk had an hour with us and in between complementing M on her blouse, my wife gave her a guided tour of the new kitchen and pool in both basements, along with showing her some photos of us all in the farmhouse over in Tuscany – one of which, was now sat in a silver frame in the dining room, which if I rightly recall, had been taken by Huddy.

Whilst Emily did the guided tour – so to speak, I got stuck into the documentary and next up was the Arsenal versus Walsall game in the Fifth Round of the F.A Cup – with the club well-up for exorcising its demons and Neill again went with the side that had stuttered against an impotent Leicester City – the same side who had recently been dumped out of the Fourth Round of the cup by Arsenal's Third Division opponents.

The big news was however, that the manager had been more concerned with the state of the Highbury pitch and had opted to blow half of what he had laid out for his recent Australian signing and had left the undersoil heating on all week with Neill telling Nigel Clarke of the *Daily Mirror*, "To hell with the cost – we can't afford to slip up against Walsall, therefore nothing must be left to chance. The pitch has been in a terrible state since the match with Aston Villa. The heating system is marvellous when there is a covering of grass on the pitch, but now there are areas that have been badly churned up and the sand we have had to put down doesn't allow the heating to function sufficiently to thaw the frost out of the ground. As a result, the top was slippery and hard against Liverpool and we couldn't really go at them 100 per cent. So, now we intend to keep the heating on to try to soften the ground."

Arsenal got back to basics, and was it not for several squandered chances the 4-1 score line would have been in double figures.

"The happiest man in the Gunners camp was 19-year-old Eire International Frank Stapleton, bouncing back from his nightmare 90 minutes against Liverpool in the mid-week League Cup Semi-Final," wrote Danny Blanchflower of the *Sunday Express*. "The young striker scored twice and was denied a hat-trick when his second half header hit the bar."

Arsenal's first came after 29 minutes when Rix and Brady worked their magic on the left and after several one-touch passes Stapleton switched the play from left to right, where Rice fed Sunderland who produced a sublime curling pass down the flank that out witted Walsall's left winger Jeff King, leaving David Price to cut inside him and pull the ball back to an onrushing Stapleton who prodded the ball home past goalkeeper Mick Kearns. 1-0 to The Arsenal.

MacDonald then knocked home a corner from Graham Rix before Sunderland struck a marvellous goal on 41 minutes.

Walsall's Alan Buckley pulled a goal back on 56 minutes, which came after a mistake by Sammy Nelson, who let in Miah Dennehy to dispossess him and play the ball across to his centre-forward, who coolly stroked the ball past Jennings.

Stapleton gave the score a more appropriate look about it, when after Willie Young mis-kicked what should have been a certain goal, he rammed home his second with a minute left on the clock. Arsenal 4, Walsall 1.

Two days later there was a twist in the Trevor Francis tale.

"Liverpool have joined British football's hottest transfer race by making an official approach to Birmingham for Trevor Francis," wrote Derek Potter of the *Daily Express*. "Ten clubs are now believed to be in the queue. Arsenal head the bids from the south and now Liverpool have emerged alongside Everton, Manchester City and Leeds as the Northern frontrunners. Every club with ambition awaits a decision from Birmingham, who have repeatedly refused to sell Francis – the player who claims his ambitions have been stifled at his only club."

Birmingham City had also knocked back a £200,000 bid from Tottenham Hotspur for their transfer-listed centre-half Joe Gallagher, whilst in other news Arsenal had been linked with a move for Falkirk's highly thought of 17-year old captain, Gary Gillespie.

Arsenal, without flu victim Alan Hudson, travelled across London to Upton Park and threw away their lead in the last minute when West Ham United's recent £180,000 signing, David Cross out jumped Willie Young and levelled to make it 2-2 and where Malcolm Macdonald was attacked by a Hammers fan who had jumped over the barrier and was said to have thrown a couple of punches, straight after the striker had tucked away his second goal.

"Arsenal were guilty of dying in the second half after taking a firm grip on the game," wrote Nigel Clarke of the *Daily Mirror*.

Macdonald's goals had come after 26 and 28 minutes, heading in off the post for his first and then racing on to a pass by Rix and through the static West Ham defence to bury his second, with the linesman initially flagging for offside, before dropping his flag, which formed the catalyst for the minor pitch invasion.

"A remarkable display of skill and spirit from Trevor Brooking inspired his team to a storming finish," wrote Tony Pawson of the *Observer*. "After the interval, Brooking bestrode the midfield or roamed tirelessly down the wings to search out the defence with probing crosses stranding David Price as he did so often and so easily he lobbed the ball deep for David Cross to head back and Alan Taylor to stab home after 47 minutes and reduce the deficit."

However, that only told half the story. Macdonald had grazed the bar, Rix was kicked out of the game, whilst Willie Young had taken an elbow in the face with Neill stating that the free kick which led to West Ham's late equaliser should never have been awarded.

The most contentious thing about the game however, had been Macdonald's electrifying burst of pace with ten minutes' left on the clock, which put him through to score, only for Tommy Taylor to wrestle him to the ground in scenes reminiscent of Willie Young and young Paul Allen in the 1980 F.A Cup Final, with Exeter-based Referee Ron Crabb booking him and awarding Arsenal a free-kick.

"That professional foul did indeed preserve West Ham a point," added Tony Pawson.

What also happened during the game was that Steve Walford had come on for Rix with 20 minutes left on the clock and that the journalist had intimated that it had unsettled the dynamics of the Arsenal side with West Ham taking off a defender to put on a forward and thereby putting pressure on Arsenal's back line – which was not too dissimilar to what it had done in the 1979 F.A Cup Final.

What both the Arsenal v West Ham game would also show is that some players thrive when playing against certain players and when playing up against David Price, Trevor Brooking always tended to run him ragged, which was something not too dissimilar to what Leeds United's Tony Currie regularly did against Chelsea's Butch Wilkins.

What was going to happen however, was that Arsenal would continue what would be a 13-game unbeaten run with some fantastic performances, which would both catapult them back up the League and take them to the F.A Cup Final as Hudson was brought back into the fold as foil for Liam Brady. However, the first match was certainly nothing to get overexcited with – and against the backdrop of lowly Orient knocking Chelsea of out the F.A Cup at Stamford Bridge and their manager Jimmy Bloomfield being rushed into hospital prior to a stomach operation – Norwich City rolled into N5.

John Bond deployed Martin Peters in front of a resolute defence, which held out for 90 minutes, with their goalkeeper Roger Hansbury saving fierce shots from both Brady and Stapleton – however, the bad news was the Macdonald had been crocked again – this time by a heavy tackle courtesy of centre-half David Jones with a few minutes remaining, which resulted in damaged a thigh to the former and a booking for the latter. 0-0.

Prior to Manchester City's second visit to Highbury on 4th March 1978, Leeds United had moved to replace the void left by Gordon McQueen and were currently going head-to-head in the transfer market with Everton for Blackpool's £300,000 valued Paul Hart. Everton had proposed a deal to The Seasiders, that involved the Merseyside club getting both Hart and Mickey Walsh with Duncan McKenzie going the other way in some *part-chop* type deal. Leeds however, had well over £800,000 of cash burning a hole in their pockets, courtesy of Manchester United's recent cherry-picking of the club and would eventually buy the defender for £330,000.

At Highbury, however, Manchester City were looking to avenge their Quarter-Final defeat by The Gunners, with manager Tony Book still adamant that they were playing some of the best football that he'd ever seen.

"City's All-stars come to town today, to play Arsenal in a match which should decide how seriously they can entertain thoughts of wrestling the Championship from Nottingham Forest," wrote Richard Yallop of the *Guardian*. "A week ago, their play had the quality of worthy contenders and their 1-0 win carried them up to within four points of Forest."

Tony Book added, "Man for man, my players have more ability than any in the country and the team's effort has never been greater."

Huddy had said something similar of Arsenal and Forest. "Man for man we were the much better side …I mean come on – Ian Bowyer and Larry Lloyd?"

City however, were second-place in the League and had only dropped one point in nine games.

"Those modern Titans of footballing inventiveness, Liam Brady and Alan Hudson, strolled through the tension and chaos of a match full of Olympian implications, bringing order to the day and total defeat to the team with Championship ambitions," wrote James Mossop of the *Sunday Express*. "And while the Arsenal fans went home, light-headed with their success, the black mood prevailed over every man in the City party."

Arsenal, without the injured Macdonald and Rix, had turned on their best performance of the season thus far, and in front of a crowd of just over 34,000 had duly ripped City a new one. After 38 minutes Hudson had collected the ball from deep, looking like he was going to play it left he sent a pinpoint through ball to the right which Rice ran on to squaring it for Alan Sunderland who stylishly – albeit with a touch of nonchalance flicked it past Corrigan. A corner from Hudson created mayhem in City's defence with Willie Young duly blasting home after 59 minutes, then following a bit of a *coming together* with Corrigan and Sunderland, David Price struck Arsenal's third on 66 minutes.

"All Arsenal's lovely, lively Liam Brady needed to do to expose City's Colin Bell was to push the ball past him, dip his shoulder to change direction and streak away," wrote Frank McGhee of the *Daily Mirror*. "In fact, Brady did much more. Some of his passes were so ambitious and accurate they were almost impudent. He was at the hub of the dozens of attacks which tore open City's alarmingly vulnerable defence. One clear reason the way Brady responded, was the presence in midfield of another considerable Arsenal talent – Alan Hudson. Far more eager to run and work, Hudson supplied the perceptive telling pass which led to the first Arsenal goal."

"Brady's long-range passing was abnormally magnificent and Hudson was having one of those games when you reflect upon what a drag it is that he is overlooked at England level, as it was his killer pass that led to Arsenal's opening goal," added Julie Welch of the *Observer*.

"Hudson tackled back diligently and was it not for several saves by Corrigan and misses by Alan Sunderland, the win could have been more emphatic," explained David Lacey of the *Guardian*.

I was just on with downloading all the footage that surrounded Arsenal's F.A Cup Quarter-Final down at the Racecourse Ground against Wrexham with Arsenal's visit fully expecting to draw a crowd of around 30,000, when M finally waved off Mrs Sosk.

"She liked your blouse then," I winked.

"Just a bit," she told me. "Although, she did have a quiet word about me not wearing a bra, though."

"I never got chance to find that out as you hit me with a big stick and split my head open."

"Sorry," she mumbled.

"It's okay," I replied, as I gleefully watched all the highlights of the Wrexham game being downloaded into my laptop.

"How's your headache?"

"Alright," I winked. "Those tablets are pretty good."

"I'm still available – yer know, if yer interested?" she said.

Fair play to Mrs Sosk, she had been dead right about the bra, or lack of – however, just as I'd ripped open M's blouse and was about to move into second gear there was yet another knock on the frigging door.

"I'm getting a bit sick of all this," said Emily as she buttoned-up her £3.96 worth of rags. "Perhaps it is time to live somewhere incognito."

"Like Tuscany?" I said.

I just loved that smile – however, I wouldn't be enjoying it for long as unfortunately, it was the ex-wife …and Paul.

And now for something completely different, I thought.

"We are thinking of getting married," Jeanette told us – before immediately noticing the cut above my eye, the fact that there was blood on M's shitty blouse …oh yeh, and the fact that she wasn't wearing a bra.

"Really," I said. "And where are the kids?"

"Chrissy's got them," she told me.

Emily was ecstatic and gave her the hug of all hugs. "That's really great, Jin," she said. "I'm so happy for you."

That was it. I had a shag cut short, my headache had come back and I was now facing a barrage of questions about the cut over my eye … oh yeah, and was I happy for her?

"Delirious," I said.

"You don't look all that happy," she said.

"Jin – believe me," Emily told her. "Lee's really happy for you."

Later that night and whilst sat on the bed my wife wouldn't shut up about it, so much so, I was thinking of gagging her and slinging her in a trunk.

"Yer can try it," she shrugged. "But I have to be honest, Lee – I don't think that'd do much for me."

That just left me shaking my head.

The excitement I think was two-fold: Her best friend was getting married and my relationship with Jeanette now looked like having some form of closure.

"Yer never talk about you and Jeanette," she said, as she slithered up to me in bed. "Yer know."

"Why, would you want me to?" I asked.

"No, I wouldn't as it'd make me dead jealous."

"You're a million times better," I told her.

"Am I that good a **cook**?" she winked.

"The best **cook** ever."

Personally, I didn't think the Jeanette and Paul getting married-thing had any *legs*. I mean, if she was that keen why did she dump him in the first place? Maybe it was a woman-thing? Or just a Jeanette-thing? One thing was for sure, however – Emily was elated about the news.

The next few weeks would be very strange indeed. At work ITV were still coming down really hard on me, especially as *The Invincibles* was now in full production with parts of it going through editing. What they were annoyed with was a couple of things. Firstly, that I wouldn't let them see it and secondly that Sky Atlantic were indeed interested and had upped the ante offering us quite a lot of money for it. In fact, we were only several *points* apart.

The Tall Dwarf had tried to be cute and I'd cut him off at the knackers, had him excommunicated and told ITV that while ever he was employed by them, they could basically stuff it.

Although, I knew I was being tested – I also did think ITV had realised their mistake.

The weekend channel had been quite easily manageable and made them a fortune. They thought going out 24/7 would work the same and earn them much, much more money. It wasn't and didn't and six matches into the football season I was summoned to see the CEO along with a load of other suits down at South Bank.

I've said before that it's always best to listen what they have to say prior to saying anything. Reading between the lines it seemed like I had been right with something that I had mentioned to Emily, whilst sat out on the patio one balmy evening over in Tuscany, in that they were doing the groundwork for a takeover, so much so, I dropped it out in conversation to my wife.

"You think they really want to buy LMJ?" she asked.

"No," I replied. "I think they are after the lot."

"Crikey," she replied.

The 25% shareholders over at White Lion, knew how much of a cash cow it was and coupled with the fact that we'd tied a few more bands up to the label and that Sky Atlantic were currently over-valuing *The Invincibles*, it made it even more so.

"What would you do if they made you an offer," she whispered.

"Faint – I think."

"What's going on?" Sooty asked me the very next day. "There's rumours flying around that ITV are on about buying you out."

"Who told you that?" I asked.

"ITV's head of sport."

I didn't tell him a much as there wasn't that much to tell and when I got home I had a most excited wife greet me along with a load of boxes of what assumed was rubbish.

"What are those?" I asked.

"Guess?" she said.

"You're leaving me – and you've packed up all your shoes?"

"I'd need a lot more boxes than that," she laughed.

I just shrugged my shoulders.

"Look in them," she said.

It turned out that the people that had bought my mum's old house had been in the loft to measure up for some conversion or whatever and had come across several boxes – some of it being my old stuff. They had contacted M and she had arranged for it to be picked up and now here I was knelt on the floor and looking through it all. More photographs, loads of news clippings, old copies of the *Shoot* magazine and every trophy and medal that I had ever won as a kid, with Emily sat on the chair with the biggest smile you could ever imagine, lovingly watching on, as I carefully scrutinized the contents of each and every box. "It's dead exciting, isn't it?" she said.

"Thanks M," I said.

She needed thanking, as this lot would have ended up at the tip if she'd not been curious as to what it was.

"Hello there, this is Alan Thompsett," the man had said on the other end of the line. "My son bought your husband's mother's house and they've just had some builders in the loft planning an extension and have come across some boxes."

"What is it?" Emily had asked.

"Just some old boxes belonging to your husband," he had said. "If you don't want it, my lad will just take it to the dump-it site."

"Keep it safe and I'll send someone up to collect it," Emily had said. "And thank you very much for letting me know."

As it turned out, Emily had had a right argument with 'Mr Man and his Van' off Donegal Street. "I just want yer to pick up some boxes in yer van," she'd twanged. "I don't want personally taking up there and back in a Limo'."

She made me laugh at times.

"Seven hundred pounds plus fuel?" she'd had growled – totally querying his figures. "You must think I was born yesterday."

Nobody pissed M around when it came to billing us – ever.

"We've just had an invoice for an extra two thousand five hundred pounds," she had said over the phone, whilst at the same time totally querying the firm that had undertaken the basement construction.

"Yes, it was for unforeseen costs," said the woman.

"Well if I were you I'd let your managing director know that this is going straight in front of our corporate lawyers who will counteract it – and when they have done totting up all the damage that your firm actually did to our property – and yes we have all the photographs and receipts, you will be paying us back in full for the basement."

I used to watch her regularly grizzling after reading the utility bills. "This definitely can't be right," she had said, whilst reading the electric bill.

The next thing I know she's on the step ladder and reading the meter and going bats over the phone and giving them a right bollocking. Then three days later we had a credit of £2,700 paid back into our account.

"Yer work really hard," she had told me in her rather matter of fact stance. "I'm not having anyone taking liberties."

"You mean like I do with you?" I'd winked.

"Definitely," she'd smiled.

I then pulled a newspaper out of one of the boxes – the one with the photograph of me with arms aloft after I'd just scored in the school's cup final, and something came over me.

"Are you alright, love?" Emily smiled.

"I've not seen it in years," I said, as I showed it her.

"We definitely have to get that put into a frame," she said, as she took it off me and read what it said.

"I think there's an actual photograph of that somewhere," I said.

"Listen to this," she said, as she read the print. "Even though reduced to ten men after only ten minutes, Janes' continual running at the defence created all sorts of problems, which more than highlighted the reason why Rotherham United are expressing an eagerness to sign him."

I just gave her a smile.

"Why didn't you sign for them?" she shrugged.

"I told you – I needed to find you."

"No, really?" she asked.

"I was made to look good because of the team I played in," I said. "Sooty, Jarv and Jack were brilliant. I was just fortunate to be part of it."

"It certainly doesn't read like that," she smiled.

"Maybe not," I said.

"And if you weren't that good – which I know you definitely were, then why were you made captain?"

"A captain isn't always the best player," I told her.

"Thierry Henry, Fabregas and Robin Van Persie were all captains of Arsenal," she said. "And they were their best players."

"That was Wenger trying to appease his star players – not because they were actual leaders like say Tony Adams or Frank McLintock."

I had been made captain in Year Nine, which certainly went against the grain as Chopper had just dropped three players to bring in Robbie Potter and Thomas Tucker along with a new kid who had moved to our school from Parson Cross called Tony Biggs. No sooner had he done that, we had started winning things, but me being captain was more because he liked me. I certainly didn't think it was because he thought me a natural leader.

"Did you play every game that season?" Emily asked me, whilst still sat cross legged reading.

"I think so."

"It says here that the goal you scored was your thirty-third of the season," she said.

"I used to take the penalties," I said. "Nothing more straightforward than booting a ball past a goalkeeper from twelve yards."

"I don't think Graham Rix thought that," she smiled, before I received a minor telling off. "Anyway, we measure in metric in this house."

"Ten …point five?" I shrugged.

"Nearer eleven," she tut-tutted, before giving me a wink. "Ten point nine-seven if I really wanted to be finicky."

I spent half the night reading those papers and one thing that I didn't know, was who the guy had been who had actually refereed that game, and it all came flooding back.

I remember the music crackling through the speakers pitch side and reverberating down the tunnel as we waited for the knock on the door.

"Remember what I told you," Chopper had said. "Keep it simple – no fancy flicks or tricks, just feel your way into the game and use the flanks."

He then walked around the dressing room and spoke with each of us, reassuring us by talking us up and in some instances rubbing our heads. Then came the buzzer and the knock on the door, which was followed by the lads banging their boots and shouting.

"Remember Shaun," Chopper had told Hilly. "Use your speed to get behind them."

Both sides were led out side by side and onto the pitch by our teacher-cum-manager's and we were met by what seemed like a deafening roar and applause from what the local papers said was a crowd of just short of 5,000 people. It wasn't like the noise that you get at a proper league or cup game, but more high-pitched. Both teams lined up opposite each other – us all in white, and the opposition in black and red stripes, and where some city councillors and head of services for sports and education were introduced to both teams.

When they approached me, all I can remember thinking about was the music which was still blaring out and crackling through the speakers – some song that was in the charts at the time, as Chopper introduced me: "And this our captain Lee Janes."

I looked up at him and shook his hand.

"Have a good game, son and do your parents proud," he said.

I nodded and told him "Thank-you", before a huge lump in my throat took over and I tightened my mouth to stop both lips wobbling.

Chopper put his arm on my shoulder, "I bet he's up there now, watching you," he whispered. "And as proud as a peacock."

I looked up into the stands and noticed some of the girls from our school singing along to the naff song as we left the halfway line and knocked the ball about and I remember the pitch being really big and the stands set back like at the old Wembley …or the old Stamford Bridge …or the old Shay –

and we had a proper referee – a coloured man, who called me to the centre circle for the toss-up.

"Are you nervous?" he asked both me and the captain of the other side.

I shook my head.

"I am," he said, rather excitedly. "I certainly didn't expect a crowd, this size."

That made us both laugh.

I looked at the clipping and it read. *Referee: U. Rennie*

The legend that was Uriah Rennie. That was certainly something that I hadn't known.

"You alright, love?" smiled Emily.

I nodded. I was. I was very alright.

"That night in Wortley Hall," I said. "You know – when you wanted a dance with me?"

She glanced me a smile.

"That was the song they were playing when we walked out onto the pitch that day."

"What – Gina G?"

I nodded.

"So, while I was probably up in my bedroom listening to it, you were scoring goals and winning cups over in Sheffield," she beamed. "It's strange where life takes you."

It certainly was.

Chapter 42

Rotherham United

The 4th October 2015, will be etched in my memory for quite some time as it had been a long time coming. Arsenal had battered Manchester United 3-0 and it was a great conclusion to what had been a fantastic weekend.

A quick rewind to the Wednesday morning prior, the head of sports at ITV had nagged me to do the prodigal son act and go and report on Rotherham United's Friday night live game against promotion favourites Burnley.

"What's this – I'm getting demoted from producer to reporter?" I asked, whilst signing off on some rosters.

"I bet you've not been to their new ground," he winked.

I hadn't. I'd been to their old ground, however. Quite a few times. I'd also been to the neighbouring scrap merchants – firstly whilst trawling every auto salvage place in the area for a thermostat housing for a Nissan 240Z and secondly with Sooty to try and flog them five and a half yards of lead sheeting on 22nd August 1998 – the exact day we saw the reigning Champions get held to a 0-0 draw over at Anfield, in a match where Nicholas Anelka beat three players on the edge of the box only to see his shot go the wrong side of the post and where the street cleaner called Derek blazed over an empty goal after Brad Friedel had made a great save from a header by Arsenal's French centre-forward.

"Where did you get that from," the guy at the scrapyard had inquired.

Sooty never answered. He had been more concerned with his sagging suspension, as his Ford Capri had carefully chauffeured half the Methodist hall roof five or six miles over to Masborough Street.

We never did tell him and the £25 he kicked up for it was hardly worth the couple of slipped discs I nearly got and the set of whistling shockers that Sooty had to replace.

"Anyway – Sky are live on this match," I told the head of sports. "What do you want me up there for?"

He then let me know exactly why. ITV wanted to make a play on Sky's ratings. They wanted me and M up there, in not too dissimilar circumstances to the UEFA Europa League game over in Germany last November.

"Rotherham versus Burnley is hardly Wolfsburg versus Everton," I told him.

"It is if you're a Rotherham fan," he told me.

It was what it was – a wasted Friday night freezing my knackers off over at the club's new £17 million New York stadium, just off Centenary Way and a stone's throw from the old Millmoor ground.

"Do you fancy going up to Liverpool tonight?" I asked my wife that lunchtime in the Coffee Shop, as I watched on as she chased after a rather fleet-footed Herbert.

"Tonight?" she shrugged, whilst wrestling with her offspring.

"Yeh, I've got to go report on Rotherham United on Friday. I thought we could make a few days out of it."

"What about the children?" she asked.

"I don't think they'd be bothered about watching Rotherham," I winked.

"Yer know exactly what I mean."

I certainly did. Unfortunately, we had been saddled with a life that didn't give us much flexibility – me with the job and kids – and Emily's pre-recorded *ITV Sessions* on a Thursday morning and her Monday-to-Thursday music classes.

"Thursday night then?" I inquired.

"That still leaves the children," she said. "And Harmony will be dead miffed if she doesn't have her Friday night with us."

She was right. My daughter had been getting ever so clingy – ever since the New York-stroke-Ross Bain-thing. Now it was something completely different – and her clinginess was due to the mum-stroke-Monty Python-thing.

"Dad, do you think mum would be stupid getting married to Paul?" she'd asked a few Friday nights ago.

"Did you think I was stupid getting married to M?" I'd replied.

"No – but M is M."

"And Paul is Paul," I'd said.

"Yeh – but M's different."

"I should hope so," I'd said. "I'd definitely not want to marry a man. Especially one who supported Brentford."

That got her laughing. And Emily come to that.

"They've asked me to be a Page Boy," I further lied.

"No, they have not," argued my daughter.

I got my standard "Behave", along with a nudge and a peck from Emily.

I must admit – it was getting as easy to wind her up as it was her wicked step mum – and when I mentioned to Emily about her going to see Rotherham United as well, she thought I was still in leg-pulling mode.

"Yeh, right," she smiled.

"Straight up," I said. "It'll be dead exciting."

"What – watching Rotherham United?" she shrugged.

"Their ground is a bit like a smaller version of the Volkswagen Arena at Wolfsburg," I said. "You'd really like it."

"Their ground must be a lot smaller than The Emirates then," she smiled.

"A bit. It holds about forty-eight thousand less – give or take a few," I told her.

I then mentioned the fact that Rotherham United had knocked Arsenal out of the 1960/61 F.A Cup and the 1978/79 League Cup, but even that couldn't entice her into coming along with me, so much so, I had spin a few yarns – one of them being that their new stadium's Kop had been named the 'Trevor Womble stand'.

"What – he's got a facking stand named after him?" Huddy had snapped, after eavesdropping on a conversation that involved me telling the head of sports one of my several big fibs in trying to get Emily on site.

"Yeh, it holds around twenty-thousand," I lied.

Having stands, bars and cafeterias named after players was apparently a bit of a bugbear for Huddy. And when Sooty mentioned that Chelsea were going to open a bar and restaurant at Stamford Bridge called the 'Colin Pates Brasserie' he went fucking berserk.

"They were originally going to name it after Craig Burley," Sooty added. "The fans voted on it."

"They'll name a facking bar after anyone," he stormed, whilst booting a waste paper bin into the bottom corner of Temporary Studio 1.

"He played under Tommy Docherty," I told him.

"Who did?"

"Trevor Womble."

"Yeh, so did I," he replied. "So, what?"

"He also played with Dave Watson." I said.

"Yeh, so did I," he said. "England versus West Germany."

"Yeh, but he also played with Neil Warnock and the Mighty Quinn – you didn't."

"The Mighty Quinn – who's he?"

"Johnny Quinn. Docherty made him the captain," I said. "Class player."

"Facking rabbish," he stormed.

"What's up with him?" Kirsty asked, in regard to our rather grumbling erratic genius.

"He's got that bit of edge that makes a good player a great player," I winked. "Or in Francis Coquelin's case – an average player into a dirty average player."

The me having to go to Rotherham-thing was doing my head in and on signing off on a few things I nipped into Temporary Studio 1 to see Huddy begin his show – presiding over two teams of five, in his highly-plagiarised quiz show, where he was a sort of an *evil* David Coleman.

"Cut," shouted Abi, before bollocking the host, much to the merriment on set.

"What's up?" I asked her.

"I told him from Day One 'no effing and blinding'," she replied. "Since he's got in his comfort zone, everything that comes out of his frigging trap is a swear word."

223

Huddy's main show – the majority of which was his idea, was based around the BBC's *Question of Sport* – but in a F.A Cup theme, where 32 teams of five (with one substitute) – all ex-pro's, who played for the actual football team at the time, got drawn against each other – with the winner progressing to the next round. In this instance, the Derby County circa 1978 quintet had been pitched against Burnley circa 1975 and three minutes in Abi had blown the whistle for dissent. Huddy had supposedly just called Bruce Rioch a "wanker and a cheat".

"Al – he's a guest on your show," I told him. "You're not supposed to victimise your guests."

It had been much worse two weeks before as Peter Shilton had been part of the Nottingham Forest circa 1979 quintet that had been knocked out by Watford circa 1978, and after he got an easy question wrong Huddy had apparently called him a "Useless great ape".

"We would have won the League if it wasn't for him," he'd snapped.

The small studio audience were all in stitches. That was until Shilton went for him and Basher had to step in.

"He's like Jack Charlton," Chris had said on the subject of Huddy's *book of many grudges*. "I'm sure he carries a black book of people he's going to *do*."

"M's told him loads of times that he watches too many gangster films," I said.

Basher's wise words had me going down all the lists and putting orange marker through anyone I thought Huddy may feel like he wanted to seek revenge on. I was just glad Terry Neill wasn't part of any team. In fact, I was even gladder that Jimmy Hill wasn't.

"I've heard that you're going to a match on Friday," Huddy inquired, around an hour or so later.

"Rotherham versus Burnley," I said. "The head of sports wanted M to go up with me and help deflect a bit of Sky's publicity our way."

"So, are you going?" he asked.

I told him I was meeting Ginge up at the ground around 6.00 pm on Friday.

"Well I'm doing the Man City – Newcastle commentary Saturday and I'm off to Goodison Park with M's granddad on Sunday, so I'll come up with you," he said.

"Hold on a minute," I shrugged. "You're going to the Everton – Liverpool match …with Bill?"

"Yeh, I got Bill Kenwright to send me down a few complimentary tickets," he said.

I had to admit it – Huddy was quite the wheeler-dealer when it came to the business end of football.

"Did I ever tell you about Stan Flashman and the seventy-eight Cup final," he grinned.

"Yeh, about a hundred fucking times," I told him.

The good thing about Huddy was his knack at arranging things and come Friday morning he'd packed all his necessities. As had Basher, Sooty, Jarv, Zak, Carter, the head of sports – oh yeh, and one of his new best mates – Dean the east coast director who had been hard at work in the editing room all week, and who in between trying to tap a ride up to Rotherham in my car, asked me if M would be free to do another couple of scenes to fill up a few gaps in *The Invincibles*.

"What sort of scenes?" I inquired.

"Just general scenes," he lied.

"Is there any sex involved?"

"No," he lied – again.

I phoned Emily, only to find out that he'd already sounded her out.

"Three scenes," she said. "One in a supermarket arguing with another woman who is supposedly one of your ex-girlfriend's mam's – another arguing with a man in a car and then sort of trying to do it in a car – and one in some room – sort of doing it …again."

I liked Dean a lot, but not only had he made my mum look like the village bike, he also appeared to be quite enjoying my wife's flourishing career in soft porn.

"He told me that there was no more sex," I said.

"Mmm, he initially told me that there was no sex as well," she replied.

"So – who's the man in the car?" I asked. "Vic Harding?"

"No – Frazer Hines," she said.

"I don't know him – is he fictional?"

"Not entirely," she chuckled.

My head was in a whirl. "So, this Frazer bloke – who is he supposed to be?

"He's an actor yer great nit," she laughed. "My mam's dead excited – she used to watch him in Emmerdale when she was a teenager."

"Christ – how old is he?"

"About seventy-something," she said.

"You what?" I gasped.

"Nothing really happens," she said. "It's all a bit rubbish really."

"So, again – who's this gadgy actually supposed to be?" I inquired.

"A man called Mr Tweedy."

Shit! I thought. *How the hell did they know about frigging Tweedy?*

First port of call – Sooty.

"Have you said anything to Dean about the story of my mum and that dirty old bastard Derek Tweedy?" I asked.

"I might have done," he replied.

"Why did you tell him about my mum – why didn't you tell him shit about yours?"

"My mam? All she did was work in a chemist," he said. "There's not much exciting about that."

I now had a frigging ageing Joe Sugden fiddling around with Emily on my mind. Oh – and Huddy insistent on wanting a lift to Rotherham in my car.

"I have to travel up alone as I'm shooting off over to Birkenhead straight after the game," I told him.

Mmm. So apparently were Huddy, Chris Wainwright and Dean.

"I rang M and she said we'd all be okay to kip at yours," winked Huddy. "She says she'll have some supper ready for us, if we're not too late in."

"Really?" I said.

"I got in touch with Rotherham's corporate manager to try and get us tickets into the players' lounge," Huddy added.

"When he found out who we all were Tony Stewart was straight on the *dog* and not only got me the tickets – but he sorted us a table in the boardroom."

"Who the hell's Tony Stewart?" I shrugged.

"The chairman."

"So, the chairman of Rotherham United has phoned you?"

"Yeh – they have a cabaret on, but Sooty said that there's a late-night bar there called *Tivoli's*, so I thought we'd watch the match and do a bit of mingling with the players afterwards – and then hit the nightclub."

"You ought to kick up a side line in event planning," I told him.

"It'll be a great night," he added. "I've had my suit pressed."

"It's a pity you weren't fucking in it," I said.

"What's up with you?"

There was quite a bit more to this, as just the other Tuesday he had called into my office and rather cagily dropped a carrier bag in.

"What's that?" I inquired.

"M told me to drop them in," he said.

"Yeh – so, what is it?"

"Just some whites?"

"Who do you think we are – a Chinese fucking laundry?"

"I'm missing having a woman around the house," he winked.

"Well you're not having mine – go find your own."

Me coming in from my jog the next day to find no coffee on and Emily upstairs doing his ironing hit a bit of a nerve – and I had to say it had me growling a bit, especially as my backlog of ironing was a gnats bollock off the ceiling.

"What's the matter?" she shrugged.

"I have to drag you into the ironing room by the scruff of your neck, throw you in it and bolt the door for you to do any of mine."

"I'll only be two minutes," she said, whilst putting creases in a pair of his boxers, that could have quite easily cut through a bar of Lurpak.

Back in real time I told Huddy that I wasn't doing any night clubs.

"When I was your age I was always in a nightclub," he said.

"I told M that I'd be home by midnight."

"What – or you'll turn into a pumpkin?" he grinned.

I just shook my head and called in to see how the pervert director was getting on with the editing of our multi-million outlay.

"It's as funny as hell," he said. "Your M certainly makes it."

"Yeh, I'm sure she does."

I seemed strange to me how a life could be made to look as *funny as hell*, yet in part, so sad? I suppose credit must not only to go to both the writers, but of course the director who takes it from paper to screen. I'd only seen the odd bits of it and I must admit – it wasn't bad.

Emily phoned me around lunchtime that Friday to see if I could skive away for an hour before I drove up to Rotherham. "Come on," she said. "You've got everything running itself."

"You what? We had to pull Huddy and Bruce Rioch apart this morning."

"Bruce Rioch – the old Arsenal manager?"

"Yeh, if I hadn't been there, he may well have had half a crutch inserted in him," I said. "Huddy carries a grudge like Nelson carried his parrot."

"Nelson never had a parrot," she laughed.

"Sammy Nelson did," I lied. "He called it Horatio."

"He did not," she said.

"Huddy's still not forgiven him trying to throw a game to get Alan Hinton the sack," I said.

"Didn't he also break Alan's leg?"

"Yeh – he's definitely not forgotten about that," I said. "He's been watching Kathy Bates in *Misery* all week."

That certainly had her laughing.

I could just imagine Huddy coldly talking down to his heavily strapped victim after finding out that his little ceramic penguin, which always faced due south, had been tampered with. "Do you know about the early days of the Kimberly Diamond mines, Rioch?" he would say. "Do you know what they did to the native workers who stole diamonds? Don't worry Rioch, they didn't kill them. No, if they caught them, they had to make sure they could go on working, but they also had to make sure they could never run away. That operation Rioch, – was called Hobbling."

The thought of a glowering Huddy complete with deadpan voice, wearing a grey pinafore dress and both standing at the end of a bed and wielding a sledgehammer, made those macabre *Rose Garden* dreams that I'd been having, possibly seem like some episode of *Bagpuss* – therefore, I had to get that frigging vision straight out of my head.

I met up with Emily and Sammy at the Coffee Shop around 1.00 pm, and on giving them both a kiss, I received a phone call, which I had to say knocked me for six. It was our lawyers, Freshfields Bruckhaus Deringer who informed me that ITV had made their opening gambit and it was nothing short of immense – and as I looked over at Emily feeding Sammy a bit of sandwich, I listened to what they had to say.

"That looked serious," Emily said, on me ending the phone call.

"ITV have made an offer through Olswang – their corporate lawyers."

"Really?" she smiled.

I gave her a nod.

"How much?" she whispered.

She nearly dropped our Sammy when I told her.

All the hard work, long hours, my shot eyesight and the excruciating headaches that came with it had apparently paid off. In just 12 months we – and I specify the word *we* – had done it. I thought back to that picnic in the woods in Northern Italy when we had spoken at length of our plans. In life, there are quite a few beautiful moments that I can recall, and this had to be right up there with them all, and the words *beautiful* and *idyllic* could never truly do it the justice it deserved.

"What are you thinking about?" Emily further whispered.

"The picnic in the woods," I said.

The smile I got back as ever, I could have framed.

"That was perfect," I said.

"No, it wasn't," she laughed. "Yer moaned like heck at having to carry all those cooler boxes."

She was right – I had. However, my moaning and groaning was about as *real* as my wife's dizzy blonde act in that we both loved to generate a response from one another. I remember putting up the long mirror in the hallway at Hamilton Square and moaning like hell about having to do it as it weighed a ton. The truth was, is that I hadn't minded at all, and chatting with Emily as she sat on the bottom run of the stairs whilst watching me do it was yet another lovely moment.

"What time are you off to Rotherham?"

"About three-ish," I said.

"Well don't go setting off too late," she said. "I don't want you speeding."

"I gather we've got some house guests tonight?" I said, whilst at the same time changing the subject.

"Not that I know of," she smiled.

"Huddy said that him, Chris and Dean were stopping at ours," I said.

"Alan's definitely pulling your leg," she said. "My mam said that Bill Kenwright has sorted them rooms at the *Radisson* off The Strand. They are all going to watch Liverpool and Everton on Sunday with my granddad."

Huddy was certainly the Dickie Attenborough of football and if he could get a foot in a chairman's door, he most certainly would.

"Did you find out that Arsenal versus Rotherham film footage that you were on about taking up with you?" she asked me.

I did and I had. Rotherham may have been spanked by Arsenal on a couple of occasions in 1972 and 1986 – however, the truth of the matter is that throughout the years they had given as good as they got and had dumped Arsenal out of the Third Round of the F.A Cup in 1959/60 and the Second Round of the League Cup in 1978/79 as both a Second and Third Division club respectively. As for the footage I'd got, I'd had it cleaned-up, so Huddy could present it to Rotherham's chairman as a bit of a *thank-you*.

In January 1960, Arsenal had travelled up to Millmoor following a 4-4 draw at Highbury with Wolverhampton Wanderers, with Arsenal needing a last-minute penalty from Len Wills to equalise. As a club, they were all over the place. During the 1958/59 season the club had been looked on as Championship contenders – however, the signs were there that they were anything but, and after the great signings of Tommy Docherty and Jackie Henderson, the manager had missed some brilliant opportunities in the transfer market and had invested badly – and as such, the George Swindin – Ron Greenwood partnership, was severely floundering.

After 25 games and lying sixteenth in the table after a terrible run of form pre-Christmas which saw them lose six games – five on the bounce and letting in a total of 23 goals: 3-2 away to Leeds United; 4-2 at home to West Bromwich Albion; 4-1 away to Newcastle United; 4-2 at home to Burnley; 5-1 away to Sheffield Wednesday; and 3-0 away to Luton Town – the club stood absolutely no chance of challenging for the title.

Amidst the backdrop, two of those clubs – West Bromwich Albion and Leeds United were having trouble with a couple of their England Under-23 players – Maurice Setters and Chris Crowe respectively. Albion's 24-year old wing-half Maurice Setters, who had a reputation as a bit of a hard man wasn't happy at the club and had turned down approaches from both Everton and Manchester City with The Baggies' chairman saying that the player didn't know what he wanted, but one thing was for sure, is that he certainly wouldn't be playing for *his* club again.

As for Leeds United's 20-year old fleet-footed inside right – the Jaguar driving Chris Crowe, he was unhappy at the club and had put in three transfer requests, being the subject of bids from both Wolverhampton Wanderers and Aston Villa – however, neither of those for clubs would get their man.

Like Jordan and McQueen some years later, Setters got his dream ticket to Manchester United, but as for Crowe –

he moved to Blackburn Rovers and on to Wolves a season later – and although he picked up a solitary England cap, he would miss out on a massive piece of history at Leeds United under Don Revie.

As for The Baggies – they would also be losing a potential England international goalkeeper in the brilliant 23-year old Clive Jackman, whose bravery had seen him suffer a series of severe injuries since his move from Aldershot. Jackman had been wanted by both Aston Villa and Coventry City and come January 1960, a severe spinal injury from a kick in the lower back forced him to retire from the game.

An injury ravaged Arsenal had silenced the 24,750 crowd up in South Yorkshire and with 19 minutes remaining they were comfortably 2-0 up. Captain Tommy Docherty – just back from an 11-week layoff from a broken leg had been in the side that had seen Jimmy Bloomfield race into the Rotherham half and provide Len Julians with the opening goal after 29 minutes and right on the hour Arsenal had made it 2-0 when a Rotherham defender put through his own goal.

Déjà vu from the season past however, would rear its head, and as Colchester United had done in the Fourth Round of the 1958/59 F.A Cup, Rotherham's Brian Sawyer reduced the deficit on 71 minutes with what Bob Pennington of the *Daily Express* described as a tremendous volley. Worse was to come for The Gunners when just nine minutes later referee Ken Dagnall blew for a handball against Len Wills. It was a harsh decision, but ex-Villa striker Billy Myerscough made no mistake and walloped his penalty past Jim Standen. Rotherham United's tails were up and they set about Arsenal big-style and in the last-minute Myerscough pulled a ball back from the by-line to see Keith Kettleborough crash the ball home. The home crowd went crazy – however, the referee had a different view and disallowed it stating that the ball had been out of play when Myerscough had centred.

Swindin was full of compliments about Rotherham's fight back and he told Derek Wallis of the *Daily Mirror*, that to produce a fight back as good as they had, showed that they had the essence of a very good team. The Rotherham defender who had put through his own goal to put Arsenal 2-0 up however, thought very different. "I reckon nowt to Arsenal," he had told Bob Pennington.

That defender? Danny Williams – the man who would go on to manage Rotherham United two years later, before taking over the reins of Third Division Swindon Town – the team that went on to humiliate Arsenal in the 1969 League Cup Final.

The replay four days later at a snow-covered Highbury was seen by a crowd of 57,598 and The Gunners saw the match as a formality after Jimmy Bloomfield had put Arsenal 1-0 up on 43 minutes courtesy of the diminutive Joe Haverty, who had created the opening. However, it was hardly the one-way traffic of the previous season's tie against Colchester United and Rotherham winger Barry Webster managed to scramble an equaliser after 57 minutes.

Arsenal offered very little and although David Herd saw his header beat goalkeeper Ron Ironside and come back off the bar and Jackie Henderson miss a clear-cut chance, Rotherham were more than worthy of a share of the spoils and that was more than evident when they caught Arsenal flat-footed with just three minutes left on the clock – however, with Standen in no man's land and the Arsenal goal gaping, Myerscough blasted over. Rotherham had spurned their chance of victory.

Extra-time played out, but after 120 minutes the game remained at 1-1.

Arsenal lost the toss which meant a trip up to Hillsborough for a second replay – something which would happen some 19 years later when Terry Neill's Arsenal would be involved in an epic F.A Cup Third Round marathon with Sheffield Wednesday. What was also interesting is that in the very same season, Rotherham United would dump Arsenal out of the League Cup in a game remembered as the one which ended the career of Malcolm Macdonald.

Prior to the second replay, was the North London bragging rights – where top of the table Tottenham Hotspur and inside forward Tommy Harmer especially, ran Arsenal ragged, beating them 3-0 in front of a crowd of close to 59,000 at White Hart Lane. Arsenal were unlucky not to score in that striker Len Julians had seen shots come back off the bar and both posts, but Spurs had been well worth their victory.

The trip up to Sheffield followed – however, Rotherham showed about as much mercy as Tottenham had, and in front of 56,920 spanked Arsenal into next week and with just 19 minutes on the clock they were 2-0 up after goals from Keith Kettlebrough and Brian Sawyer.

"Make no mistake, this was humiliation and almost disgrace," wrote Frank McGhee of the *Daily Mirror*. "Kettleborough underlined for the rest of his team-mates that this Arsenal team were just a bunch of ordinary players. He ripped and tore them apart and schemed and scored a dramatic opening goal in the seventh minute and after that Rotherham dominated the game. I still don't know how Arsenal got off so lightly."

"Arsenal were mighty fortunate not to have been whipped by about half a dozen goals," added Desmond Hackett of the *Daily Express*.

The star of the show had been the relatively unknown 24-year old Kettleborough – a player who would go on to make Alf Ramsey's *squad of 40* for the 1966 World Cup.

"With his balding head, pallid features and scuttling gait, he didn't cut a glamorous figure on the football pitch," wrote Ivan Ponting of the *Independent*. "The slim Yorkshireman was one of the game's true craftsmen, a subtly constructive midfield general who brought to his work an appealing cocktail of artistry and industry, which prompted the England manager Alf Ramsey to call him into his squad. Operating as a deep-lying link-man between defence and attack, he proved to be a passing master who could stroke the ball accurately over long distances and short, always probing for openings. He was endowed with remarkable stamina, too, revelling in his box-to-box remit, and he was also a feisty tackler, leaving his imprint on any uninformed adversaries who deemed, perhaps from his somewhat studious appearance, that he was easy prey."

"It's a really nice gesture," smiled my wife, regarding our presentation of the film footage.

It was, and as Emily would certainly tell you, as a couple we never liked to go anywhere empty-handed. You could say that Huddy is the same. At first, he used to fetch a decent bottle of wine around – now he just drops in his washing!

"What time do you think you'll make it home?" Emily asked.

"Just after midnight, I reckon."

"I'll wait up for yer then."

I got back over to the studios to find that word had got out – not about the offer from ITV, but the fact that there were a few of us going up for the Rotherham match and Dave Faber and Stevie Kell who were in the building also fancied indulging in a bit a corporate hospitality. As did Stevie's mate – Baso, who was one of football's characters in that he generally tops most polls on the Internet's full-kit wanker scene, as he has both home and away kits specifically cut and tailored at the beginning of each season, to wear in a half-and-half scenario at every game.

There were also three of the crew who were working on *The Invincibles* set and a lighting technician who fancied tagging along as well, so much so, it was looking like we needed a transport manager.

"We'll be able to *take* their fucking Kop at this rate," a rather irate Sooty had said, as he tried to arrange which person was actually going with who.

"Did your legal people phone you?" inquired a rather officious Abi.

"They did. Me and M are going in on Monday."

"Why – what's happening Monday?" asked Sooty.

"ITV have made an opening offer for LMJ and White Lion," I said.

That certainly got him thinking!

Faranha had wrapped me the DVD that contained all the Arsenal versus Rotherham United footage from both 1960 and 1978 – the latter which showed a Dave Smith-inspired United, dump Arsenal out of the League Cup on 29th August in what was basically *A Tale of Three Headers*.

Smith set up two goals in two minutes. The first by tormenting Pat Rice before putting left-back John Breckin through to provide striker Dave Gwyther, who was an extremely capable player in the lower leagues, with a diving header at the far post, which was followed by a free-kick where United's centre-half, John Green out-jumped Willie Young to head home and put the Millers 2-1 up.

Rotherham's play had been extremely opportunistic as Stapleton had given Arsenal the lead after seven minutes and then after 18 minutes headed against the bar. Throw Macdonald missing a sitter from six yards and Rix being denied a nailed-on goal by a brilliant save from Tom McAllister into the mix and it was always going to be one of those days where Arsenal had created yet had failed to convert and after 65 minutes the writing was on the wall when Rotherham got their third goal after an overhead kick by Gwyther came back off the bar for Richard Finney to head home.

The trip up north was interesting in that Huddy was riding shotgun and had the chair – and it would be here that he mentioned something about his failed move to Hércules de Alicante Club de Fútbol and one of the reasons it fell through.

"I received a phone call from Ken Friar," he said. "He told me that Arsenal had received an offer for me from a Spanish team – which I obviously thought was either Real Madrid or Barcelona. I walked into Ken's office to a very warm welcome. He was all that was good about the club and knew that deep down, I loved Arsenal. As the offer sunk in, I began to think that it couldn't be any worse than working under Terry Neill. I was cock-a-hoop and sought him out to tell him the good news. Rub it in a little bit, if you like. I wouldn't say it backfired but it was clear there was no way he was letting me leave unless he got a drink out of it."

I looked through the mirror at Chris who returned a shrug of his shoulders.

"There was bad blood between Sammy Nelson and Neill, with the left-back inferring that his manager wanted a cut out of his move to Brighton," I said. "And George Armstrong –

he supposedly offered Neill a sweetener to let him leave ...according to Neill that is ...and there was all that stuff in the papers when he was at Tottenham about irregular payments."

"Everyone has something very different to say about Terry Neill," said Huddy. "He was a complete facking idiot!"

Malcolm Macdonald had told a similar tale.

"Alicante had made a firm offer for Alan," Macdonald had told Jason Pettigrove – the sub editor of English version of the Spanish football magazine *Marca*. "I remember waiting outside Highbury to see Huddy coming out. I've never seen a man so angry. What had happened was that he had discussed the deal with Hércules and they were going to pay him a big whack up front – a signing on fee. Huddy was all for it – however, he made the mistake of telling Terry Neill what they were offering him. The upshot was that Neill wouldn't allow him to leave unless he got a cut of some of that money. Huddy, as you can imagine, was livid, angry, upset and frustrated. 'I'm not giving that fucking bastard any of my money, why should I?' he told me. That was perhaps the final straw for him – being taken for a mug on top of everything else."

I must admit – having Huddy in the car with us made the near-three-hour drive quite tolerable.

The match itself was nothing to write home about with Sam Vokes scoring Burnley's winner right at the end – however, listening to Huddy with their chairman was something else and how he never got an interview for Rotherham's vacant manager's job was anyone's guess.

"Do you have any suggestions?" one of Rotherham's directors asked me.

"One thing I like about your setup and not including the lovely new ground, is the fact that you have a core of players from the British Isles," I said. "Personally – and whatever you do, don't mention this to Huddy – I'd have Graham Rix up here for an interview. He has the South Yorkshire roots and was a sound coach with Chelsea. He'd jump at the chance."

He listened, but considering the Ched Evans-thing being big news in this area, I knew that Rix at Rotherham would be a no-no ...as was trying to get Huddy and Chris out of the players' lounge afterwards, so much so, I ended up leaving them there.

I rang M to tell her that I was on the M62 and like in the Simon and Garfunkel ballad – *Homeward Bound.*

Emily stayed on the phone from Hartshead Moor over Saddleworth Moor and on to Birch Services telling me about the kids plans for Halloween, them picking their outfits for a scary night of trick or treating in Birkenhead along with this, that and the other, before reprimanding me for only having eaten some toast and marmalade with her and Sammy at daft o'clock that morning.

"Lee yer body can't function right on twenty cups of coffee and a bit of bread," she said. "I'll have some food on for when you get in."

When I say that I had needed someone like M all my life – I really did mean it.

Chapter 43

The Sooty Show –*Episode 9*

I woke up in a hotel room in the centre of Sheffield to find my roommate and last nights supposed designated driver shaving in the bathroom, whilst at the same time humming Frank Sinatra's *Fly me to the Moon*.

We had been in Rotherham United's 1925 suite until chucking out time and ended up at a knocking shop in some old refurbished steel mill off the A61 bypass and had come back to the hotel at stupid o'clock, where we had a few frames of snooker downstairs before retiring about what felt like ten minutes ago, as England's finest midfielder ever, had had enough and needed to catch up on some beauty sleep. In between all that, Buzzy's missus had called me when I had been in the chairman's office *talking shop* – hence the ten missed calls and about as many texts on my phone.

Huddy's idea was to do a *Lee* and drink Perrier water all night and offer deep meaningful insight into what was a shit game of football and then drive us to the hotel in my car. That train of thought lasted all of ten minutes after he had presented the chairman pitch side with a gift of some old TV footage from ITV 7, which was immediately reciprocated by the chairman and two of his directors furnishing him with a trip to the bar.

I couldn't believe that I'd fell for Huddy's patter.

"So, I've now got to go and pick up my car in Rotherham?" I said, on sitting up in bed.

"I offered to drive," came a voice from the bathroom.

Yeh – that much was true. He had. Huddy must be the only person in the world that can look quite sober and still be seventeen times over the limit.

I nearly fell for his patter, but after hearing how he *beached* his Jaguar on some roundabout in Newcastle-under-Lyme, I'd told him, that he'd got "no frigging chance".

"I'm alright," he'd said. "I once spent the night in a nightclub and just a few hours later hit the winning goal at Highbury."

"I know – I saw the goal," I'd told him. "The Arsenal defence were that shit then, that you could play against them in the state you are now and still have fucking scored."

The goal had come on the 23rd August 1975, and totally summed up the brilliant Arsenal side that Bertie Mee had destroyed. A stupid back pass by Brian Kidd and lousy defensive work by Sammy Nelson, paving the way for the designated driver and our erratic genius to lash a ball past Jimmy Rimmer.

"Did I tell you the story about the Spurs-supporting copper that pulled me up for drink driving after John Pratt's testimonial?" he'd then asked.

"Yeh about twenty times," I'd replied.

"As soon as he saw who I was, he dragged me out of the car and slung me over the bonnet."

"I know – you've told me," I'd said. "About twenty times."

"The cheeky bastard tried buying my car afterwards," he'd chuckled, still merrily sharing his tale. "And I told the guy in the garage – 'If you sell it him, make sure you *do* the facking brakes'."

"You're missing one," I'd said, waiting for his next sentence to compliment the tale.

"I even had Don Howe back my corner in court," he'd added. "Telling the judge that after losing in the F.A Cup Final I'd had a miserable few weeks and that I was someone who takes pressure hard."

"That's the one," I'd nodded, before enlightening everyone that it had therefore been my 21st time of hearing it!

Back in real time I rang concierge and asked them to sort me a taxi. As it happened Basher had been down there at the time after coming from breakfast and relayed me some news over the phone. "There's some bird down here asking for you."

"What is she – a reporter?" I asked.

"I doubt it mate – she's dragging around a suitcase and a couple of carrier bags."

I didn't like the sound of that – however, Huddy hobbling out of the bathroom suddenly caught my attention.

"Who are you – Windy Miller?"

He was decked out in a red and white tracksuit with the tags still on it courtesy of a midnight raid on Rotherham United's club shop, whilst cracking a couple out and stinking the room out at the same time, with what I assumed was the essence of last night's lamb kebab.

"'You going out for a jog?" I inquired.

"No – down for some breakfast," he said.

"Well open a frigging window or summat before you do."

Huddy had spent half the night semi-angling for Rotherham's vacant manager's job and then interrogating one of the directors about *The Trevor Womble Stand*. He was still on about the latter whilst we were over at Paradise Alley or whatever they called it – and when I thrashed him five frames to nil at snooker.

The snooker game had been really funny. He'd been getting the hump with me as I kept on leaving the cue ball at the far end of the table and snookering him behind any one of the coloured balls. In fact, at one time he was on minus 32 before he had even managed to hit a red. I must admit, snooker was a game that I played quite well. I've had half a dozen breaks of just over 100 and won a few quid in the process – including the £50 per frame off Huddy.

"I don't play at this level," he'd snapped.

"What are you on about?" I'd said. "It's a pub game."

"What's that supposed to mean?"

"It means that with you always being in the pub, that you should be good at it."

"Stan Bowles was always in the bookies – it doesn't mean he was any facking good at riding horses."

Huddy was one of those people who always had something to say – always!

Whilst I racked up the balls he'd been spinning a yarn in a bid to outdo the Leeds-hating gob shite that was Dave Faber. Dave had told us that while he'd watched Huddy turn the League Cup Quarter-Final around against Manchester City and putting in one of his best-ever shifts in an Arsenal shirt, he'd had had his car nicked from Highbury Fields.

Rather strangely, one of the Arsenal historians Andy Kelly had his car stolen from Green Lanes near Turnpike Lane Tube Station – the exact same place where me and Annie Dixon had been the subject of a botched robbery, and whilst he had watched a game against City in 1992. Maybe both their cars ended up on Moss Side. Who knows?

As for Huddy, you get him on a roll and there was no stopping him.

"I've got a story for you," he'd kicked off. "You remember that programme – *Upstairs, Downstairs?*"

"You're definitely not going to tell me that you were fucking in it?" I'd winked.

"No," he'd snapped. "Gordon Jackson's character – Hudson. He was named after me."

"What a load of bollocks," I said.

"It's straight up," he'd said. "One of the show's writers was a big Chelsea fan. Mrs Baldwin was named after Tommy Baldwin."

"Well why wasn't there a Mr or Mrs Osgood in it then?" I 'd asked.

"He might have something there, you know," Dave had added. "Alfred Harris was a character in it too – he could have been named after Ron …and Mrs Bridges maybe she was named after Barry Bridges."

That got us all thinking, with Dave straight on his iPhone googling all the characters. "There was a Jean Marsh in it as well – maybe she could have been named after Rodney?"

"I actually met the writer after a Play-off match between Stoke and Leicester City around at Terry Conroy's house and he revealed that the butler was actually named after me and that Mrs Baldwin was named after Tommy," Huddy had told us. "I wished I'd had known that at the time, as my mum used to watch it. She would have loved to have told all her mates at bingo."

The last bit of the conversation was what Lee and M both loved about him – his humility. I rarely saw that side of him. With me, it was as if he was always trying to rub me up the wrong way?

I managed a shower before I got the dreaded knock at the hotel room door and lo and behold it was the woman with the suitcase.

"I've been thinking about what you said," she said.

Why – what did I say? I thought

She didn't reveal the intricate details of what I'd supposedly said and just slung me the edited highlights – *Match of the Day*-style. No boring back passes, no wasted crosses and no time wasting by booting the ball out of play. Just the goalmouth action. "I'm pregnant and it's yours," she said.

"So, what's with the suitcase?"

The reasoning behind the suitcase was that their Kev had kicked her out.

"I took the car," she shrugged. "And these are just some of my things."

"You've come in your car?" I inquired.

I received a nod.

"Nice one – I can cancel the taxi and you can drive me over to Rotherham to pick up mine."

I let Huddy and Basher know what was appertaining – however, the awkward part was telling Lee …mmm and Lib …and Maggie come to that. "I've got Buzzy's missus with me," I told him.

"How did that well-executed come-together happen?" Lee inquired.

"She phoned last night."

"And now she's with you. You'll be telling me next that she's pregnant."

"Well I wasn't going to mention it, but yeh, she is," I said.

"And it's definitely yours?"

I had been down this route quite frequently of late and what pissed me off about it, was his regular line of interrogation – mainly the 'Is it yours?' barb.

I never ever asked him if he was sure that his kids were his and I said as much.

"M nor Jeanette are porn actresses and nor were they trying for a baby with other men," he said. "Believe me Sooty, it's a valid question."

It pissed me off how he could do what he did and everything turned out great. At the minute, I was like King Midas in Reverse in that everything I touched, not so much turned to shit, but complicated my life another ten-fold. As for him – on Monday he'd be negotiating what we – or more to the point what Jeanette, understood to be a £100 million-plus deal that would see him and M sitting pretty for the rest of their lives. My relationship with ITV 7 was totally different – a hundred fucking million times different.

I looked over at Buzzy's wife standing there and something hit me. Maybe Debbie was my version of M? Just maybe, this was what I had been looking for? I mean, hooking up with a married bit of skirt had worked for him. We chatted for a bit, but nothing jumped out at me to tell me that she was on par with M, apart from the fact that she was pregnant.

She did however, run me over to the New York Stadium to pick up my car and we arranged to meet in the Midland Hotel in Manchester around 8.00 pm – however, that wouldn't happen as M stepped in with a phone call.

"I can't believe that I've just been talking to Emily Janes," Debbie gasped afterwards.

What was strange is that I never thought anything of the *fame* that came with our jobs. Maybe that was because there was a lack of *fortune* attached to mine.

That weekend I was all over the place and to make matters worse Leeds got mugged by Birmingham City at Elland Road – having nearly 70% of the play and losing 2-0, which made the afternoon along with my show, quite unbearable.

What happened with Buzzy's missus is that M had given her the directions to their house in Liverpool and the phone call I received from Debbie after my show was one of pure happiness and total disbelief. "Have you seen their house," she told me. "Aw Sooty, it's absolutely gorgeous."

I had never been to Birkenhead – ever, never mind invited over to Hamilton Square and I told her as much.

I still didn't have a clue what I was going to do with her, as Libby and Maggie were taking up all my time – however, what had been made clear was that Lee wanted nothing to do with any of them – Lib and Maggie that is.

Debbie Burrows on the other hand, was a completely different proposition.

I met her in the foyer of the Midland Hotel around 8:45 pm.

"Okay," I shrugged. "So, what do we do now?"

"No idea," she told me. "Perhaps we ought to discuss us – that's of course if you feel that there is, any *us*."

I let her know about the structure of my current situation – in that there wasn't any.

"Do you love your wife?" she asked.

That was a relatively easy question to answer. "No, I can't stand her."

"What about the foreign one?"

"No."

"Well, I quite like you," she said. "Although I don't have as much baggage."

"Three carrier bags and a suitcase is enough for me," I told her.

That made her laugh.

"So, you got on with M okay?" I asked.

"She's really, really lovely," Debbie told me. "We had lunch together with her little ones and she introduced me to her mother and father."

"Did she inquire about the *bump*?"

"Only if I was sure that it was yours."

That made me grind my teeth a bit.

"Did she mention anything else about me?"

245

"Not especially – just that you were a bit lost and hadn't a clue what you wanted," she said.

I knew exactly what I wanted. I just couldn't have it.

"She's really pretty, isn't she?" she asked me.

"Who – M?" I asked.

She just nodded.

I don't know why I asked the question as I had known exactly what she meant. In my mind, M was everything that personified the perfect woman and the only thing that I could think of, that perhaps blighted the said *perfection*, was that she had come to the union via some failed marriage.

"They have a great life," I told Debbie. "Everything you could imagine has been put in their path to mess it up but it never has and if I'm being honest with myself, I'd love to be loved like that."

She listened to what I said, but I had no idea if she understood what I meant.

"Two years ago, Lee was ready for imploding," I told her. "His life was a right mess."

"A bit like yours," she shrugged.

"No, mine's a fucking disaster," I laughed. "He'd been kicked out by his wife, had his kids kept from him and was on a road to nowhere. He'd met M, but even then, it wasn't straightforward as she was married to some psycho. They both saw something in each other and fought like hell to keep it and make it all work."

"You talk with such an affection about them," she smiled.

"Maybe," I replied, before changing the subject. "So, what did you spend the afternoon talking about?"

The next bit was interesting. M had sounded her about a couple of things, one of which was Derek Tweedy, the other – Donna Harding.

"Donna Harding?" I shrugged. "I've not seen her in years."

"M says they were like pen friends for a while."

That was certainly a lot more than I knew.

"What did you tell her about Tweedy?" I asked.

"Just about the *thingy*," she said. "You know?"

246

I did know. Now M did. That made me laugh.

The stories surrounding the man got exaggerated the more they got told, so much so, that he became something of a cult figure rather than a figure of hatred. He never did half the things people claimed – however, the things he did, we certainly got to know about.

Tweedy was a little guy – about 5'5 and from what our old man told me he was originally from Elland in West Yorkshire. He was also a qualified physiotherapist and chiropractor, but something happened that made him leave the area. I have no idea what, but I could certainly hazard a guess. He relocated somewhere to the east of Rotherham and ended up managing a clothing factory in the town centre for a bit. At that time unemployment in the area was rife and being that 99% of his employees were women, he made his position crack.

However, in 1991 the firm that owned the factory went belly up and he returned to physiotherapy and took up residence in a rundown medical practice off Moorgate belonging to a Doctor's Tyrell, Bird and Wheeler. After a while it became common knowledge that some players from Rotherham and Sheffield United were going to him as part of their rehabilitation post-injury. The fact was, that he was an extremely clued-up bloke and certainly knew his stuff and more to the point, knew how to interact with people – young mum's especially. And he made a point of always being overly concerned and knowing the names of their children. He also carried a big Orange mobile phone on his hip like some gunfighter, and made sure that if any of his patients needed him, he would be there at the drop of a hat.

I never had to see him but both Jarv and Lee did. The former due to an ankle injury and **Numb***nuts* as he had fell off the outhouse whilst trying to paraglide with some contraption he had made with some canes and one of his mam's bedsheets. I'd told him that it was a fucking stupid idea. He ended up hanging himself on his mam's washing line before nearly breaking his back.

On being checked out at hospital he had to do some physio and on getting there and seeing all the signed football photographs, he had been in his element. That soon changed after he'd had been checked out, as Tweedy copped his mum and ended up with her on the table and getting treatment for what he claimed was a possible inner thigh strain.

I remember Lee telling me the tale. "He told me to wait outside," he'd said. "'Just step outside son, while I see to your mum'."

According to Lee she had been in there a good half an hour!

"So, when do you have to start calling him daddy?" I joked on him telling me.

He went scats – but not as much as he did after he'd found out that I had told the director on the set of *The Invincibles*, the exact same story, and who in his wisdom immediately ordered a slight rewrite.

"Just step outside son while I see to your mum," I told Dino. "The scriptwriters have definitely got to get that fucker in."

"Won't he go mad?" Dino had asked.

"Yeh – mental," I laughed.

On first getting here, Dino had appeared quite a straight-laced young kid. However, after only a few weeks in *The Warehouse* – the rubbing of shoulders with Lee and Huddy, getting his arse kicked by Jaime and Kirsty and his continually drooling over M, he had become somewhat contaminated by the overall setup at ITV 7.

"Where's Sinead?" Lee asked one morning, whilst looking around. "And Kirsty, come to that?"

"Dino's hijacked them," Faber told him. "…And Becky and Abigayle."

He had. He was using all Lee's *Fox Force Four* as extras – Jarv's *alleged* family of Lesbians from Greasebrough, with Lee popping his head into Temporary Studio 4 to find all four of them under a duvet, with Sinead slightly perturbed in that it was only a ten-to-fifteen second screenshot and not a 30-minute romp.

"I suppose we could make it a little bit raunchier," Dino had said.

Kirsty kicked that train of thought into touch, straight away and gave him a rather resounding, "I suppose you effing could not."

As for Tweedy, he got rumbled after Edgar Kennedy's wife complained about him. Not so much because of the X-rated massages and numerous seeing-to's that he had given her over the course of eight months, but more to do with the fact that he had got bored and had moved on to another object of desire – in this case, the extremely fit elder sister of Brinie Hood. I liked Edgar. He lived three doors away from us and was totally fucking stupid.

"There's something not right," he had told my dad one time – and in earshot of me.

Really?

It had been the talk of the street, and I had seen Tweedy many a time calling around to theirs when Edgar had just left for work around 5.00 am in the morning. At 8.00 am on the dot I had then seen the good *doctor* and Edgar's lingerie clad missus stood necking on the back step before he left to go massage the groins of Curtis Woodhouse, Dane Whitehouse, Brian Deane or whatever part of their body he actually did massage.

His Crown Court trial involved more people coming forward than in the Jimmy Savile case and made all the local headlines that late-September in 1998. Paulo Di Canio's comical assault on referee Paul Alcock and his clubs last minute 1-0 victory against a star-studded Arsenal side never even got a look in. Tweedy got struck off and jailed for a few years.

As for Edgar? We still get a card off him and his wife every Christmas.

"So, what did M say, when you told her about Tweedy?" I asked Debbie.

"She was really shocked."

That night was strange in that I had as many texts and missed phone calls from Lib as she had Buzzy.

"I'll not answer mine if you don't answer yours," I said.

Chapter 44

The Invincibles

The production of *The Invincibles* was very special. I had never done mainstream programming before and the lump I got in my throat as I watched it, was unreal.

"It just needs some more tweaking and a bit of fine-tuning," Dean told me.

Emily had spent more time absorbed in watching my reactions than she had her performance, which I had to say was both fantastic acting and nothing at all like my mum.

The lovely thing Dean had done was to install some of Buzzy's dad's video camera footage into the programme and cut into the actors both talking and playing on the pitch. I had to admit – it was all quite amazing and looked very real.

"We should celebrate," Emily told me. "Just me and you."

I thought that was a brilliant idea, as did Basher who in his wisdom insisted that he and his wife Kerry should join us.

His *Terry Neill Years* documentary had been put on the backburner for a couple of weeks – however, when I got out of *The Invincibles* first screening I let him know that I'd be moving forward on it as the head of sports now wanted it to show it on ITV 7 between 9.00 and 10:00 pm between the 25th and 27th of November.

"They'll pay you a hundred grand for it," I told him.

"Er, how much do you get?" he inquired.

"Nothing," I told him. "I did it for you as a favour."

"Does M get anything?"

"One hundred grand," I said. "Fifty-fifty."

"So, if I'd put all the thirty grand up instead of fifteen I'd have two hundred grand?" he asked.

"No."

"How's that then?"

"One, I wouldn't have done it – and two, ITV wouldn't be showing it."

That had him thinking.

"And remember – you get the net profits from DVD sales."

"What about M?"

"Yeh, she'll get fifty percent of the net as well."

"So, when do I get my hundred grand?" he inquired.

"One, when I finish it – and two, when Annie bills ITV."

"We should celebrate," he said. "We could do the Three Horseshoes over in Laleham or the Caffe Gondola."

"I'm not driving all the way down to frigging Staines for a steak or pasta."

"What are you on about – it's only twenty-odd miles," he said.

"Yeh, by frigging helicopter."

The thing with Basher is that he was very persuasive, therefore, whilst Jeanette and Paul watched over Sammy, we had to endure a massive tailback on the A40 Western Avenue and driving at snail pace all the way up to the M25, where the traffic was slightly better in that I managed to get the car up to 40 mph at one point. Then Chris insisted that we pick him and his missus up from their house in Egham.

"Why do I have to pick you up?"

"Because I'll be having a drink."

"And?"

"And you won't."

I didn't have an answer to that.

It also transpired that although he lived within a stone's throw from Junction 12 of the M25. There was a slight snag in that you just couldn't get to his frigging house from it unless you drove another ten miles down the M3 to Sunbury-on-Thames and another thirteen miles back on a loop to get back. A tip for you. Don't live in Egham – it's like in that film *Children of the Corn* where all the roads lead to anywhere but the place that you are heading for.

"Where are you?" he asked, via my hands-free.

"I've just come of Junction Twelve," I said. "How the hell do I get to yours?"

"Not by getting off there – you should have got off at Junction Thirteen and gone down the A-thirty over Runnymede Roundabout and down the Thorpe Bypass."

"Why didn't you tell me that before?" I asked. "You just told me you lived next to Junction Twelve."

We finally made the torturous journey to his home – a quaint little house with Georgian windows on a cul-de-sac – correction: a very well-hidden cul-de-sac.

"I'm surprised you actually manage to get home on a night," I said on picking them up.

All I got back from him, was that I was late.

The evening was quite nice. We spoke of Arsenal and the god-awful performance that they had just put in against Sheffield Wednesday in the League Cup, along with the arrogance of the Frenchman in charge in fielding a couple of his towel boys to make up the numbers.

"There was no midfield," I said, whilst at the bar. "They were worse than useless. That Iwobi runs like *Square Bear* off Hanna Barbera's *The Hair Bear Bunch* and I wouldn't employ that Kamara to sweep out the yard."

"We had over seventy percent of the possession," Chris added.

"So, does Sooty's missus and look how well that one's worked out," I said.

"Where is he anyway?" asked Chris. "He's not been in all week."

That was a question well worth an answer. He had finally walked out on Libby and their house was up for sale.

Back at the table, Emily had been roped into a discussion – firstly, about *Live at The Warehouse*, which was an extremely touchy subject as it had been one of the stipulations of ITV's opening gambit, in that she host the 12-week run. Them being given *The Invincibles* was the other.

I stood firm on both – however, if ITV wanted something, then they generally got it, and the carrot that they had dangled us, was far too good for us to turn down. In just three days ITV would own everything – including us. When I told Chris, he was gobsmacked.

Basher was one of those people in life that when you get to know him, comes over totally different to the person that you initially perceive him to be. The first thoughts are – don't mess with him as you'll end up encased in concrete as part of the foundations for some new junction on the M25. However, if you look beneath the surface you find an extremely caring guy – which is one of the many reasons why M, Abi and Jaime think the world of him. He's also very humorous. Just ask Huddy: about him being chucked out of the Mitre in Fulham for passing dud twenties – or better still, about having one of his crutches hack-sawed down a good five inch.

Huddy had been walking around in circles a good ten minutes before he cottoned on that something wasn't right. "Has somebody been facking around with one of my crutches?" he'd snapped.

All the upstairs studios had been pissing themselves with laughter.

"But the set-up and everything is great," Chris said. "Why would you want to sell."

"Because they want to buy," I shrugged. "And the price they've offered is extremely good."

"That's not entirely true, Chris," Emily told him. "Lee's eyesight is failing and he has been having blackouts. He's had six of them in the past four months."

I added to that by confirming it with a nod.

"The doctors say its stress-related," Emily told him, "although I'm not so sure."

Chris shrugged his shoulders.

"I had my skull fractured when I was a little lad," I said. "I only found out a month or so ago after M made me go for an MRI."

"How did you do that?" he asked.

"It could have been several things," I lied.

I then thought back to Chopper talking to me after a football game while I was in Year Ten. "You ought to head the ball a bit more, Lee – You've got the natural height and the power, but you seem more interested in getting it down on the floor, and that can lose you valuable split-seconds."

I used to head the ball and the pain I got was unbelievable. That was the main reason why I rarely indulged in headers and why the Cup Final had been so special.

"I told you that you should use your head more," a delighted Chopper had beamed on hugging me after the final whistle had gone. "One in the bottom corner and another off the bar."

As for Sooty. "Brilliant goal mate – and dead unlucky with the second," he said. "How's your head?"

"Banging like hell," I told him.

It was. It had taken five paracetamols and a good couple of hours to get shut of it.

"You once asked me why I never signed for Rotherham United," I said to Emily, whilst driving back into North London.

She looked at me and nodded.

"Their manager – Archie Gemmill – he came to our house to try and persuade me," I said. "He was a brilliant little footballer – played with Derby County and Nottingham Forest. I turned them down because I knew that I had a problem with my head."

"You knew back then?" she asked.

There was a silence for a few minutes and then I told Emily the truth. "My Auntie Margaret did it when I was ten or eleven – she hit me over the head with something."

"What?" she asked aghast.

"I can't remember," I said. "But whatever it was, it was really heavy."

Emily was staggered.

"It's not bothered me for years," I said.

"Didn't you tell your mum?"

"No – I thought I'd get into trouble."

"Trouble – trouble for what?"

I just shrugged my shoulders.

Later that night and as ever, I had her sat cross-legged on the bed. The main conversation being about my auntie and then about my head – mainly what hurt it and what didn't.

"M, as much as you like shuffling about on it, you're definitely not doing it tonight."

"I never even asked," she grinned.

"Yeh – it's before you do."

"I right like the feeling of power," she winked.

"I thought you liked it the other way around …and liked the thought of being powerless?"

"Yeh – I like that as well."

As I've said, I couldn't fathom her out at times.

"The power bit makes me feel right dirty," she winked.

"I'll definitely go along with that – it makes me feel right dirty as well. I had to get a shower and change my pillowcase last time you were on it."

"You like it though," she grinned.

I did. I liked it a lot. I just didn't like the fact that she got so carried away whilst doing it, so much so, that it totally whittled down my options. Either death by asphyxiation or death by drowning.

"I'm surprised I've not got a nose like Freddie Mills with all the hammer it takes."

"What – the Ipswich Town full-back?"

"You know exactly who he is," I told her.

She did, as not only was she there that night when I had given the Tottenham Hotspur chairman Daniel Levy a colourised and framed photograph of the boxer knocking Len Harvey through the ropes at White Hart Lane on 20th June 1942, we had also seen him as this *Waxy Lister* character in a pile of shite black and white film called *Kill Me Tomorrow* during one of M's cuddle and TV nights.

I got up early the next day to get stuck into Basher's *Terry Neill-Years* documentary and to try and collate all the bits and pieces together – however, I immediately dropped on something.

Graham Rix, who had come off injured during West Ham United's fight-back at Upton Park – had missed the Norwich City (0-0) and Manchester City (3-0) games and would also miss the F.A Cup Quarter-Final match at the Racecourse Ground against Wrexham, with the press citing both a groin and ankle injury. However, one thing that I hadn't known is that prior to that he had broken bones in his spine. Two vertebrae in autumn 1976 that required the player to wear a plaster cast for three months. There was an upside to that however, in that he'd had to give up golf. An Arsenal fan called Jamie Hunt told me that!

The game was billed as a possible upset with the Welsh side sitting comfortably at the top of the Third Division with two games in hand. There had also been an Arsenal connection in that their former inside-right Arfon Griffiths was the Welsh clubs' player manager.

Griffiths was signed by George Swindin in February 1961 and was shipped out by Billy Wright on 17th September 1962, playing only 15 times for The Gunners.

There was a story behind Griffiths's transfer out of Highbury in that Billy Wright was looking at a deal which involved Wrexham's 21-year old goalkeeper, Kevin Keelan going the other way.

Arsenal had major problems with the position of goalkeeper following Kelsey's retirement from the game at the beginning of the 1962/63 season with neither Ian McKechnie nor Northern Ireland international John McClelland being to Wright's liking and both eventually being shipped out – McKechnie to Southend United in March 1964 and McClelland to Fulham on Boxing Day that year.

The Griffiths-Keelan story was picked up by Ken Jones of the *Daily Mirror* – however, what happened a day after is that Wright would put £47,500 signing George Eastham on the Transfer List with the player telling the journalist, "It seems obvious to me that my style no longer suits the club and after talking to Denis Hill-Wood, I now know that this is the case."

Jones added: "With Wright's quick-passing and hard running play, Eastham's ball-playing skills have no place in such a pattern."

Griffiths – who was understudy to Eastham, had inferred the exact same. "I felt I had a future at Arsenal, then we got a new manager who changed our style completely," he told the journalist. "I don't care what people say, I still think there is a future for a ball player in British football and I hope to be able to play my own game with Wrexham."

What was strange in Arsenal getting rid – or trying to, in Eastham's case, of two talented ball playing inside-forwards and replacing them with brute force and graft, was that only a few days earlier the club had not only just been humbled, but totally humiliated by possibly the best ball-playing side in world football. Real Madrid had come to Highbury to play in a friendly, and in front of a 32,574 crowd had soundly beaten Arsenal 4-0, with goals by the brilliant left-winger Francisco Gento who hit two and had one disallowed, and Ferenc Puskas and Yanko Daucik. They also had another goal disallowed when midfielder Felix Ruiz's effort was ruled out by Dutch referee Leo Horn.

"Real Madrid crushed the power and hope of Arsenal with strolling nonchalance," wrote Clive Toye of the *Daily Express*. "And that makes the Arsenal failure all the more bitter, for they flung themselves with frenzy at men who were able to control them without breaking into a trot."

Arfon Giffiths the manager had been to see Arsenal in their match against Norwich City – a game where former teammate Keelan had sat out the match as he had still been injured after he had sustained a broken hand down at Ashton Gate, and candidly stated to John Lloyd of the *Daily Express* that his club would certainly give Arsenal a game to remember. He also told Harry Miller of the *Daily Mirror*, that if they played their normal game it could be enough to see them through to the Semi-Final.

The Wrexham side contained three players in Bobby Shinton, Dixie McNeil and Graham Whittle who certainly could put the ball away. Their 26-year old right-winger Shinton would eventually join Malcolm Allison's strange, albeit expensive revolution at Manchester City in a £300,000 move a year or so later, whilst 31-year old Dixie McNeil had a reputation as an extremely predatory striker in the lower leagues with an impressive 1:2 goal per game ratio; whilst 24-year old Liverpool born striker Graham Whittle possessed a 1:3 – and those statistics weren't one-offs either, as they would go on to total over 800 League games.

There were also more Arsenal connections in Wrexham's line-up such as ex-Arsenal and 22-cap Welsh international centre-half John Roberts, who played a part in the club's Double success and the 23-year old diminutive albeit brilliant Mickey Thomas. After his £300,000 transfer he would go on to play for Manchester United and 51 times for Wales; and would also play against Arsenal in the 1979 F.A Cup Final before his journeyman career would some 14-years later take him full-circle and back playing for Wrexham, who even though they were lying in eighteenth place in the old Fourth Division, would knock Arsenal out of the F.A Cup – helped on with an equalising goal by the left winger and directly from a free-kick.

Wrexham's goalkeeper in the 11th March 1978 clash, was the 19-year old Eddie Niedzwiecki who would go on to join Chelsea with Thomas and help them to the Second Division title, before retiring from the game at 27 years old through a horrendous knee injury. He would eventually go on to join Arsenal in late 2000 as reserve team coach – the man who he replaced? George Armstrong, who had tragically died from a brain haemorrhage during a club training session.

Rewind back a bit to Arsenal's goalkeeper John McClelland – he sadly died at the age of 35, from a brain tumour. And if you want another Arsenal connection – Ian McKechnie, who Wright drummed out of the club due to him both being overweight and having a nightmare game against Staevnet of Denmark. He ended up playing for Hull City … and under none other than Terry Neill.

Those coincidences and parallels just wouldn't let up.

McKechnie's time at Hull City was a fantastic story as he held legendary status – not only due to him saving a penalty from Denis Law in the 1970 Watney Cup Semi-Final and then missing the final one from the spot, but also the events surrounding a F.A Cup Third Round match on 4th January 1969, against Wolverhampton Wanderers, where The Tigers went down 3-1.

Unwittingly, he started a cult craze among Hull City fans of throwing oranges into his goalmouth before kick-off and at half time. "This began after two young fans, with whom he exchanged greetings, spotted him one day in the street near Boothferry Park eating an orange," wrote Jack Davidson of the Scotsman. "At the next home match, a couple of oranges were thrown into his goalmouth whereby he peeled and ate them during the game. From that point on, the craze grew and continued for years with the Hull fans regularly throwing hundreds of oranges towards his goal in tribute to the popular keeper. At times, it reached epidemic proportions as at the game against Wolves, when about 600 oranges cascaded on to the pitch at half time, necessitating a late second-half kick-off as the whole ground staff were deployed with bags and brushes to remove them."

Football and its beautiful history, eh – who could not love it?

"I can't believe you are on your laptop at half-four in the morning," Emily said, as she came into the kitchen.

"Jesus Christ, M," I said.

"Did I scare you," she grinned.

"Yeh, slinking around the house like some frigging ghost."

That made her laugh

"Anyway, make yourself useful and make me a coffee."

"Why are you up so early?" she asked, whilst dutifully doing as she was told and rooting around for some coffee beans to grind.

"I couldn't sleep."

"Yeh, yer could," she smiled. "You were flat out until Sammy fell out of bed, and then when I put him in with us I saw you doing your creeping and that was about three o'clock."

I wasn't having that and I totally denied being a creeper.

"Yeh, yer do," she grinned. "Which of my shoes don't you like?"

"None," I told her.

"There you go," she said. "That's creeping as I know yer definitely didn't like those boots I bought the other week."

"That's only because I prefer to see your legs and your ankles."

"Uh – that's okay then – I'll let you off," she smiled. "Anyway, why are you up so early?"

"I need to get this Terry Neill-thing finished."

"I can't believe you're still working so hard," she said, as she snuggled up at the side of me to take half my chair.

I'd never considered doing a documentary on Arsenal to be work, and I told her as much.

"I'm not relishing having both our lives taken off us over the next few weeks," she sulked, regarding her having to do *Live at The Warehouse*. "I've got to go in for some publicity shots today."

"Offset the stuff what you don't like, with the stuff you do," I said. "Go treat yourself."

"That's a bit like exorcising me demons," she twanged.

"A bit," I said. "I see coming home as the thing that I like the most."

"You always say right nice things," she smiled.

"I can definitely offset that train of thought," I winked.

"Well, I'm definitely not doing the ironing."

It was strange how she could always *read* me.

That morning I called in to see her doing the said publicity shots and had a natter with her number one fan – Dean, who told me that he would like to ask her opinion on the soundtrack of *The Invincibles*.

"She'd really enjoy doing that," I told him.

The publicity photographs I thought, were nothing short of great.

"I know *The Warehouse* has a sixties theme, but I think I'm getting a bit too old for all the short dresses," M told me.

I disagreed totally and demanded a personal catwalk show at 7:00 pm.

"Well, I can definitely do that for you," she smiled.

Meanwhile, I had more pressing business and a date with Wrexham. The highlights and goals never do a game of football the real justice it deserves, just as the match on television can't – even as good as the camera work is. The Wrexham versus Arsenal match itself was an astounding cup tie and as good as you could possibly get. We were fortunate in that we didn't just have the five-minute segment – we had the whole 90 minutes-plus and I descended into the new TV room in the studios to go back in time. And when I say go back in time I really mean it.

Terry Neill had told Harry Miller of the *Daily Mirror* prior to the game that after seeing Wrexham a few times that he thought them a very well-organised side that played what he termed as "smashing football".

"The Wrexham fairy tale is over. Arsenal, London's pride and the bookmaker's favourites, had too many guns and too much power for the famous cup-fighters from the Third Division – but only just," wrote Richard Bott of the *Sunday Express* after the game. "If Welsh fire and passion had been enough, then Arsenal would have gone the same way as so many other distinguished clubs before them."

Arsenal had beaten them 3-2.

Malcolm Macdonald had been extremely praiseworthy in his assessment. "They do everything so simple and they created more problems than any other side this season," he said. "My opinion is shared by all the other lads in the dressing room – they will walk promotion."

"Against a team prepared to run until they dropped, tackle as if their lives depended upon it and vociferously backed by a partisan crowd of 25,547, Arsenal showed the class which separates the divisions," wrote David Miller of the *Daily Express*. "With that superb footballer, Liam Brady directing proceedings they were able to raise the tempo of their game whenever necessary."

Brady had an input in all Arsenal's goals floating a diagonal cross for Stapleton to have a header palmed away by Eddie Niedzwiecki only for MacDonald to tap home after 24 minutes.

Wrexham had what looked like a legitimate goal ruled out in the first half when they sprung Arsenal's offside trap and put the ball in the net via what was a three-man move. The reasoning why referee Tommy Reynolds ruled it out was a strange one. It was left to 27-goal Dixie McNeil however, to equalise and notch up his number 28 on 66 minutes – which was more an uncustomary Jennings fumble and an own goal than anything else. Brady provided the cross for Alan Sunderland's looping back header on 70 minutes, which was not too dissimilar to Billy Hughes's goal against Arsenal in the 1973 F.A Cup Semi-Final. Three minutes later Liam Brady slung a high cross over from the right, which resulted a beautifully executed pull-down and right foot drive from an acute angle by Willie Young to put Arsenal 3-1 up. However, it didn't end there, and as with the Walsall match in the previous round, Arsenal's Sammy Nelson was duped into a mistake as Mel Sutton took a diagonal pass from the former-Coventry City and Welsh international midfielder Les Cartwright and duly turned Nelson inside out before crossing for Graham Whittle to reduce the deficit and have Arsenal under pressure for the remaining few minutes of the tie.

I then had a visitor – my wife still dressed in her publicity-shot garb.

"I thought you'd gone home?" I said, whilst still totally engrossed the match.

"What without me saying ta-ra?" she shrugged. "I'd never do that."

"You look nice," I noted.

"Je ne peux pas attendre jusqu'à ce soir," she said, as she locked the door behind her. "Je veux que tu me jettes sur le canapé – et baise ma cervelles dehors."

"What's that mean?" I inquired.

"Tu devries essayer de le traduire," she smiled. "Try and translate it."

"I got the sur le canapé bit – as I remember le poulet sur le table – the chicken is on the table, that you were learning the kids the other day," I told her. "Does canapé mean biscuit …or bread?"

She clipped and clopped around me before kicking off her shoes and clambering over me.

"Oh right – obviously, it doesn't mean biscuit or bread, then?"

I ended up missing what was Les Cartwright fluffing a sitter from five yards and what was Willie Young's winning goal after 73 minutes and ended up with my hair all over the place, a face and shirt full of lipstick and make-up – and half the studios looking at me when I finally got out of the room. As for M? She just waltzed out, totally unperturbed and without a care in the world.

I learnt a few things during that steamy 11-minute encounter: 1) that canapé didn't mean biscuit and meant couch; 2) that cervelles meant brains; 3) that baise meant a *yer know*; and 4) that I had do number four on number one, in order to dislodge number three. If you get that?

Like Benny Hill in one of his early 1970's clips with model Jenny Lee Wright, I was "Learning all the time".

"Seven o'clock and don't you dare be late," she winked on leaving the room.

I managed to scrounge footage of every league game prior to Arsenal's appointment with Orient in the F.A Cup Semi-Final, none of which they lost and all of which they should have won – however, the injury to Graham Rix had just been the start of the injury pile up that Terry Neill could have never ever have envisaged and which showed the perils of having a small squad with a manager who had a nil-philosophy for rotation. What would happen during this short period of time would be thought about the following season, when Arsenal would ease up and lose silly games in their run up to the 1979 F.A Cup Final, winning only two games out of a possible nine between the Semi and the Final.

On 18th March 1978, Bristol City came to Highbury looking to replicate their result in the previous season after their promotion into the top flight, but witnessed an Arsenal performance that literally blew them away.

Whilst the Orient manager Jimmy Bloomfield was recuperating from an operation to remove the cancer that would eventually take his life, acting manager Peter Angell and chairman Brian Winston were treat to a masterclass that blew Arsenal's recent performance against Manchester City out of the water.

"Some of their football was a joy to watch and it is easy to see why they have done so well this season," Angell said afterwards.

"If anyone imagined Arsenal were about to take the next few days at a light canter in pre-preparation for their F.A Cup Semi-Final with Orient, then they were shown to be heretically wide of the mark," wrote Robert Armstrong of the *Guardian*. "Arsenal clearly regard the position of runners-up in the League Championship against a place in Europe next season, should they fail to justify their rating as cup favourites. Bristol City must have wondered what marauding demons had taken possession of Arsenal as they raced into a 3-0 lead in 21 minutes. Arsenal hit their stride so perfectly with a blend of precise passing, clever running and accurate shooting that proved virtually irresistible."

"The performance was typical of some of the stuff that we have been playing this season," said Terry Neill after his sides 4-1 win – which really could have been doubled.

"Bristol had no answer to the languid left foot magic of Liam Brady, the fastidious passing of Alan Hudson, who looks like he is back to stay and the fierce drive of the fair-haired David Price," wrote Alan Hoby of the *Sunday Express*.

On 11 minutes Alan Sunderland dribbled down the right before laying off the ball to Macdonald whose dummy trickled to Stapleton who duly stabbed home. Four minutes later Arsenal were 2-0 up after Sunderland chested down a weak clearance by City and smashed the ball past Stirling-born goalkeeper John Shaw, who was once on Leeds United's books. On 21 minutes David Price latched onto a cross by Macdonald and executed a what was described as an imperious goal – a diving bullet header to make it 3-0.

"It was good to see Price – the underrated guy in Arsenal's engine room who keeps the big wheels of Brady and Hudson turning, so hungry for the ball," wrote Hoby, before adding. "Once again the red wave swept down on the Bristol goal. From Brady to Hudson the ball flowed and a magnificent Hudson through-ball found Stapleton in the box and despite the presence of three defenders the striker turned so sharply, that he created an opening before shooting diagonally into the net."

This was Arsenal's most dominating game thus far under Terry Neill and was perhaps the best first half of football that I had ever seen them play.

"Hudson came out for the second half with his socks down," wrote Tony Pawson of the *Observer*. "However, no one on the Arsenal side seemed to be taking it too seriously until Sunderland stretched Shaw to two instinctive saves."

There were a few rumours knocking about the following day, one of which was confirmed by Ray Bradley of the *Sunday Express* in that Arsenal were to hot up the chase for Blackburn Rovers' John Bailey – a target, for Aston Villa, Forest, Everton and Birmingham – the latter of who Arsenal were due to play up at St. Andrews on the Tuesday night.

Arsenal had been looking at left-back Bailey since the New Year – and had what was described as a "big bid" turned down by Rovers, which was something that was confirmed by Bradley in a later edition when The Gunners turned their attention to Sunderland's Joe Bolton – who reported, that they were ready to offer a player in part-exchange. That player – Sammy Nelson?

The other rumour was that with Butch Wilkins side-lined through a niggling groin injury, new England manager and former number two at Arsenal, Ron Greenwood was considering giving Alan Hudson his third cap for the forthcoming international with Brazil.

Arsenal travelled up to Birmingham, who as a club were all over the place at the time, with their supporters so upset with how the club was being run, that they were planning a mass walk out 15 minutes from time. A crowd of 22,087 saw Trevor Francis claim an early lead for his club after latching onto some uncertainty by Willie Young on 18 minutes, whereby following a lofted pass into the area from defender Gary Pendrey it bounced off him for Francis to take the ball, race past him and lash a shot past Jennings.

The truth was, that Birmingham were absolutely outclassed – however, Arsenal's supremacy in possession couldn't give them a return in goals with Macdonald forcing three tremendous saves from goalkeeper Jim Montgomery before half-time. As with last season's preceding fixture,

Francis wasn't done and with The Blues boardroom under pressure from the supporters and with Arsenal lying in wait with a planned half million raid, he knew that he was well and truly in the shop window and could have had a second after 44 minutes, but saw his shot hit an upright.

In the second half Arsenal upped the pressure and Brady hit a 25-yard shot against the post before Hudson dispossessed midfielder Terry Hibbitt and looked odds-on to get his first goal for the club – however he was crudely brought down in the area by a combination of the player that he had dispossessed and the maker of the first goal – the 29-year old Pendrey.

Brady converted the penalty and Arsenal were level.

"With Brady, Alan Hudson and David Price in control of the midfield, it was remarkable that Arsenal needed a penalty to get the ball in the net," wrote Dave Horridge of the *Daily Mirror*.

That much was true, however it could have been worse for Arsenal when after 82 minutes, a fierce shot by Francis deflected off Sammy Nelson and on to a post.

For all Arsenal's work rate and effort, Francis could have had a hat-trick – however, there was more to his game than just scoring goals with Patrick Barclay of the *Guardian* stating after the game, "Trevor Francis once again allied his effervescent skills to unselfish commitment."

The journalist's words rang very true. Francis was one hell of a player.

Next up were West Bromwich Albion – the team who had been rather prematurely tipped to meet Arsenal in the 1978 F.A Cup Final and a team who were only five points behind their hosts. That being the case they were expected to give Arsenal a much sterner test than they had done during the Christmas fixture down at The Hawthorns.

"If Arsenal do meet West Bromwich Albion on the more important occasion of the F.A Cup Final at Wembley they have established a clear case with this win for staging the presentation of the trophy in a dramatically different fashion," wrote Frank McGhee of the *Daily Mirror*. "The Arsenal players should be allowed to climb the steps to the

Royal Box before the match, collect their medals, do their lap of honour waving the big silver pot and then kick off. That way, Albion fans could empty one end of the great ground and set off for home as the first whistle blows. It will spare them the humiliation of seeing their team speared by Liam Brady's passes, chopped up by Alan Hudson's lazy-looking expertise and swallowed by the swaggering Macdonald."

Arsenal put on their best performance of the season – even better than they had performed against both Manchester City and Bristol City. Everything was now falling into place. As a team, they were on fire.

On what was a quagmire of a pitch and against intermittent weather – including howling rain, Macdonald hit a hat-trick – however, it was a pure team performance that helped him get it. His first goal was a header after 35 minutes, made firstly by Young and Rice playing the ball out of defence and from a pin-point right-wing cross by Alan Sunderland, who had outpaced left-back Derek Statham to get it in. However, something would unknowingly define the remainder of Arsenal's season and on 47 minutes, Sunderland was involved in a challenge for the ball – again with Statham, and had to limp off the field, being replaced by Graham Rix. An X-ray would prove conclusive in that he had sustained a stress fracture in his right leg and would miss the next seven games including the F.A Cup Semi-Final through injury.

Rix however, proved more than a capable deputy and by taking over the left of midfield it appeared to give the side a much better balance and allowed Hudson and Brady to boss the centre of midfield, and boss it they certainly did. On 56 minutes Rix played the ball to Hudson who from an impossible situation made a lovely jinked pass to Brady, who took it to the by-line and from what Julie Welch of the *Observer* stated was a "devastating angle", whipped the ball back to Macdonald who lashed the ball home with a fierce left foot drive. 2-0.

Four minutes later Brady provided a beautiful through-ball to Macdonald who blazed through the West Bromwich defence, rounded Tony Godden and smashed the ball home with his right. 3-0. However, Arsenal weren't done and on 76 minutes Willie Young headed a glorious fourth from a corner by Rix.

"There was something more important than the goals and the victory that happened for Arsenal – something deeply involving the erratic genius of Hudson," added Frank McGhee. "This man appears to have learned at last, the lesson that however good a person is at what he does – and Hudson is very good indeed – life, from its limitless deck of cards, can always turn up someone superior. Hudson's own considerable talent has been trumped by Brady's, and the encouraging thing is that Hudson appears to both realise and accept it. Hudson, the player who always used to insist on running the show, because nature, instinct and ability prompted him to do so, is now quite happy to lift his head, look for Brady and Arsenal have become all the better for it. They were superb and if they carry on like this, all the other teams could be trailing and gasping next season."

"Macdonald obviously deserves much credit since he was responsible for three goals," wrote Julie Welch. "However, the two men chiefly responsible for this win were Brady and Hudson. Brady's contributions have always been vital and now that Hudson has opted to play out of his skull, Arsenal are producing some excitingly unorthodox stuff and West Bromwich Albion could not live with them – they are marvellous players."

David Lacey of the *Guardian* was in a similar mindset. "Brady and the new Hudson, an industrious revelation now that he's started running again, dominated the field between the penalty areas," he said.

As for our erratic genius?

"I can't remember any of those games," Huddy told me.

The studios were a hive of activity and after piecing together more of the documentary and signing off on a few things I decided to knock off around 6.30 pm – my remit of things to do had been made plainly obvious, but what I would get home to I had no idea.

Whilst I was with Jeanette I knew exactly what I'd be coming home to – me generally getting nagged. With Emily, I never knew what to expect and this evening would be no different.

"Wow – you look beautiful," I said.

That smile!

"You didn't have to get all dressed up in your posh clothes," I added.

"Yeh I did," she said. "We're going out."

"Are we?" I shrugged. "Who's watching Herbert?"

Mmm. The erratic genius with the languid lazy-looking expertise, whose whiter than whites were spinning around inside our washing machine and who was on the sofa at the far end of the new kitchen both bouncing my youngest on his knee and talking him through the Wrexham game.

"Where did you get that from?" I asked, about him being in possession of the Wrexham v Arsenal game. "That was in my office."

"Yeh, I know – I got one of the girls to make me a copy and seeing as you won't let anyone in the TV viewing room at work – I thought I'd watch it here – you know, as your house is the nearest."

"And you'd kill two birds with one stone, so to speak," I said. "And drop in some more washing?"

I had a nod returned my way.

"So, why are you babysitting?"

"M made me some tea after she'd done arguing with Sooty's wife, so I suggested she take you out," he said. "I've booked you in at the French Relais on King's Road. They know me down there."

"Sooty's wife – what, Libby?" I shrugged. "She's been around here?"

"Yeh, not half," he said. "I would have offered to chuck her out – however, I couldn't get a word in as M was too busy telling her off for all the nasty things that she had said to you."

"Listen mate – she'd still be here getting told off now, if it really was for **all** the nasty things that she'd ever said to me."

"I've never seen your M get mad before," he said. "It was quite an eye-opener."

"I have," I told him. "Useless tradesmen or call centres are her forte."

"Phew – that looks, phew," once phewed a plumber.

"Look – can you do it, or can't you? If you can – do it, if you can't – then I'll get a real plumber who can," she'd said.

Paying bills to automated voices were her biggest bug bear however, and I'd often here her growling through all the promotional shit and all the 'Please press 1. Please press 2. Please press 3. Please press 4 and Please press 5 …or if you would like to speak to a real person with a brain just stay on the phone and somebody from Pakistan who can't speak a single word of English will assist you."

Then, they have the gall to say that it's progress.

I picked up Sammy and gave him a cuddle as Huddy pointed out a few things – one of which was that the Wrexham game hadn't been one of his better ones. "Brady won the match almost single-handedly," he said. "His performance was flawless on a pitch that was reminiscent of a mud heap."

He also told me a story about Wrexham's left-winger that day, in that he visited him open prison towards the end of his 18-month stretch for counterfeiting money. "I was gutted that we never played together," Huddy said. "He would have been a great Arsenal player, because I have never known a player so revered at every club he played for."

Huddy was quite right. He was a lovely player, but a player's head must be in the right place and Mickey Thomas's most certainly was not.

"My life has had some real highs and lows," Thomas told Henry Winter of the *Telegraph*. "I was a kid growing up on a rough council estate, we didn't have much money and I was thick. The former Wrexham manager John Neal understood that I had demons in my system. I used to hate walking the streets. I felt intimidated. Although I came over happy, boisterous and cocky, I wasn't. That was a front. On the opening day of one season for Wrexham, against Walsall, I had an outstanding game, but I couldn't handle the pressure. I walked out. John found me and brought me back."

"Thomas's industry, flair and eye for goal meant some manager was always ready to sign him, regardless of his disciplinary baggage," wrote Duncan Mackay of the *Observer*. "Most lived to regret it. Perhaps his non-conformism explains why such a talented and hard-working player won very little: A Third Division Championship with Wrexham and the Second Division title at Stamford Bridge."

"I must have been eight or nine when I remember seeing Mickey Thomas on the left wing for Manchester United with that long, flowing black hair," Ryan Giggs had told Robin Turner – a journalist with *Wales Online*. "He was left-footed, skilful and entertaining, and what was even better – he was also Welsh. From that day, I wanted to be Mickey Thomas."

You had to hand it to Giggs. He did exactly just that. He too had dark hair, was left-footed, skilful and entertaining, played left-wing for United and got 64 caps for Wales. The only thing he did slightly different to Thomas was that he shagged his brother's wife and not the wife of his brother-in-law.

We definitely ought to do a documentary on the player, I thought.

Chapter 45

Mr Spock goes to Washington

"How dare you come around here after what you said to Lee about his children, you horrid woman," was M's opening line on Libby coming to the house in search of her missing husband.

I certainly knew where he was, but as Emily rightly said, there was no way on earth that I wanted neither Sooty's bullshit nor her around. Nor was I overly happy that Kev Burrows had been ringing me in search of his wife. There had certainly been some tête–à–tête between me and M surrounding the subject and even more so, after Sooty had arrived at work one morning.

"Who the hell are you – Mr. Spock?" I asked.

The stupid git looked like he'd gone Mach 2 and had only gone and indulged in some back-street Botox. Looking a pillock aside, he and his new beau – Kev's wife, had moved into some rented house on Washington Road top side of Upton Park and Libby had been scouring the streets for him. His advice to her prior to him changing his phone number was: "I'm filing for divorce – get the house put up for sale."

He had tried angling me for one of the flats over on White Lion Street – however, with ITV soon to be taking over, that certainly wasn't happening.

On the Jeanette front, she'd been surreptitiously tasked by Libby to locate Sooty through me, however M had told her straight: "I want nothing to do with it Jin – I know she's your friend, but she's certainly not mine."

I thought with her getting Paul back in tow, that things would go back to how they were – however, they hadn't and she was still a bit stand-offish. With me that is and not with M. Neither of my kids were ecstatic about how things were, especially my daughter, who had started giving her mum some grief by way of a bit of back chat. Emily revealed very little of what was said between them outside of the kids, but I certainly knew the main problem. Her life was going in the exact opposite way that she had wanted it to go. She looked at both me and M and truth-be-known, wanted Paul like a hole in the head. Ross Bain was back touring and the bullshit that came with him was what she wanted – not feeding from the scraps I gave her. ITV's buyout of LMJ and White Lion plus all its assets also pleased her about as much as did Sooty. The thing with Jeanette was, as much as I loved her – and I did, the more you gave her, the more she would want. Ross was a rising star and she jumped on board expecting to enjoy the journey. However, it hadn't quite worked out like that.

A few weeks ago, we had braved a wet Wednesday evening to watch my lad play his first full game of football – a friendly against some under-nine's from Barnsbury and she had stood well away from us and had said very little.

"Are you okay?" I inquired afterwards.

"Fine," she lied.

"Dad, can I come back with you and M?" whispered my daughter.

"You can for me," I said.

On asking Jeanette the question, I saw her expression change, so much so, I thought she was going to explode – however, my lad coming over and asking my opinion on something, cut dead what could have been a volatile response.

"Was I rubbish, dad?" he'd asked me.

"No, you were brilliant mate," I told him. "Why would you ask that?"

The game had been a bit like the Wrexham v Arsenal F.A Cup game – all end to end stuff and tactically very Billy Wright-stroke-Les Shannon, with his team coming out 6-5 winners, along with my lad scoring at the wrong end after his weighty back pass had bounced over the goalkeeper while he had been trying to tie his bootlace.

All things considered, they obviously needed to tighten up their defence.

"Do they need a hand?" Huddy had asked, on me telling him the result.

"You start coaching them and they'll boozing in nightclubs by the time they're eight."

That had him growling at me a bit.

When he was at Arsenal – Huddy that is, and not my lad, he had been applauded by Denis Hill-Wood on several occasions for taking time out to take five-a-sides with the club's youth players. Huddy's situation was not too dissimilar to that of Charlie Nicholas a few years later – in that the press are only after headlines, and as crass as it sounds, and it does – Huddy taking time out to take youth training sessions or Charlie visiting sick kids in hospital doesn't carry the weight of the former in a night club hours before a match or the latter humping either Samantha Fox or Suzanne Dando. That's the tabloid media for you – very agenda led.

We had walked to the car and it had been a case of both kids with us and not their mum, which must have been extremely hard for her to take. It would only get worse too, especially after Ted the Head rang M to let her know that my lads school football matches would be played at 9:30 am on a Saturday morning.

"Will I have to pack it in?" asked my lad.

"No – why would you say that," I replied.

"You'll never get to Manchester before one o'clock if you watch me – especially the away games as we have to travel miles."

I sat him down and told him straight. "If an old lady could brave the hail, wind, sleet and snow to watch her grandson play football, then so can I with you," I said.

"Your dad would never ever let you down," smiled M.

"Really, dad?" he asked.

"Really."

It was one thing saying it – however, it was another actually doing it, as my daughter duly informed me.

"Dad it's going to be really, really hard for you," she said.

"I suppose you could go up to Liverpool with M on Friday night and we could travel up Saturday after the match."

"That's certainly not happening," my wife informed me. "We have certain rules – don't we Harmony?"

"We do – we don't split the family up," smiled daughter. "Ever."

"Too true," said Emily, whilst giving my daughter a cuddle.

"New York told us exactly that, didn't it M?" added my lad.

"It certainly did," she said, before thinking about it a bit. "So, how would ITV feel about you turning up late as you'd not get there until half-past two, maybe three o'clock?"

"I run a football channel," I said. "It would be a bit hypocritical of them denying me from watching my lad play school football, whilst at the same time trying to promote the sport."

"That's a good point," said Emily.

Good point or not, when I told the head of sports he hadn't been that enthusiastic about it.

"ITV 7's football carries itself," I told him. "I'll be there before each kick off and if needs-be, I'll have some hi-tech webcam or something rigged up in the car."

That swung it – that, and him taking a step back and thinking about it a bit more. The family aspect? Grass roots football? He knew there and then that he was on to a winner. A dad watching his son play primary school soccer and then travelling over 200 miles to do his job. That was a pretty cool dad. It also sounded a pretty cool TV station for letting the pretty cool dad do it!

"We wouldn't be able to have our Friday nights up in Liverpool, though M," said my daughter.

"We would still have our Friday nights – but here," she smiled. "Just like before. Just so long as we are all together and we all have each other, nothing will ever change."

"I suppose we could travel down Monday morning's," I said. "We've done that before."

"That's definitely do-able," said my wife.

There it was. Until Jeanette decided it wasn't.

"You've had a hair up your arse ever since you turned up in Italy," I told her, on dropping off the kids.

"Rubbish," she lied.

"I really don't think it is Jeanette," I said. "You're a fantastic mother and I mean that – but don't go ruining that by using the kids as pawns."

That was a bad move by me as she went ballistic.

I got back in that night and let Emily know what had been said, and the reply I got was one of silence.

"What?" I shrugged.

"Nothing," she lied.

"M, if you have something to say – say it."

"She wants you back."

"What – she told you that?" I asked.

"Jeanette doesn't have to tell me a thing like that – I know. I've always known."

"Why?" I shrugged. "We made each other miserable …well she certainly made me miserable."

That had her laughing.

It didn't have me laughing – Jeanette had insisted that both kids had to be back at hers by 6:00 pm Sunday. That was until M told me different a few days later when I got in from work to see her in *mad professor*-mode with all the kids down in the kitchen.

"What are you all on with?" I asked.

"Spud got stung by a bee at school and M's showing us about alkaline's and acid's," said my lad.

Emily had put some vinegar in a glass and dropped some bicarbonate of soda into it – my kids absolutely loving the reaction of the explosion of carbon dioxide that it made.

"If a bee stings you it injects an acid," explained my daughter. "If a wasp stings you it injects an alkaline. M's showing us how to neutralise it."

"Neutralise it, eh?" I winked. "That's a dead cool word."

"If a wasp stings you, you put vinegar on it and if a bee stings you, you can use bicarbonate of soda – but M says toothpaste is probably better as it's a sort of cream," added my daughter.

"I think I'm going to be a scientist when I get older," added my lad.

"Yeh – right," my daughter replied. "Last week you were going to be a racing car driver for Ferrari and the week before that you were going to be a drummer for Guns 'n' Roses."

"I think they are ace," said my lad.

"You only like them because M told you that their guitarist was called *Slash*," argued his sister.

"No I didn't – I have a great taste in music," said my lad, before needing a bit a reassurance from his wicked step mum. "M said, didn't you M?"

"I did love," smiled Emily.

"You're a right divvy," said my daughter. "You thought Foo Fighters were a Chinese football team."

Half the time they had Emily creased with some of the things that they said to each other.

It transpired during our bedtime routine – Emily sat on the bed yacking until gone quarter-past one, that she had been around at my ex's that afternoon and there had been some *clear the air* talks and rather strangely I was informed of some of their content.

"Jesus Christ, M – you actually said that?"

Oh yes – she actually had.

Emily had stayed close to Jeanette – even during the *Ross*-thing, which at times had her grinding her teeth such was the bullshit that came our way. I would say it was because of the kids, which to some extent it was – however, there was a little bit more to it than that. They liked each other immensely – especially as they had quite a few things in common – me obviously being the main thing. However, in the background, it was like in one of Huddy's *Godfather* movies in that you keep your friends close, but your enemies closer still. Although Emily never saw Jeanette as a threat with me – and she didn't, she was more than aware of the manipulation tactics my ex often used with the kids and she had seen that at first hand over in Italy and more recently with school football. Most wives would have possibly thought – *Nah, I can't be doing with that shit* – however, M wasn't just any wife – she was one that backed my corner 100%. Emily had stayed close – had involved her, kept her in the loop, and even kept her parents in the loop. I'll make no bones about it, Emily wanted her close and that familiarity and friendship meant that M was possibly the only one who could ever get away with talking to Jeanette as she did. "You can ask me Jeanette as I've certainly no problem with telling you," Emily had told her. "However, if you are afraid that you won't like the answer then I'd urge you not to."

"I messed up with Ross," she'd initially said.

"Big wow," had been Emily's response. "I'd consider that a good move, not a bad one."

"And I've lost Lee and now I feel I'm losing the kids," she'd added.

"How are you losing the children? Have mine if it makes you feel better," she had joked.

"I look at you and I feel such a bloody failure," Jeanette had said. "How do you do it?"

"How do I do what?" Emily had shrugged.

"How do you keep him so happy."

"Who, Lee?"

Yip – that was the one!

"So, how did she react to that little snippet of sizzling-hot information?" I grinned.

"As soon as I coaxed her in from the ledge and stopped her gibbering, I put a call in to The Samaritans," she lied.

That was M for you. Never ask her a question if you don't want to know the answer.

Back on to the Sooty problem. We'd had Libby stalking both studios, with Basher and Tony told that under no circumstances whatsoever should they let her in, which after turning her away for the seventh time had her stood screaming in the car park, so much so, I had Faranha ring the Met to have her forcibly removed.

I ended up visiting the young lovers in their Washington Road residency to relay all the goings-on, seeing as I had shifted Sooty out of the way – and put him out on the road interviewing former Arsenal players for Basher's documentary. I had to admit – Buzzy's wife was ten times better than Libby and another ten times better than the Romanian harlot with the foul mouth that was Maggie.

"So, what's happening then – you're making a go of it?" I asked.

As it turned out – they were.

"She reminds me of M," he said.

"What's that supposed to fucking mean?" I snapped.

"Nothing – just that she's nice."

An "Oh" was about as much as I could muster.

"So, how far have you got on the documentary?" he asked me.

"I'm still on with trying to put it over that this is where Arsenal actually peaked under Terry Neill," I said.

"I thought they peaked around the time they beat Juventus in the Cup Winners Cup?" he asked.

"No – they peaked in the spring of seventy-eight," I said. "Neill just never built on it and then lost one of the most prolific centre-forwards and one of the most cultured midfielders of their era."

That had Sooty laughing.

"What's up?" I inquired.

"It's just hard to imagine Huddy being cultured at anything he does the way he goes around effing and blinding at everyone."

There was a story here, which starts off with me bumping into Ray Parlour the street cleaner and sort of ends with an *Huddy-ism*, if you like …oh, yeh – and Sooty being the first to get it.

I was just loading up some gear in M's car one day when I ran into him kerbside and loitering around our bins. Ray Parlour the street cleaner for Camden Council that is, and not our erratic genius with the lazy languid expertise.

"'You okay, mate?" I said.

I got a nod, but that's as much as I did get.

"I first saw you play against Leeds at Highbury when I was about eleven," I told him. "We drew one-all. Lee Chapman scored for United and Merson equalised."

He never said a deal.

"You came on as substitute for David Hillier. It was the game where Nigel Winterburn got kicked in the face on the build up to their goal and instead of getting on with it and tracking back to cut out the cross, he went over to argue with the referee."

Again, he never said a deal.

"We played them in the cup the season after and were two-down at half time," I said. "You came in from the left running at their defence and slid one under John Lukic to pull one back and Merson hit a twenty-yarder for the equaliser."

Again, he never said a deal.

"A lot of Arsenal supporters gave Lee Chapman a hard time, but almost every time he played against us, he was a right handful," I said. "Him and Gary Speed scored."

"The defence was all over the place that day," he mumbled.

"Strange season that," I said. "Arsenal played crap, yet won two cups and both Ted Fenton and Bobby Moore died."

"Tommy Caton died as well," he nodded.

"Yeh – I forgot about him," I said. "That was tragic."

We both stood there in the street looking at each other.

"Your career could have been a bit different if Andy Sinton would have joined Arsenal that August, instead of Sheffield Wednesday," I said. "I bet he regrets his move."

"He was a left midfielder – I played on the right."

"I knew you were frigging Ray Parlour," I told him.

"Piss off," he said as he pushed his cart away. "My name's Derek."

I went back in the house scratching my head.

"What's the matter?" Emily shrugged.

"Ray Parlour was skulking around our bins again," I said. "He nearly admitted he was Ray Parlour as well."

That made her laugh.

"He told Madge that his name is Derek Wilton," she said. "Yer know, like in *Coronation Street*."

"He died recently, didn't he?"

"Who – Derek Wilton?" she smiled.

"I'm sure he did, as I remember Kirsty on about it," I said.

"He was married to Sarah Long who did *Play School.*"

"No, he wasn't – he was married to Mavis Riley," I argued. "I definitely know that as my mum used to watch it all the time."

"No, I mean in real life, yer twit," she grinned.

It was getting hard at times, to separate the fiction from the fact, as some of the things that were happening to us bordered on the surreal. Huddy knocking on the front door didn't help matters either.

"That Ray Parlour bloke is on the street again," he said.

"We've just been discussing him," said Emily, as she gave Huddy a peck on the cheek. "His real name is Derek Wilton."

"Like the carpet-bloke?"

"No, he was a character in Coronation Street," she chuckled. "In real life, he married Sarah Long who presented *Play School.*"

"*Play School?*" he shrugged.

"Yeh the pre-school children's programme with Floella Benjamin, Johnny Ball and Brian Cant," she said.

"Brian Cant?" he asked. "What – there's actually someone called that?"

"Yeh?" said Emily. "What's up with it."

"I'm certainly glad I'm not called it," said Huddy. "Although, I know a few who should be called it."

That was it, and from thereon in, if Huddy was pissed with you – you were a "Brian" – Sooty being the first to get it – and back in real time he mentioned it. "And for some reason, the git keeps on calling me 'Brian'," said Sooty in regard to the era's most cultured midfielder.

"Brian – or a *Brian*?" I inquired.

"A Brian?" he asked. "What the hell's 'a Brian'?"

I definitely felt like telling him – however, I didn't.

"We had him babysitting the other day," I told him. "He'd got Faranha to copy him the full ninety minutes of the Wrexham game."

"He also got her to copy him the full ninety minutes of both the West Bromwich Albion and Manchester United games," said Sooty. "And the Orient and Queens Park Rangers games."

"That's a lot of viewing," I said.

"He intended watching them in the new TV and Media Room after work," said Sooty. "He was going mental because you had locked it."

"He mentioned that the other day," I shrugged. "I wondered what he was on about."

"Yeh – him and Basher were trying to pick the lock for nearly an hour," laughed Sooty. "I watched them for a bit and then didn't have the heart to tell them that the door opened outwards."

That had me laughing.

"Fucking Huddy," Sooty said, shaking his head. "The erratic genius."

The erratic genius had been well-worth his moniker when two days after the trouncing of West Bromwich Albion Arsenal travelled south of the River Thames to play an Easter Monday afternoon fixture against a Chelsea side struggling in seventeenth place in the League.

The match, which was watched by a crowd of 40,764, looked nothing more than a formality for Arsenal on the windswept Stamford Bridge, with Alan Hudson to inflict the most of the problems to his former club's five-man defence, which had midfielder David Hay employed as a sweeper. Huddy had created chance after chance after chance during the first half where Macdonald put a fierce trademark left foot drive just past the far post as well as getting on to a pin-point corner by the midfielder and having his header brilliantly turned around the post by an ageing Peter Bonetti. And just for good measure, Frank Stapleton – who had been the victim of some heavy tackling, also rattled an upright.

"The 0-0 result failed to reflect the superiority Arsenal enjoyed," wrote Harry Miller of the *Daily Mirror*. "Arsenal pushed Chelsea after the interval with a series of quality build-ups that continues to suggest they can dominate the First Division next season."

"My dad was raging about the way how Arsenal treated me when I first signed for them and when they kicked me out of the hotel," Huddy had told James Lawton of the *Daily Express*. "However, he came to me after the game and said – 'Look Alan, I honestly think you would be a fool to leave Arsenal, as it can really work out for you'."

The upshot was that Huddy had still been on the transfer list and was attracting interest from Derby County – whose manager Tommy Docherty had just had a huge public spat ...with none other than Bruce Rioch, after a game at the Baseball Ground against Liverpool in which they won 4-2.

"Any manager who allows his position to be undermined by players is asking for trouble," Docherty had told Joe Melling of the *Daily Express*. "I believe in taking strong action right from the start with players who try it on, no matter how big they are."

Rioch had been criticised for his recent performances by his manager and had even walked off the field of play without permission after allegedly feigning injury in his clubs 1-1 draw at home against Newcastle United. The player had told the press that Docherty had told him that he would put him out of the game, adding that they had a right "Up and downer" with his manager aggressively poking him in the chest.

"I may have got some things wrong in my career," Hudson told Lawton. "It's time to prove just one thing now, and that is how good I am out on the field."

That is exactly what happened when the expensively assembled Manchester United side rolled into town on 1st April 1978, as Arsenal ought to have hit them with half-a-dozen goals – however Alex Stepney had played out of his skin and Bridgwater-referee Alex Rees had waved on-play after a stonewall penalty appeal was turned down after Gordon McQueen had bundled over Frank Stapleton in the box.

"The Gunners sunk United with some of the most sophisticated football I have seen this season," wrote Alan Hoby of the *Sunday Express*. "Once Arsenal began surging forward they slipped into a Rolls-Royce brand of football where dream-like approach work split United's defence like rotten timber and only some fine positional saves by Alex Stepney and brilliant covering by Martin Buchan kept United afloat."

"Arsenal are steaming unstoppable as a train in the direction of Wembley," wrote Frank McGhee of the *Daily Mirror*. "However, the most remarkable aspect of their recent success has been their ability to cope without key men. When Malcolm Macdonald dropped out recently they looked just as effective with Alan Sunderland as their main striker. When Sunderland was ruled out of the United game, Arsenal looked at least as lively; thanks to the contribution of the tricky Graham Rix who gave them the width of a natural winger. It tempts me to believe that not only will they win the F.A Cup they will also be outstanding challengers for the Championship next season."

"This was a contest of the highest all-round quality," wrote Robert Armstrong of the *Guardian*. "Arsenal thrusted forward with the confidence and sense of economy that suggests Orient's bubble is about to burst."

"Arsenal played the most superb football that I've seen this season," wrote David Miller of the *Daily Express*. "The left-sided penetration of Liam Brady, Graham Rix and Malcolm Macdonald with support from Frank Stapleton, David Price and Alan Hudson was as good as anything I've seen. It was so fluent, that it even drew spontaneous applause from the main bevy of United supporters."

Arsenal were well worthy of their 3-1 win in what was a brilliant, albeit bad tempered match where Sammy Nelson aimed a swipe at United forward Stuart Pearson, elbowing him in the face and Liam Brady and Joe Jordan had a continual spat throughout the game, not at least after Jordan had equalised Arsenal's opening goal after only 60 seconds whilst being offside, where amidst the jeers, he had stuck two sets of two fingers up at the North Bank.

Willie Young sought some recompense after being hacked down by the striker and head-butted him at the back of the head, whilst Pearson carried it on a little and elbowed Young in the face – whilst in other news, Rix sprang Manchester United's offside trap and it was left to Brian Greenhoff to Rugby tackle him to the ground.

The first goal had been scored by Macdonald after 36 minutes latching onto a beautifully struck right-foot shot by David Price which came back off the woodwork. This was after Rice had had two attempts within as many seconds to put the ball past Stepney, whilst Nelson for the hell of it tried to do the same, but minus the ball.

"Arsenal's midfield was magical. Brady and Rix bewitched on the left, whilst Hudson dominated with his shrewd passes whilst on the right," added Alan Hoby. "David Price played a positive role as well, helping to lay on two goals. Twice bad finishing by Stapleton ruined Arsenal's sophisticated build up. From one lightning Brady-Rix move the Arsenal striker completely missed the ball, before he lobbed the ball wide after a beautiful move involving Hudson, Brady and Macdonald."

The best goal of the match came after 68 minutes when from a free-kick, Alan Hudson played the ball to O'Leary who played it to Price who nodded over to Macdonald, who in turn nodded it into the path of Brady who scored from the edge of the box with a left-foot volley of sheer arrogance that went straight into Stepney's bottom left hand corner, giving the keeper no chance.

Macdonald sealed the 3-1 win after 83 minutes when Rix floated in a cross to the far post where Rice was on hand to head across the area and where the England striker beat Buchan to the ball to prod past Stepney.

It was here that Arsenal under Terry Neill had peaked. They were untouchable, although unbeknown to Neill and Don Howe at the time, a series of injuries would hinder them all the way to Wembley.

Next up however, was Jimmy Bloomfield's Orient and a game where Alan Hudson would again go back to the place it all started – Stamford Bridge.

"Of the four best passers of the ball in the game, three play for Arsenal," wrote David Miller of the *Daily Express*. "Football is primarily a passing game and Liam Brady, Graham Rix and Alan Hudson are in a class apart."

"Arsenal's back four don't mark tightly enough when the game changes and they may not react quickly enough to stop Peter Kitchen nicking a goal," former Orient manager George Petchey told Malcolm Folley of the *Daily Express*. "Of course, if Arsenal play to their full ability, men like Liam Brady and Alan Hudson will have too much for them."

Much like Dixie McNeil of Wrexham, Peter Kitchen was a prolific striker in the lower leagues and whilst at Doncaster Rovers, had been trailed by a few clubs, one of which was Ipswich Town – the team who were playing in the other F.A Cup Semi-Final against West Bromwich Albion.

Mexborough-born Kitchen had been brought to Doncaster by Lawrie McMenemy and had scored one of the goals in his clubs 2-2 draw in a F.A Cup Third Round match back in January 1974 against the current League Champions and that years eventual F.A Cup winners – Liverpool at Anfield – a game which saw his lobbed shot come back off the underside of bar in the final minutes of the game.

A £40,000 signing for Orient in the summer of 1977, Kitchen had proved to be a snip and had Kevin Moseley of the *Daily Mirror* pointing him out as "Arsenal's big talking point" and "The man Arsenal fear most" stating, "Kitchen has scored in every round of the Cup taking his season's tally to twenty-seven and this week has collected the *Mirror* Sport's Footballer of the Month award as another accolade in a season, which has brought him fame and glory."

As in the 1971 F.A Cup Final against Stoke City, referee Pat Partridge took control of the game, which was both watched by a crowd of 49,698 and which was basically over in the first 19 minutes – David Price having a vicious shot palmed away, Willie Young crashing a header against the bar, before two wicked deflections from the shooting of Malcolm Macdonald gave Arsenal a 2-0 lead – one crashing in off defender Bill Roffey's chest and the other from the face of ex-Arsenal youth player, Glenn Roeder.

"This was a muted annihilation," wrote Hugh McIlvanney of the *Observer*. "Arsenal disposed of Orient at a canter and yet had to rely for their victory on three dishevelled and unmemorable goals."

"Every probe of the Arsenal intelligentsia – Brady, Hudson, Rix and Price bore warning and after 16 minutes the threat became reality," wrote James Mossop of the *Sunday Express*. "Hudson – a man who will bring grace to the Wembley stage created the first, taking a pass from Rix and playing for a one-two off Stapleton to hone in on the goalkeeper, had the return ball played behind him and over to Macdonald, whose shot took a wicked deflection into the goal."

"For practical purposes, Orient were wholly reliant on the success of their carefully constructed defensive system in holding Arsenal's players who are producing the best attacking football in the country," wrote David Lacey of the *Guardian*. "Apart from the excellent control shown by Hudson, Rix, Brady and Stapleton, so essential in the defeat of tight marking, a notable feature of Arsenal's performance was the varied running to support the man in possession."

"Brady and Hudson flaunted their class in the midfield with relaxed and justified presumptuousness and at the front Macdonald swerved and darted among the opposing defenders," added McIlvanney. "When Arsenal became more profitably aggressive it was mainly through Macdonald, who was in one of those moods when his muscular and mobile presence is liable to make the most composed defenders panic. Hudson who has rediscovered the vigour and delicacy of touch that once made him one of the greatest prospects of British football was another insistent aggravation."

Graham Rix's mazy run from midfield and shot from the edge of the area after 63 minutes, wrapped up a comfortable 3-0 victory and a date at Wembley with Ipswich Town.

Arsenal had now gone 13 matches unbeaten and were nailed-on favourites to lift the F.A Cup with Hudson giving James Lawton of the *Daily Express* something to smile about by telling him, "I'm not playing bad, am I?"

I had a couple of coffees with Sooty and drove back into North London where a somewhat bemused wife would have probably greeted me if it wasn't for the fact that she had been stuck in the loft for the last hour and a half. "Is that you, Lee?" she shouted.

"Where are you?" and "What are you doing in there?" were obviously my initial lines of inquiry.

It turned out that the ladders had refused to stay in one place while she had been up there and that she had left her phone in the kitchen, so therefore couldn't S.O.S her predicament.

"Where's Herbert?" I inquired, whilst lifting her off the bottom rungs of the re-erected ladder.

"Jody and her mam took him for a walk," she said. "So, I thought I'd give the loft a bit of a tidy out and put some of his stuff up there."

"Her mum?"

"Yeh – they came over in Jody's new car," she said. "I never knew she was Irish."

"That figures," I winked.

"Don't be mean," she chuckled.

It still beat me how Jody had actually managed to pass her theory test.

"Are there many spiders up there?" I inquired. "I'm just asking as you've got a bit of cobweb in your hair."

I received a "Yuk", which was swiftly followed her shaking her head and her inquiring to why I was home so early?"

"I nipped over to drop off some stuff for Sooty. I did text you to tell you."

"I didn't have my phone, did I?" she mumbled.

"He's filed for divorce," I said.

"Yeh – Jeanette told me this morning. Libby was around at hers all last night really upset."

"She's not upset about Sooty – more upset about her having to flog the house."

"Has his face returned to normal," she grinned.

"Normal-ish," I said. "His eyebrows are still half way up his forehead though."

That had her smiling, but not as much as the next bit.

"It's done," I said. "The takeover."

"Aaaaagh!" she screamed before, giving me the hug of all hugs.

"I'm in with the legal people tomorrow – that's the real reason I'm home early."

"I just can't believe it," she said.

Nor could I – but there you go.

"Can you remember telling me off for that time I looked in your purse, when we first started seeing each other?" I asked.

"I've never told you off," she smiled. "I was just dead embarrassed about never having any money."

Well she certainly had quite a bit now.

This had been the big game plan. The Tall Dwarf's meddling in our affairs were what started it and during our holidays, M and myself decided to put our strategy in motion. When I got back I immediately tied everyone to three-year contracts and set about reeling ITV in. They saw LMJ along with its colourisation and White Lion and how it made money – and a lot of it, but they also wanted a 24/7 football channel, *The Invincibles* …and they wanted M back in *The Warehouse*. I could give them the lot. In return, I would get no more 6.00 am starts and 10:00 pm finishes, no more working throughout the night and more to the point – no more missing precious time with my family. The *no more worries* factor was also quite appealing, too.

Chapter 46

Trick or Treat?

The 2nd November 2015, was the day that everything was finalised – with ITV taking full control of both LMJ and White Lion. It was a strange feeling. Everything that we had built was now in the ownership of someone else. As for me, I was now just the producer of ITV 7 – an employee. Fortunately, however, with all the bits and pieces surrounding the build-up to what was an extremely intense transition, I had been given Friday and Saturday off.

Emily had not said anything to her parents the whole way through, so it was therefore something of a shock when they, along with Lucy had come down on the Friday afternoon and whilst cracking open the skulls of a few pumpkins, their Emily told them of the intricate details of scale of the deal.

I didn't get to know the details of what had actually been said, as I had been tasked with picking up the kids and then nipping to a *Sports Direct* opposite the entrance to Poland Street to pick up my lad some new football boots.

"I want white ones like that Alan Ball used to wear," he said.

"They don't do those anymore," I told him. "You'll have to make do with those silver Messi ones."

"They are rubbish," he replied, before some rather fetching blue boots with red soles took his eye. Or rather fetching blue boots with red soles, the accompanying Adidas logo and the rather exorbitant price tag, I should say.

"That's a lot of money for a pair of kids boots," I said. "They'll most likely be too small in six months."

"If M was here – she'd buy me them," he said.

"Yeh – only because you're a creep," noted my daughter.

"I'm not a creep," he argued, before requesting some enlightenment from yours truly. "Dad what's a creep?"

"Someone who says nice things in the hope of getting things," I winked. "Or in your mum's case – in the hope of not getting things – mainly me not being shouted at."

That had my daughter laughing.

"Dad always says nice things to M as well," said my lad.

"No, he does not," grinned my daughter. "The other day he told her that she stunk like an old bat."

"Yeh, but M always knows Dad's kidding," he said.

"If he said that to mum she'd have gone mental," laughed my daughter.

That much was true!

In Emily's case, she had got Mrs Sosk a birthday present – in this instance, some perfume and as women tend to do they dab a bit on their wrists …or neck …or ears. In M's case I thought she'd had a bath in the stuff, such was the audacious stench of it.

"It's *White Musk* from Body Shop," she'd told me, as she carefully went about wrapping it.

"I can well understand her husband leaving her if she wore that," I said. "It stinks rank."

"I can definitely see where you're coming from," said Emily. "It is a bit on the heavy side."

She wasn't lying and later that evening, the quilt, quilt cover and all the pillows stunk of the stuff, so much so, I had to open a window.

"What's the matter?" asked Emily.

"The smell of that stuff is everywhere," I said. "The bedroom stinks like an old folk's home."

"I can't smell it," she sniffed.

"No – that's because you're covered in it."

"Give me two ticks," she said, before nipping over to the bathroom.

Post flannelling it still stunk as bad, if not worse.

A tip for any woman: wear that and men will never bother you again! It's about on par with growing a beard or having massive feet.

291

Back in real time, we ended up getting some assistance from one of Mike Ashley's alleged overworked and underpaid employees – and I don't mean Tim Krul. "These are brilliant boots, mate," the sales assistant told my lad. "But the Adidas Purechaos are better."

"What colour are they in?" asked my lad.

"Black and red – or orange," he said. "They are the best boots in the shop."

"Are you on commission?" I inquired, post-seeing the price tag.

He didn't answer and was more interested in getting the boots on my sons' feet.

"Sound," said my lad. "These are mint."

"I want at least a couple of goals if I buy you them."

"I'm a team player," he told me as he ponced about in the mirror. "Alan told me I'm the pivot."

"Really?"

"Alan says, that when things aren't going to well on the pitch that the other players will look to me."

"Really?" I said.

"Alan says that if I work on my passing a bit more, I could end up like him."

Mmm, that was something to think about, I thought. *Erratic genius or serial boozer?*

Huddy had been spending more time down at the school than half the teachers – nominating himself as Mr Bone's right-hand man – coach, trainer, tactician, dietician, physio, talent-spotter and agent, with all the kids hanging on to his every word. If you can imagine a cross between Brian Clough and Fagan out of *Oliver Twist* …well, that would have been Huddy.

I'd known Jimmy Bone quite a few months and had never heard him swear. Since meeting Huddy however, it was as if he had caught Tourette's as every other word that came out of his mouth was a profanity – with the 'u' vowel being totally dismissed and intricately substituted by an 'a'. I wouldn't mind, but Jimmy was from East Fife.

Perhaps you can now see why Huddy kept on calling Sooty a *Brian*?

After being relieved of a penny under two-hundred quid, we walked back to the car with both kids elated when Emily told them over hands-free that Granny and Granddad were down – especially when she told them they had come bearing gifts …sort of.

"Why – what have they brought?" asked my lad.

"About twenty meat pies for Halloween," she said. "From that butchers, you like in New Ferry."

"I hope they brought some black pudding," added my lad, post phone call.

"I didn't know you'd even tried black pudding?" I inquired.

"Yeh, it's brill'," he said. "'M got the butcher up at Highbury Park to cut me some off. The butcher said that it's made from pig's blood."

"That's right," I said. "It is."

"'M also told us that there was a television programme from the olden days where they wore flat caps and smacked each other over the head with it."

"What – with black pudding?" I shrugged.

"Yeh – it had that man with the beard in it, who likes birds."

"Who – George Best?"

As it transpired, it certainly wasn't George Best as my wife duly explained when we got in. It was the bearded ornithologist that was Bill Oddie during his far eastern adventure to Rochdale, where he learned the martial art of *Ecky Thump* and fought a Kung-Fu expert who had an uncanny resemblance to the supposedly daft one out of The Monkees and a middleweight boxing champion who possessed a rather striking resemblance to one of the Black and White Minstrels.

"Goodies – goody, goody, yum, yum," Emily winked.

The reality was, that it had been Emily who had been the one bearing gifts and she told my lad to look in what she termed as the *something drawer*, which was a place in the kitchen that each time the kids came to the house, there would be *something* in it that would be both *something* of a treat, but *something* which they would also have to learn about.

"Wow!" exclaimed my lad on opening it.

It was the dead scary *War of the Worlds* DVD, which had both he and my daughter immediately on their respective laptops surfing the Internet and trying to find out everything they could about it.

"It says here that H.G Wells wrote it," said my lad, as his finger followed the text on the screen. "That was him who did the *Time Machine* with them Morlocks – wasn't it M?"

"That's right love," she said. "He did."

"It says that he also wrote the *Invisible Man*," he added, before doing a bit of pondering. "I wonder what that one's about?"

"Probably a man who's invisible you divvy," eloquently stated his sister.

"What about you Harmony," chuckled Emily. "Can you tell me something about it?"

That was no problem, as when my daughter swotted up on a film, she really swotted up on it.

"Steven Spielberg directed it," she said. "He did that *Catch Me if you Can* film that dad likes because it's Christmassy …and *Jaws* with that shark."

"Shark?" inquired my lad. "What shark?"

That was it. My lad was fascinated by them. Shark's that is.

"It's about a really big shark that terrorises a seaside town," Emily told him.

"What – like Blackpool?" he inquired.

"No, it's in America," his sister told him. "You don't get Great White Sharks in the Irish Sea."

"I once read somewhere that there had been sightings of them," Emily said, which certainly caught both kids' attention, before having them both diligently reading up on not only H.G Wells and Steven Spielberg – but of all the different kinds of sharks that swim in Britain's waters. And all that from a DVD, that Emily had bought off eBay for just £1.98. I had to hand it to my wife – she stimulated the minds of both my kids and made everything seem extremely interesting.

As for *War of the Worlds* – it had been extremely compelling viewing, so much so, that we ended up with both kids in bed with us.

"Dad – just imagine if those big wind turbines off Burbo Bank near Granny Sil's were them Tripods," whispered my lad. "That would be dead scary, wouldn't it?"

"Mega," I said.

"Where would we go if they did come alive?"

"Probably down Hamilton Square Tube station," I told him.

I got up around 5.30 am and managed a jog before coming intp the house to the smell of coffee and the radio on, along with the pure perfection of what was a gorgeous wife griddling bacon and sausage and a not so gorgeous second son slinging cereal everywhere.

"It's a bit foggy out there," I said.

"It'll be right good for Halloweening," she smiled.

"How long has Herbert been up?"

"Just after you."

"He's got some really disgusting table manners, M," I said, after picking a spoonful of Weetabix out of my hair

"Yeh, he takes after his real dad," she lied.

"Why – was he disgusting?"

"Oh yeh," she said, as she slithered up to me. "Right filthy."

I was just about to inquire into a little bit more of Emily's totally and utterly filthy and disgusting second life when we were somewhat interrupted as her mum came down the flight of stairs and into the kitchen.

"I didn't hear you get up, Mam," noted her daughter.

"Obviously," grinned Sil', post-earwigging of our conversation and walking over to her grandson to remove an upturned bowl of cereal from his mitts and to give him a cuddle.

"Definitely to be continued," whispered my wife.

The foggy start to the morning continued and school football was delayed by a few minutes – not so much because of the visibility on the pitch, but because the referee had been stuck in traffic near Essex Road Train Station, which gave Mike plenty of time to get acquainted with the use of the video camera.

"Remember what I told you," Jimmy Bone said to his players prior to the referee arriving. "Always look for a man to pass it to and don't panic when in possession."

Obviously, my lad didn't adhere to a thing he said and once *Clive Thomas* had arrived on site had set off the scoring, putting through his own goal after only three minutes.

He had a right knack for it. From an in-swinging corner from the right, my lad caught it full on the toss with his left-Peg and volleyed it straight into the top corner.

"Oi, you great pudding – you're supposed to put the ball in the other net," I told him.

Huddy made his presence known exactly twelve minutes in – shuffling up to the side-lines, taking a cup of coffee off M and seeing his tactics in motion.

"They're one-down," I told him. "Anyway, I thought you were covering the West Brom v Leicester game up at The Hawthorns?"

"I swapped with Dan Betts," he said. "I'm due over at Stamford Bridge for the quarter-to-one kick off."

The next thing I know he's hobbling up and down the touchline with his cup of coffee in one hand and doing a bit of pointing with the other, both telling young Irving to unfold his arms and take an interest and calling the referee a "Dickhead" for not blowing for a rather blatant handball in the oppositions area, which amidst the laughter on the touchline, duly earned the rather angelic-looking ex-England midfielder a booking.

After fifteen minutes, my lad's team equalised, and then went 2-1 up – and then scored another – and another – and another, so much so, I started to lose count. "What's that five or six?" I asked Emily's dad, whose teeth were now chattering.

"Five," he said.

I would have asked Huddy, but he was still busy galloping up and down the touchline barking orders and arguing with the referee. Nothing changes!

At half-time, the score was 5-1 with my lad extremely pissed off that he'd scored an own-goal – again.

"It happens," I told him. "Most players score an own-goal at some point in time."

"What every week?" he grunted.

"Well not every week, no," I said. "That in itself is a little bit special."

"Did you ever score an own-goal?" he asked me.

"I don't think so – but even if I had, it wouldn't have been as good as yours," I told him. "Not even Peter Cech would have stopped that."

Whilst Jimmy Bone and his Cockney-number two – or in Huddy's case, his *Namber Two*, talked tactics, Emily gave my lad some moral support. Firstly, by giving him a cuddle and secondly by slipping him some illegal doping material in the guise of a cereal bar. "I shouldn't really be telling you this," she whispered. "But this contains honey."

"Honey?" he whispered back, whilst looking cagily around. "Why, what does honey do, M?"

"Honey has loads and loads of glucose in it," she told him. "Glucose makes your brain think quicker, so when the other children get tired you won't."

I'll tell you something – *Popeye the Sailor-Man* wasn't in it. He wolfed that cereal bar straight down and a few minutes after kicking off the second half, he slid in to make what look like a career-ending tackle on the other team's centre-forward at the edge of his own box to retrieve the ball, before seemingly looking around to lay the ball off for what felt like an eternity.

"Carry the ball, Jamie," shouted Huddy. "Run at them with it."

He more or less did exactly that, although it certainly wasn't a quick attack – more thoughtful than anything, and as he nonchalantly carried it forward looking for that all-elusive pass he evaded four challenges, before metaphorically donning his cape and bursting into the oppositions area, half-rounding the goalkeeper and smashing home the ball off a post.

I was literally gobsmacked. We all were.

"Granddad," he shouted post-his arms in the air celebration. "Did you get that one?"

"I did, lad," laughed Mike.

"Aw – he looks just like you in that photo," smiled Emily.

Emily was right – he looked exactly like me.

Huddy gave his Brian Clough-type thumbs-up and wink and that second half my lad literally ran the other team ragged and although he didn't score again, the referee gave him man-of-the-match.

"Thirteen-one, eh?" I winked, as I rubbed his head and a smiling wife zipped up his coat.

"We need the goals just in case we're level on points at the end of the season, M," he said, before wanting it confirmed by yours truly. "Don't we, dad?"

"You do mate."

He wouldn't shut up and on getting in the house he asked Emily for some polish and a duster, so he could buff-up his man-of-the-match cup.

"Was it a really good goal, dad?"

"Possibly the best I've ever seen," I told him, as I copied the digitalised footage onto my laptop before ripping a DVD.

"Are you going to save all my matches on DVD?" he asked.

"Of course, I am," I said. "It'll be something I can look back at and show your kids when I get old."

That certainly got him thinking.

That afternoon, whilst Emily and the kids watched Dr. Jekyll and Mr. Hyde – Rouben Mamoulian's 1931 version with the dead scary Mr. Hyde who possessed the tousled mullet and horrible great big set of choppers, which combined made him look like a rather unkempt and even nastier Gabriel Paulista – if that's even possible, I had been setting up a camera in the lounge.

It had been the very first-time ITV 7 had ever run without me. On ITV's head of sport's recommendation Abigayle Gibbs had taken the anchor and was showing everyone that she was absolutely first class, whilst my lowly remit was to preview the Swansea City versus Arsenal game via my front room. Possibly a first for TV? Who knows.

All I did know was that Emily had made sure that the lounge was absolutely spotless and that the vase on the piano had been freshly replenished with flowers and that all the framed photographs had been both washed-down and meticulously arranged.

"You're going a bit overboard, aren't you?" I inquired, as she dragged the stepladders around the lounge, as she had dusted the coving the day before, making it plainly obvious that I was the only one who could ever call her a "dirty cow".

"I'm just glad yer actually told me what was happening," she had said, whilst jiffing down the piano legs before ever-so slightly exaggerating. "I would have died of embarrassment if you hadn't."

"I was thinking of doing the match preview from the ironing room," I'd winked.

Emily's face had been a picture after I'd said that!

As for my Swansea-Arsenal preview?

"I'm really not sure which Arsenal will turn up," I said. "They were absolutely dire against Sheffield Wednesday and I have a feeling that they will get slaughtered over in Munich."

"What do you think the problem is?"

"I really think it's the manager, Abigayle – he has too many favourites, never seems pick the right side and his body language reflects the lack of fight or bottle in his players."

"How do you see today's game going?" she asked.

"Knowing Arsenal – they will survive a few early scares and batter Swansea," I said. "Giroud will definitely score and Fabianski will show everyone, both his technical agility and the reasoning behind why he never made it at Arsenal."

"The score, Lee?"

"Three-nil to The Arsenal."

What a guy?

Over at the coffee shop, Fosis had put £500 on exactly that score line and got both his money back and a return of £7,000 – and the phone call I got off him bordered on something else. "You and your family come to my house for dinner."

It was a fine gesture but Halloweening took precedence and as such, by the time all the results had come in, we had a house full, including both Jeanette and Paul, with my ex being coaxed by a rather scary – albeit totally racy-looking Emily, to get in the spirit and doing a bit of dressing up.

"You have got to be joking?" Jeanette told her.

"No – come on Jin," she grinned. "It'll be great fun."

"What really?"

"Yeh – sure," M told her.

Emily and my ex spent the next twenty minutes' upstairs, the latter scratching her head at the fact that my wife actually owned a nun's costume. "Put it on – you'll look really scary," Emily grinned. "Lee nearly had a heart attack when he saw me in it."

"What would you want something like this for?" probed my ex.

"It was a silly idea really," Emily told her. "He thought I looked like Vanessa Whitlock."

"Who's she?"

"A witch," she said.

"Yeh, but why would you want it?" Jeanette asked, whilst looking through a few more oddities in what was M's fully loaded walk-in wardrobe.

"So, I could be a nun," Emily told her. "What d'yer think I'd want it for?"

In the end and still scratching her head, my ex succumbed to become one of the Magdalene sisters, which was something that my daughter thought was brilliant. "Wow, you look really scary, mum, but you haven't got a hat," she said. "And witches definitely don't wear high heels."

"I'm not a witch – I'm a nun," she said.

"Dad, do I look scary, dad?" my lad had asked.

"Yeh, *shit-your-pants* scary," I lied, which totally had him laughing – especially as I immediately got told off by Emily for swearing.

Lucy initially considered herself far, far, far too mature to even think about going Halloweening until she saw her big sister and Jeanette dressed up in all the spooky clothes and then had the witch who was supposedly a nun, asking her why she didn't want to go *Trick or Treating*?

"I'm too old," Lucy had said.

"You're not too old?" Jeanette shrugged. "Look at me? Look at your M?"

"Yeh – but you're doing it because of our Harmony and Jamie."

"And you'll have children at some point and you'll be doing all the things that me and your M are doing now."

"If they don't give us any treats, we egg their windows," enthused my lad.

"We definitely do not," laughed his mum.

"Dad used to – didn't you, dad?" he asked.

I had to admit I had slung a few in my time, the last being at Sooty's house a few years ago – when one of the eggs actually went straight through a downstairs window and which was something that shocked me as much as its occupant.

"You never told me that," grinned Emily.

"I do have a few secrets."

"I haven't any costume, though," Lucy told my ex.

That soon changed when Mrs Sosk poked her head through the back door. "Are you all having a party?" she asked.

I wouldn't have described pie and peas, hot hogs, chilli con carne and pumpkin soup as a party – however, my daughter certainly did. "We are," she said. "We are all going trick or treating first, though."

"Aren't you going with them, Lucy?" asked Mrs Sosk.

"I've not brought anything down," she replied.

"I reckon I've got a few things over in my house for you," she winked. "That's if you want?"

"That'll be great Madge," Emily beamed.

Mrs Sosk having a few things in her house was an understatement as she was something of collector-maniac-stroke-hoarder-stroke-professional mourner – and when Lucy returned, Morticia Adams or Lily Munster weren't in it. Sil' nearly had kittens. All in black and wearing a hat with a mourning veil.

"Wow – you look great," said Jeanette.

"No – you don't," said my lad. "You look dead scary."

Mrs Sosk had also put a white cake make-up on her face, which had made her look ten times scarier, so much so, my lad was a bit reluctant to look at his young aunt.

The rather scary quintet trawled up and down Frederick Street across Ampton Place and down Ampton Street and then back again, with all the kids and undertook some mega-*Trick or Treating*. As for Emily and Jeanette? They even got propositioned by some young University student in one of the flats near the corner of Grays Inn Road for a rather unearthly Ménage à trois.

"Calm down and take it as a compliment," the lad had said after Emily had threatened to have me come around and "Pan his face in", as she so eloquently termed it.

"Talking like that in front of the children," she had chuntered.

An hour out traipsing the cobbles and £135.61p and a bucket of sweets later – with absolutely nil amount of eggs thrown, the so-called Halloween party ensued, whereby my lad immediately showed his Granny Sil' the fine art of saucing up a jumbo hot dog in between trying to work out his one-fourth share of the *Trick or Treating*.

"Nearly thirty-three pounds Gran," he smiled. "I'll be able to buy more Beezer comics from the Christmas jumble sale."

"No, you will not," said his mum.

Over a short period of time, half my lads stash of Beezer's had worked their way from ours down to Clerkenwell, where Jeanette had been tasked with finding a place for them in his bedroom, which was already packed to the rafter's.

"You don't need these," his mum had told him.

"Yeh – I do," he'd said. "They remind me of my dad."

"How do they remind him of me?" I'd asked Jeanette a few days after he'd supposedly said it.

"You and your grandma," she'd told me.

I never paid it any attention until I had seen him multi-tasking with the hot dog and Halloween money, whilst at the same time talking to Mike. "Which comic did you read Granddad?" he inquired.

"*Tiger* and *Roy of the Rovers*," he said.

"Were they funny?" asked my lad.

"Not really, they were action comics," his granddad told him. "They had stories about football and other sports in them."

"He's even started rolling them up under his arm and taking them into the toilet with him," Jeanette told Emily. "He's in there, ages."

That certainly sounded like me at my gran's.

"Have you fell down the thing?" my gran would often shout.

It was a great night and after everyone had retired – or in Jeanette and Paul's case, gone home, Emily had changed from being Yutte Stensgaard's dead sexy character out of Hammer Horror's *Lust for a Vampire* and back into my wife, and as such, we sat chatting into the night.

"What do you think is the best time we've ever had together?" she asked me.

"We've had loads of great times."

"Yeh, I know – but one that sticks out in your mind," she said.

"What – all of us together – or just me and you?" I inquired.

"Me and you," she smiled.

"Pick a date – any date?"

"Christmas Day."

"Apart from Christmas Day," I said.

"Okay then – er, the twentieth of April," she smiled.

I picked up my phone – checked a couple of things on it and had a bit of a think. "You picked me up from work around six o'clock and you'd had your hair done," I said. "I remember you picking me up in my car as you were having yours serviced. I watched you make fish in parsley sauce, new potatoes, cauli' and broccoli and we had a TV and cuddle night. We watched Peter Sellers ...possibly the *Smallest Show on Earth*."

She was gobsmacked. "I can't believe you can remember all that."

"The exact same date the year before I remember taking a beautiful woman up to Hull to watch Arsenal, and after seeing how she was with my kids that weekend I knew there and then that I would have to marry her."

"That's so lovely," she said.

"I just checked the dates with the Arsenal matches and I can sort of remember the times we had around them. I don't have specific nice times – I always have them."

"Paris was good, wasn't it?" she said.

"It was definitely up there."

"That smelly cheese in the bedroom," she grinned.

"I remember – I thought it was your feet."

"You did not," she gasped.

"That night we'd had a meal opposite the Seine and you'd wore a tight black dress and a pair of shoes with no backs in them and you had to walk back to the hotel barefoot as they'd been crippling you," I said. "You ordered veal cutlets and I had a fillet steak and the waiter brought you a Sauvignon Blanc instead of a Chardonnay and you were telling me about one of your auntie's hysterectomies."

"I can't believe you can remember all that," she smiled.

"Nice times are fairly easy to remember, M."

"Mmm, unfortunately, bad times are just as easy."

"We keep having nice times and soon the bad times won't have any room to rear their heads," I winked.

"So, we keep on doing what we are doing now, eh?" she smiled.

I got up early Sunday morning as I had what felt like a thousand and one things to do – a couple of Premiership matches and a full round up of matches through Europe –

however, my orders from the ITV's head of sport were to stay at home.

"Stay at home?" I asked. "Why, what's the matter?"

I didn't really receive an answer – although he did mention Chris's *Terry Neill Years* and the fact that ITV had picked up on the invoice and had wondered what the head of LMJ's security and my wife were doing owning a company that were producing a documentary – an Arsenal documentary at that.

ITV had just coughed-up an unbelievable amount for all or assets and now here they were appearing to haggle over some poxy proforma invoice for a documentary, which I had been working on since the spring.

"Well just quash the invoice if it bothers you that much," I said.

"What's the matter?" Emily asked, on walking down into the kitchen.

"ITV have rumbled the Basher documentary," I said. "And that I've been putting it together with their assets, partly during their time and partly using their employee's."

"But you've spent hundreds of hours on it working from home," she said.

She was right – I had. Fortunately, Emily had marked those said hours down – over 400 of them – although half of that would have been watching football matches, which in my mind could hardly be construed as *work*.

"I told you my fastidious, finicky and secret scrawling down of man hours would come in handy," she winked.

"No, you didn't. You just wanted to use them as a bargaining device in a bid to negotiate more TV and cuddle time."

"Yer know me, then?" she grinned.

As it transpired, it wasn't the invoice. The CEO and a few suits had wanted me in London and had demanded they see me on Monday morning – at 8.00 am sharp.

I wonder what that's all about? I thought.

I slipped back into the spring of 1978. Arsenal had been unbeaten in 13 matches, had a date in the F.A Cup Final pending against Ipswich Town and had just dished out a series of heavy defeats: 3-1 v Manchester United, 4-0 v West Bromwich Albion, 4-1 v Bristol City and 3-0 v Manchester City.

Their opponents Queens Park Rangers however, had major problems. Not only were they in a precarious position in the League and staring down the barrel of relegation, they also had internal problems including having some unhappy players – one of which was the enigma that was Stan Bowles.

Bowles had publicly criticised some of his team-mates work ethic and said that he couldn't see himself playing in the old Division Two. I mean, why should he? He was not only Malcolm Macdonald's nemesis, but a truly gifted player who deserved much better and against an in-form Arsenal, he helped gun them down – his side coming out 2-1 winners.

"Stan Bowles showed the skilful side of his split personality last night, to halt Arsenal in their sophisticated stride," wrote Steve Curry of the *Daily Express*. "The mercurial little man who declared just two days ago, that he would not follow Rangers into Division Two has almost certainly saved them from that fate."

"On a cold Loftus Road evening, and with England manager Ron Greenwood in the director's box, Bowles showed the form that will remain Rangers' trump card in the remaining matches," wrote Harry Miller of the *Daily Mirror*. "Bowles scored one goal, manufactured another and made sure that the relegation pressure is heavily back on West Ham and Wolves. The super Bowles show started as early as the third minute. He threaded a pass through the middle and as Arsenal's defenders hesitated Don Shanks scored with a low shot."

Bowles' goal came after 68 minutes after he seized on to a wayward back header by Sammy Nelson to makeshift defender David Price to put Rangers two-up.

There was more to the story than Arsenal's casual manner in self-belief of the adulatory headlines given to their recent performances, which Richard Yallop of the *Guardian* had suggested. Arsenal had lost centre-half Willie Young to a hamstring injury after a heavy tackle from Don Givens, with

Price having to drop back and substitute John Matthews taking his place in midfield.

"Many of Arsenal's patterns in the first half were a delight to watch with Hudson, Rix and Stapleton playing their way out of the congested areas with slickly executed five and ten yard passes," wrote Yallop. "Arsenal displayed such an abundance of talent in such casual manner in the first half that it was almost as if they were playing in an exhibition match."

Arsenal had the ball in the net after 75 minutes when Rangers keeper Phil Parkes had been confronted by 18-year old and soon-to be-remanded to a detention centre Arsenal fan, James Porter – however, referee Tom Bune strangely stopped play and re-started the game with a drop ball leaving Arsenal to reduce the deficit a minute from time after Dave Clement had brought down substitute Matthews, leaving a rather inconspicuous Liam Brady to score a penalty.

Terry Neill said that his team played some delightful one-touch football with Hudson going close in the first half and Brady and Rix extremely unlucky not to see goals – the former producing a great save from Parkes, whilst the latter had a shot skim the cross section of the upright and bar.

Sometimes in life, you don't get the rewards one's endeavour deserves. And this was one of those instances. The truth was however, that Arsenal's bubble had burst and injuries – firstly to Alan Sunderland and now Willie Young, were firmly underlining the fact that Neill's decision not to build on his squad earlier in the season was coming back to haunt him.

The following Saturday, Newcastle United were due down at Highbury, with Steve Walford drafted into central defence for his first ever start in an Arsenal shirt since his low profile move from White Hart Lane in the summer.

With just four minutes on the clock Stewart Barraclough had picked up on a loose ball in the Arsenal midfield and had fed Alan Kennedy out on the left to square the ball past an onrushing Jennings – however, Newcastle's ex-Burnley midfielder Geoff Nulty failed to hit the net and saw his shot come off the underside of the bar.

"It was a shabby first-half performance," wrote Bernard Joy of the *Sunday Express*. "There was sloppiness in The Gunners' passing and a lack of fight by the men up front who were too often caught in the offside trap."

"Confidently expected to canter away with it, Arsenal instead played nowhere near the marvellous standard that we have now come to expect," wrote Julie Welch of the *Observer*. "They spent an embarrassing 75 minutes being given the run around by a side who were one of the season's earliest write-offs."

"It's a devastatingly familiar story. Teams cruise to Wembley, fancy themselves, lose the final and waste the season," wrote James Lawton of the *Daily Express*. "And Arsenal looked utterly locked into that problem for most of the game."

The most Arsenal had mustered were three headers by Walford, two cleared off the line by John Blackley and Alan Kennedy, with the third coming back off the bar, whilst Hudson had dropped in three pin-point crosses for both Macdonald and Stapleton – all of which were headed over.

Newcastle took the lead after 60 minutes when a speculative 30-yard cross-cum-shot by Mickey Burns confused not only Pat Jennings but Geoff Nulty, and hit far post before nestling in the back of the net to send The Magpies contingent of travelling fans in the Clock End delirious with joy. It had been coming. This however, forced Arsenal into kicking up a bit of momentum and Liam Brady equalised from close range after Macdonald had had a shot blocked and Stapleton's follow-up had been mishit.

"Fortunately, Arsenal have three players in Alan Hudson, Liam Brady and Graham Rix who find playing badly too much of a strain," added James Lawton. "All three picked their feet up to remind their colleagues that a place in European football next season might be at stake and if Hudson and Rix continue to dovetail so neatly around the brooding talents of Brady it could be bad news for Alan Sunderland, who expects to be back in action prior to the F.A Cup Final. Hudson's ambling control always threatened to turn this low-key game and he sent in a beautifully floated cross from the right with all the nonchalance of flicking a speck of dust off his lapel, for David Price to ram home the winner.

"Alan Hudson produced another performance to suggest that he has booked his place in the F.A Cup Final," wrote Nigel Clarke of the *Daily Mirror*. "His second half display and the ball that set up the winning goal had the stamp of class about it. Hudson's performance lifted Arsenal when it seemed like they would never score."

The man of the match that day made all the headlines a couple of days later.

"Alan Hudson, whose career in English football seemed at an end earlier this season, when he was playing for Arsenal reserves could well be back in the England side for the game against Brazil at Wembley," wrote David Lacey of the *Guardian*. "Hudson has only played for the full England side in the spring of 1975 when he had an excellent first half against West Germany and was retained by Don Revie for the European Championship game against Cyprus, only to withdraw from later games that season because of injury, and England manager Ron Greenwood has been trying to contact Arsenal for permission to call the player into the squad. "

"Alan Hudson was called up by England last night," wrote Harry Miller of the *Daily Mirror*. "And he joins the squad for the prestige international against Brazil at Wembley, with every chance of playing. So, in a season that started in ruins for the talented midfield man, could be about to end in glory. Little more than a week ago, Hudson helped Arsenal reach the F.A Cup Final and late yesterday England manager Ron Greenwood decided to bring in Hudson."

"Ron Greenwood last night sent out an emergency call for Alan Hudson, Arsenal's former problem star," wrote David Miller of the *Daily Express*. "Hudson will team up with Tony Currie in midfield for England against Brazil – his first full international since 1975."

"Revie had played him in an Under-23 game against Hungary in Budapest the following year but then dropped him because he was disappointed in the players general attitude," added David Lacey. "Only recently has Hudson started to turn in the sort of committed performances that marked his early days at Chelsea and at Stoke City, but it cannot be denied that he has played a considerable part in taking Arsenal to this year's F.A Cup Final."

"Alan has re-emerged with the help of Don Howe," the England manager told a packed press conference. "He is 26, which is when a player should be at his peak. If he is willing to show total involvement, then the opportunity is there for Alan to be a big part of the England set-up. Players' attitudes change by their performance on the field and not by talking about it."

Hudson's hard work had brought him an England call-up – however, the return for his endeavour would be short-lived.

Legend would have you believe that there had been crossed lines with Greenwood's phone call – that he took the call in a pub – that he told Greenwood to "fuck off". The truth was that although Hudson still didn't feel that he was playing at his peak, he had picked up a throat infection, that not only ruled him out of the England game, it also forced him out of the following League game up at Elland Road – a fixture where Arsenal had not won in 40 years – the last time being a 1-0 win in front of a crowd of 29,365 with the winning goal in the last minute coming from none other than Bremner …Arsenal's Gordon Bremner, that is.

The prelude to the Leeds match was extremely interesting, not at least in the last six meetings where Arsenal had been spanked 3-0, 6-1, 3-1, 2-0, 3-0 and 2-1. More recently however, Liam Brady had been voted runner-up in the 1977/78 Football Writers' Association Footballer of the Year and Pat Rice had been badly injured in a training ground incident, where he went into a tackle with David O'Leary and injured his right ankle, with suggestions being made by John Lloyd of the *Daily Express* that there would be little or no chance of the player making the F.A Cup Final.

"It was a complete accident," explained Rice. "However, I have always been something of a quick healer, so who knows?

There were also a few other Arsenal connections elsewhere. Graham Rix made his first start for the England Under-21 side in the Semi-Finals of the European Championship – a 2-1 defeat in the Vojvodina Stadium, Novi Sad against Yugoslavia. This was a match he played both alongside Steve Williams and under none other than Dave Sexton.

It was also a match in which he had played against Red Star Belgrade's 23-year old midfield schemer, Vladimir Petrovic – the player who would ultimately sign for Arsenal and who would be seen by many as the player who would replace the void that was left by Liam Brady. It is strange how things work out, as neither the mentioned transfer fee nor the player himself turned out anything like the way Neill or Arsenal thought it would.

Football's politics initially scuppered the transfer and once he did play for Arsenal, the hustle and bustle of the English First Division and the player's lightweight frame made Neill re-think his strategy and the player ended up going to Royal Antwerp – even though some of his performances in the Arsenal shirt at times, bordered on an outlandish kind of brilliance.

At Red Star Belgrade, Petrovic was considered as one of only five legends of the club. He was captain of both club and country and had won the 1980 Yugoslav Footballer of the Year award picking up 34 international caps, five Yugoslav League Championship titles, six Yugoslav Cups and through a very defensive-style of football, reaching the final of the 1979 UEFA Cup, knocking out Arsenal in the Third Round 2-1 on aggregate (1-0 and 1-1), and losing to Borussia Mönchengladbach in the final by the exact same scoreline. A contentious penalty after 15 minutes, which was converted by one time Arsenal target Allan Simonsen settled the affair at the Rheinstadion in Düsseldorf. This was after a 1-1 draw over in Belgrade.

It was in the 1978/79 UEFA Cup tie that Neill had taken his first real look at Petrovic, a man Harry Miller of the *Daily Mirror* had described as Red Star's most outstanding player.

"The goal was started by a sharp exchange of passes between Muslin and Petrovic – two of Red Star's best players," wrote Richard Yallop of the *Guardian*. "Duško Lukić crossed from the right flank and with Pat Rice unable to cut out the cross, Yugoslavian international Left-winger Miloš Šestić knocked it back into the goalmouth courtesy of Willie Young's head for Cvijetin Blagojević to drive the ball home after 13 minutes.

Arsenal had been trailing Petrovic for seven months and on the actual transfer being finalised, the player had told Joe Melling of the *Daily Express*: "I am fulfilling the dream of every Yugoslav footballer in joining Arsenal. I regard the club as the most famous in England and I hope to make them as successful as Liverpool have been in recent seasons."

On 28th July 1982, the *Daily Express* reported that Arsenal must wait 10 days for the Yugoslav F.A to forward Petrovic's playing permit.

"I am still waiting for clearance from Yugoslavia and I am sorry that it is not here already," Petrovic explained. "Some top officials in the Yugoslav F.A have told me that there would be no problems, so I hope all will be well."

All wasn't well, however.

The player had been training with Arsenal and was due to make his debut in the friendly match in the Rotterdam tournament against Feyenoord on 6th August 1982. However, the Yugoslav F.A convened an emergency meeting in Belgrade and decided against the sanctioning of two high profile transfers – that of Petrovic's £450,000 move to Arsenal and fellow 54-cap international attacking midfielder and 1979 Yugoslav Footballer of the Year Safet Sušić's £400,000 move from FK Sarajevo to Paris St. Germain.

In another Arsenal connection, the Yugoslav F.A also accepted the resignation of Arsenal's former managerial target and the man Hill-Wood and the board originally wanted to replace Bertie Mee with – Miljan Miljanić.

"Due to the Yugoslav national teams' abysmal showing in the World Cup, their F.A are looking for scapegoats," Arsenal secretary Ken Friar told Steve Curry of the *Daily*

Express. "Terry Neill was devastated and his heart bleeds for the lad. He said that it is going to be extremely difficult to explain the situation."

Petrovic would have to wait until 1st January 1983, to play for Arsenal – and then it wasn't the suggested transfer fee, but a £40,000 deal with an option to buy.

On kicking off what was his short Arsenal career, which consisted of 19 starts, he was considered a marquee signing – however, his main problem was that he wasn't Liam Brady and was it not for the lack of backtracking and tackling he could be possibly described as *more* Alan Hudson.

"I don't have any hard feelings about Terry Neill," Petrovic told Steve Curry of the *Daily Express* the day after the news broke of his former managers sacking. "However, I don't think he gave me a proper chance at Arsenal – a club that was my great love."

In other news and prior to the showdown at Elland Road, Leeds United had moved to replace Joe Jordan and had gone and raided Terry Neill's former club Hull City and paid £75,000 for none other than 23-year old John Hawley.

With Hudson sick and Rice and Sunderland out, Neill brought an unfit Willie Young back into the side in place of Steve Walford – even after the youngsters' impressive full debut the week before, the latter of which would be the start of a relationship with the manager that would force several transfer requests – the first of which would come to light in early October 1979, with his manager flatly turning it down. "He's under contract and he will honour it," Neill told the press.

Walford – a target for West Ham United at the time, would also be joined by both David Price and Alan Sunderland in wanting a move away from the club, with Malcolm Folley of the *Daily Express* also stressing that Willie Young wasn't entirely happy about being dropped from Arsenal's starting line-up. "If I'm dropped again, I'll have to have a chat about my future," he told Folley.

John Matthews and John Devine were also drafted into the Arsenal line-up – the latter making his full debut for the club and before a crowd of 33,263 – just ten more than what had watched them labour against Newcastle United the week before.

Leeds attacked from the off with Tony Currie dictating the game for the first 20 minutes, only for Arsenal to hit them on the counter attack and score three goals in a devastating 11-minute spell.

"Arsenal suggested that they were going to take the afternoon off. They simply handed the ball over to Leeds and dared them to do something with it," wrote Don Hardisty of the *Sunday Express*. "Leeds proceeded to do everything with it, except score – with Tony Currie as supremo they stroked the ball about with consummate skill. In one move they strung together more than 20 consecutive passes. As a knitting pattern, it would probably be superb, as a winning tactic it was useless, because for all Currie's prompting, the other forwards just could not finish."

A free-kick by Liam Brady was glanced into the net by Frank Stapleton, which opened the scoring on 23 minutes. Just two minutes later a powerful corner by Graham Rix and pressure by Frank Stapleton forced new signing Paul Hart to head into his own net and after 35 minutes Liam Brady put Macdonald through, who raced past Trevor Cherry and hammered a left foot shot past goalkeeper David Stewart and into the bottom corner. From nothing Arsenal were 3-0 up.

"Tony Currie was too good for the rest of the Leeds team," wrote Michael Morgan of the *Daily Express*. "He was always thinking several seconds ahead of them."

This was also huge feature, if not the main *problem* with Jon Sammels', Jim Baxter and indeed Alan Hudson's play.

The quick-thinking Currie did pull a goal back after 37 minutes, driving the ball into the roof of the net – however, Arsenal held on with future-loanee Ray Hankin having a header well saved by Jennings and after 78 minutes having an effort ruled out for offside, with Arsenal eventually coming out 3-1 winners.

Next up, Liverpool at Anfield – the team who had been extremely fortunate to put Arsenal out of the League Cup – however, as with the closely fought Semi-Final, this was another game that would dictate the course of Arsenal's 1977/78 season.

"Liam Brady, star of Arsenal's midfield, was the centre of an injury scare last night – and with the F.A Cup Final only ten days away," wrote Derek Wallis of the *Daily Mirror*. "He was carried off after 37 minutes, returned a couple of minutes later, but was replaced at half-time by John Matthews."

"Double blow as Brady limps off," wrote Alan Dunn of the *Guardian*. "A greasy pitch made many of the players tentative on the turn. Brady – the man who gives Arsenal's midfield character and substance, injured his right ankle late in the first half and joins Rice and Sunderland as the other walking wounded."

"Injury to Liam Brady has put Arsenal on the Wembley torture rack," wrote Derek Potter of the *Daily Express*. "Brady limped out of last night's 1-0 defeat at Liverpool with an ankle injury that will begin an anxious 10-day countdown to the F.A. Cup Final. Arsenal and England physio Fred Street, said 'I don't want to talk about odds. We'll just have to treat the injury and hope'."

David Fairclough hit Liverpool's winning goal after 24 minutes, after latching on to a weak back header by the still-struggling Willie Young and although Hudson helped Arsenal pick up the momentum in the second half, Arsenal were never really in the match.

However, what all the tabloids had not been told – but what had become in certain parts obvious, was the sudden drop in form of Pat Jennings.

Against Liverpool he had made a brilliant save to tip over a 25-yard screamer by Jimmy Case, but against Newcastle United he had made an uncharacteristic mistake of misreading the play that let in Geoff Nulty – the player who Case would eventually end the career of – to have a clear shot at an empty goal. Jennings had also let in goals in the match against Queens Park Rangers that he would have normally saved.

"Arsenal's secret, hidden for two months has been revealed," wrote Nigel Clarke and Tony Stenson of the *Daily*

Mirror. "Pat Jennings has been playing with an injured right ankle and has been having intensive treatment – playing with the aid of a pain killing injection and having his ankle heavily strapped."

Arsenal's drop in form and injuries, were indeed related.

I watched ITV 7 from home that afternoon and was invited – this time by Becky Ivell, to preview the Everton v Sunderland and Southampton v Bournemouth games from our lounge – both of which I called correctly, although I certainly never expected The Toffee's to put six past Watford-bound Costel Pantilimon.

It had been a strange weekend, which would get stranger the following morning post-meeting with ITV.

In other news, the Derek Tweedy show starring his very special guest star M, had hit more than a few buttons, not at least my wife's, who when I got up to *The Warehouse* was sat at my desk, both crossed-legged and rather deep in thought.

"You're done early," I said.

She was. I had been in with the ITV's hierarchy since early doors and I fully expected to see Emily still acting out her last scenes until daft o'clock, with me having to pick up Herbert from Paul's sister Chrissy's – however, she had completed them all before lunchtime.

"I didn't really have to do a great deal of acting to be honest," she said. "I'm just hoping that you'll not be too mad."

Mad – why should I be mad? I thought.

Uh. After seeing the face of an extremely bullish and smug-looking ex-West Riding farmhand when I'd arrived on site, I should have known that there had been something a bit untoward.

"Why, what's happened?" I inquired.

I then got the intricate details or my *supposed* mum's appointment with the *supposed* chiropractor and muscle specialist – including his chaise longue substitute – i.e. a long leather bench, complete with arm, leg and thigh restraints along with the other prop – namely a multi-speed magic frigging massager that looked like one of the great big microphones that Jody uses on set and which the *supposed*

316

chiropractor and muscle specialist used to iron out my mum's *supposed* thigh strain.

"You what?" I gasped.

"My knees *went* as soon as I saw it, Lee," she told me. "I couldn't help myself."

"I can't believe I'm hearing this."

"I'm glad we only had to do three re-takes," she said. "I could hardly walk afterwards."

"Are you making this shit up?"

"No, of course not," she said.

"I'm just asking, as at times you do have a tendency to embellish certain aspects of your alter ego," I said. "Mainly that of you being an unfaithful wife and nymphomaniac when out of my company."

I was then given the intricate details of the said ironing out process.

"Anyhow, Dino said I was brilliant," she said.

"He would do – he's a bigger frigging pervert than Sooty."

"So, if you're looking for any ideas for Christmas present's," she grinned.

I made a point of giving our rather fruity director a kick up the arse until I saw him in the editing suite along with Abi – and diligently dropping the extremely hot scene into the timeline of events.

"Wow," I said.

"I've never known an actress get so engrossed in a scene," Dean told me. "M's ad-libbing is sheer perfection – she makes it all look so very real."

You didn't have to be fucking Hercule Poirot to work out the answer to that one, I thought.

"I'd like her to try out for a part in a film that I'm due to do," he said.

"Oh yeh – like this, is it?" I asked, whilst still watching at my heavily restrained wife squirming about at the hands of Doctor frigging Lovelace.

It turned out that Dean, was due to direct some film in the spring about some low rent gangster during the 1950's called Johnny Holiday – the story of which, was to be set in

Philadelphia being that the character has to go on the run after killing a loan shark that is tied to the mob, but whose life is made ten-times more complex due to his promiscuous wife – the latter obviously being Dean's shoe-in part for my rather weak at the knees wife with the *so-called* superb acting skills …mmm, or so I thought.

"What d'yer reckon?" he asked.

"She's not even starred in anything on screen and she's already frigging typecast as some brain-dead blonde who can't say no to sex," I said.

"It's not like that at all," said Dean. "I'd like M to try out for Desiree."

"Desiree?" I shrugged. "Who's Desiree?"

"She's a career girl with an extremely high intellect who falls in love with his wife."

"Girl?" I sort of cagily inquired. "His wife?"

"The wife has a bit of an affair, the upshot being that she – Desiree, eventually kills the gangster to be with his wife."

This sounded an absolutely brilliant film – 1950's America, gangsters, unfaithful wives and more to the point – sophisticated lesbians.

"You're casting for Desiree," I told my wife some twenty-seven minutes later.

"Am I?" she shrugged. "Who's Desiree?"

Chapter 47

Six

The **6**th of November was never my favourite date and after ITV's *Live at The Warehouse*, Emily and I sat looking at each other down in the kitchen.

"Only another eleven to go," she said.

The *Live at The Warehouse* show was the one thing that Emily didn't want to do. It was also the one thing that I didn't want Emily to do. What made it even worse is that I wasn't even the show's producer anymore. ITV had other things in store for me and as we sat across the kitchen table from each other, we knew that the next few months could test our marriage more than anything – however, her show wasn't the real problem. ITV had bought out a struggling, albeit minor TV station over in the United States that ran with stuff such as *The Wendy Williams Show* along with naff re-runs of *Hart to Hart* and *Hardcastle and McCormick*, and as such had a business plan that would entail a major investment and a huge rebranding exercise. ITV America was the project and I was to become its CEO.

It was a fantastic move, if indeed I was a career-driven person. However, as anyone who really knew me would tell you – being *career driven* wasn't me at all. I had been foolish to think that the tail could wag the dog in that I could manipulate a buyout of my firm and then run out my contract doing the job I loved the most. With ITV, it is plain and simple: they are a multi-billion-pound corporation that have a game plan and as such, they always get what they want. They wanted a foothold in the United States and they knew with me as its face, they stood a great chance of getting exactly that.

Our life was nothing short of perfect and to be told that I would be living Monday to Thursday in New York wasn't really something I was happy with.

"Fly back Thursday night, and you have your weekend," ITV's CEO had told me.

That was hardly the point. I had fought tooth and nail for my family to stay together and here I was now being told that out of every seven days – I would lose four, plus the thirteen-hour flying time along with all the dead time such as the waiting around in Departures and Arrivals. I'll be honest about it – I wanted to walk away, but for now, ITV had me firmly amongst the suits and temporarily working at their headquarters on the South Bank and trying to put together some form of business plan.

Imagine, after being used to watching programmes such as the *Sons of Anarchy*, *Fargo*, *The Soprano's*, *The Shield*, *Mad Men*, *The Blacklist* or indeed *House* and then getting ITV's flagship programmes such as *Coronation Street* or *Emmerdale* or any of the reality garbage that's rammed down our throats on a daily basis?

"Do you actually watch TV?" I was asked by one of the suits.

"No disrespect and please don't take this the wrong way," I said. "Ask most people with half a brain and they would tell you that **six**ty percent of what's currently on UK TV is shite."

I was sure that my candid and forthright input wouldn't be welcomed – however, this is where I would be wrong, as I was asked to elaborate.

The answer was simple. Back in the day there were four channels – now they are hundreds. Add the likes of Sky, NetFlix and Amazon into the equation and that runs into thousands.

"Me and M make a point of just watching films on DVD," I said. "Even the kids would rather watch a Hanna Barbera cartoon from the **six**ties or seventies on DVD than any kid's programmes that are currently shown on TV."

That much was true as they even watched **six**ties and seventies drama. Just the other week Emily had taken the kids up to *The Range* on Suez Road in Enfield – as according to form, it was the only place that stocked Flat Mop Refill Pad's and my lad ended up buying three or four cheap DVD's from some bargain bucket. I got in from work and the first thing he asked me post-the handing out of kisses was: "Is Frank McLintock a Mexican?"

"I doubt it," I told him.

I never thought any more about it until I started eating my dinner – and whilst M was rattling on about Olivia Cook trying to issue Sooty with legal documentation over non-payment of maintenance, my lad was sat cross-egged and totally engrossed, watching a cowboy drama on TV – a cowboy drama on TV with a couple of Arsenal connections, I may hasten to add.

"See – it is Frank McLintock," he said.

For as versatile as Big Frank was, I never really had visions of him dressed like Johnny Cash and trying to negotiate a truce with the Apache Indians.

"What's he got on – *Bonanza*?" I asked.

"*The High Chaparral*," grinned Emily.

"It's right rubbish," said my daughter. "He's had it on for the last two hours."

"Frank McLintock moonlighting as a Mexican cowhand called Manalito during the run up to the 'six**ty-nine League Cup Final," I winked at my wife. "No wonder Swindon Town beat us."

"And that Blue Boy looks right like that David Price," added my lad, whilst chomping at his sandwich.

Mmm, he did a bit, I thought.

Back in the meeting, I was then asked about *Coronation Street* and *Emmerdale*?"

"I'm definitely the wrong person to ask," I said. "M's mum likes them – but as for me, they are what they are."

"And what's that?" asked one of the suits.

"They are shit programmes with shit scripts, shit characters and shit acting," I said. "However, a soap opera is an outlet from real life to the normal working man or woman – and for the unemployed and unemployable, it can be quite entertaining."

"What about *Eastenders*?"

"The same," I said. "It was okay when it started out and like *Emmerdale* and *Coronation Street* at times it generated major interest such as the Den Watts character getting Michelle Fowler pregnant or in the case of *Coronation Street* – Mike Baldwin having an affair with Deidre Barlow. As for *Emmerdale* – for its time, I suppose that broke the mould with the two gays."

"Two gays?" shrugged one of the suits.

"Yeh – Amos Brearley and Mister Wilks."

"They weren't gay," he replied. "Henry Wilks was married."

"So was Elton John," I said.

I was hoping that ITV would see that my heart wasn't in it, but the more I opened my mouth, the more intrigued they became.

Each day I got home I'd have M sat across from me both smiling and listening – however, me being away from home for the next ten to eleven weeks was an extremely touchy subject. Emily had gone through every permeation possible – however, my penchant for dirty scouse EasyJet stewardesses, French maids, strict schoolteachers, her ever-purring *cat* along with the implementation of both rules number one, made my being away from home, non-negotiable.

"I've had a long think about it," Emily said.

"Oh yeh?"

"We are definitely coming with you," she said. "We can come home and spend the weekends in London or up at Hamilton Square."

"We can't have Sammy spending half his childhood jetting backwards and forwards over the Atlantic," I said. "It's not fair on him and it's not fair on you."

I also mentioned that she hadn't been that up for us moving to The States, the first time I received an offer.

"We'd just got married and I'd just had Sammy," she said. "The timing back then was all wrong."

"What – and now the timing is right?" I shrugged.

"Everything is right," she smiled.

"What about the kids?"

"Whether we go together, or you go alone, the outcome is unfortunately still the same," she said.

"And then there's you contract with ITV."

"The *'Sessions* programmes are pre-recorded," she said.

"*Live at The Warehouse* frigging isn't," I told her.

The pain in the arse that was *Live at The Warehouse*, hung over us like some dark cloud and every time we wanted to move forward, it held us back.

In the end, I told ITV's CEO about Emily wanting to come with me and the problem that surrounded her programming.

"Can't she wait just a few weeks?" he asked.

Another one of the reasons about her not wanting to do *The Warehouse*, was the fact that she was heavily pregnant, and according to the woman carrying it – fit for bursting. She wasn't as such, but at nearly **six** months pregnant you could certainly tell that there was a bun in the oven.

"Eleven weeks isn't a few," I told him. "It's three months – she could end up dropping the kid on set."

As exciting as this sounded – M's water's breaking live on a Friday night was what made ITV think about pulling in another host for the programme. Jeanette? Nope. Jody Reeves.

"Well, good luck with that one," I said, knowing full-well that Jody reading from the autocue would be highly illuminating.

We had managed to keep the lid on it and somewhat schtum regarding the America-thing – however, me going M.I.A from the ITV 7 set up was more than noticed.

"What's going on, Lee," asked Abi. "Everybody's talking about it."

Sooty was the same – however, it was when Jeanette put the feelers out during the pre-recording of the *ITV Sessions* that my gob shite of a wife told her what was happening.

"ITV have offered him the job as CEO of ITV America," Emily told her.

"So, you're going to America?" she asked.

"He's not signed anything yet, as there are a few things that need ironing out."

"So again – you're going to America?" re-asked my ex.

"Lee was on about commuting," Emily told her. "Monday until Thursday."

Jeanette certainly liked the sound of that. Especially the thought of me spending four days a week away from Emily and in a foreign city with a great job and money in my pocket – her obviously thinking that this would be the start of the eventual break-up of our marriage.

"However, I told him that was definitely not happening," Emily winked.

"What – don't you trust him?" my ex inquired.

"Of course, I do," she said. "However, it's my job to look after him and keep his mind occupied and I can't do that if he's thousands of miles away."

"So, the kids will lose him during the week?" Jeanette asked.

"That was one of the *said* things that needs ironing out," Emily told her. "The children …and you of course."

"Me?"

"We are a family," Emily said. "What we have all learned is that no matter what happens, we all stay together."

"Okay then," shrugged Jeanette. "How does that work?"

"We were hoping that you would fancy coming, seeing as you were dead set on going during the summer."

Emily had played her hand and Jeanette for once was lost for words. Which was a good thing – I think?

I still had several obligations with ITV 7, one of which was the completion of the *Basher project* and while Emily was on her laptop house-hunting in New York, I tried to sum up the rise and fall of what should have been Arsenal's greatest era – however, I kept on getting side-tracked by a continually yapping wife.

"Am I annoying you – yer know, me talking?" she inquired.

"No," I said.

"Fibber," she winked.

"So, what's the matter?" I asked.

"I know living centrally isn't an option," she said, scratching her head. "As everywhere is dead expensive."

"What are you looking at – something in the country?"

"No. What's the point in living in New York if you're not in New York? It's like wanting to live in London and ending up in Barnet."

"True," I said.

"Plus, living in the country would drive you scats," she said.

"What – you reckon?" I winked.

"No – I know," she grinned.

I just let her get on with it and kicked up my laptop.

The success of Arsenal's 1977/78 season didn't just depend on the outcome of the F.A Cup Final, but the 29th April showdown at Highbury against a twelfth-placed Middlesbrough. A win would mean qualification for Europe – strangely the first time since 1971.

In 1971/72, Arsenal had competed in the European Cup as Champions and one would have thought had managed to claim a UEFA Cup spot the very same season with a fifth-place position in the League – and only **six** points behind Champions Derby County. The following season they were even more sure of European qualification as they were pipped to the League Championship by Liverpool and ended up runners-up, yet still failed to qualify.

Tottenham Hotspur may feel hard done by with events that succeeded the first World War, whereby the First Division got extended and in an alleged *cash for votes* scenario with the-then Arsenal chairman allegedly pulling all the strings, they got relegated and fifth-placed Arsenal got promoted. However, Tottenham robbed Arsenal of entry into the UEFA cup two years on the trot due to the *one club per city* ruling at the time. Spurs gained entry as winners of the competition in 1972 – beating Wolverhampton Wanderers in the final, and then by winning the League Cup in 1973 – beating Norwich City 1-0.

"North London breathed a sigh of relief with the news that Arsenal's brilliant young Irish midfielder Liam Brady will be fit for the F.A Cup Final with Ipswich Town at Wembley on May 6," wrote Kevin Moseley of the *Daily Mirror*. "Brady had an X-ray which revealed only a slight sprain."

"The leg is still sore and heavily strapped but it's just a case of rest," added Brady. "I'll miss Saturday's game with Middlesbrough, but the break will make all the difference to my fitness."

The scenario with Brady, was not too dissimilar to that of Peter Storey in the 1971 F.A Cup Final and his comments to the journalist surrounding the ankle injury were also not too dissimilar to that of his captain – Pat Rice. "I'm usually a quick healer, so I'm hoping I'll be training normally next week," he said.

History will tell you that neither Brady nor Rice had something as trivial as a sprained ankle – they both had torn ankle ligaments – and that along with Alan Sunderland's hurried return from a stress fracture of the fibula were things that a good manager should have seen through – as was the indifferent form of Malcolm Macdonald, whose recent lethargic performances had been overlooked by his goal tally. In reality, he had been carrying a nagging injury since the crunching 3-1 victory at The Hawthorns during the Christmas period, having to be withdrawn in later games against both Everton and Norwich – and post-F.A Cup Semi-Final he had become quite inconspicuous on the pitch.

Whereas Brian Clough omitted the not 100% fit Archie Gemmell and Martin O'Neill from the 1979 European Cup Final, Neill initially made the mistake of rushing back Alan Sunderland from a seven-match lay-off telling Nigel Clarke of the *Daily Mirror*, "He went like a bomb in training – he did really well and I'm now considering him for the game against Middlesbrough. If he does play and comes through safely, there is every chance that he will play at Wembley."

History will tell you that all he was doing was clutching at straws and after just five weeks out Sunderland was nowhere near ready – certainly nowhere near being ready for Arsenal's biggest game in years – the fiftieth F.A Cup Final at Wembley – exactly **six** years to the day, the hour and the minute since the 1972 Centenary F.A Cup Final, when Arsenal went down 1-0 to Leeds United. Strange?

Also, prior to the Middlesbrough game, Ray Bradley of the *Sunday Express* had just recently broken the news on what would eventually form an integral part to Arsenal's biggest ever move in the transfer market, stating that the club had made a £60,000 move for Plymouth Argyle goalkeeper Paul Barron and had approached Crystal Palace for their £200,000-rated, 19-year old left-back Kenny Sansom, the latter of whose manager, Terry Venables would have him tied to a new five-year contract come the end of July.

What has possibly never been mentioned before is that Arsenal were also looking at Burnley's Northern Ireland international winger Terry Cochrane, who had been a shoe-in replacement for Leighton James and whose scintillating displays at the relegated club had attracted a huge interest from a whole host of clubs, including Arsenal's opponents that day – Middlesbrough, who on 11th October 1978, would splash out a record £210,000 on the player. Coincidentally, the Teesside club had just had a £100,000 bid for Scottish international goalkeeper Alan Rough knocked-back by Partick Thistle, whose chairman Miller Reid told John Lloyd of the *Daily Mirror*, "We find Middlesbrough's offer completely unacceptable."

A crowd of 32,138 watched on as Frank Stapleton connected on to a left-wing cross from Graham Rix and sent a diving header past goalkeeper David Brown in first half stoppage time – time which had been added on due to a cockerel being thrown into Jennings' goalmouth. 1-0 to The Arsenal and qualification for Europe. That Tottenham connection again!

"We were determined to keep Sunderland on the pitch no matter how tired the player felt," Neill explained after the match. "He had to prove himself fit to face Ipswich."

Sunday plus the first ever May Day Bank Holiday – a day when it slung it down with rain – to rest up, would precede a four day build up to the big day. The major questions surrounding Arsenal before their warm-up at Wembley the following day however, was: would Brady be *fit* and what would be Neill and Howe's line up? To offset that somewhat, a war of words between Ipswich and Arsenal kicked off when Alan Hudson came under fire from opposition skipper Mick Mills.

"Mills – Ipswich's model professional and Hudson, Arsenal's rebel hero, are just about as far apart in terms of character and temperament as two footballers could be," wrote Steve Curry of the *Daily Express*.

"There are one or two players in football with whom I cannot see eye to eye," Mills had told him. "One of them is Arsenal's Alan Hudson – and I nearly ended up rooming with him in the England hotel before the international with Brazil. There is no doubt that he has got terrific ability – I think it is because I don't feel he has made the most of it that I get a bit angry with him."

"I don't really want to answer Mills as I don't feel anything for him anyway and if he dislikes me, then so what? He's not the only one," Huddy had told the journalist.

Ipswich Town's preparation for the final was to initially be on the end of a 6-1 mauling by Aston Villa up at Villa Park, which added further weight to the bookies prediction of Arsenal being made 8/13 favourites to take the Cup with some – David Miller of the *Daily Express* in particular – suggesting that Ipswich could be on the end of the biggest Cup Final defeat since 1974.

The Tractor Boys' 1977/78 season however, had been a one-off to a degree, in that they'd had to blood new players as the club had been ravaged by injuries.

"Arsenal, on their day are one of the most attractive teams in the country," wrote David Lacey of the *Guardian*. "Ipswich, in contrast have had a poor season, having previously finished fourth, fourth, third, **six**th and third in the First Division. They had hoped to challenge for the Championship, but injuries and indifferent form swiftly wrecked this ambition."

David Miller added further to the clamour surrounding Arsenal by stating that The Gunners were only two or three players short of "Europe-winning quality", something similar to what had been said by Nigel Clarke of the *Daily Mirror* around the time they were looking at Francis, Wilkins and Statham.

Apart from the long-term knee injury that ruled out Trevor Whymark, Nigel Clarke explained that there was doubt surrounding the fitness of the central defensive unit of Allan Hunter and Kevin Beattie, with the talk being that 19-year old Russell Osman could be drafted in – however, there was a huge degree of bluster taking place and manager Bobby Robson was doing quite a bit more than playing his cards very close to his chest and as Pat Rice would eloquently put it – he was playing his "Crying game" to great effect.

Robson was due to assess the fitness of both defenders along with midfielder Colin Viljoen in a reserve game against Queen's Park Rangers down at Loftus Road – however, the game got postponed due to a waterlogged pitch. "This is typical of our luck," Robson moaned. "We specially set up the reserve game to help us sort out our injury problems."

Viljoen, who had netted a brace of goals in his clubs Fourth Round demolition of Hartlepool United back in late-January, suggested to David Lacey of the *Guardian* that other players had purposely played him out of the reckoning during his team's 6-1 defeat at Villa Park and as such there was a huge degree of acrimony when Robson would eventually name his squad of 16.

"I understand and can sympathise with his disappointment at being left out, but I deny any inference that certain players influenced my decision not to include him in the squad," Robson said. "There is no unrest in the camp. I played Colin against Villa because he is one of the most skilful players in the country and his style would have been suited to Wembley. However, I had to change the team to accommodate him and it didn't come off, therefore I will revert to the midfield trio that has served us so consistently in the last few weeks. I pick the side and the only player who sometimes has a say is the captain, Mick Mills."

Midfielder Roger Osborne was however, one of the said influential players. "I am not a glamour player and I don't have that much skill but I'm the type of player that every team needs and I was upset and angry about being left out of the side against Villa," he said. "I didn't think it was fair. Colin Viljoen is a good player, but you can't expect to come back after six weeks out and play in a F.A Cup Final."

Maybe Terry Neill should have taken note?

History will also tell you that Viljoen, who was capped twice for England during the Home International's in May 1975 – strangely taking the place of Alan Hudson, would never pull on an Ipswich shirt again.

Both teams trained at a rain-soaked Wembley, with Robson stating that Hunter missed the session due to him having fluid drained from his knee and that centre-forward Paul Mariner and goalkeeper Paul Cooper both trained light due to muscle strains. "I honestly don't know when I will be able to name a team," groaned the Ipswich manager, post-training session.

Wembley groundsman Don Gallacher put over a completely different perspective, somewhat suggesting that Robson was being more than economical with the truth and complained about the East Anglian club churning up his lovely wet pitch. "Ipswich were practising under match conditions and making sliding tackles," he said. "It was completely different to Arsenal, who themselves took it easy."

Arsenal had been the first out and trained for 75 minutes, with the most notable thing being that they trained without Liam Brady who told David Miller afterwards, "I'm okay – the boss knows that – I just didn't want to get involved out there."

The truth was that Brady was still injured and his inclusion would rob a fit player of a place in the starting eleven, the exact same as Storey's inclusion robbed both Jon Sammels or Eddie Kelly of a start at Wembley in 1971.

Miller rather interestingly, suggested that Arsenal might line up with a 4-2-4 formation with Brady and Hudson playing centrally and Rix and Sunderland being deployed on either flank and dropping back as and when needed – however, the journalist emphasised the fact that in Mick Mills, Kevin Beattie, Allan Hunter, Brian Talbot and John Wark, Ipswich Town had five players who were "apt not to distinguish between brick walls and opponents when running through them", and the thought of Arsenal lining up with just the two schemers in midfield, could on one hand, make them a very attractive proposition – however, on the other, it could also make them extremely vulnerable.

"A midfield of Brady and Hudson could have wilted in the face of Ipswich power the way West Bromwich Albion did in the Semi-Final," added Miller.

As for Graham Rix, the player told Nigel Clarke, "I badly want to play. I think I deserve to play and I'll be terribly disappointed if I don't play."

"It is one of the most difficult decisions I have ever had to make," Neill told David Miller. "It is simply a question of what will be best for the team."

There were similarities to the situation in picking the team for the 1968 League Cup Final when Bertie Mee dropped his then-club captain Terry Neill to play the 21-year old David Jenkins – a player who had only made five starts that season.

Graham Rix had played the first 39 games of the season before he got injured, missing **six** starts at the beginning of Arsenal's purple-patch, before coming back into the side at the expense of the injured Alan Sunderland.

"Rix deserved to play as he had been playing out of his skin," said Huddy. "The truth was that Terry left him out because he was the youngest."

"The revival of Hudson – the real reason for the unlucky Rix being substitute – has been equally important to Arsenal's all-round improvement," wrote David Lacey of the *Guardian.* "Now, instead of playing with the ponderous rhythm of a Victorian steam engine, monotonously pumping in high crosses, Arsenal's football is full of subtle changes of pace, clever variations of flight and angle, and deep plots as Hudson loiters alongside or just behind Brady."

Alan Hudson was down at 33/1 to be the first scorer – the exact same price as *Roland Gardens* – the winner of the 2000 Guineas at Newmarket, just half an hour before kick-off. An omen, maybe?

"The odds favour Arsenal. They appear to be more skilful, more experienced, better balanced and tradition supports them," wrote Frank McGhee of the *Daily Mirror.* "Tactically they are better equipped for an occasion that can play havoc with the best laid plans and they have players like Brady and Hudson who can dictate the pace of a game. The final verdict must favour Arsenal, but it will be close."

McGhee had edged his bets somewhat and added, "Both Rice and Nelson can be impetuous and Clive Woods – the only authentic winger on the park, has the pace and skill to exploit them both and the job Osborne does on Brady will be vital."

"Arsenal have been growing stronger all season," wrote James Mossop of the *Sunday Express*. "In their midfield, there are players that can turn the pattern of any match. Liam Brady and Alan Hudson are in delightful form, Macdonald's scoring touch is undiminished and Pat Jennings is the safest goalkeeper in the land."

The referee for the game was 47-year old Christchurch-based Derek Nippard, who along with Gordon Hill, Pat Partridge, Clive Thomas and Ron Challis are immortalised in 1970's folklore, as apart from refereeing the 1978 F.A Cup Final, he had also refereed an ill-tempered match at the Baseball Ground on 1st November 1975 – a game in which he sent off both Francis Lee and Norman Hunter for fighting, during Derby County's 3-2 win.

Bob Driscoll of The Sun broke the news to confirm that Rix would indeed be substitute and that both Alan's – Sunderland and Hudson, would occupy a place in the starting line-up, with the latter waking up on Cup Final morning to embarrassingly find himself the subject of an open letter in the Daily Express. "Dear Alan, I hope this finds you well this morning," wrote James Lawton. "No sore throat? No depression? No chip on your shoulder? Well, that's terrific! I am so pleased you're in good shape, mate, because it seems to me that there comes a day in everyone's life when they have to say – 'Right, this is it. This is my big chance to prove something'. Well this is such a day for you. I know what you think of your talents. I know you think that it's a joke that you played for England so briefly. You feel ill-used, don't you? You feel that over these last 10 years there has been a conspiracy to do down Alan Hudson. The truth is Alan, is that it only seemed that way. Some say the chip on your shoulder was outstripping the talent in your boots around the time you were downing your first lager along the King's Road. That for every perfectly placed pass you've delivered there has been a failure of will, a subconscious copping out of a difficult situation. Yes of course there have been difficulties. Of course, a lot of people in English football get twitchy when they come to deal with extraordinary talent. It disturbs them. Because of the climate of the game in this country they often see such talent as a threat rather than an asset. And when they hear stories of how you turned up for training in your Chelsea days 'smelling of drink' that is just about 'Goodnight Vienna' to your reputation. But that is not the sort of stuff you should be dwelling on this morning, Alan. You should think of the faith of Tony Waddington when he ransacked Stoke City's resources and bought you at a time when the rest of big-time English football fancied you about as much as they did cholera. You should also bury your conviction that Arsenal manager Terry Neill itches to give you the elbow at the first loss of form. This may or may not be true, but the fact is he too, showed a bit of faith. He brought you to Arsenal. Bertie Mee – Neill's predecessor, wouldn't have taken you with a warehouse full of gift stamps. You should also think of Ron Greenwood. It was a small tragedy that you weren't fit for the Brazil match. Greenwood's selection of you was more significant than you thought. A few years ago, he too, for all his love of skill, had measured your talents against your reputation and came to the popular unfavourable conclusion. But the greater tragedy has now been averted. By now you might have been on your way to earning a fortune with Alicante or picking up the easy dollars in North America. But you are too good for that Alan Hudson. I hope you think of that when you come out of that dark gloomy old tunnel this afternoon. You have been in the wilderness too long, son."

There was nothing like having a fucking monkey on your back.

The 1978 F.A Cup Final went exactly as planned for Arsenal – well for the first 10 minutes anyway, with O'Leary an inch away from making it 1-0 to The Arsenal after Hudson and Brady had combined on the right via a lovely series of interlinking play, which resulted in a deft reverse-pass from Brady, which Hudson played over to the central defender, who was highly unlucky not to score.

It was a blinding game of football played by two teams that possessed hugely contrasting styles – Arsenal's being the more patient European-style against Ipswich's very much "up and at 'em" British-style of football. However, what was immediately noticed was that not only did Paul Mariner have the pace and aerial ability to continually outstrip and outjump an uncomfortable albeit still-struggling Willie Young – Arsenal also had several players out there that were playing whilst injured.

What is true is that Terry Neill had been blindsided.

History would have you believe that Roger Osborne, who had done an exceptional job of man-marking Johann Cruyff in Ipswich Town's 3-0 win against Barcelona some **six**-months earlier, had shackled the unfit Brady until his substitution – however, the reality wasn't quite like that.

Brady for his part interlinked well with Hudson in midfield, but it wasn't so much that the Arsenal midfield was being overpowered, it was the fact that Macdonald was static – only winning one aerial duel all match. Sunderland also appeared completely out of touch and Stapleton was raw to the point of naivete – and that being the case, the ball kept on coming back at them, with Ipswich's play purposely bypassing central midfield with them utilising the both flanks and the pace and skill of Clive Woods, who had been given a free role by his manager.

Mariner hit a shot past Pat Jennings's far post after a knock down by Woods, before hitting the bar some minutes later after Woods had crossed into the area and had created some uncertainty in Arsenal's defence. Ipswich were upping the pressure but Arsenal didn't panic and kept on playing it out from the back, with Hudson in part, utilised as a sweeper in front of the back four – a back four that only had one fit player in it.

Two of Arsenal's defining moments came in the first half.

The first was after a nine-man move out of defence, which saw Sammy Nelson race onto a ball laid back by Macdonald and into space between Ipswich's central defenders – and with their goalkeeper well off his line and the goal gaping, he had the chance of putting Arsenal 1-0 up – however, he bottled what was a golden chance, opting instead to play the ball out wide to Sunderland, who failed to control the ball before Ipswich cleared.

It was a glorious chance and the big question was – "Why didn't Nelson take on the shot?"

Not only had he missed his chance of glory, he had also lost possession and was out of position as Arsenal were again put under pressure from a long ball out to the flanks where Mariner again created problems, winning a corner, which Arsenal cleared – Hudson winning a tackle against John Wark on the edge of the area and taking the ball out to the left flank where he delightfully evaded three challenges from George Burley, David Geddes and Mills before feeding the ball through to Macdonald who was immediately, albeit aggressively dispossessed by Allan Hunter.

This was the Ipswich *blueprint* all the way through the game. Arsenal's forward line just couldn't hold up the play and Ipswich continually gained possession and the one time that they did, Nelson had failed to capitalise on it.

It was then 19-year old Geddes' turn, and he unleashed a 30-yard shot which Jennings managed to turn around for a corner.

As the first half wore on both Brady and Hudson were giving a fair account of themselves in midfield – however, what would happen next would be the other defining moment of the first half.

Ipswich broke from their own half and Brady *took out* an onrushing Geddes around 40-yards out, which not only gave Ipswich a free kick but was something, which following a short pass by Hudson, gave John Wark his chance to effectively seek recompense for Brady's poor challenge on his teammate – the Scottish midfielder and 1981 PFA Players' Player of the Year sliding into him with an X-rated lunge that effectively put Brady out of the game.

This was a major turning point as Brady would come off early in the second-half having further aggravated his ankle.

Brady and Hudson in midfield had hardly been overrun, more bypassed by Ipswich's tactics, but on Arsenal's midfield duo retrieving possession they had little to aim for and on the other occasion Arsenal had been presented with a clear sight of goal – Alan Sunderland had fluffed a one on one with goalkeeper Paul Cooper.

As for Malcolm Macdonald, he only managed only one real shot on target, with the truth to come out later, that he had been badly troubled by his knee, in that it had been continually locking – as had a rather out-of-sorts Willie Young, who had assisted in setting up Roger Osborne's winning goal on 77 minutes with a slide-rule clearance straight into the midfielders' path.

It was never going to be Arsenal's day and was it not for Pat Jennings – who was still carrying an ankle injury, Ipswich Town's 1-0 slaughter of Arsenal could have been much worse with Kevin Beattie candidly stating afterwards that they ought to have put five past them.

That much was true but it could have been so much different if Nelson had put his foot through the ball when presented with the chance – however, what was to come out afterwards was that the Northern Ireland international left-back had broken one of his ribs early on in the game.

With seven players carrying or returning from injuries, Neill's man-management had failed. The aura of the biggest game in English football had not only massaged his ego but had severely blurred his vision. And these injuries weren't just a Bobby Robson-type excuse – Rice, Nelson and Jennings would not only miss the last League game of the season, they would also be unfit for all three Home International's between 13th and 19th May 1978, whilst on 26th May, John Morgan of the *Daily Express* reported that Liam Brady would have to be fitted with a plaster-cast to completely immobilise his ankle.

Willie Young would also miss the last game of the season, where a makeshift Arsenal side would go down 3-0 away to a Charlie George-inspired Derby County – the only plus point for Arsenal being a 30-yard screamer of a free-kick by Graham Rix, which was brilliantly turned away by goalkeeper John Middleton.

As for Macdonald, his condition was far more serious and by the 31st August 1978, his career would be in tatters. He would later-on be diagnosed with Stage 4 of Osteoarthritis of the knee, something that would come after several cartilage operations, which ultimately resulted in the complete replacement of one of his knees.

The 1977/78 season was a season where Arsenal had played some of the best football ever seen at the club, but it was also the season that Terry Neill should have built on. However, he didn't and by 1st September 1978, the signs were ominous. They would be four of five players short of "Europe-winning quality" and come summer 1980 they would be at least **six**.

Chapter 48

The Kids are United

"You run just like your dad," Jarv had told my lad after a school football game.

Much to the displeasure of Huddy, Jarv had been given the job of doing the match report at Stamford Bridge and had therefore called down to see what all the palaver was about regarding the ex-England schemers candid assessment of what he had termed as *the best kid's team in British football.* And while the erratic genius was grating his teeth at having to report on the Brentford versus Nottingham Forest match that afternoon, he and Jimmy Bone's lads had turned in yet another fine performance – winning 15-2 at Surrey Square Park just off the Old Kent Road, with my lad scoring two in the process. And the good news was that they were both at the right end.

"Why – how did dad run?" asked my lad, as he guzzled from his bottle of orange.

"A bit like Robert Pires," Jarv told him.

"Uncle Sooty said that dad was really lazy."

"He could look lazy," Jarv replied. "But believe me – it only looked that way."

He was right – some players have a languid look about them, which can appear as though they aren't trying and in the early days Chopper had pulled me up a few times about it. I think it was a confidence thing with me. I may have been extremely cock-sure in the final two years of school, but on first going up to the big school, that certainly wasn't the case.

It was about that time that my gran had told him the story of my dad – her son, and Chopper who would have been about the same age as my dad, began to put his two and two's together and understand about certain things and the encouragement I began to receive was unbelievable. Some teachers can be less useless, but Chopper wasn't. He was a bit of a rarity for a teacher – and just a brilliant guy.

I think it had been Hilly who had been struggling with some assignment at the beginning of the second to the last year in school and Chopper had sat him down and explained everything to him and as Hilly was pig-thick, he eventually ended up doing the assignment for him. As soon as word got out, Chopper began doing half the football teams homework until the penny finally dropped.

"Do you lot think I'm stupid?" he once asked, whilst counting heads on the bus before a trip to an away game and after Jarv had handed him some homework – logarithms, if I rightly recall.

"No, sir – none of us think you're stupid," I'd said – speaking on behalf of all the team.

Me saying that must have it a nerve, as I got an "Okay, Lee" and a nod.

My gran told me that it would be a good idea to get the lads to club together and buy him something as a bit of a *Thank-You* for all the time he took with us. We did, and raised about nine and a half quid, which was enough for Jarv's mum to put to it and buy him the *Godfather I* and *II* DVD from HMV.

"We got you this to say sorry for you thinking that we were mucking you about and to say 'thank-you'," I told him, on handing him the badly wrapped gift.

"Oh yeh?" he replied. "And whose idea was all this then – your gran's?"

I nodded. "It was a good idea, though."

On opening it, his bottom lip went and he got all emotional.

That year was the start of something very, very special and it got as though we would run through a brick wall for him – and the sight of him on the touchline jumping around and punching the air when we had scored, was certainly something else.

Our respect for him was immense, as was our not wanting to disappoint him.

I look back at him and then at Arsène Wenger's body language during Arsenal's 2-1 defeat at The Hawthorns later that day and can only shake my head in comparison. It is passion that drives us and to see what is quintessentially a dithering old man sat in an anorak on eight or nine million a year is extremely hard to take. Chopper got paid absolutely nothing for all his hard work and commitment and showed a passion that was quite unmatched.

I had taken Jeanette's father down to see his grandson play football – for the first time ever, and he had been absolutely overawed with it all – especially the fact that a heavily bundled up Emily had been there too. "Woo-woo – go on our Jamie," she had shouted, after he had tucked in what had been a poor back pass that had bounced off the goalkeeper.

"Do you go every week," Michael had asked her.

"Of course, I do," she'd replied. "I wouldn't miss it for the world."

M's liking of being a soccer-mum was two-fold. She also got to know a lot of gossip and made several friends, whilst keeping an ex-friend somewhat at arms-length – that of young Irving's mum, Sally Nattrass. It was a shame, but it was what it was.

"Dad, can Erv' come to ours?" my lad had asked on a regular basis.

Both Emily and I liked the little lad and certainly had no problem with him – however, Sally used it to get her foot back in the door – as did Tony, offering us smoked cod, crevettes, langoustines and lobsters on picking up his stepson.

"Can we be friends again?" Sally had asked my wife.

In my mind a pair of swingers can't be ever classed as *friend* material. I mean, their game was one of deceit in trying to get us at ease prior to them making their move. If it happened once, it would happen again.

Emily had run it past me, and for as much as I had enjoyed their company in the early days – and I had, to me their end game would always be the same. "Do what you feel is right, M," I'd replied. "However, in my mind they can't ever be trusted."

"And Sooty?" she shrugged.

"I've known Sooty nearly all my life – I've known them for ten minutes."

It wasn't so much Tony that was the problem, it was Sally. His problem however, was that he basically let her do what the hell she wanted. Nevertheless, Emily decided that being civil, would be the best way forward – especially as both kids thought the world of each other and there was only a short time-frame prior to me moving jobs.

We got back home, only for Emily to lose me to ITV 7 for the afternoon – having to answer questions surrounding the days' fixtures from the lounge and piecing together part of the *Basher documentary*, of which the first installment would air in midweek.

The blarney that surrounded Terry Neill wasn't just exclusive to the pre-season and first few months of the 1977/78 season, it was also more than evident the following season – and even more so.

On 2nd June 1978 – one day after the start of the 1978 World Cup and on the day Argentina came back from one-down to beat Hungary 2-1, with goals from Leopoldo Luque and Daniel Bertoni, the goalposts moved slightly. At its annual meeting, the Football League voted to allow two continental players per club – something that would put Arsenal – and more so, their North London rivals, very much in the spotlight.

Although there was a certain acrimony surrounding the 1978 World Cup – not at least with how the hosts firstly got awarded the competition and then how they progressed to the final, hundreds of millions of viewers witnessed what was quintessentially a set of mobile midgets and possibly the most un-South American of football teams – amidst waves of paper confetti, lift the trophy after an extra-time win over a Cruyff-less Holland. Ally's Army's poor showing aside, the competition had been a huge success and brought several players to the attention of a whole host of English football clubs – some of who had had decent international players cherry-picked by clubs from the North American Soccer League, who had offered them huge sums of money along with a quite fantastic lifestyle's.

Players such as Dennis Tueart from Manchester City, Kevin Hector from Derby County, Willie Johnston from West Bromwich Albion and what would be the most notable – Alan Hudson from Arsenal.

Straight after the competition Arsenal were offered two soon-to-be 26-year old's – Osvaldo Ardiles from Huracan and Ricardo Villa from Racing Club, for a combined fee of $700,000, but after thinking about it, Arsenal's rather loquacious boss knocked the idea on the head with Neill saying that although he was having huge problems with Alan Hudson and that he did need a midfielder, he didn't need two.

He had been quite excited about the prospect of Ardiles, but he was also skeptical about how they would fit into the fast-paced aggression of British football – him thinking that Ardiles, although extremely technical, may have been a bit too lightweight – and Villa, possibly too inconsistent.

The original fee supposedly quoted to Neill was some way off with what Tottenham Hotspur actually laid out, with its former club captain, Northern Ireland manager and journalist for the *Sunday Express*, Danny Blanchflower stating that the actual transfer fees were £335,000 for Ardiles and £359,000 for Villa.

There was also the chance of Arsenal getting River Plate's 29-year old big-name striker Leopoldo Luque for a fee reported to be around £400,000 – however, the Arsenal manager wasn't that keen. "On the continent, all the best players tend to be mercenaries," Neill had said. "Going from country to country and being employed on short-term contracts."

Ardiles had looked an extremely capable player – however, Mario Kempes and Daniel Passarella were the real stars – and Kempes was already in Valencia and on around £3,000 a week, whilst Passerella – although a brilliant player – at 5'8 was possibly considered too short to be a centre-back in England and as such, later-on ended up playing in Serie

A with Fiorentina and Inter Milan.

However, that wouldn't stop Manchester United trying to lure him and the brilliant Argentinian goalkeeper Ubaldo Fillol from River Plate in a £1 million deal come December 1978.

The beaten Dutch side however, provided Neill with plenty of targets – six of who Arsenal would be linked to, with the club supposedly *going hard* for Ruud Krol in September of that year.

Arsenal, with Hudson and Macdonald about to conclude their employment with the club – the former because he loathed Neill and the latter as he was about to become severely crocked, needed reinforcements and on 14th May 1978 and just eight days after the club's no-show in the 1978 F.A Cup Final, Ray Bradley of the *Sunday Express* broke the news and reported that Arsenal were in for Brian Talbot. "Talbot has the drive the Gunners seek as they set their sights on Europe after a season tinged with disappointment," he wrote. "Arsenal have eyed Talbot all season and are now ready to move in with a big bid."

Some 11 days later, and with Macdonald recovering from a cartilage operation, a £500,000 bid for the current Scottish Football Writers' Player of the Year and Rangers' 24-year old Derek Johnstone was allegedly being tabled – however, chairman Denis Hill-Wood, calmed this down by telling Kevin Moseley of the *Daily Mirror*, "I think it is most unlikely that there will be a bid from Arsenal in the next twenty-four hours as Terry Neill is going away on holiday."

Johnstone was a remarkable player and in a similar situation to Mel Charles nineteen years earlier in that he could play at either centre-forward or centre-half – that he had refused to sign a new contract and had handed in a transfer request – and that Arsenal and Tottenham Hotspur were the two clubs that were in for him.

However, what history will tell you is that the move never happened.

With Terry Neill wrongly indicating in the press that Arsenal had a big enough squad, it soon became apparent they would be a man light when the *Daily Mirror* ran its back-page headlines on 22nd July 1978.

"Alan Hudson has walked out on Arsenal, telling the club he will quit football unless they sell him," wrote Kevin Moseley. "This threat is the outcome of a personality clash between Hudson and manager Terry Neill that reached a climax towards the end of last season. This week he failed to report for pre-season training. He later had a talk with Neill, who promised to sell him for a bargain £100,000 fee."

Hudson, whose impressive form in the tail end of the 1977/78 season had helped Arsenal to not only challenge for three trophies, but also earned him a call-up to the England squad, had told the journalist that it would be a waste of his time and the club's, saying he would not enjoy his football without mutual respect between him and the manager.

Hudson's appraisal of his club's F.A Cup Final defeat against Ipswich Town possibly being the straw that broke the camel's back.

"There was a team meeting on the Monday after the F.A Cup Final which was called by Don Howe," Huddy had told me. "Don being Don, wanted the players to be honest, forthright and passionate. He sat us all down in the Highbury dressing room and asked everyone what they thought about their performance and why we had played so poorly. When it got to me, Don was looking me in the eye with Terry Neill peering over his shoulder and asked me what I thought and I said: 'Don, to be quite honest I thought that *he* lost us the game' – and pointed at Terry. I then turned to Alan Sunderland and said, 'Sorry Alan, but you shouldn't have been picked'. I then looked at Don and said, 'Graham Rix is playing brilliantly, but he left him out because he is the youngest' and before I knew it Terry was trying to get over Don's shoulder at me – 'You're a disgrace, Hudson', he shouted."

Hudson's honesty had been a continual thorn in his managers' side, so much so, he had been fined five times in 12 months for speaking his mind. The truth of the matter was, that if it had been a League game, half the Cup Final starting line-up would never have played due to injury.

The very next day on 23rd July 1978, Ray Bradley of the *Sunday Express* broke the news that Sheffield United manager, Harry Haslam – the man who along with his coach Oscar Arce, had helped broker what the press claimed as *the most sensational deal in British football history* – had also themselves shelved out £160,000 on an Argentinian midfielder – River Plate's Alex Sabella. He also needed a player to link up with him, that player being Arsenal's unsettled and in and out midfielder John Matthews, who went for a fee of £90,000 some 25 days later, making Arsenal's midfield another man light.

That however, was only part of the story.

"Arsenal plan £1 million coup," Steve Curry of the *Daily Express* had headlined the Tuesday prior. "Arsenal manager Terry Neill is ready to splash the cash to get Chelsea's Butch Wilkins and Ipswich Town's Brian Talbot to match the signing by Tottenham of Argentinian's Ardiles and Villa."

"I have made inquiries for several players and it stands to reason that they would have to be big names to improve on the staff we have at Highbury," Neill told the journalist. "So far, my inquiries have proved abortive, but I shall continue to push for certain players in the hope that there is a price at which their clubs will release them."

Three of the other players had been Kenny Sansom of Crystal Palace, John Bailey of Blackburn Rovers and Joe Bolton of Sunderland – which as with the Derek Statham inquiry in the pre-season of 1977/78 not only backed up Alan Hudson's claims in that the club needed a top quality left-back, it told its own story in that Neill didn't quite fancy Sammy Nelson – a player who the Northern Ireland manager Danny Blanchflower had publicly labelled a "cheat" after his country had gone down 5-0 against West Germany in April 1977.

Chelsea's chairman Brian Mears had told Alan Hoby of the *Sunday Express* that he had met with Denis Hill-Wood the previous weekend and had made it abundantly clear that he was wasting his time making any further inquiries about Wilkins, as there was no way Chelsea would sell.

"One of the things I resent is the suggestion that some critics have made in that Wilkins would only develop into a world-class player if he moved to a more successful team," Mears had snapped.

"Wilkins is not, and never has been up for auction," added Chelsea manager Ken Shellito. "I am angry that because Arsenal have made a formal inquiry, that it's inferred that we are about to pack him off to Highbury. He has a year of his contract to run and we shall be offering him improved terms during the course of this season."

Arsenal had known that Chelsea were strapped for cash and would have to sell, and it was only a case of when – however, the Talbot to Arsenal story was interesting in that the player had recently extended his contract and that the inquiry Neill had made, had turned the players head and had unsettled him.

"Bobby Robson will today launch a personal crusade to restore top soccer's tarnished reputation," wrote David Moore of the *Daily Mirror*. "The Ipswich boss-plans a showdown with £400,000-rated Brian Talbot to tell the England midfield man wanted by Arsenal, that he must stay at Portman Road."

"Talbot was happy to sign a four-year contract with Ipswich only 12 months ago and if he finds himself with itchy feet now, then that's his problem," Robson had said. "I have already offered him a new five-year agreement ensuring that he will not lose money by being denied a move to another club, yet he has so far turned it down. I respect a player's rights, but I am not going to let the tail wag the dog. Ipswich will not sell their top stars and if Brian, for one, does not like it, then he can lump it. He has three ways of approaching the situation – his way, my way or preferably, our way. And *our way* means that he stays at Ipswich and helps us build an even better side."

Another major difference between Robson and Neill was that the Ipswich Town manager was an astute man-manager and saw the bigger picture and as Huddy had said on Arsenal prematurely getting rid of Alan Ball – you build on the good players you have – you don't just go and replace them.

"I am totally convinced that Arsenal with me, Ball and Brady at our best would have been the best midfield in the history of the game," Huddy had said. "I would have loved being the anchor man to those two. It had everything: Brady's wonderful ability to take on and beat someone like they weren't there and Ball with his incredible one touch play and knowledge – experiencing two World Cups, something that Terry Neill should have took as a pleasure to be involved with instead of being jealous, if that is indeed the right word."

Would Arsenal making a world class signing such as Ardiles had made Hudson change his mind about leaving?

"The damage was done with Terry Neill," Huddy had told me. "I truly could not take any more of him. I was spoiled under Tony Waddington and had gone from the wonderful heights of both playing and getting on with a great manager to being managed by an absolute buffoon. I think playing with Ardiles would have been something special, but I think Terry getting rid of Alan Ball was the initial problem, which had me thinking 'How can he want a great team if he can let a fantastic player such as Ball go?'"

Neill had done a similar thing whilst manager with Tottenham Hotspur and sold another World Cup hero for what was quintessentially chump-change – Martin Peters to Norwich for £50,000 and had readily admitted in later life, his dislike for what he termed as "star players".

"Those who can't stand the heat – and there are one or two, will end up in the reserves," Neill had told Kevin Moseley of the *Daily Mirror* after just five months in charge of Tottenham Hotspur and after being on the end of a rather embarrassing 3-0 mauling by Leicester City. "Some of the players aren't used to working for a living and as such, they will have to learn damn quickly or they will not play for me."

Tottenham captain Martin Peters had had numerous run-ins with Neill, in much the same way as Alan Ball had.

Neill insinuated to the journalist that money could be raised to strengthen the squad by selling his skipper along with Martin Chivers, Ralph Coates and Phil Beal.

Coates held firm at Spurs, but Neill swept out the rest along with The King of White Hart Lane – the enigmatic albeit extremely talented Alfie Conn, a player who David Emery of the *Daily Express* expected Arsenal to move for with a £100,000 bid.

On being released from Arsenal, Alan Ball would help Southampton firstly get promotion from Division Two and then help get them to the 1979 League Cup Final, whilst playing some of the best football of his career. Martin Peters' swansong at Carrow Road had been similar – helping them reach the summit of Division One come September 1979, with manager John Bond even offering to extend his 35-year old captain's contract a further three years.

With both Ken Shellito and Bobby Robson holding onto their prized assets, Terry Neill began pushing in a different direction and on 8th August 1978, Ray Bradley of the *Sunday Express* ran with the headlines: "Arsenal want Steve Daley".

What he also slipped into the article was, that so did Manchester City.

"Arsenal have already made an approach for unsettled Wolves and England 'B' midfielder Steve Daley, but they will have to await the outcome of this week's board meeting by the Midlands club," he wrote. "Daley has made six transfer requests in as many months and Arsenal see the £350,000-rated Daley as a replacement for Alan Hudson, after failing to get Brian Talbot from Ipswich."

The move for 25-year old Daley however, didn't quite make sense. He was a fine player – in fact, Wolverhampton Wanderers' star player – but he was certainly no Alan Hudson. He was also considered by David Lacey of the *Guardian* to be one of the few genuine left-halves in the country, which posed the question of – if Arsenal did buy him – where would he actually play?

That aside, there were others that thought that he just wasn't a good enough player for Arsenal.

"I don't think he can hit the ball and I don't think he can tackle," Arsenal's ex-captain and former Manchester City and England manager, Joe Mercer had said. "Now and again I suppose you see a flash of brilliance, but to me he's just an ordinary player."

Ray Bradley had also stated that Arsenal were looking at securing the services of £500,000-rated Dutch forward Johnny Rep, from French club Bastia.

Just like it is now, Arsenal's inactivity in the transfer market was big news and a day after Robson had publicly told Brian Talbot he could lump it, Peter Batt of the *Daily Express* ran with the back-page headlines, "Francis is set for dream deal."

Arsenal had been trailing Trevor Francis for quite some time and had had several inquiries rebuffed so it was hardly new – *news*. However, this was quite something else. This was former England captain and Queens Park Rangers midfielder Gerry Francis – a player who had been plagued by injury and who was destined to go Manchester United back in January, with United eventually getting cold feet and knocking the deal on the head and focusing their attention in going all-out for Gordon McQueen.

"Gerry Francis could be an Arsenal player within days," wrote Batt. "For Arsenal are the new leaders of an elite clutch of big-spending clubs who are ready and waiting to tear the £400,000 'for sale' tag from Francis – who two years ago, was considered one of the best midfielder's in Europe."

Letting Hudson go for £100,000, when lesser players were now changing clubs at £400,000 would be a decision that would come back to bite Neill in the backside – something that was more than noted when Macdonald hobbled off during the embarrassing 3-1 defeat by lowly Rotherham United on 31st August. The squad was light of quality and it needed addressing. Still the news of Neill trying to bring in players was making back page headlines, but that's all it was, as after the shock League Cup exit Denis Hill-Wood was quoted as saying that although Arsenal had made several formal inquiries, they hadn't actually bid on anyone this season, before going on to add: "Maybe one or two players will become available in a months' time."

Strangely however, the player who Neill was negotiating with was not a midfielder – but Ruud Krol, Ajax

Amsterdam's Dutch international sweeper, who could also play left-back and who was considered one of the best defenders of his generation.

"The directors of Ajax are meeting tomorrow to again discuss the offer made by Arsenal at the weekend for Rudi Krol – the sweeper who captained the Dutch World Cup team in Argentina," explained David Lacey of the *Guardian* on 5th September 1978. "Arsenal are prepared to break the British Transfer record for Krol with a fee of more than £500,000, however judging from a comment made by the deputy chairman of the club Dick Boering, the chances of Krol moving to Arsenal are slim."

"Rudi Krol, the world's best defender, wants to play in England," wrote Harry Miller of the *Daily Mirror* on the very same day. "Krol is disillusioned with club football in his own country and that could be the key factor in an effort by Arsenal, to bring the 29-year-old Ajax star to Highbury. Krol, one of several top Dutch player's Arsenal manager Terry Neill has watched and inquired about, told me from Amsterdam last night: 'I have had twelve years with Ajax and have always done my best for them, but perhaps the time has come to move on. In England, I have many friends. I am interested in Arsenal – very interested."

"We haven't given up hope of signing someone before the weekend because you never know what might develop in the space of 24 hours," Terry Neill told Malcolm Folley of the *Daily Express*, a day later. "We have made inquiries about certain players in Holland – however, it would be wrong to assume that our next signing will be a foreigner."

It had also been reported by Folley that Arsenal were also looking at the Van Der Kerkoff twins.

Denis Hill-Wood, told Steve Curry of the *Daily Express* the very next day that there was a meeting on Friday 8th September to discuss transfers and said: "Terry is over in Holland to check on one or two things. He knows what we want and how much we are prepared to pay for it. It is no secret that we are anxious to strengthen our staff and that we are looking to Holland to provide us with what we want."

The Ajax board met and its chairman Tom Armesen told Patrick Barclay of the *Guardian* that Krol's move to Arsenal had been blocked and that the player would be seeing out his contract – something which was more than echoed by Steve Curry of the *Daily Express*. "Arsenal will not be allowed to invade Holland and pick up quality players like tulips," he had written the following Monday after interviewing AZ 67 Alkmaar's manager Hans Kraay prior to their European Cup Winners Cup match against Ipswich Town.

Kraay had told the journalist, "It's not easy to see Rudi Krol or Willie and Rene Van der Kerkhoff going to Arsenal as we have a strong contract system over here."

Malcolm Folley of the *Daily Express* and Harry Miller of the *Daily Mirror* also ran with similar stories of Krol's move to Arsenal being blocked – however, the respective £300,000 and £500,000 transfer fee's that were reportedly being offered by Arsenal, were well wide of the mark.

Arsenal's negotiations, which were conducted by both Neill and club secretary Ken Friar, broke down due to both the size of the transfer fee wanted by the club and the players' salary. Ajax wanted £500,000 and Krol's current wages – even though his club were regularly playing in front of gates of less than 10,000, was in excess of £1,000 per week and according to the chairman of Ajax, Arsenal were just being Arsenal. The reality of it was, is that Arsenal had only offered £225,000.

Strangely, the weekend the Krol to Arsenal story broke – or broke down rather, Arsenal had been linked with 19-year old Sunderland midfielder Kevin Arnott – the player who had been attacked by an Arsenal supporter during a dreary goal-less draw at Highbury in early February 1977 – a match which also saw a shot by Sunderland's 18-year old substitute Alan Brown narrowly miss its target and come back off the underside of the bar and one which certainly did hit the target – namely Wilf Rostron landing a punch on Bobby Kerr.

It was also reported that Arsenal had been tracking 21-year old Danish midfielder, Michael Schafer from Lyngby BK and according to Harry Miller of the *Daily Mirror*, that the club had tried to sign Aston Villa's midfield general Dennis Mortimer before the season had started.

Mortimer was another player whose face didn't fit – and like Jimmy Greenhoff of Leeds United, Stoke City and Manchester United, he was often described *as the best player never to get an England cap*. That summer Mortimer had just been made Villa's captain and would be one of the few players to lift both the League Championship trophy and of course the European Cup – in 1981 and 1982 respectively.

"Arsenal have only got one player in midfield – Liam Brady," Mortimer told the journalist after his much-depleted sides 1-1 draw at Highbury on 7th October 1978. "We have found that he goes deep to collect the ball, so he doesn't always do it in the danger areas and this gives you time to recover. They badly need someone."

It was apparent that Brady was now negating the job he was good at – to do Hudson's job.

"Arsenal manager Terry Neill must rue the fact that Arsenal will take the field against Lokomotiv Leizpig in the UEFA Cup without Alan Hudson, a player ideally equipped for the rhythms of European football," wrote Richard Yallop of the *Guardian* on 13th September 1978. "Hudson it was, who helped make Arsenal such an attractive and effective force last season and it is readily admitted at Highbury, that his absence has disrupted the blend, which promised so much this season."

What had happened was that Neill and Howe were forced to toy with similar system that the latter had used in the 1970/71 season – the same system as which catapulted Pat Rice into the first team following the pre-season injury to Jon Sammels. In this instance, Rice was moved into midfield to cover the loss of Hudson, whilst John Devine covered at right-back.

It appeared quite tangled web with Alan Hoby of the *Sunday Express* hitting the nail on the head by stating, "With their European commitments Arsenal should have bought long ago and need to strengthen their first-team squad quickly."

What has possibly never been said, is that in early November Arsenal were one of a few English clubs linked with a £500,000 valued Uruguayan international – the 26-year old free scoring Nando Morena from Penarol – a player who would firstly have a move to Real Madrid blocked in 1975 and then ended up going to another club in Madrid a couple of years later – Rayo Vallecano, before signing for the 1980 European Cup Winner Cup Winners – and straight after they had defeated Arsenal.

As I said, I just loved connections.

Football aside, Emily had been out during the late-afternoon and had got in around 5.30pm.

"Where have you been?" I inquired, on looking up at the kitchen clock.

"Just at my boyfriend's," she lied.

"I wondered why you looked a bit flush."

"I'm probably a bit flush as our Sammy's totally been on *one*," she said. "And I've had the estate agent on the phone for the last half hour, with Jeanette's mam trying to eavesdrop every word."

"You've been over at Jeanette's?"

"Yeh – where else would I see her mam?" she grinned.

I would have threatened to put her over my knee for being a trifle flippant – however, she would have only enjoyed it.

"So, what was up with Herbert?" I further inquired, before looking around. "Where is he by the way – and my other two come to that?"

"Kate and Michael asked if they could take Harmony and Jamie to the cinema – and Sammy kicked off, so they ended up taking him as well."

"Wow – that's a right result," I said.

"Better than Arsenal's," she said. "I heard on the radio that Cazorla missed a penalty in the last minute."

"He showed about as much passion when he struck it as Wenger did in the dugout," I said. "There's no motivation whatsoever."

"Talking about motivation – we do appear to be childless until tomorrow."

"What – they're staying as well?"

"There's a method in Kate's madness," Emily smiled. "She can't interrogate them about your new job while they're over at ours, can she?"

She did have a point.

The job in The States had gathered a bit of momentum as Emily had picked a property just off Atlantic Avenue – sort of between the Cobble and Boerum Hill's areas of Brooklyn, which was around ten miles from JFK and a five-minute walk to Bergen Street Underground Station, which runs straight into Manhattan. The downside was that the houses at both Hamilton Square and Frederick Street, not only blew it away – they had also been a lot less expensive to buy – and when I say a lot – I mean it.

After a couple of weeks, Emily had now got her head well and truly around the fact that we were set for another adventure – however, the down-side was that I knew Jeanette would dig her heels in. When she was destined to go to The States, she had been totally up for it. In this instance, she was very much totally not up for it. There is a story here, however.

ITV needed not only an angle for their new station but an anchor programme – and although that would be down to me, it would also come via an unlikely source.

Emily was always scouring the Internet with both my eldest kids looking for something or other and just a few weeks ago, she had come across some old ITV footage of a Saturday morning kids show, that had run its course around the time Emily had been born. How they got to that YouTube clip was anyone's guess, but they got to it all the same. *The Phantom Flan Flinger*, *Houdi-Elbow*, *Trevor McDoughnut* and *Spit the Dog* were all part of an anarchic ATV programme that was called *Tiswas* – and some of the clips had had all three of them in stitches.

"Yer've got to come and watch this, Lee," a rather creased-up Emily had said.

For the life of me, I could never ever recall it and I said as much – but between us, we did a bit of research, which had us both looking at each other.

"An updated and more-wilder version?" Emily said.

"I don't think any TV station would go for that."

"Yours would," she smiled.

"What – with you as the *Phantom Flan-Flinger*?"

That certainly had her smiling.

Sometimes that is exactly how things start. I looked back at the Sammy documentary and what seemed an age ago and who would have thought it would have led to where it had?

Chapter 49
Abi's Tales – *Take 8*

Change can both be a good thing and a bad thing – however, in the case of ITV 7, I just couldn't put my finger on it. Everything was changing, that was for sure!

Lee was still down as producer and its head, but he hadn't been in the studio's for weeks and Christmas would soon be upon us. There seemed to be people everywhere, and I had gone from being Lee's *Número dos*, to just another body in what was an ever-growing TV station.

I'd made a few friends, but it was nothing to what we had. I saw absolutely nothing of the crowd down at White Lion Street nor did I have any input in the *ITV Sessions* or *Live at The Warehouse* programmes, as I had done before. Like I said – everything was changing. I wasn't working as hard as I had, that was for sure – but nor was I enjoying it the same.

I'd kept in touch with M by text and the odd phone call and I'd called round at Jeanette's a few times, one of which had been quite odd as her mother had been there and you could have cut the atmosphere with a knife. Jeanette's life had become something of a mess since she had split with Ross and she now had some guy in tow that she had previously dated. I thought it was that, what was the problem, however it wasn't.

TV studios are full of rumours with the big one at ours being that Lee had been cherry-picked to either take over one of ITV's other channels or set up an ITV 5 or 6. As is with rumours, there is no smoke without fire and that being the case, there is generally a smidgen of truth in them, and this was no different.

I'd met Jeanette's mother a few times and in my mind, she was your archetypal controlling mum –basically the exact same as mine. She looked at her daughter's life and wanted nothing more than to manage it. The fact that Jeanette's marriage had broken down and the man who had been her husband had remarried, taken stock of his life and done a little bit more than just moved on, apparently drove her mother absolutely dotty.

"Lee's got a job offer in America," Jeanette told me, whilst pouring us a coffee. "That's what all the fuss is about."

"America?" I gasped.

"M only told me the other week," she said.

"He'd never leave you and the children, Jin."

"I wouldn't blame him if he did," she shrugged. "We were going to leave him, weren't we?"

Neither Lee nor M were like that. They would never just up and leave with no thought for anyone else, and I told her as much.

"I'm only kidding," she smiled. "My mother's brainstorm is that he's doing it to teach me a lesson."

"Well that's certainly not true either," I told her.

"I know that and she knows that. She just can't admit it."

"So, what is he doing – about the job, I mean?"

"He's taking it," she said. "Both Lee and M want me and the kids to go with them."

"And that's what your mum's upset about?"

"And that's exactly what my mother's upset about," she smiled. "Lee made things worse by offering to fly them out once or twice a month."

"How the hell would that make it worse?" I asked.

"She feels that it's her job is to hate Lee and he keeps on doing nice things."

I got told as much as she knew about the said job offer and I felt gutted that he would be leaving. I felt even more gutted that he hadn't asked me to go with him.

The next day when I got to the studios I was immediately met by Basher who was a bit fuller of himself than usual. The first instalment of his and Lee's *Arsenal: The Terry Neill Years* documentary had been aired last night and the *Daily Express* had been extremely complimentary about it.

"Did you see it?" enthused Chris.

Nope. But seeing as I'd been tasked with downloading hundreds of hours of footage to help make it, the last thing I had wanted to see was Liam Brady's ugly mug again – unfortunately however, on getting inside I got Huddy's. "Lee's been in and was looking for you," he said.

I therefore sent the main man a text. "Where are you?"

"Home – why?" he texted back.

"Huddy said you were looking for me."

I was waiting well over five minutes for a *Beep-Beep* from my phone. Instead however, I received a call. Apparently, he had been tied up – or so he claimed.

"So, when did you decide that you were not going to tell me about going to America?" I asked him.

"Who are you – my wife?"

"I may as well be, the way you treat me," I said, on shutting the door to my office and sitting on the edge of my desk.

"Did you see the documentary last night?" he asked.

"No."

I then got a silence on the other end of the phone.

"Lee?" I asked.

"What are you wearing?" was his rather strange follow-up question.

"A rubbishy dress," I said. "Why?"

"Is it short?" he inquired.

He surely can't be wanting phone sex, I thought. *Could he?*

"Not especially," I said. "Why, would you want it to be?"

The backside nearly dropped out of my pants with his next line.

"Well put a clean pair of knickers on and meet me at the Café Royal Hotel at one o'clock," he said. "There's some American's I want you to meet – I'll be in the Ten Room."

A clean pair of knickers and a date at a posh hotel. Something certainly to misconstrue, eh? Read on.

When we were at the old firm, the amount of hotel bills Sooty and Lee had to soak up in the business had been nothing short of unbelievable – however, none of these were anywhere near as posh as the Café Royal.

I made room in my itinerary for an afternoon out and seeing as Mr Chris Windley esq. wasn't doing anything constructive I commandeered his vast talents. "Chris – have you got ten minutes."

"For you, ducky dear, I've got eleven – what do you want?"

"I want you to make me beautiful."

He took me into his parlour, put his hands together Archbishop of Canterbury-style and asked me exactly what my mind desired. "I am your slave and your wish is my command," he said.

"I want to look as sophisticated as Jeanette and loads more gorgeous than, M," I said.

"Fuck me – I reckon it'll take a bit more than ten minutes to do that, lovey."

The thing is with male gays is that they are twenty-times more-bitchier than women. Well this one certainly was.

"What did you put your mascara on with?" he inquired, whilst he wiped the canvas blank with the aid of what could only be described as some heavy duty industrial wipes. "This lot looks as though it has been put on with a trowel."

Grrr.

"You should look after your skin a lot better," he added.

"To say your only thirty, your complexion is shocking."

"I'm nowhere near frigging thirty, you, cheeky swine – I'm only twenty-five."

"Oops," he grinned.

Double grrr.

"Milan brought in some beautiful dresses for Jeanette's wardrobe this morning," he added.

"Yeh, I know, it was me who signed for them."

"If you were a bit slimmer, you could have borrowed one," he further bitched.

Triple grrr.

"There's a nice red one in there that would really offset the blotches on your neck."

"Do you say this shit just to annoy me?" I snapped.

"What?" he rather innocently shrugged.

"I'm only a size frigging ten, and I definitely don't have blotches on my neck."

"Suit yourself," he said.

"I am a ten – I've always been a ten," I mumbled.

You wouldn't have thought he was one of the outreach volunteers at the Angus Street branch of The Samaritans down in New Cross. His line of patter certainly wouldn't entice me off a roof – perhaps, maybe only to strangle him.

"So, where are you off to ducky?" he inquired.

"I'm meeting Lee at the Café Royal," I rather proudly stated.

"Where are you meeting him?"

"Room Ten," I said.

"He's booked you a room?" he rather inquisitively inquired. "That sounds interesting."

"I don't know," I shrugged. "He just said to meet him there at one."

"I hope you've put on a clean pair of knickers."

Talk about giving you an inferiority complex! I thought.

After a 40-minute session of verbal torture, I looked nowhere near as sophisticated as Jeanette nor as beautiful as M. Nor could I fit into any of Milan Baros's really posh dresses – red or frigging otherwise. And just for good measure, Chris enlightened me with the fact that Lee hated bare legs.

That was strange, as during my three-day Tuscan adventure, everyone had bare legs – even Basher.

"What really?" I asked.

"That's what M once told me," he said.

Mmm, that was interesting, I thought.

I made my way across the landing where I got accosted by the frigging *Six Million Dollar Man* – or Huddy, rather. He had caught wind of my not-so secret planned liaison down at the Café Royal with Lee – and the bottom line was, could he come?

"I think you need to work on trying to adapt your social skills a bit more, before we unleash you in a posh hotel," I told him.

Last night's *Huddy Show* starring the main man himself had more fucking bloopers than a show made up and crammed full of them. Having Rodney Marsh on his version of *Question of Sport* was like a red rag to a bull. In between throwing sexual superlatives at him and continually referring to him as "Brian", he must have threatened to kick his head in at least five times.

"Him and Bruce Rioch were the most hated men in football," he snapped.

"Yeh – hated by you," I said.

I went into my office to pick up a few things only to find Sooty rooting around in my drawers. My desk drawers that is.

"Oh – I thought you were out," he said.

"No doubt," I replied. "What exactly are you after?"

"The keys for the TV and media suite."

"You can't have them," I told him.

"Why?"

"Lee says no-one can have them, especially you."

"When did he say that?"

"You know exactly when he said that as you were there when he said it," I told him.

The TV and media suite was the only place in the building which you couldn't see into and which at one time was never locked. That was until Lee went in there with a few suits from Sky Atlantic only to walk in on Sooty and one of the Temps that had been hired-in on a supposed two-week jobby to categorise and reference loads of film footage. Obviously, Lee got the ready-made answer of why it had taken them nearly two months to actually complete the job.

Not even Sooty telling me that I looked drop dead gorgeous could offset the bollocking I gave him for rooting through my stuff.

"So, where are you off to – you know, all dolled up?" he asked.

"None of your frigging business," I said, before asking if I could borrow his overcoat.

"What do you want to borrow my coat for?"

"I can't go on the Tube dressed like this – can I?"

The acting head of wardrobe (until ITV set on a proper one) – Jaime Hudson, had sorted me out a brand-new dress from M's *Live at The Warehouse* set. The thing worth noting is that although M dresses quite reserved off set, on it she's anything but.

"If I can't get into Jeanette's stuff I'm hardly likely to fit in one of M's," I said.

"They're new ones," Jaime said. "Designed to cover her bump."

Even with her three months off having a baby I still found it one hell of a squeeze to get into it. There was also another thing too. With her only being a short-arse and me being some six inches taller, the hemline was rather high to say the least.

As *Live at The Warehouse* promoted indie bands from what was often termed as the North London sound – most of who wore circa 1960's type clothes, the thing I currently had on my back was of a similar ilk, so much so, I'd certainly caught Kirsty's attention. "Wow – you could audition for *The Benny Hill Show* wearing that," she said.

Hence me requesting the use of Sooty's overcoat.

"I'll have it back to you before you leave," I told him.

I got on the Tube at Bounds Green and by the time it had reached Turnpike Lane I had two young lads firmly pushed up against me, both of whom possessed rather wandering hands.

"Do you mind?" I said to one of them.

Obviously they didn't and me actually saying it was fairly pointless as they didn't speak one word of English – however, I have to say that Chris's bare leg revelation saved me from maximum satisfaction come the Finsbury Park interchange, where a further four lads who obviously belonged to the self-same professional groping outfit got on the train and who set about doing their job with meticulous focus – that was until the British Transport Police boarded the train at King's Cross and arrested them all.

I was in quite good company on that score. Even the totally unfrigginggropable Liam Brady had been accosted by a few lads whilst getting off a Tube at Finsbury Park Station on 18th January 1979. According to the player he had been called an "Irish bum" and had been smacked in the mouth and suffered a cut lip and a ripped shirt.

As for me, I had been accosted by twice as many youths and been called a "very sexy lady", had my ear blown in once or twice and not even suffered as much as a ladder in my tights.

"We have it all on CCTV, Miss," one officer said. "Would you want to make a statement?"

Sex with males for me is like the London bus scenario. You're waiting for ages and get absolutely **none** and then seven *come* at once. I obviously never said that, although I certainly thought it.

"I have a business meeting in the city," I jabbered to the officer, whilst rooting around for a business card in Sooty's coat. "However, if you ring the office – I'll gladly make one."

"Diva Escorts?" shrugged the policeman, on reading the card.

Fucking Sooty, I thought.

"Sorry – it's not my coat," I told him. Not that he believed me, however

By the time, I got off the train at Piccadilly Circus I was a bag of nerves, with me totally hoping that I still looked drop dead gorgeous after being the subject of a systematic fumbling, and post-grope it being very much insinuated by a British Transport Policeman that I was indeed some prostitute.

I'd be just glad of getting to the hotel and having some of the old vino blanco.

"Yes miss?" inquired a guy on the Concierge.

"Room Ten," I said.

I got pointed the way and felt absolutely happy in the knowledge that the drop dead gorgeous Abi Tyson looking back at me in the mirror in the lift, would soon be guzzling wine and tête-à-tête-*ing* with the man I admired the most. Outside the door, I opened up Sooty's coat and did the job of the *repositioning of assets*, which the synchronised gropers had managed to shift out of place and brushed myself down, before knocking on the thing.

The door was opened by some well-heeled American with a bald head and Michael Caine-type bins. "You look absolutely fantastic," he said, which definitely cheered me up. "Doesn't she honey?"

I walked in to be met by a very affluent female, who looked much younger than him. "They weren't understating it when they said how beautiful you were," she said, as she offered to take my coat. "And I can't believe how prompt you are."

I'd only been in their company a matter of seconds and felt totally at ease.

"I'm Abigail Tyson," I told them. "My friends and colleagues call me Abi."

"Well Abi," said the bald bloke in the rims. "We certainly weren't expecting anything as lovely as you."

"You're so kind," I told them.

"Would you care for a drink?" asked the lady.

"I don't mind if I do," I smiled. "A white wine would be very nice."

"I'm Connie and this is Larry," smiled the lady.

This was the life, I thought. *Wined and dined by a couple of wealthy Americans.*

"Your clothes and make-up are first class, Abi," said the lady, as she handed me a drink.

"I cheated really," I told them. "Chris, the make-up guy at work did my eye shadow and hair and I borrowed one of M's dresses."

"You have an in-house make-up guy?" inquired Larry.

"Yeh, he's very Julian Clary," I told them. "Very good at his job, but a right bitch."

"It sounds quite a professional set-up," added Larry.

"I think with advertising and sales we're looking at close to four hundred million," I told them.

"Gee Whizz," he said. "That's one hell of a turnover."

"It's been hard work, but we still try to be as professional as possible."

"So, you work long hours?" inquired the lady.

"Sure – sometimes fifteen hours a day, dependant on what Lee wants," I smiled. "He's a brilliant boss, though."

"I bet," said the man.

"Sit down Abi," said Connie, as she tapped a seat at the side of her, "Take a load off – we have all afternoon."

Indeed, we do, I thought.

"Do you mind if I have a drink?" asked Larry.

"Not at all," I said. "Fill your boots."

I couldn't believe how polite they both were, me thinking that if they thought I was this good, no wonder Lee had got the gig.

"So, where in The States are you from?" I asked.

"Philadelphia," said Larry. "Although Connie is from Nebraska."

"We had a film producer from Philadelphia in over the summer," I told them. "He was shooting what will be a six-part serial, which is looking absolutely brilliant."

"So, your company do films as well?" inquired Larry.

"We've got a few shows under our belt," I told them. "But I must admit, doing the fictional drama was a bit special."

"So, these shows?" asked the lady. "You found them interesting?"

"We did one as an exposé of the British porn industry," I told them. "That's up for some award. Sooty who now works for us, was like a director of the company at the time."

"Sooty?" inquired the man.

"Yeh – Tim Sutton," I told them. "He's certainly a character."

"Do you act in them?" asked Connie.

"No, I direct," I said. "I couldn't act to save my life. M on the other hand is absolutely brilliant."

"She sounds great," said the lady. "Is she pretty?"

"Gorgeous," I said. "She's having to take it easy of late as she's pregnant."

"I bet it's Lee's," said the lady.

"Yeh, of course it is," I said.

"Perks of the job," Larry smiled, as he poured me another glass of wine.

"Yeh – I suppose," I shrugged. "She'll be casting for the lesbian character in a film being shot in Philadelphia that's pre-titled *Desiree.*"

"Well I think she's passed the interview – don't you Larry?" smiled Connie.

Interview? I thought. *That's the easiest interview I've ever had.*

"We need a screen test, though, Connie," said the man. "Don't forget the screen test."

"You want me to do a screen test?" I smiled. "I really didn't expect this."

"We have to give everyone a screen test," added Larry.

If M could stride through one, then so could I, I thought.

"Do you have a script?" I asked. "Or aren't there any – words that is?"

Larry explained the scenario. "Just ad-lib," he said. "But it has to be really romantic."

Wow! I thought. *This is mega.*

"Imagine that Connie's wildly in love with you and her husband has retired to bed, kinda worse for wear," he told me. "Just use the couch and I'll shoot it."

"Is she in love with Connie too?" I excitedly inquired. "I'm just asking, so I can act accordingly."

"Madly," he said. "But the husband doesn't know."

"Wow, it sounds really intriguing," I smiled.

Larry got out what was a Sony PXW-FS5K camcorder, which although it wasn't the best, it was still a natty piece of hardware to chuck in a holdall.

"We use the PWX-Five Hundred's for stuff such as this," I told him. "You get a better variation with the lighting and the picture is far superior, especially for the close-up stuff that you're planning."

He seemed more than impressed, so much so I thought he appeared to be getting a bit excited about it all. Me personally – it would have to be a Sony F65RS/VF F65RS to get me that giddy – but there you go.

I then remembered exactly what M had told me. "I just try to think that I'm with Lee," she'd said.

I suppose I could do that – however, the Connie lady wasn't that bad, sort of in her early-forties and quite appealing in a brash American-kind of way ...probably.

"When you are ready ladies," said Larry.

This was extremely exciting and as I kicked off my shoes and got quite comfortable, Connie started talking about something, which I have since totally forgotten about before hitting me with a kiss and what a kiss it was. She had a tongue like a frigging anteater and her hands were everywhere.

"Kiss me back," said Connie.

I did, but trying to focus when her hand was rubbing between my legs, was a bit hard as all I had on my mind was my recent Tube ride post-Finsbury Park, which was about as nearly as romantic. After a good three or four minutes of tongue-in-mouth action, I fully understood what M had meant when she had told me that she was aching all over. My jaw felt like it was going to seize up and we were only on the first frigging take.

"You've got to tell me you love me," said Connie.

Fucking hell – it was hard enough trying to breathe, without having to dialogue, I thought.

I then remember noticing some movement in her upper set of teeth as the palate came loose and then over at the cameraman out of the corner of my eye ...and that did it. I threw-up all over my supposed female lover.

"Ugh," I choked. "Sorry Connie – it's not your teeth – he's got his thing out."

I wasn't lying. While his wife had been forcefully trying to remove my tonsils, he had been at the other side of the room – one hand on his camera, and knocking one out with the other.

Connie was livid at the bowl of Cocoa Pops, Vanilla Slice and about six cups of coffee that she had to brush off her dress. As was I, when a knock came at the door.

"Hiya – I'm Gail from Capital Escorts," said the girl, on Larry opening it.

Just then my phone started ringing. It was Lee.

"Where are you?" he asked.

"Where you were supposed to be – in Room Ten with a pair of fucking idiots," I told him.

"I'm down in the Ten Room, you twit," he said.

I must have got in that lift looking like I had been dragged through a hedge backwards. I'd only been out less than an hour and I'd been captured on Transport for London's CCTV as well as a camera you could buy from Argos, being sexually assaulted by a load of frigging foreigners – and then having the pleasure of seeing some egghead of a cameraman having a wank, whilst his deranged wife dislodged her teeth trying to choke me with her tongue. I'd certainly had better days, that's for sure.

I managed to find the stinking Ten Room – I mean, which idiot would think of calling a dining room in a hotel something as stupid as that?

"Are you okay Abi?" M asked, post-my arrival.

"If I told you what's happened to me in the last hour you wouldn't believe it," I told her.

"You look really nice," she smiled, before looking at me a bit closer. "Although your lip gloss is a bit all over the place."

"Yeh – I've just had some old woman in Room Ten try her best at licking it off," I gibbered.

M did no more than rip a make-up wipe out of her handbag, carefully wipe my face and reapply some lippy. As for me? I felt like bursting out crying.

"What's up with you?" asked Lee, on seeing my bottom lip wobbling.

"Nothing," M told him, before turning to me and smiling. "Are you okay to have some lunch and listen to what's happening?"

I nodded. It was getting as though M was turning into my mum.

Chapter 50

The Sooty Show – Episode 10

It was all happening and of that there was absolutely no doubt. The bane of misery that was my wife had finally agreed to proceed with the divorce and Lee and M were off to The States – and rather strangely taking Jeanette with them.

"How does that work?" Debbie asked me.

"I'm not really sure," I shrugged.

Although we spoke regularly, Lee had kept me firmly at arms-length since the Wortley Hall-thing, and as such, outside of work I got to know very little.

ITV 7 was now the real deal and completely blew Sky Sports out of the water. It was that good. Lee had to take all the credit as he had put a team together, lost half of, it only to come back with an even better set-up. *The Sooty Show* and *The Huddy Show* that ran a couple of nights a week formed an integral part of its success and I couldn't grumble – I was now being paid twice what I had earned and since the buyout, my workload had eased-up immensely, but that was down to the fact that Lee's demand for 110% wasn't around anymore, as some suit from South Bank had been temporarily put in charge.

On the home front, we had been doing a lot of moving around and had moved from a rented semi in West Ham to a flat overlooking Joseph Grimaldi Park before settling on a broken down four-storey shithole on Ritchie Street, just top side of the White Lion Street Studios.

"This'll take some work," Debbie had said to me.

She was right. Getting a mortgage for the thing had been the hardest bit of graft that I had ever had to undertake and only the promise of getting half he profit from the house at Holland Park had managed to swing the deal.

That aside, I'd never been as happy. Although they were worlds apart and looked absolutely nothing like each other, Debbie was my version of M and there was nothing that she wouldn't do to make things run smooth. She also got on quite well with her alter-ego, and one particular day I got home from work to find them both emptying M's Range Rover of standard lamps, rugs, kitchen utensils and a load of other pointless stuff.

"You ought to be ashamed of yourself," M told me. "You can't have the girl living in squalor."

Squalor? I had a brand spanking new 55" TV, DVD and surround sound and the best home entertainment system on the planet along with a really modern black leather three-piece suite and a great big bed to kip in.

"You want to get my dad to come down and get the place sorted for you," she said.

"Why – will he do it for nowt?" I asked.

"Don't let him kid you, Debbie – he can afford it."

The big problem with M was that she knew far too much as her gob shite of a husband told her everything – including the figure of what ITV now paid me, which was something which had Huddy pissing in my ears most days.

"How come we do the same amount of work, yet you get paid more?" he had asked me.

"Because I'm super talented and indispensable and you pissed all yours away and are only here because Lee felt sorry for you."

I got my random "Fack off" and ten-minute sulk, until he completely forgot about it. He was either getting Alzheimer's or that Henri Charrière book that he often carried around with him like some boring Jehovah's Witness, was rubbing off on him and making him more philosophical about life.

"Haven't you read that thing yet?" I asked, regarding the novel that was *Papillon*.

"Those who haven't been exposed to the hypocrisies of a civilized education react to things naturally, as they happen," he answered in a rather aloof tone. "It is in the here and now that they are either happy or unhappy, joyful or sad, interested or indifferent."

Yeh – definitely fucking Alzheimer's, I thought.

As with Lee, I had both my kids a couple of days through the week, but in the background, I had the haunting figure of Olivia Cook pushing the courts to further shake me down in her bid to make me penniless, with the Donald-kid being the most effective tool in her armoury. DNA has got a lot to answer for.

"Dad, what does our brother look like?" our Zooey asked me the other week.

"No idea," I said. "I only pay for him."

Debbie urged me to make contact and play the woman at her own game – that of going for full custody.

"Yeh – and what if I end up getting lumbered with him?" I said.

"That's awful," she said.

She was right – it was, and after some deliberation we had a drive up to Harpenden one evening and Debbie's intuition had been spot on. The kids' grandma and granddad may have wanted my financial input, but they certainly didn't want me in his life. What pissed me off most wasn't so much the fact that they didn't want me, but the fact that the woman had been well up for having **Numb***nuts* as his dad and M his step mum. With me it was a case of "Thank-you, but fuck off" and I didn't get past the front door.

"Maybe it's a good thing," I said.

"Why would you say that?" Debbie asked.

"Well look at me – my life's all over the place."

"M told me that Lee's was the same when she met him – and look at them now."

I was sick off looking at them, and ten-times sicker when someone used them as a yardstick – especially when that particular yardstick was used to measure my failure against his success. I mean – if he fell in a pile of shit he'd come out holding a string of pearls. If I fell in a pile a shit, I'd just stink.

"Dad will you take us to see Auntie M and Uncle Lee?" the kids regularly asked on me picking them up.

"Why, what's up with just being with me?"

"Nothing," shrugged our Mia.

Kids aren't stupid and they know what they like and what they don't.

When Harmony and Jamie used to come to our house, they were generally itching to go home after ten minutes. When our Mia and Zooey go to theirs, they need dragging out with a tirfor.

"Aw dad, can't we stay longer?"

Although they love Lee – mainly because he acts like a pillock, it's M that makes their house a home. You go into their house and its always noisy and there's a hive of activity with the TV and radio on, two ferrets racing around the floorboards and smell of cooking or baking coming from the kitchen. The house at Holland Park was never like that and all you could hear amidst the ticking clocks was Libby whining on. As for this house, it's currently about as homely as a holding cell and even M's moving-in present of a coffee maker couldn't offset the smell of damp.

I knew Debbie wanted more movement in the relationship, so I did as M had said and got Mike over – who came mob handed with both Sil' and Sammy.

"We've come to see your Uncle Sooty, haven't we?" his granny smiled at him – Sammy that is and not Mike.

"He doesn't half look like your M," said Debbie, as she took him off her.

"He's just as bad tempered," laughed Sil'. "It took three screaming fits and the enticement of a Milky Way for us to get his coat and hat on. Our M and Lee must have the *patience of Job* to put up with that every day."

"So, what are you after doing with the place, Sooty lad?" asked Mike, as he looked around.

I looked over at Debbie who was still cutchy-cooing with Sammy and I said the next bit without really thinking. "Deb – Mike wants to know what you are after doing with the place?"

"Me?" she shrugged.

"Yeh – it's you who'll be trying to make the place liveable," I said.

She hadn't said much about one thing nor the other, but I knew with M rattling on in her ears that she wouldn't be devoid of ideas.

In the meantime, I took the opportunity to grill Sil' about *Silly bollocks* taking both his wives and three kids to The States.

"I'm certainly not ecstatic about it," Sil' said.

"What about Mike?" I inquired.

"If it was up to Mike he'd go with them," she smiled. "He's fairly excited for them, to be honest."

"So, why are they dragging Jeanette along?"

"Hasn't he told you?" she shrugged.

"I've not really seen him," I lied.

"Our M and Jeanette will be doing the *ITV Sessions* from New York and are to host some three-hour children's programme on a Saturday morning."

"Kid's programme?" I shrugged.

"*Tiswas*," said Mike.

"What the hell's that?" I asked.

"YouTube it," he grinned. "The original was as funny as heck."

"My mam and dad were *Swap Shop*," said Sil'. "They thought *Tiswas* was a bit over the top."

That was interesting, I thought.

That aside, the Arsenal documentary that everyone was raving about had me on it as its *face* this particular night.

"With their European commitments, they should have bought long ago and need to strengthen their first team squad quickly," wrote Alan Hoby of the *Sunday Express*, following Arsenal's 1-0 win over newly promoted Southampton in late October 1978.

Amidst continual booing from the crowd and the currently manager-less Leeds United publicly trying to entice Lawrie McMenemy from their opponents, Arsenal looked both weak and shabby and were described as extremely lucky to take any points from the game.

The same could have been said after the clubs 0-0 draw with Norwich City at Highbury on 9th December 1978.

"Arsenal need to spend a million pounds if their ambitions extend beyond mere respectability," wrote James Lawton of the *Daily Express*. "Terry Neill accepts the problem and talks of the search for quality players – however, he may have to reach some swift compromise if Arsenal are to keep pace with the First Division's dwindling elite."

Neill had wasted chance after chance of building on the previous season and had instead let Alan Hudson walk out of the club and had seen Malcolm Macdonald suffer an injury from which he would never recover.

In the 1978/79 season, Arsenal were light and heavily reliant on Liam Brady – and after getting sent off in the UEFA Cup tie against Hajduk Split, his suspension would show the Arsenal supporters exactly what the team would be like without him. For all Neill's foibles in losing Hudson and failing to secure the services of Ruud Krol, Arsenal would exit a competition in which they could have quite easily won with the squad of the previous season, with Neill himself stating later-on in life that, that was indeed the case.

The tactics of Don Howe could only take the club so far and what was needed were major signings – however, Arsenal not only underbid for players – they also failed to offer them top wages.

Brady inferred that if the ambition would have been there, he would have stayed. To let Alan Ball go showed a lack of ambition as did the failure to man-manage Hudson along with their failure to firmly move for their three main targets – that of Francis, Wilkins and either Sansom or Statham.

As Lee had already said, Danny Blanchflower hit the nail on the head when he said that when Chelsea were finally prepared to listen to offers for Wilkins, Arsenal's valuation of him fell well short of the players real worth, therefore they moved for Brian Talbot. Arsenal were still trying to negotiate in the two and three hundred thousand bracket at a time when bids of half a million were to become commonplace.

Trevor Francis would have been a major success at Arsenal and would have readily fitted into the system –

however, and as history will tell you Arsenal valued him at £500,000 when firstly Coventry City and then Nottingham Forest posted bids of £900,000 and £1 million respectively.

It was the same with Ray Wilkins – Arsenal's value of the player was in the region of £400,000, whilst Manchester United would need more than double that to secure the players services.

Arsenal valued Wolverhampton Wanderers' Steve Daley at £350,000 and inquired about the player around the same time as Manchester City had, and whose larger than life coach publicly unsettled the player in the media, with the-then Wolves manager John Barnwell responding by saying that "Malcolm Allison could go to hell".

Money as ever, talked – and even though there was a hatred of sorts between the two, Daley did eventually go to City – and for over £1.1 million more than Arsenal had initially valued him at.

Both Neill and Bertie Mee before him had insisted that agreeing transfers was an "extremely hard business".

If you have the cash and are willing to spend it, it fucking isn't – as Brian Clough, Dave Sexton and Malcolm Allison proved at the time.

It took Arsenal until January to make a move in the transfer market, where more brinkmanship was evident between Terry Neill and his nemesis Bobby Robson. As already stated, Neill's public interest in Brian Talbot after the F.A Cup Final had more than unsettled the player, something which Robson had readily admitted to journalist Alan Hoby.

"Ever since I was a boy I've wanted to play for Arsenal," Talbot had told Tony Stenson of the *Daily Mirror* on him finally putting pen to paper to complete his £450,000 transfer. "They are a tradition, a part of history and being a southerner they are a Mecca for any player who wants the best."

The Talbot to Arsenal transfer, could have quite easily never happened, as Arsenal had threatened to pull the plug on the deal when Robson was about to Cup-Tie the player by playing him in a previously postponed F.A Cup Third Round match against Carlisle United.

The upshot was that Arsenal had the money, but wouldn't part with it, which was something that saw Frank McGarvey's move to Arsenal break down and which saw Arsenal firmly move into the driving seat to negotiate a deal for a player they had supposedly been trailing all season. Arsenal had been linked with Glasgow Rangers centre-forward Derek Johnstone, since the spring and on 16th December 1978, a contingent from Highbury had watched him bag four goals in his clubs 5-3 defeat of Heart of Midlothian.

What should also be noted is that Bertie Mee had tried to sign Johnstone as a 16-year old in December 1968.

"Arsenal and Spurs are ready to mount a £500,000 battle for the signature of Glasgow Rangers and Scotland strike ace Derek Johnstone who has surged back to top form," wrote Ray Bradley of the *Sunday Express*. "With a big question mark hanging over Malcolm Macdonald's future at Highbury, The Gunners are now ready to go back for 24-year old Johnstone after having a bid rejected in the summer."

Although the player had submitted a transfer request, legend has it that Rangers manager, John Greig persuaded him to stay. As for Arsenal being serious in acquiring the players' services – they needed a striker of that there was no doubt and there was even a story by John Davies of the *Daily Express* stating, that Arsenal could be prepared to do a deal with Coventry City, and one which would see Macdonald go to Highfield Road in a player plus cash deal with the unsettled Mick Ferguson going to Highbury.

What was also in the news was that Manchester City were wanting to offload their ex-England striker Mike Channon and according to Steve Curry of the *Daily Express* a bid of £200,000-plus would have secured the 30-year old's signature.

Arsenal had reportedly been interested in Channon in mid-July 1975, around the time of the players transfer request – a move which had been rejected by Southampton.

However, on being told of Channon's availability in late-January 1979, the journalist explained that Arsenal along with a few other London clubs had given a "not interested" reaction, with possibly his age, form and wages scuppering any potential deal.

Two months later Channon would come to Highbury and earn the man-of-the-match award after firing home a fiercely driven free kick after 25 minutes to earn Manchester City a 1-1 draw, which was also a game where he and O'Leary had clashed in the final few minutes with the Arsenal defender insinuating that Channon had gone over a little too easy in the penalty area after running on to a pass from Asa Hartford.

According to the press, it was Charlton's 24-year old Mike Flanagan that Arsenal were supposedly serious about – however, the timing of a transfer suddenly became awkward after he was infamously sent off for fighting with his own player in a F.A Cup Third Road match against a Dickie Guy-inspired non-League Maidstone.

"Tampa Bay Rowdies have outbid the English First Division and come up with £700,000 for the transfer of striker Mike Flanagan," wrote Steve Curry of the *Daily Express* on 15th February 1979. "Charlton manager Andy Nelson and Tampa boss Gordon Jago were negotiating late last night on a deal that would deprive English Soccer of one of its most colourful players. Arsenal were widely expected to sign Flanagan, but Terry Neill's valuation fell short of Charlton's asking price."

Mmm. Was it bad timing or was it the money?

According to Ray Bradley of the *Sunday Express* on 31st December 1978, Arsenal had had two bids knocked-back and were expected to go back in with another bid of £400,000, with Don Howe telling Terry Smith of the *Daily Mirror* some 13 days later that Arsenal were going to spend again and if they could get another quality player before the March transfer deadline, they would stand a great chance of pushing for the title.

As regards Mike Flanagan, he turned down the move to America and walked out on Charlton Athletic, which along with his high-profile sending off showed something of a *conducting unbecoming* and caused something of a backtrack from the Arsenal chairman Denis Hill-Wood who told Harry Miller of the *Daily Mirror* that he and Terry Neill weren't interested and hadn't spoken about the player in ages, having recently got the man they really wanted in Brian Talbot.

"My ambition has always been to ply my trade in England and if a First Division club comes in with an acceptable offer, I will be happy to join them," Flanagan had told the *Daily Express*. "The trouble at the moment, is that Charlton are quoting one price for me to one club and a completely different price to another and the overall effect is placing me out of the reach of the First Division."

Watching me on TV was something which Debbie found extremely interesting.

"I think it's brilliant that I'm living with a football presenter from off the telly," she smiled.

"Hazel Hall probably had the same mindset, but in the end probably wished she hadn't," I said.

"Hazel Hall?" she shrugged. "Who's she?"

"The wife of Stuart Hall – after fifty-odd years of marriage she ended up filing for divorce after her husband got sentenced to five years for fiddling about with nine and ten-year old girls."

An "Ugh" was as much as I got back.

What was strange about the Hill-Wood quote is that it was common knowledge that Arsenal needed to strengthen, and Arsenal's annual "He'll be as good as a new signing" raised its deflective head one month later when the *Sunday Express* ran with Ray Bradley's scoop of "Super Deal for £4 million Gunners".

Arsenal weren't actually in for anybody, they were just letting their fan base know that they should be grateful, as they would be tying both Liam Brady and David O'Leary down to new contracts with Hill-Wood adding comment: "They are two of the greatest players in Britain and I wouldn't take £4 million for the pair of them."

Terry Neill's blarney was apparently rubbing off on his chairman!

Chapter 51

Tiswas

"I want to go Lee, but I've just bought a new house and everything," Abi told me.

I had just offered her a job as my number two at ITV America along with a substantial financial package and explained to her that it was a chance in a lifetime. She had taken just twenty seconds to knock it back.

"Think about it," I said. "This is *the* ultimate career move."

"What do you think, M?" she asked my wife.

"I think you should do what you feel is best for you, love – only you can make that decision."

A move of both home and career may look exciting looking in from the outside, but the amount of problems it can cause is quite unbelievable. Acquiring property, sorting schools for the kids, kitting out a new home, feeling your way into a new job, along with trying to embrace a totally different culture. Like I said, it's anything but straightforward.

"Christ almighty, Lee – have you seen the cost of houses over there," was Jeanette's first shriek. "I couldn't ever think about moving there until I sell our house."

I remember the discussion at our kitchen table with the word "vividly" being an understatement. Everything I proposed, being questioned, before getting knocked back – and as we had chosen Brooklyn as a base, she had got her awkward head on and was looking at places as far away as Long Island.

"Come on Jin," said M. "We are going out there as a family – we need to stay close."

"It's okay you saying that – I don't have your financial clout to just up sticks and throw a few million at buying a big new house."

"Lee's not asking you to," Emily told her.

I wasn't and I offered her a similar deal to that of Abi in that the job would provide her with an apartment.

"What – some flat?" she had initially said, before rather nonchalantly turning her nose up at every one that had been on offer.

In the end, I upped the ante and she agreed on some extremely plush albeit overpriced apartment on Furman Street, close to the Brooklyn Bridge, which had a great view of both the East River and the New York skyline – however, more importantly, it was just five minutes away from where we were looking to locate.

"It's still a flat," she grumbled.

"It's not a frigging flat," I told her. "It's got over four thousand feet of space, which makes it much bigger than the house in Clerkenwell."

"And this apartment or whatever is free?" she asked.

"Yeh – to you it is," I said.

That wasn't really the deal breaker I thought it would be as she hummed and erred for a good hour about a boat load of other shite.

"Crikey – and I thought that I panicked a bit," said Emily, later that night whilst sat cross-legged on the bed. "She certainly wants you to do everything for her."

Emily was right, she did – and trying to factor an extra ten-grand a month rent as part of her salary, I knew would be problematic and I have to say that my wife wasn't best pleased after I'd succumbed to her demands for a bigger and better place and then agreed to personally go into my own pocket to get it for her.

"You must be mad, love," she said. "You spent half the summer both worried and upset about her taking away the children and moving them into a much lesser place and now you're just caving in to her demands."

"I just want my kids, M – what can I say?"

"I know you do, love – but just be careful, she's playing you."

I didn't need Emily to tell me that.

My lad was certainly in two minds about the move – his school football being the root of his concern.

"They'll have football teams in New York," I told him, as I walked back from training with him. "And think of it this way – you will be the star player, being from England and having been coached by Huddy."

"Can't I just fly back for the matches?" he asked.

"Who do you think you are – Ronaldhino?"

That brought a giggle.

"Alan's a bit upset about me leaving," my lad had told me. "He said that his long-term plans for the team revolve around me."

I knew there was a reason why Huddy was being a bit *off* with me. I thought it was because I hadn't offered him a job as a co-host on the all new *Tiswas* – you know, a sort of aged Chris Tarrant with Tourette's.

"Why do they call it *Sucker* in America, Dad?" he asked.

"It's Soccer, not Sucker," I told him. "It's probably because they have their own type of football that involves wearing crash helmets, slinging a rugby ball around and trying to break each other's necks."

"Will I have to play that?" he asked.

"No idea – but whatever sport you do, I'm sure that you'll be brilliant at it."

A couple of days later when I got in from work, I found him sat watching DVD's of me playing school football on the TV down in the kitchen. It transpired via Emily that he didn't really want to leave behind what he had described as his "brill' life".

"He's just being stubborn," said his sister. "M told him that while ever we are together everything will always be great."

Both Emily and myself knew exactly what he meant. He was extremely popular at school, had loads of friends, had two pairs of grandparents and a set of great grandparents that he dearly loved, as well as a pair of ferrets that he had been whittling about ever since New York had been first mentioned.

"Your gran and granddad will see you nearly as much as they do now," Emily told him. "Your dad will fly them over and me, you and our Harmony will be able to pick them up from the airport – like we do when they come down on the train. Same goes with your Granny Kate and Granddad Michael."

"What about Erv'?" he asked.

"I can't fly him over as he's just a kid," I said. "And I'm certainly not having his mum and stepdad over."

"We'll not be in New York all the time," Emily told him. "We will be going back to London, so you will be able to see him then."

"What about the house in Liverpool?" he asked.

The house at Hamilton Square was the one thing that Emily had never wanted to leave behind. The house which she had adoringly put together piece by piece to create what was the perfect weekend home for us all. A home in the town where she had grown up amongst all her family and friends.

Quite unbeknown to me, when Jeanette had first planned to move Stateside with Ross – the place that they were planning on living in wasn't actually in New York City, but in the State of New York – and was some house in the country overlooking Irondequoit Bay in Rochester County.

"I thought it was in Manhattan, the way he was talking," I said to Emily, after she had enlightened me about the rather sketchy description that I had been given by Ross.

"Nah," she shrugged. "Some wooden hut near the 'label's studios on Lake Ontario."

"I wonder why I thought it was in the city?" I shrugged.

"Probably because he's dead boring, so you never took any interest when he was drolling on about it."

"Possibly," I said.

"Who are you talking about – Ross?" asked my daughter.

Rules 20 through to 50, never talk about grown up stuff or use grown up words in front of my kids – ever.

"What did you say?" Jeanette had once asked on me taking the kids home and after my lad had mentioned the fact that Emily had said a sentence that had been sprinkled with the odd innuendo or two.

"Maybe he was on about M complaining about the workmen in the basement and the cracks in the plaster that they'd caused," I'd replied, on first being interrogated.

"Bollocks, Lee," she'd snapped. "Do you think I'm effing stupid?"

Emily had duly requested that a couple of holes could do with filling upon my immediate return.

"Well I hope you didn't disappoint her," sniped my ex.

I couldn't remember off hand.

Emily was often creased-up at some of the scrapes they got us into. "I'm sorry for laughing, love – it's just dead funny."

Apparently at some point I must have told Emily that she must take after her mum in the bedroom department, and that snippet of information was relayed by my daughter.

"Dad said that M **cooks** like a rabbit," she shrugged. "And that she must definitely take after you, Gran."

Sil' was gobsmacked.

"I'd really take that as a compliment, mam," their Emily had said, once she'd gained her composure and stopped pissing herself.

As for me – I nearly died on the spot. It wasn't just resigned to us and grown-up sex talk either. It was normal grown up gossip that at times could well get both repeated and misinterpreted.

Back in real time and to my daughters' question.

"Yes, love," said Emily. "We were talking about Ross."

"Mum was on the telephone to him last night," my daughter told us.

"Who – Ross?" Emily shrugged.

"But I'm not supposed to say."

"That's okay," said Emily. "Anything you want to tell us, you can – and I promise you that I would never ever say anything that could ever get you in trouble with your mam."

"I heard mum telling him about that big apartment we're going to move into," she mumbled. "And that we would be just over six hours away."

Emily just gave her a cuddle.

"He must have been asking lots of things about you," she shrugged. "I don't really know what, though."

I hadn't heard a thing of Ross Bain since ITV's buyout of LMJ and White Lion – Emily had however, and once both kids were in bed I got passed that snippet of information. According to my wife he was indeed just over six hours away – but by car, not by plane. He was still in New York State.

"How do you know that?" I asked.

"Jeanette – who else?" she shrugged.

"So, she's still talking to him, then?"

Emily nodded.

The pact that Emily and my ex-wife had formed and which at times kept me firmly out of the loop was beginning to get on my nerves – as I was also unaware that since our planned move to New York had been mentioned, Paul had been re-dumped.

"So, she's back with Ross?" I shrugged.

"To be honest Lee, I don't think she's ever *not* been with him."

I've said it before – I had no problem whatsoever with whatever bullshit Jeanette got involved in – however, I certainly did when it came to my kids being thrust in the middle of it. I also felt slightly stupid in the fact that if they were indeed an item – again, then I had just set them up in a $250,000 a year love nest, of which half of that I was about to personally kick up.

Emily's *me caving in to her demands* conversation now made total sense.

The very next day I was due to do a *talk* on Sports Journalism at the London College of Communication – *Arsenal: The Terry Neill Years* documentary being the subject matter. The talk itself had been set up by the suits at ITV, which had meant an early start that included driving down to the ITV Studios at South Bank for a 7.00 am meeting and then having to drive over to the Elephant and Castle to give a five-hour lecture, which had been inconveniently pencilled in for kick-off at 9.30 am sharp.

"I'm dead proud of you," Emily said, as she fastened my tie and ruffled-up my hair.

It was great having a wife who was your number one fan.

"Are you okay dropping the kids off at school?" I asked.

"Yeh, of course I am," she shrugged.

The meeting at ITV was very much of a muchness and we would have all learned more if we had stayed in bed and the only good thing about it was the fact that my new contract was ready to sign.

The suits at head office had loved the idea of the totally revamped and an even more anarchic *Tiswas*, especially after seeing a clip of Emily on the behind the scenes of Electric Ladyboy's European Tour where she had mimicked the lead singer of Transvision Vamp, whilst both spoon feeding me my birthday cake and then *flanning* me on the conclusion of the song.

The original programme was said to have lacked an educational element and appeared more slapstick than anything – however, I for one never really saw that. Nevertheless, it would be something that that I would certainly try and rectify. There was another thing in that, you couldn't really recreate Bob Carolgees' alter-ego and puppet and nor could you really have a Trevor McDoughnut or a David Beh-whammy – as these were all lost to the era.

Part of the answer? Well, that was found in the *Beezer*.

"Colonel Blink," grinned Emily. "A fifteen to twenty-minute segment recreating his adventures and have him as a regular on the show. The possibilities are endless."

It was a brilliant idea as was re-creating the Child Catcher out of Chitty, Chitty, Bang, Bang in a surreal world where the kids would help form the basis of the programme.

A lot of our ideas were, as with *The Huddy Show*, highly plagiarised – however, good ideas can be always be built on and ITV seized on the opportunity and had me drag Emily into the Bounds Green Studio's and re-record her antics over in Tuscany with some sexually charged and explosive mimickery, if that is indeed a word.

We then staged a 30-minute promo with a load of kids from school, which we had the screen writers behind *The Invincibles* part-draft up.

It was hard work – but the satisfaction element surrounding it was nothing short of immense.

I edited what we had got down to just under four minutes and whereas we had shots of Electric Ladyboy backing up Emily over in Tuscany, we had some kids from school miming playing the instruments in the studio – one of who was our studio director's eldest – yeh and dressed as Elvis, with my lad extremely pissed off that he wasn't part of it all, as unfortunately his name hadn't come out of the hat, whilst we'd been drawing lots.

I had never done anything like it before and I couldn't believe what I was seeing.

I went back and forth splitting the screen from one into four, six and eight segments with Emily continually singing the whole way through and moving around within each of the these whilst we had various other clips such as a *Ready Steady Cook* with four kids and a celebrity chef – a take on the *Generation Game* with Jeanette as Bruce Forsyth along with the contestants who were four celebrities and four kids – having about twenty kids dressed as The Proclaimers chase and flan the Child Catcher – along with the Colonel Blink character armed with a pair of pliers and a monkey wrench and dressed up as a surgeon with four kids as his assistants and performing some operation on Jody Reeves. The finished article was nothing short of brilliant with explosions of cream and custard everywhere.

A new Tiswas logo was made by Arsenal-nut and graphic design artist, Steve Wade and was inserted into the four-minute promo, which we were informed was currently being shown in the U.S and which was creating a huge, huge interest, so much so everyone who was anyone was lining up to be on it.

"It's done," I told M, over hands-free whilst driving down Waterloo Road.

"What – yer've signed it?"

"You can move forward on the house and sort the flights," I said. "I move into the new job on the eleventh of January."

"I meant it yer know – what I said."

"What?"

"That, I'm dead proud of you."

How could you not love her?

I made it to the University and was met by my point man – or woman rather, as she was a young lady with a skirt up her arse.

"You must be Lee?" she beamed. "I'm Aisha."

I was then introduced to a few people including the lady who was head of the college before being taken to some lecture room, which was crammed full of students.

"Morning," I said, on being handed the podium. "I'm up for some conversation, so anything you want to ask me – and I mean anything, please feel free to chuck me a question."

Boom! Loads of hands went up.

"Where did you meet your wife?" one lad asked.

"Which one – the one I'm with now, or my ex?"

That raised a few laughs.

"Both," said the lad.

"I met Emily at some charity bash and I met Jeanette at some pub in Derby, while she was still at Birmingham University," I said.

"Why did you and Jeanette split up?" asked some girl at the front.

"Because I was a rubbish husband," I told her. "I've worked hard on that issue since and Emily says that I'm brilliant."

Again, there was laughter.

"ITV Seven?" asked another girl. "I read somewhere that it was your idea."

"Ah – and that's where poor journalism rears its head," I said. "ITV Seven was ITV's idea. I was asked the question of could it work and if so, did I fancy making it work?"

"Would it have worked without you?" asked another girl.

"Quite possibly – although it certainly wouldn't have been the same. What I did was put my faith in a lot of *bright young things* that I knew I could trust."

"Who's the most interesting footballer that you've ever met?" some lad asked.

"Most of today's footballers are about as interesting as a round of golf," I said. "You need to look back to the golden era of football – the fifties, sixties and seventies. It's the same with the journalists of that era. There was a beautiful honesty about it all. Nowadays, we live in a world where it all revolves around money and you must watch what you say – and that's not just football players, but journalists too. If any one of them steps out of line and says something damning about say Wenger, Van Gaal or Mourinho and the like, there's every chance that he or she will be ostracised – and that's why we end up reading a lot of sycophantic journalism when it comes to the Premier League."

"Do you get shunned?" asked a young girl, two rows back.

"Only by my ex when my kids drop me in it," I winked.

Again – I got more laughs.

I was starting to feel like Denzel Washington in that film, and I said as much.

"*Man on fire?*" someone shouted.

"No, *Devil in a Blue Dress*," I winked.

I got more laughter aimed my way.

"But to answer your question," I said, to the girl sitting two rows back. "I'm not a tabloid journalist, but if I was, it wouldn't really bother me. The idea is to have an angle but never an agenda and never shirk responsibility or indeed the issue – and the rule which continually applies, is to always be as honest as possible."

"The Arsenal documentary – the one that's just been shown on ITV Seven," asked a lad. "A lot of that revolves around Alan Hudson – the ex-Chelsea player who hosts *The Huddy Show*, why is that?"

"That is a marvellous question," I said. "Huddy as we refer to him in the studios, is possibly the most candidly spoken person you could ever meet. If you can handle all his effing and blinding and steer him onto the questions you want answering, rather than the subject that he wants to talk about you're left with an extremely humble and honest guy who deep inside knows that he wasted what was a wonderful talent. Was that down to him? Possibly, possibly not. We can't change history but we can supposedly learn from it, but what he has shown, is that despite everything that has gone on before, he still has character and is an extremely genuine guy, which is something that no-one can ever take away from him."

"Do you get on with him?" asked the same lad.

"Yes, of course I do, but that's really a question you need to throw at my seven-year old son," I said. "Huddy spends a lot of his free time coaching at grass roots and the football team that my lad plays for and to say my lad thinks the world of him would be a huge understatement."

"The documentary makes out that his walking out on Arsenal crippled the club in the seasons thereafter," said a girl at the front.

"It did, and he should have never been allowed to leave," I said. "Although they are totally different players, the signing of Brian Talbot saved the following season and the maturity of the squad the following season had them pushing on four fronts and took them extremely close to the Treble. Unfortunately, Arsenal being Arsenal, they failed to invest in the squad properly and come December eighty-three after the club had been dumped out of the League Cup by Walsall, Terry Neill was pleading for Alan Hudson to come back to the club to help save his job. Now that is not only journalism – it is history."

Strangely, I was asked a question about Arsenal's tracking of Celtic's powerful 20-year old defender Roy Aitken in the 1978/79 season – a player who could also play the holding role in midfield. "Was he being looked at as a replacement for Alan Hudson?" asked some lad with glasses, sort of left of centre.

"It's hard for me to answer something that I'm not really sure of," I said. "Arsenal had been reportedly scared off by the three-hundred grand asking price for Dundee United's

David Narey around November and were then were linked with Aitken in December, so I'm surmising they wanted him as a defender."

Both would have been impressive acquisitions for Arsenal as Aitken would go on to play 57 times for Scotland, whilst the extremely gifted Narey – some two years older, would go on to play 35 times.

Around 12 months later Arsenal would also make their first inquiry for another Scottish central defender, the-then 20-year old Alex McLeish – a player who would outdo both Aitken and Narey in the international stakes and would go on to play 77 times for Scotland.

"Arsenal had both O'Leary and Young as the mainstay of central defence with Steve Walford drafted in as cover as and when he was needed, therefore it would have been interesting to see where either of them would have fitted in," I explained. "The versatile Aitken however, could play in any position along the backline – including the clubs problematic left-back position, which Birmingham City manager Jim Smith had also had problems with – not at least after he had filled it with what was one of the most ambitious, if not audacious moves in British football at the time."

"We offered £220,000 for Blackburn left-back John Bailey and they turned it down. We asked about Kenny Sansom but Crystal Palace wouldn't even listen," Smith had told Harry Miller of the *Daily Mirror*. "We therefore went out and paid £295,000 for Alberto Tarantini who is 22 and has played 34 times for his country and anyone who saw him in the World Cup knows that this is one hell of a good player."

Tarantini was indeed a good player – however, moving to a very poor Birmingham City wasn't really the best move for the fiery full-back and he made 23 appearances and scored one goal during his ill-fated spell at St Andrew's, where Manchester United's Brian Greenhoff was made more than aware of the players' dark side, after he was knocked unconscious by the left-back, following an elbow in the face during the Blues 5-1 thrashing of United in November 1978.

I could talk about football and its history all day and come 3.35 pm I would say that I was all talked-out, but that could never be the case and as I gathered my things to leave, I was collared by Aisha who introduced me to one of her fellow students, who I'd certainly not seen during the talk – a blonde haired girl who was introduced to me as Rémy. "I'm part of a magazine journalism and publishing course in which I hope to get my B.A," she told me.

"Rémy along with a few others from the college run an indie magazine," said Aisha. "It's extremely good."

"That sounds interesting," I said. "What are we talking – digital or hard copy?"

"Just digital at the moment," said Rémy.

"What is it – music, fashion?" I shrugged.

"Real life," she replied.

It transpired that they conveniently resided at some nearby student accommodation – which was some place off the vibrant Walworth Road and just a stone's throw from the college …or a dice with death whilst trying to cross the A3. How did I know? My car had been blocked in by someone's VW Camper Van and I was invited over to see the indie magazine's H.Q, which of course doubled as the girls flat.

I had always maintained that both Emily and myself were extremely wary about being given a false sense of security before being led into what was the lion's den, and as such, I was more than reluctant to take up the offer of a cup of coffee and have a look at any magazine set-up – be it run by attractive girls or otherwise.

"Tell me, Mr. Janes," thus inquired the detective. "What made you believe that the two nineteen-year old female accusers had wanted you in their flat?"

"M, I'm blocked in at campus and I'm just nipping over the road to have a look at some indie magazine that's run by some students," I told her, whilst trying to negotiate a safe passage across the A3 Newington Butts.

"Yeh, okay love," she replied. "Give me a call when you're on your way home and I'll put some food on."

The words "He nearly didn't go", could be inscribed on loads of tombstones, the length and breadth of the country. It was hardly a case of David Blakely nipping over to the pub on South Hill Park for a packet of fags – probably more

Robin Van Persie going over to the Tulip Inn to help some damsel in distress find a set of missing garments.

"You went to what was some teenagers flat above a Chinese restaurant because you thought it was what?" further inquired the detective. "You were led to believe it was the national headquarters of …some magazine?"

To contradict that, I suppose there was also the story of Decca's Dick Rowe.

Needless to say – me getting in the elevator with two teenage *bits of fluff* and being invited into some flat that had all the hallmarks of Bohemian squalor along with an unmade bed, which I was invited to sit on, had me feeling a bit uneasy. A couple of years ago, it certainly wouldn't have, as I would have probably been debating which one of them I'd be doing first.

"I won't bite, you know," said Rémy, as she crawled about on her hands and knees trying to plug the five-socket extension into the sole plug hole in the oversized closet, which doubled-up as her bedroom.

"I'm certainly not frightened of the being bitten bit," I said, looking around. "More frightened with falsely being accused of biting either of you."

That had her laughing.

"Tea's up," said Aisha, as she walked into the bedroom, before passing me a cup of brown stuff and plonking her arse down alongside me.

On her kicking-up the computer a screen-shot of a magazine titled Rémy came up, which I had to say, looked about as professional as any I'd seen. "We have an Internet site where we publish the mag' as a flash file," she said.

I had taken off my jacket and spent a good half an hour trawling its pages, whilst being pandered over by the flats two tenants and on drinking my third cup of coffee I thought it prudent to ask the million-dollar question of – where did I figure in all of this?

"We just wanted you to see it," smiled Aisha.

"Okay then – and now I've seen it?" I asked.

Neither of them let their guard drop, but it was obvious that I had been asked over for a bit more than three cups of

Kenco and a quick shufti at an Apple Mac in some birds' bedroom – especially by the way that they were looking at each other. Again – a couple of years ago, they wouldn't have had time to hum and err.

"I can't help you if you don't tell me what you want," I said. "That's one of the first rules of journalism."

"Your wife," Rémy said. "Emily – I'd really like to interview her and have her photograph on the front cover."

I thought about it for a few seconds before taking a business card from out of my jacket and then scribbling the Frederick Street address down on the back. "Come around at seven o'clock tomorrow evening," I said, looking at them both. "And one of the first rules of journalism is to always protect your source – therefore, I don't want my address nor mobile phone number bandying about willy-nilly."

On me getting home and me telling my wife about my tea-time adventure at some student accommodation flat opposite the ongoing enabling works on what will be the tree-lined Elephant Park, she appeared slightly taken aback.

"So, you went back to a flat with two teenage girls," she asked.

"Yeh – I told you," I said, whilst chomping away at some dry fried chicken and greens.

"I quite rightly recall that you mentioned the word *students*," said Emily. "I certainly don't recall you mentioning the word *girls*."

"Why – are you jealous?" I inquired.

"I'll tell you tomorrow after I've met them," she said.

Chapter 52

Rémy

Unbeknown to me the next few days were going to be rather strange – something which kicked off with a sort of one-two, buckle my shoe and three-four, knock at the door scenario, but the opposite way around as at 5.30 am there was a rata tat-tat on the front door and as I ran down the stairs to answer the thing, I fell over three boxes of M's shoes, which had for some strange reason been placed on the second step from the bottom.

"It was so I wouldn't forget them," she grinned.

"Forget them for what?" I inquired.

"I don't know – I've forgot."

She amazed me at times.

The person at the end of the knock on the door at stupid o'clock, was Bondy – who appeared in quite a cheerful mood. The sole witness in the case against him had passed away. Mainly the kid he had allegedly shot.

"That's convenient," I said. "How did he cop it?"

"He O.D'd."

"Fair do's," I said, as I made him a coffee. "So, what now – 'you back for good?"

"My brief let me know a few days ago, that there was no real case, so I here I am."

"Yeh – and here you are," I said, as I passed him his coffee. "So, what do you want?"

"That money I borrowed," he said.

"What about it?"

"I'll have at back to you at the weekend – that's if you want it?"

"Why wouldn't I want it?" I asked.

"I have some business out of town and it would be handy if I could sit on it a bit," he said. "I just wanted to clear it with you first."

"Sit on it for as long as you want – we are out of here in the New Year."

"Where are you off to?"

"New York – ITV want me over there."

"So, it's a relocate?"

I nodded.

"What about Jeanette and the kids?" he asked.

However, before I could answer the question, Emily walked down into the kitchen and copped our guest.

"Oh hello," she said. "You are the man we met in Morocco, aren't you?"

"Yeh, the *Man from Marrakesh*," he winked. "How's that big piano?"

A great smile beamed across Emily's face. "Brilliant."

After I'd bollocked her for the shoes that she'd put on the stairs, so as not to forget, but had forgotten why she put them there, so as not to forget in the first place, she poured herself a coffee and put on the radio and nonchalantly eavesdropped as much as possible as she made some breakfast – with Bondy eventually getting handed a first.

"This is bacon," he said.

"Yeh, I know," said Emily.

I don't know whether he had been mesmerised by the dippy blonde in the Arsenal shirt or the pig in the bap – whatever it was, he ate it!

Apart from him wanting to sit on the money – as he put it, the other thing he needed was Annie Dixon's swift removal from his flat, as apparently, he didn't want to be attacked again – however, me being the bearer of bad tidings up in Cockfosters certainly wasn't at the top of my *bucket list*, therefore I asked Emily to sort it.

"I can't believe that you're both frightened of her," she grinned.

"She won't attack you as you're pregnant," I told her.

"You're pregnant?" shrugged our guest. "You can't tell."

That bit pleased my wife immensely.

The removal of Annie wouldn't be that straightforward as you can't just go and kick a woman and two kids out on the street. Therefore, the first thing to do was to do was to check out some property that was 'To Let' in the area. However, there was the other much bigger problem in that Annie didn't actually pay any rent. So basically, it was a case of kicking her out of a nice flat and putting her in some shithole that she would have to cough up around £1,200 a month for. The more I thought of it, the gladder I became that I'd tasked Emily with the job.

"Mmm," Emily hummed, after realising the permeations of the devilishly dirty deed that had been bestowed on her in the eviction of the psychotic female who had both stabbed our guest and who had beaten Sooty up in full view of half ITV 7. "Maybe I should go up to *The Warehouse* and tell her there – yer know, there'll be plenty of people about and that."

"So, is Jo still doing the accounts at the other place," Bondy inquired.

Emily's ears certainly pricked-up after he'd said that.

"Why – do you know Johanne?" she asked.

"Yeh – another psycho-bitch," he said. "All she ever wanted was the unfrequented love bit – you know, total commitment, undying loyalty, etcetera, etcetera."

"What's wrong with that?" Emily asked.

"She just didn't want it with me," he said.

"What – you two were an item?"

"I wouldn't go that far," he said, before bringing me into the conversation. "She just tortured the hell out of me with him."

"Who – Lee?"

"Yeh, she just used me to get to him – but he was with Jeanette at the time," our rather big mouthed guest added. "She wanted Lee to leave her."

"You never told me that," said Emily.

There was a lot of things I'd never said and that were best left unsaid, and this was one of them.

"So, yer did do it with her," was the first question I had hurled at me from a rather pissed-off wife, once Elvis had left the building.

"No," was always going to be the answer, as that was indeed the correct answer to what exactly happened. Nothing.

"But he said she said that she wanted you to leave Jeanette," Emily shrugged. "How does that even work? It doesn't even make any sense?"

"She wanted me to leave Jeanette before she would consider anything," I told her. "I wouldn't and nothing happened. It ended before it could even begin."

"Apart from the bra," nodded Emily. "I do, in fact, know about the bra."

Christ on a bike, I thought. *Being me was fraught with problems.*

"What about her bra?"

"You took it off in your car – everybody knows. It's Jo's favourite ever story. If you took the *you and her and the bra story* from her life she'd have absolutely nothing to talk about. The structure of her life is founded on that flipping horrible, *you and her and the flipping bra story,*" she said, before giving me her grand finale. "Aaaaaaaagh! Emily's dead mad and she's not talking to you."

Wow, I was impressed – me knowing that a mute Emily would certainly be interesting.

That stance lasted a bit longer than I thought, and whilst in the middle of a meeting down at the South Bank Studios and at exactly 11.27 am I received a telephone call to tell me that my mobile was switched off – which I already knew, as it was me who had switched the thing off, and to ask if I fancied meeting up at the coffee shop at 1.00 pm.

"I thought you weren't talking to me?"

"Yeh, I know – I'm sorry," she mumbled. "I was horrible with you and you certainly don't deserve it."

"While you're on the phone, you might as well know that we're booked on the first flight out of Heathrow in the morning," I said.

"Why – where are we going?"

"Two nights in New York – so, get your toothbrush and knickers packed."

"Yipee," was what the other six suits and a secretary heard, whilst all the conversation had been going on via the intercom. "...As if you ever let me wear them."

Yeh – and that bit.

ITV America was firmly on the agenda – however, we could use some of the spare time to have a look at the property and the area we were looking to locate to, whilst at the same time check out one or two restaurants.

When I got to the coffee shop Emily had been on the *bat phone* to her mum, who I was told was on her way down with Mike to undertake both the duty of babysitting Herbert and knocking three of Sooty's walls out. Obviously, Mike doing the wielding of the sledgehammer meant that Sil' had indeed drawn the short straw.

"I hope he's good for her," said his mum, as we watched on as he smashed up his crisps and tipped pop everywhere. "He's been dead naughty of late."

He had a bit. His favourite past time had become the emptying of the fridge. He was like lightning – turn your back for ten seconds and half its contents were on the floor including all the stinking chucky-eggs. It was like having some frigging Poltergeist in the house with the continual opening of all the cupboards and drawers.

"Oh yeh," quipped Emily. "Do you remember those two from Tuscany?"

I just gave a shrug.

"The caretaker and his wife," she said. "They are back in the UK and asked if they could pop in to see my mam – it turns out they've had some kind of family tragedy."

"Really?"

"Yeh – Hazel's younger brother – their Derek, has apparently run away from home and her mother is at her wits end."

"Runaway? How can he have run away – she said he was fifty-six?"

"Yeh – that's what I thought," she shrugged. "Dead strange, eh?"

It certainly was.

"Oh – remember," she winked. "You've got your two new *girlfriends* coming around tonight."

I had completely forgotten about that and was going to cancel, was it not for an inquisitive wife.

"I suppose the competition will keep me on my toes," she said.

Rémy wasn't her real name, it was her chosen name – and that means chosen by her. We were to eventually find out that Rémy had actually been born Claire Rimaldi, one day after New Year's Day back in 1997 and to a 15-year old girl named Serena Topping, who currently resided south of the river in some high-rise flat on Restell Close, but it would be here that I would be getting ahead of myself.

On first meeting her I thought Rémy as just a rather outgoing *bright young thing* with a great future ahead of her and after calling to the house at 6.58 pm that evening, nothing changed that opinion. Emily however, had been a bit put out about some of the questions that she had asked – some of which inferred that she knew quite a lot about us.

"She's an extremely clever and assertive young girl," Emily told me later that night. "However, I wouldn't trust her as far as I could throw her."

The interview had been littered with questions of a quasi-sexual nature: about M's role in *The Invincibles*, being invited to cast for *Desiree*, along with the events surrounding our relationship …part of which included Emily's miscarriage back in the spring.

"There's something that I can't quite put my finger on," Emily said. "Only our close friends and family knew about that."

I thought nothing of it at the time.

"Maybe she just fancies you," I told her.

"Yeh, you wish," she smiled.

With an early start for New York and the excitement of flying out to a different country, I'd say the Rémy interview – or interview for *Rémy*, rather, had been forgotten about – however, that's where I'd be wrong. "Why would you call a magazine after yourself," Emily asked me on the flight over. "Don't you find that rather narcissistic?"

As for me? I was more concerned with the fact that I'd awoke that morning to find that some git had run a key down the side of my car – however, I answered her question all the same. "I would if I knew what it meant," I winked.

"Vain – yer nit," grinned Emily.

Although the magazine title was quite striking, Emily had hit on a valid point – it was a bit of a vanity project, but if you know you're good and you're not afraid to state it – then so what?

Emily had offered her loads of press photos from *The Warehouse* – however, she had insisted that they did all their own work, therefore they took all the shots themselves, which I again thought was quite impressive – although my wife certainly didn't as she'd had to piss around putting on make-up and being photographed all over the house.

Like I said, it certainly had my wife scratching her head.

New York never failed to surprise me and every time I visited the place I enjoyed it, not at least with the current company I was in. Emily had been born to live in here. Her face, hair, clothes and the overall aura that surrounded her were all very New York and on jumping in a cab at JFK she asked the driver to drop us off on Pacific Street in Brooklyn – bags and all, so we could meet the lady from real estate company and view the property.

Inside it wasn't too dissimilar to our house on Frederick Street, but minus the pool and came with a price tag which would have both made you gibber at the thought of it and just about wiped out all the money I received when the old business had been bought out. A year in anyone's life is a long time, but in ours a hell of a lot had happened – and Emily, although financially very prudent, had said about buying the house in New York: "What the heck, Lee – let's just go for it."

Moving forward is always exciting, but looking back at those you are leaving or have left can also be quite choking. "Lee's one of those people who has to keep moving," Emily had told her parents on my purchase of some half-renovated old building off Bounds Green Road in the early autumn of 2014. "And there's no way on earth that I'm going to hold him back. I signed on for the ride and I'm going to enjoy it."

It had been their Lucy that had told me that.

It was the most ambitious thing that I'd ever done and having M at my side give me the impetus to make the decision. If I'd still been with Jeanette I really don't think that I would ever have had the guts to do it for fear of being continually nagged and balled out. Emily's outlook was to back me unconditionally and her outlook on the move to New York had been no different. How could you ever knock someone who both loves and has confidence in you?

"There are other houses if it's not quite what you want," I said, on us looking around the place.

"I think I could drag myself to live here," she winked.

As I said, moving can also be quite exciting – but New York? That had to be the ultimate move in the right direction. We left the cases in the property and had a walk up and down a couple of streets. You just had to see it, there were shops and restaurants everywhere.

"It'll take some getting used to, but I'm sure we'll manage," smiled Emily.

"There'll be really hot summers and some very cold winters though," I said.

"Lee – I think it's perfect."

Even my migraines had eased up since I'd left the setup at ITV 7 along with the dreaded colourisation department that I'd spawned after watching a Burnley versus Chelsea game and which seemed like years ago – so M's description of "perfect", wasn't that far wide of the mark as summations go.

"Won't yer miss yer football?" Emily asked.

Mmm?

It was another valid question as of course I'd miss it – however, nowadays I was a watching-on-television-and-monitor buff as opposed to catching the Tube up to The Emirates. And it had been quite some time since I'd been one of the real supporters who follow the club all over the country. Anyhow, I could see all Arsenal's games as overseas viewers have better access to the Premiership than people in the UK.

We eventually got to the hotel and checked in before going over to the new ITV offices and studios on Lafayette Street. New York being like London, you can't really dictate the flow of the traffic nor the speed of the hotel concierge, which often knocks any kind of punctuality out of synch, and that being the case we were around 30 minutes late. However, on walking through the doors we had everyone tearing around after us like blue arse flies. "Welcome to America," said one of the Stateside suits as he greeted us and shook my hand. "We're all very pleased to meet you, Boss."

"Boss, eh?" whispered Emily, as she both linked my arm and leaned in to me as we were escorted into a press conference, and where a fantastic buffet had been laid on in our honour.

"You can still call me Lee, though," I whispered back.

It was all too much to take in and to say Emily was impressed with surroundings ...well she was impressed – especially as there was a huge poster in a frame advertising *Tiswas*, with her complete with a cheeky smile, wearing a sparkly cream dress and a bow in her hair and with half a Black Forest gateau in her mitts.

"Hiya Lee," said one of the pressmen. "What's your main focus going to be with the new ITV America network?"

"I'd say to make it the number one channel in the USA – however, that would by quite an arrogant statement being that I'm a guest in your country," I told him. "Therefore, Emily and I are going try and embrace both the lifestyle and culture of your country and try to understand how the America-thing works, and over the next few months maybe we'll make lots of new friends and hopefully be able to give something back."

"What a lovely thing to say," said one of the female reporters.

The *When in Rome* speech always goes down well, and even more so, when he or she who is actually saying it, means it. As for me? I certainly meant it.

As for Emily, she got pulled to one side to be interviewed by some lady from the *New York Times* and all I can remember was her continually looking over at me with a great smile, whilst she was giving her interview. Never had I seen her so happy.

That afternoon was all one big haze, and maybe jetlag and the time difference had thrown both our body clocks as come 7.00 pm we were both cream-crackered – however, when you are in the city that apparently never sleeps, an early night isn't really on the agenda.

"I thought you were tired?" I asked, whilst watching on as Emily multi-tasked, undertaking a teeth cleaning exercise, whilst checking out the contents of the bathroom.

"I am – very, but there's no way on earth that I'm not wearing my posh frock and new shoes and you aren't taking me into Brooklyn for an Italian," she garbled.

"You always complain about food in Italian restaurants," I said.

"When in Rome, dearest," she said, on coming out of the bathroom still brushing her teeth and looking like she'd contracted hydrophobia. "No one knows that better than you."

The drive in the cab from the Astoria and through the Midtown tunnel dropped us off in the Williamsburg area of Brooklyn, which was absolutely nothing like the place in Boerum Hill, where we were destined to reside. Overseas visitors going to London possibly think that the city is all Knightsbridge, quaint Mews cottages on cobbled streets and Trafalgar Square – so much so, the arse would drop out of their pants if they got dropped off in say Harlesden, Brixton or Tottenham. The Brooklyn area of New York was no different as it has both the affluent and not so affluent neighbourhoods and the restaurant we got dropped off at was definitely in the latter.

"Maybe I should have brought a gun," I winked.

On us going into the restaurant however, our mindset immediately changed as this was something that wouldn't have looked out of place in any of Huddy's gangster movies and had an ambience that was second to none – and with me in a dark blue suit and M dressed to kill, we certainly drew some attention.

"I phoned earlier," my wife explained. "I booked a table for two – Mr and Mrs Janes."

"You're English?" smiled the waiter, as he took Emily's coat.

"Yeh – at the moment," she replied.

Tourists might be the order of the day in Manhattan's commercially reprocessed and manufactured Little Italy, but here there were none.

"Would you like to take a seat at the bar while I sort your reservation?" asked the waiter.

"Wow, this is dead good," whispered Emily, as she looked around.

"You won't be saying that when all they have is stodgy tasteless pasta with no meat in it," I told her.

"Due bicchieri di vino rosso, per favour," she smiled at the bar man. "Secco, se possibile."

The barman returned her a steely half-smile.

"My Italian's a bit all over the shop," Emily told him. "I did a bit of swatting up when we went to Italy in the summer, but because you're not talking it all the time, you tend to forget the way sentences are constructed."

"Stop flirting and just order us a drink," I told her.

"I just did?" she grinned.

"Chianti, Brunello di Montalcino or Vino Nobile de Montepulciano?" asked the barman.

"I definitely could do a Chianti," she smiled.

The night barring the food was brilliant.

"It still beats me how these Italian places get away with serving you ten bob of produce and turn it into a dish that robs you of sixty quid," I said, as we were driven back into Manhattan.

"It tasted alright," Emily said.

"The only real meat dish they had was a Steak Fiorentina and that was a meal for two which you wouldn't have as it had got Thyme in it."

That had her chuckling. "How was your eggplant?" she asked.

"Again – ten pence for an aubergine and another forty for the bits of cheese, basil and tomato sauce," I said. "No wonder the mafia over here were so successful!"

"Stop moaning, as I know you don't really mean it," she told me.

She knew me too well!

Chapter 53

Closure

The run up to last Christmas had been nothing short of brilliant and we were hoping that this one would be the same – however, there is always something around the corner, which can hit you head-on and knock you out of your stride, and that is exactly what happened to us.

I got in this particular evening after picking up my freshly repainted car to find Emily all bundled up, complete with Arsenal scarf and hat – you know, the original one with the dark red bars and not the general R&W garbage that the *plastics* wear and which could easily double as a Manchester United scarf when the going gets tough, which sort of had me thinking that I was in for a veritable treat.

It can't be a proper game though, as we haven't got one on, I thought. *Mmm, maybe it's a reserve game up at Meadow Park.*

My glee was cut short when Emily threw me a googly. "I'm just waiting for the gas man," she said.

"The gas man?" I inquired. "Who's he?"

"The gas man, yer great nit," she chuckled. "The boilers on the blink."

"Uh, I thought you were treating me and taking me up to see a reserve game," I said.

"Lee – I love you loads, but the chance of me volunteering to stand in an empty pavilion over in Borehamwood for nearly two hours whilst you discuss the finer points with some old man and a dog of why Chubby Acton (Chuba Akpom) will never ever make the grade at Arsenal, is absolutely nil. I've done it once – and that dearest, is quite enough for anyone."

"I thought you enjoyed it," I told her.

"A bit more than doing the ironing and slightly less than having a cervical smear," she smiled.

"Anyway, what's up with it – the boiler?"

"I told you – it's broke."

"Do you want me to have a look at it?" I asked.

"Not particularly – that's what we pay the six hundred pound a year for."

"Where's Herbert?" I inquired.

"With his brother and sister at his Auntie Jeanette's."

"Well at least something good has come out of it," I said. "Get the boiler bloke to fix it and then we can nip out and cop a curry."

The boiler bloke however, decided that it wasn't a straightforward case of taking a broken bit out and sticking a new bit in, and as such he did a bit of head-scratching and pondering, so much so, he got the laptop out of his briefcase before trying to work out how to split the atom.

He finally cracked the code about nine o'clock that night. That was after he'd replaced nearly every device within the boiler – i.e. the heat exchanger, pump, thermostat, pressure relief valves etc., and then gave us the sales patter about us maybe procuring a new all singing and dancing version of our boiler, which according his sister over in Gallions Reach, was the Maserati of all boilers.

As for me I had nipped outside into the freezing cold for a bit of warmth and I immediately noticed that the white plastic cover on the gas meter in the back yard had been tampered with.

"That shouldn't be like that," the gas man told me post-scratching of his head. "I thought there was a gas flow problem. Have you been messing with it?"

"Me?" I asked.

"It looks like someone has been messing with the meter," he said, whilst at the same time and according to my wife semi-implying that one of us had been trying to pilfer a few doubloons from the coffers of the multi-billion-pound conglomerate that is British Gas. That was indeed a mistake as Emily's expression changed completely and she gave him two short sharp blasts of verbal.

"You've definitely picked up a bit of nasty streak since I met you," I told her afterwards. "I reckon you're regressing back into a Scouser. You'll be shoplifting next."

"No, I will not," she grinned. "I just don't like anyone insinuating things that are *not nice* about us."

"I didn't really think he did, did he?"

"Uh – maybe I am getting a bit cynical," she said. "It might have something to do with me feeling right fat."

"You don't look fat," I told her, which from past-experience I knew was the most perfect answer in the world. And indeed, I was right.

"You're just saying that to cheer me up," she smiled.

There was certainly no way at all that I was carrying on that line of conversation, therefore I changed it. "So, do you fancy nipping out and getting a curry?" I asked.

"I was going to make us Chicken Cacciatore and green salad," she shrugged.

That was an even more brilliant reason to nip out for a curry, and as such I mentioned the fact that there were a few new pairs of shoes that I hadn't yet seen her in, which totally made her rethink her Chicken Cacciatore, green salad and washing-the-pots-up-afterwards strategy.

"I love it when you take an interest," she smiled.

Yeh – right, I thought.

King's Cross is quite a vibrant place in that everything is available 24/7 and nothing at all that goes on in the area could ever surprise you; and whilst tucking into our starters we had the pleasure of watching a gang fight that was going on outside the station through the window of the curry house, and by the time we got to the main course, three riot vans had arrived on the scene.

"I'm going to miss coming here," I said, as we watched on at a couple of coppers slamming some innocent looking thug against the van and then stamping on his head prior to handcuffing him. "It's like having an executive box down at Millwall."

That made her laugh – which was certainly something that she wouldn't be doing early next morning.

"Lee – Giroud and Arteta have gone," she shouted, on coming in from the back yard.

"Gone?" I shrugged.

"Yeh – they're not in their house."

They weren't. I looked everywhere for them – and she was right, they were nowhere to be seen.

What was odd was that they hadn't escaped since the first few months of us getting them and as with dogs and cats, you generally find that if you look after your pets properly, they tend not to want to go elsewhere. The ferrets were no different: they loved being handled and were always lively and entertaining when the kids brought them indoors and both played with them and bathed them; and more importantly they were also extremely well-fed. In fact, M eventually applied for them their own *Waitrose* club card due to the large amount of shelf-expired chickens she'd been purchasing from the The Brunswick store down in Bloomsbury – so much so, that if wasn't it down to the fact that they scuttled around twenty miles a day through a series of 132mm diameter pipes which formed their *run*, they would have both been the pole cat equivalent of Alan Brazil.

I'd often come in from work and Emily would have them both on the kitchen top hand feeding them chicken. She didn't actually get them to sit and give a paw, but all the same, they had fairly good table manners in that they never snatched the food out of her hand. They also tended to dress quite sophisticated too – especially when the kids came over and put them in their best gear – mainly a pair of turtle-neck neck sweaters that Granny Edie had knitted them.

"Dad, Giroud looks like Choo-Choo out of *Top Cat*," giggled my lad.

Arteta certainly didn't. The jersey that he wore made him look more like Wilfred out of the *Bash Street Kids*, and as such and whilst racing around the kitchen tops he either ran into things or fell off them.

With both animals missing, Emily was nothing short of devastated.

"Can't we just buy another pair?" I said. "The kids would never notice."

That was a mistake as I didn't half get a bollocking for suggesting that.

"I was only kidding," I lied, before duly volunteering to trawl a couple of streets in my quest to appease a rather upset wife.

I spent more time looking for those ferrets than I had on the Sammy documentary, such was the task – including asking all our neighbours ...oh yeh, and Derek the street cleaner who kept insisting that he wasn't Ray Parlour.

"Have you seen two ferrets – both white?" I asked.

"I haven't got them," he said, as I watched on as he sauntered up the street with his cart.

"I'm not saying you have."

"No then – I haven't," he said.

When I got in, I then had another one of my wife's brain-waves to deal with.

"I need these posting up in the shops," she said, as she showed me a computer print-out that advertised a £1,000 reward for any information leading to their swift return.

"Fuck me M," I gasped. "Who are they Hannibal Hayes and Kid Curry? They'll be getting nicked and returned every week just for the reward money if we put those up."

"Money doesn't come into it," she told me.

"They only cost me a fiver apiece," I mumbled.

"Lee, they're part of the family. We've had them more or less since the first day we got together."

We also had to cart them everywhere with us – including up and down the M6 each weekend, and as such they'd got nearly as much mileage under their belts as Alan Whicker.

It was then Emily dropped on something that I had just said. "Why – would you think someone would steal them?" she asked.

"What – a pair of ferrets? I doubt it."

Nevertheless, that had Emily's head ticking, especially as there would be no way at all that either of them could jimmy the lock. She was right, you know – something just didn't sit right.

"I'll check the cameras," I said.

"What – so, you think that someone could have stolen them?"

I didn't know, but that was what I was going to find out. Since the *Live at The Warehouse, ITV 7, Sessions* etcetera, people had got to know who we were and as we moved around quite freely amongst the public we had got to be quite recognised in and around the area where we lived, so much so, I thought it prudent to get the house both fitted with CCTV and a burglar alarm. Some mornings however, it became a pain in the arse due to me forgetting to disable the alarm on going downstairs, which of course, immediately got me a bollocking in the way of an "Aw Lee", as it awoke Herbert from his slumber and set about the start of another twelve hours of toil and torture for his mum.

The cameras were interesting in that they brought a 48" screen TV into the bedroom, which I thought was great until I was informed that it wasn't for watching football and was solely for security. That was until Emily thought about it a little bit more and on my return home one evening I'd been seductively enticed into the bedroom by what I was told was an admin officer from Legal & General, sporting a pair of glasses, high heels and an even higher at the hem dress, only to find a few thousand-quid's worth of digital equipment sat on a tripod.

"You've got to be joking?" was my first expression.

"I thought it'd be fun," Emily grinned.

I wonder if Jeff Stelling's wife gave him as much grief?

Back to the case of the missing ferrets.

Although we had the cameras and could run them forward at speed – it was still a time-consuming business of watching their house – the ferrets house that is, especially as we couldn't break it down into a certain time-frame as they generally slept all night, so it was a case of running the recording from the time we'd last fed them up until the time we found they were missing. Like I said – very time-consuming.

"I can't sit here all day waiting for someone to abduct them," I told her, after ten minutes of fast forwarding.

"We can't just do nothing, Lee."

The search got that intense that when I got in from work that evening there were two of the Met's finest in our kitchen, with some female detective and her male counterpart taking a statement from a rather flustered wife, along with an ex-England midfielder offering comfort by making cups of coffee. It transpired that the ferrets had indeed been kidnapped.

"Someone's taken them," Huddy nodded. "About half-four this morning."

Not only that, but on the previous morning the CCTV had also picked up on someone tampering with the gas meter outside – which, was it not for the coincidence of the boiler going down, we would have never known about the leaking gas pipe – well not until we either received a gas bill for around ten-grand or a wayward dog end from a chain-smoking Jody blew us all up.

Now the coppers had a time-frame it would be quite easy to follow the kidnapper's course of direction as at the end of the street there was CCTV everywhere, not at least all down both Grays Inn Road and King's Cross Road. Unfortunately, however, the two plodders must have had a more pressing engagement as that was the last we ever saw of them. Emily was unperturbed and asked a couple of shopkeepers if she could check some of their CCTV footage around the time of the abduction, whilst Huddy made an excuse for a mini pub crawl and checked the CCTV outside all the local hostelries in the area and between them they started putting some form of movement of the ferret-snatcher together.

Although our kidnapping hardly possessed the stature of the Charles Lindbergh case, I had to admit it became interesting after Huddy had followed the trail as far as the Calthorpe Arms on Wren Street, whose landlord had kindly stated that around the specified time he had seen some van driving away.

"Can we see it on CCTV?" our erratic genius inquired, whilst carefully jotting it down in his notepad à la *Dixon of Dock Green*.

We could – however, his wife was the only one who knew how to download a recording and had told him over the phone that when she got in she would sort it and bring it around.

Over in Clerkenwell the kids had got wind of the abducted rodents and were in mourning.

"Can we come over and help look for them?" my daughter had asked over Skype.

As for my lad, he'd put on a black armband and was busy drafting up a memorial service.

"Me and your dad will find them," Huddy reassured them.

"I hope you're right, Alan," Emily said, post-Skype. "I can't believe that someone would do such an awful thing."

"Why nick a pair of ferrets, dislodge the cover of a gas meter and split a pipe or if it's the same kid – run a key down the side of your car," shrugged Huddy, whilst sipping at his glass of wine. "If you're going to do something – then why not do it."

"How d'yer mean?" asked Emily.

"If you are going to be malicious, why not put a brick through your windows or kill the ferrets?"

"That's really, really awful," gasped Emily.

"I didn't mean it like that, M," he said. "However, if you're asking me it all sounds a bit gay."

"What?" snapped Emily.

"It sounds all a bit – you know, gay."

There was a sudden silence, which had me and Huddy looking at each other. Strangely if I'm being honest, especially as Emily left the kitchen.

"Did I say something wrong?" whispered Huddy.

"I'm not sure, Al."

I wasn't. Huddy can't have offended her as in my mind he had said nothing untoward. That aside, we were a straightforward and frankly spoken set of people. Although Emily never swore or really said anything non-P.C, we certainly did and it certainly never bothered her. That was obviously up until now!

"You're pissed with Huddy because he said 'gay'?" I asked afterwards.

"No."

"Well what is it then as he feels he's done or said something wrong."

"It's not Alan," she said. "He's like one of the family."

"Well, what is it then?"

"Can we leave it, Lee?" she asked. "Please, love."

Me? I was at a loss. Emily however, was not and had been extremely quiet, which I had rarely seen before and for the life of me I couldn't work it out. She wasn't mad with me – it was more a case of her being mad with her ...I think?

A couple of days went by and on the evening of Friday the 11th of December I got in from work expecting a house full of kids and a drive up to Birkenhead – however, Emily had knocked that on the head and I found her sat down in the kitchen dressed in a black leather motorbike jacket, black leggings, black stilettoes with a silver heel ...mmm, and a pair of big black sunglasses on her head.

"Where are all the kids?"

"Jeanette has them," she said, post-peck on the lips. "Me and you are going out."

"What – dressed like that?"

"Why, don't I look nice?"

"Yes, of course you do, you always look nice. I've just – you know – never seen you dressed like that before."

"Well yer've seen me now," she said.

"And it is miles too dark to wear sunglasses."

"Just be a good lad and please don't ask any questions," she said. "Go and get changed – I've laid your clothes out on the bed."

How old was I – ten? I thought.

The next bit was interesting. A new black suit and black polo shirt?

"Is there any reason for us both to be dressed in black?" I asked.

"Yer'll look right smart – now be a good lad and drive me."

"Where to?"

"I'll show you."

And she did. An evening drive in pre-Christmas and bumper-to-bumper traffic through Holborn and down New

Fetter Lane along the Thames Embankment over Westminster Bridge and into South London, where she had me park up close to some very dodgy looking flats and a stone's throw from the Vauxhall arches.

"Is it a party we're going to?" I inquired.

"Shush," she said. "Just be a good lad and look after M."

That was three "good lad"s in the last half hour, and I knew from past experience I only tended to get called a "good lad" when something rubbish was going to happen, like me having to eat greens or something of that ilk. Thinking about it – I was fairly hungry, as I'd not had anything to eat apart from the toast and marmalade I'd had to make myself this morning. And that was because I'd had a wife who had still been in mourning and pining for the safe return of our two stinking minks: namely the French international ferret and the uncapped Spanish ferret with the Action Man-style painted-on barnet.

"If I park here the car will get nicked," I told her. "Or scratched – again."

"Be a good lad and stop moaning."

Uh – that was four "good lad"s, so I definitely knew something rubbish was going to happen – and bless my cotton fucking socks it did.

'Live Tonite – Men in Black Ties' - the huge poster on the viaduct read.

"Men in Black?" I asked. "Is that why we had to get dressed like this?"

"Shush," she said. "And be a good lad and pay us in."

I looked around and exactly who we were queuing up alongside and then it hit me. "M, there's no way on earth that I am going in here," I exclaimed. "Really."

She just looked up at me.

"M – this a frigging gay bar," I whispered.

It was no use, as when Emily had her mind set on something she generally got what she wanted and as we walked beneath some railway arches we were met with noise of techno hip-hop reverberating off the walls and people jumping around pretending that they actually enjoyed listening to it. Emily however, dropped her shades and mingled with the crowd.

"What the hell are we doing in here?" I asked her.

"Shush – just be a good lad," she said.

I was sick of being a good lad and told her as much, especially as I had some black leather clad Farrokh Bulsara-lookalike writhing up against me. Don't know who he is? Then google him!

"Oi pal – fuck off," I told him.

As I've said before – I can totally cope with good looking lesbians but I draw the line at some bloke with a moustache rubbing his crotch against my arse.

"You look like Becks," he told me in his rather camp voice. "Sexy Becks."

"Yeh – I am," I lied. "Posh found out that I caught syphilis off Lily Allen and booted me out."

"What really?" he asked.

Some people were just stupid.

"Lee – behave," said Emily, as she dragged me away.

This had to be the most masochistic choice of venue ever – however, I was to eventually be met with quite a surprise as Huddy of all people was here – and dressed in some black velvet suit and dickie-bow and talking at length with one of the doormen – and knowing Huddy as I did, quite possibly describing his first half showing against West Germany in 1975.

"Who are you, then – the compère?" I asked.

I'd never seen him in a suit before – and certainly not one that had possibly belonged to either Terry Griffiths or Doug Mountjoy.

"...Or are you nipping to the snooker club later?"

"Don't be a smart arse," was as much as I got back.

I followed her into the pack before we were met by another three faces donned in their whistle and flutes and who I knew only too well – Chris Wainwright, Tony Baker ...and rather strangely, Ginge.

"What's going on?" I asked.

"This is all frigging Huddy's idea," said Basher. "He just told us that it was some Black Tie *do* at some men's club. I had no idea that we were coming to some faggot bar."

"I've never been here before," exclaimed Ginge. "It's right good."

"Yeh – I'm sure you would like it. How's Rachel?"

"Sound – she was watching Jasper Carrot and Danny Dyer on *The One Show* when I left," he told me.

"So, what's happening," I asked, whilst at the same time trying to keep track of a wandering and extremely up-the-duff biker chick. "I'm in the dark on all this?"

"Cagney and Lacey worked out the case of your missing pets, this afternoon," explained Chris.

"Cagney and Lacey?" I shrugged. "Who are they?"

"Your M and Huddy. That's why we're in this dump."

"We are your back-up," grinned Ginge.

"Backup?" I shrugged.

"At Huddy's request, we were supposed to be coming down here mobhanded," said Basher. "Stevie Kell and Baso were due down, but got held up."

"Held up?" I inquired.

"Huddy got Jody to pick them up," he said. "They're currently somewhere in Stratford."

"That figures," I said, with one eye still on my ever-wandering wife. "Hold on – Jody drives a Fiat One-Two-Four – they'd never all fit in it."

"Yeh, that was another thing I was going to tell you," Chris added. "Stevie's just had me on the phone pissing himself. Baso's stuck behind both seats and the fire brigade are now on site trying to get him out."

How the hell he got in there in the first place was an even bigger mystery as he must weigh a good 20 stone.

"I really, really don't think he'll fit in there," Stevie had grinned.

"I won't Jody," a rather adamant Baso had added, whilst looking behind the seats. "It's too small a space."

Jody's powers of persuasion managed to get him in there, but even with both seats forward and Stevie's face pressed firmly up against the windscreen it was still a tight squeeze –

and the fact that Jody drove her car nearly as good as she could read and write had caused something of a stir.

"Take your next left," the Sat-Nav had said.

"Left, Jody," Stevie had told her. "Left – fucking left."

"Shit, I sometimes get my hands mixed up," Jody had informed her passengers.

According to Stevie, Baso had quickly become a bag of nerves and by the time they had got in the Blackwall Tunnel, claustrophobia had well and truly set in.

"Aaaaaagh – Jody I've got to get out," he'd shouted.

"Take your next left," the Sat-Nav had said.

"Shit – the wrong one again," Jody had said.

"Jody – I really, really need to get out," panicked Baso. "I'm feel like I'm suffocating."

"...And that was about fifteen minutes ago," Chris told me, back in real time.

As the noise rebounded against the interior of the arches, seeming to get louder and louder, Emily pointed over. "He's there."

The next thing I knew, there was a scuffle as all three of them leapt into action and had dragged some big bloke into a corner, with Tony eventually locking the guy's arm behind his back.

As for me? I couldn't believe it. I really couldn't frigging believe it. I was lost for words.

"Where are they?" Emily asked the guy.

He said nothing, and for that matter nor did I. Like I said, I was nothing short of dumbfounded.

"Take him outside and just smash his face in," Emily told Chris.

Smash his face in? I thought. *Did I hear that right?*

With everything going on around me I couldn't get my breath and all I could remember was Chris and Tony marching the guy out of the bar, whilst Huddy was gesticulating to a couple of doormen, that everything was under his control.

I had to admit – Huddy's connections were extremely far-reaching and not only covered nearly every football league club, race track and boozer in London – it also covered the city's gay scene. The perks that go with Chelsea, eh?

Tony had always been in his element when it came to a ruck and Chris certainly wasn't nicknamed Basher for nothing.

As for the guy – it was Emily's ex-husband.

"So, he's gay?" I asked my wife.

I received no answer

"So, he's gay?" I asked – again.

Again, I received no answer, as I watched M watching her ex being removed from the venue.

Outside, Emily again repeated her question. "Where are they?"

"Where are what?" he replied.

All I can remember was Basher using some of his persuasive powers – firstly some Vulcan death grip followed by some deft ninja move, which had my wife's ex writhing around on the floor. And then within the melee I caught sight of a pair of shiny shoes, which belonged to none other than our erratic genius doing their best at trying to boot the man on the deck.

"Hey twinkle toes – will you fucking pack it in?" said Tony. "You've booted me twice."

I had to admit – Huddy was quite impressive. For someone with bad legs you could have quite easily put him in a frilly dress and he wouldn't have looked out of place in the Moulin Rouge. As for me, I didn't know if I wanted a shit, shave or haircut and I was just glad this wasn't being picked up on CCTV as ITV would have really been pissed off.

"Answer the lady," shouted Huddy.

"They're at Serena's," he said.

Me? I was all over the fucking place. "So, he's gay?" I shrugged.

Unbeknown to me, Emily had been on some dark crusade that had firstly involved running her theory past our ex-England midfielder over a cup of tea and a slice of my cherry pie and then dragging the editor of the *Rémy* magazine out of her lesson and confronting her about a 1973 VW Camper van that had been seen driving out of Wren Street early Tuesday morning and which had incidentally blocked me in at the college campus the week before and had threatened her with the police.

It hadn't just been something Huddy had said, but also something in the *Rémy* interview that had hit a nerve.

"You miscarried at eleven weeks," she had asked my wife. "Were you under any undue stress at the time?"

She certainly was, but she never said.

"Is it true that your ex-husband wanted a paternity test done on your son?" Rémy had asked.

"How did you know that?" Emily had inquired.

"It's just something I picked up from the media," she lied.

"That has never been in any media – ever," Emily had said. "I'm ninety-nine point-nine percent sure of that."

Emily was anything but stupid and her and Huddy had trawled through the records of every student on campus – and there wasn't anyone with the Christian nor surname with that of Rémy.

"Oh, you're on about Claire," said the woman in administration. "Claire Rimaldi."

Bang. Emily was now a woman on a mission.

Why? Why indeed. Not only had Emily found out her name but she also had an inkling of exactly who she was.

"So, he's gay?" I asked, for the umpteenth time.

"I don't want to talk about it, Lee," she mumbled.

I frigging did!

Rémy's father was one Terence Rimaldi of Varburgh Hill in Greenwich, which meant very little to anyone – that was with the exception of Emily. It transpired that at one time he had been both a colleague and an extremely good friend of her ex-husband – and in more ways than one.

"Lee, our Sammy's yours," Emily had told me prior to the miscarriage. "He knows that."

I also remembered the conversations early on in our relationship. "He can't have children," she had told me.

"Why – what was up?" I'd asked.

"He just can't have them," she'd said – and that was sort of that.

Perhaps it was just a touchy subject, I'd thought.

Emily didn't tell me an outright lie, she just led me to assume – the same as she had done about many other things in her life. Her ex-husband had been gay and she just couldn't handle it.

"Do you want us to come with you?" asked Chris.

"I can take it from here," I told him. "And thanks."

As for Emily, she was extremely upset. And I mean really upset.

"Are you okay, M?" I inquired a few minutes later.

She just shook her head and kept quiet – however on driving over to Greenwich, I finally got a muffled sentence out of her before she burst out into tears. Even distraught couldn't have described how she felt.

"I tried to tell you ...and wanted to tell you, but I just couldn't," she said. "I'm really, really sorry and just feel so mad."

"M – you're with me now, it's okay," I told her.

"No, it's not – it's all dirty and horrible," she said.

"That's his problem," I said. "You're anything but."

There was a good few minutes' silence before she added to that. "He always made out that everything was my fault."

Making everything her fault, isolating her from friends and family, using money to control and the jealousy is all the standard M.O for an abusive husband and I told her as much. "What he did was try to pass the blame for his own failings."

"He wasn't like that at first," she said.

"It's how all the manipulation and abuse starts," I told her. "Him leading you into a false sense of security."

"But he never looked nor acted gay," she said.

"They don't all look like Chris in make-up or Eddie Izzard," I said, before trying to exert some levity. "Look at Sooty?"

That brought a smile.

"He told me that I made him turn gay," she mumbled.

"That's total bullshit and I'm sure you know that" I said. "You didn't make him turn gay – he will have always known he was gay."

"What really?"

"Yeh – of course really," I said. "He will have just used the being *married with you* to hide the fact."

That seemed to cheer her up – I think?

"That's how I always knew that our Sammy was yours," she said. "I just felt so embarrassed to tell you."

"I understand," I said, as I looked out of the car window and up at some high-rise.

"Do you really?" she asked.

"Just stay in the car, M," I said.

I got out of the car and walked over to the building and up three flights of stairs and rattled on the door of a flat, which was answered by some woman in her early-thirties who had a new-born baby in her arms.

"You have my kids two ferrets," I said. "I'm here to pick them up."

"Who is it, mam?" shouted a voice from inside.

The voice? That of Rémy.

The closet gay that was M's ex-husband, was living with his best friend's ex-wife who was her mum, and as such, the baby in her arms I assumed was his – maybe, maybe not. As for Rémy's father, there was a story here that was possibly best left for another day – however, the upshot was that he – her father, had *come out* years ago, and around the time he and M's ex had both been discharged from the police force after an incident near Plaistow Park, which was something that forced Emily to leave her first teaching job. Like I said, it is a story best left for another day.

The kids were elated because their best friend and uber-hero M had retrieved their pets and my wife was upset due to the fact that her past had come back to haunt her again.

"Why do people keep on being horrible to us?" she asked, as the kids had the ferrets running around the kitchen.

"Look around you," I said. "Not everyone is horrible."

She did, and for the first time in nearly a week a big smile represented itself.

"There's nothing wrong with you – you've proved that by everything you've given us."

"New York will be a fresh start, won't it?" she said, as she climbed on to my knee and gave me a hug.

"Not really, M," I told her. "The fresh start started long ago."

She then looked around at exactly what she did have – and that was everything.

The End

The Characters

The Janes'
Lee Janes – Producer and Head of *ITV 7*. Owner *LMJ* and *White Lion*,
Emily "M" Janes nee Orr – Lee's wife. Presenter, *ITV Sessions, Live at The Warehouse*
Jeanette "Jin" Janes nee Karelis – Lee's ex-wife. Presenter, *ITV Sessions*
Harmony Janes – Lee and Jeanette's daughter
Jamie Janes – Lee and Jeanette's son
Sammy "Herbert" Janes – Lee and Emily's son

The Orr's
Mike Orr – Emily's father, Granddad Mike
Silvia "Sil" Orr – Emily's mother, Granny Sil'
Stuart Orr – Emily's brother – Trainee Cameraman, *ITV 7*
Lucy Orr – Emily's sister
Bill Kane – Emily's Granddad Bill
Edie Kane – Emily's Granny Edie

The Sooty's
Tim "Sooty" Sutton – ITV 7, *The Sooty Show* – Lee's best mate and former business partner
Libby Sutton – Sooty's wife
Zooey Sutton – Sooty and Libby's daughter
Mia Sutton – Sooty and Libby's daughter

The Karelis's
Michael Karelis – Granddad Michael, Jeanette's father
Katherine "Kate" Karelis – Grandma Kate, Jeanette's mother

Bounds Green Road Studios *(The Warehouse)*
Abigail "Abi" Tyson – Head of Studios / Assistant Producer *ITV 7*
Jaime Hudson – Studio Director
Annie Dixon – Finance Director
Dean "Dino" Moynahan – Director, *The Invincibles*

Becky Ivell – Head of Colourisation, *ITV 7*, Foxy Fab Four
Chris "Basher" Wainwright – Head of Security
Chris Windley – Head of Make-Up
Jen Steward – Head of the Contract Cleaning Company
Kirsty Burns – *ITV 7*, Foxy Fab Four
Sinead McAnnerny – *ITV 7*, Foxy Fab Four
Abigayle Gibbs – *ITV 7*, Foxy Fab Four
Mark "Jarv" Jarvis – *ITV 7*
Dean "The Unstoppable Sex Machine" Carter – *ITV 7*
Zak "Z Cars" Carr – *ITV 7*
Faranha Farooq – P.A to Assistant Producer
Georgia Clayton – P.A to Lee
Cat Ulchenkö – Colourisation
Becky Sharpsott - Colourisation
Sam "Ginge" Antwi – Cameraman
Andy Marden – Commentator
Dan Betts – Commentator, Journalist
Jonathan "Jono" Greaves – Trainee Cameraman, Live prop, Stuart's mate
The Tall Dwarf (Harold Tirford) – Head of Programming, *ITV*
Stacey Tirford – Wife of The Tall Dwarf, one of Lee's ex-girlfriends

White Lion Street Studios
Johanne Edgington – Head of White Lion
Scott Tighe – Engineering Manager
Tony Baker – Head of Security
Jet Marchione – Head of PR
Jody Reeves – Artist, friend of Lee and Emily
Peter (Pedro) La Greave – Artist, Electric Ladyboy, friend of Lee and Emily
Ross Bain – Artist, The Queen & Pistol, Jeanette's boyfriend
Dee Man – Artist
Joe "90" Aitkin – Artist, Red & White

Others
The Inner Sanctum of ITV 7 (The research)
Stevie Kell – Arsenal Supporters Cub, Gunflash magazine, Arsenal fan
Gary Lawrence – Arsenal fan, Gunnerstown blog
Brian Allan – West Ham United fan
Ian Smith – Arsenal fan
Ian "Chappy" Smith – Arsenal fan
Martin Whittle – Arsenal fan
Tony Fisher – Arsenal fan
Paul Hatt – Leeds United fan
Dave Faber – Arsenal fan, Goonerholic blog
Steve "Stevo" Knight – Arsenal fan, Gooner 24/7 blog
Kevin Whitcher – Arsenal fan, Editor, Gooner magazine
and **Baso** – Arsenal fan, Gunflash magazine

School
Ted "The Head" Marsden – Headmaster at School
Jimmy "Bonesy" Bone – P.E Teacher, Manager of School football team
Joanne Peters – Class Teacher
Irving "Erv" Nattrass – Son of Sally Nattrass, School friend of Harmony and Jamie
Bobbie Hudson – Daughter of Jaime Hudson, School friend of Harmony and Jamie
Charlie Hudson - Daughter of Jaime Hudson, School friend of Harmony and Jamie
Thomas "Spud" Tate - School friend of Jamie
Faisal Mohammed - School friend of Jamie
Wendell "Wendy" Jones - School friend of Jamie

Some friends and relations
Fosis – Owner of the Coffee Shop off Euston Road
Ray "Derek Wilton" Parlour – Street Cleaner
Donna Harding – One of Lee's former girlfriend's
Mark Smith – Emily's ex-husband
Yusuf "Bondy" Elias – Lee, Sooty and Jeanette's longstanding friend

Madge "Mrs Sosk" Solskjaer – Lee and Emily's Neighbour

Tony "Flash" Gale – Friend of the family

Sally "Mrs Tuppy Wuppy" Nattrass – Friend of the family, Tony's girlfriend and 'Erv's mother

Maggie – Sooty's girlfriend

Kevin "Buzzy" Burrows – Lee and Sooty's old schoolfriend

Debbie Burrows – Buzzy's wife and Sooty's new girlfriend

Jimmy "Wuffy" Shepherd – Lee and Sooty's old schoolfriend

Robbie "Beatrix Potter" – Lee and Sooty's old schoolfriend

Reverend Frederick Bain – Ross Bain's father

Mavis Bain *nee Woodruff* – Ross Bain's mother

Leighton Bain – Ross Bain's brother

Fletcher Woodruff – Ross Bain's uncle

Reverend Cliff Kay – Ross Bain's father's friend

Kerry Wainwright – wife of Basher Wainwright

Jimmy Wainwright – Basher's son

Paul Knight – Jeanette's ex-boyfriend

Chrissy Knight – Paul's sister, babysitter to Sammy

Brinie Eely *nee Hood* – One of Lee and Sooty's former girlfriends

Carl Eely – Brinie Hood's new husband

Andrew "Digger" Gardner – One of Emily's ex-boyfriend's

Adebayor – Decorator and Ginge's brother-in-Law

Olivia Cooke – Grandmother of Sooty's DNA

Bambos – Son to the owner of the Coffee Shop off Euston Road

Patricia Park - Old friend of Emily's

And **Alan "Huddy" Hudson**,
Diane Abbott and **Fraser Hines** as themselves

Chapter 41a

Abi's Tales - Take 4

Deleted Chapter

4.55 pm, 20th September, 2015. I remember the date and the time. I'd had an email that told me that I had to go into the solicitors and sign for a property on Rydon Street that I was buying. I was ecstatic.

"Nice one," said Lee. "You should tell M – she'll be really pleased for you."

I did and she was.

It felt great. I had the best job in the world and I would soon have a lovely house. I called my parents to let them know and my dad told me how proud he was of me. That was twice in nearly ten months that he had said that, which was exactly twice more than he ever had done – but that was dad for you.

I then realised when I got the keys to the house, just how much it would take to fill the thing. All I'd had at the flat was a Television, DVD, a bed, my clothes and an iron, as the washing machine, dishwasher, cooker and fridge freezer all belonged to the landlord.

Cue: M. Since summer I had gone from being held at arms-length, to being like one of their family and within a couple of days she was stood in my front room hands on hips and giving orders to Chris Wainwright and his young lad – Jimmy, about not scratching any of my freshly painted architraves with a big square-armed leather sofa that she had given me. As for Lee, he got in that night to find that there was something not quite right on him going through the front door.

"Where's the settee gone?" he asked, whilst looking around. "And the chairs come to that?"

"It'll be here by Thursday," M told him.

"What will – our settee?"

M just gave him a peck and a nod.

"Why – who have you lent it to?"

"I've given it to Abi," she told him.

"Why?"

"Because she needed one."

"So, what do we sit on until Thursday?" he asked.

"Shurrup moaning," she grinned. "We are always in the kitchen anyway."

Always being in the kitchen sounded strange, if I'm being honest. That was until I inquired about it.

"I like to think of our kitchen as the heart of the house," M had told me. "There's always something going off whether it's me cooking, the children drawing or watching TV …or Lee on his laptop."

"So, don't you ever sit in the lounge?" I asked her.

"Maybe if I need to talk to my mam or any of the children's parents – but apart from that, no not really."

I loved her way of thinking – simplistic yet beautiful and I thought back to Tuscany and how they both interacted with each other. There was always a rich dialogue. Even at work, she'd often be sat on the side of the desk in his office both gesticulating and laughing.

Over a short period of time, I knew that M was Lee's life and I loved watching them. "What do you both find to talk about?" I remember asking her.

"We're probably trying to catch up for all the years we missed," she smiled.

That was another thing I didn't understand, until one night at my new house, when we were both hanging some drapes – or trying to, she explained it a little. "I once told Lee that if I could turn back time to me being sixteen years old I would find him out and demand for him to marry me on the spot," she said. "I then thought about what I'd just said and I could have eaten myself."

I listened as she shook her head.

"I was being selfish. I hated who I was and the life that I had and I was putting my own wishes first. The upshot was, is that I couldn't have ever imagined our life without the children, so much so, I ended up apologising to him for what I had said."

"I know how much you love them," I said. "We all do."

"Lee just told me that I had to do what I had done for him to find me," she smiled. "How do you respond to something as sweet as that?"

I thought their life was nothing short of perfect and I said as much.

"Not always Abi," she said, whilst juggling with a curtain clip in her mouth and trying to pin the curtain itself to the rail.

"My ex was extremely controlling and abusive, and there were times when I just wanted to end it."

"End it?" I inquired.

"Mmm – end it, end it," she said.

"Wow," was all I could say.

"There were a lot of dark days," she said.

"Sorry about that M – I never knew."

"I did some pretty stupid things, one of which was angling for something of an old flame to help me get away from him, which was one of the stupidest things that I had ever done in my life," she said. "I wanted out, but all he wanted was sex. In the end, neither of us got what we wanted, and when my ex found out he made his point. The ex-boyfriend ended up in hiding and I ended up with renal trauma courtesy of a ruptured kidney and a fractured pelvis."

"God – that's awful M," I said. "Does Lee know."

"Lee knows a lot, as a true relationship has few secrets," she said. "However, as Lee will tell you, some things are best left in the past. But as for your question – no, love, he doesn't."

I just looked at her, as she continued clipping the curtains to the rail.

"It caused loads of complications when I had Sammy."

"I'm really sorry, M."

There was also something else that I had noticed. Not only did M never wear any jewelery apart from her engagement ring, wedding ring and maybe the odd pair of pair of earrings, she also never seemed to where anything with short sleeves.

Prior to Tuscany, I had seen her in loads of dresses both on and off set – some long, some short, some off the shoulder, some not – but they always had long sleeves. It was over in Italy, that I had noticed that her left elbow was out of synch – not much, but I noticed it all the same. Her ex had twisted her arm so much that he had given her what she termed as an Olecranon fracture.

"He knew how to hurt people and without it showing," she told me. "Anywhere apart from the face was fair game to him."

"Does it still hurt?" I asked her.

"I don't really feel pain like normal people," she said.

"Mentally I would – say if Lee left me, cheated on me or whatever, but physically Abi – I'm off the scale, so much so, I quite like it."

I couldn't believe what she was telling me.

"I told you that one in confidence Abi," she said. "Jeanette is the only person that I've ever told about the violence from my ex."

"What about the pain-thingy?" I inquired.

"That's never really been brought up," she smiled.

"However, at times I will admit that at times it drives Lee batty."

I loved hearing her speak. The candour and the hones-ty. I could listen to her all day.

"My ex knew he was losing me and did whatever he could to keep me in my place," she said. "Until I met Lee my life was like being in a dark tunnel with just that glimmer of light at the end."

"And that light was Lee?" I inquired.

When I first met him, I found myself pouring my heart out," she said. "Unfortunately, his life was nearly as bad as he was all over the place."

"Yeh – but you ended up together."

"We did," she laughed. "I think we both needed looking after."

"I actually remember when he first met you," I told her.

"Yer can?" she beamed.

"I can certainly remember you leaving him," I winked.

"I never really left him," she said. "I just wanted him to show that he loved me and to come and find me.

"And he did," I said.

"He did, and I had never felt so proud in all my life," she smiled.

"I knew there and then that I definitely had to marry him and have loads of his babies."

"I'd love children," I told her. "However, having a fear of you-know-what's makes going down that route a bit awkward."

"It's also a bit awkward not having a boyfriend," she winked.

"Yeh – a bit of a bummer that," I laughed.

The **Arsenal**

The Return of the Prodigal Son. *10ᵗʰ August, 1977.*
Against the wishes of some of the directors, 41-year old Don Howe re-joined Arsenal, which proved to be a major turning point for the club.

Don was certainly no manager, but tactically was without doubt, the best coach in the country and perhaps saved Terry Neill's job.

1-0 to The Arsenal. *24ᵗʰ January, 1978.*
League Cup Quarter-Final Replay. Arsenal 1, Manchester City 0

In front of a crowd of 57,960, Liam Brady converts a penalty
against Manchester City and then swings on the bar to celebrate.

"They were doubling up at the turnstiles all around the ground –
there must have been well over sixty thousand in that night." Nat
Young, ex-Tottenham Hotspur Youth player and Arsenal Supporter

In Neill's Defence. *David O'Leary was who Neill and Howe wanted to build their defence around. Neill spent much of the 1976-80's season's continually looking to replace Sammy Nelson and made several inquiries for Kenny Sansom, Derek Statham, John Bailey, Joe Bolton and Kevin Hird.*

Neill was also looking to replace Willie Young and made inquiries for Gordon McQueen, David Narey, Roy Aitken and Alex McLeish, and even had a £225,000 bid for Ajax's Ruud Krol turned down in early September, 1978.

The problem was that Arsenal wouldn't pay the money.

The Future is Bright. *8th March 1978.*
The F.A Cup Semi-Final. Arsenal 3, Orient 0.

Frank Stapleton and Liam Brady congratulate scorer Graham Rix.

"This was a muted annihilation," wrote Hugh McIlvanney of the Observer.
"Brady and Hudson flaunted their class in the midfield with relaxed and justified
presumptuousness and at the front Macdonald swerved and darted among the
opposing defenders. When Arsenal became more profitably aggressive it was mainly
through Macdonald, who was in one of those moods when his muscular and mobile
presence is liable to make the most composed defenders panic. Hudson who has
rediscovered the vigour and delicacy of touch that once made him one of the greatest
prospects of British football was another insistent aggravation."

The best first half of football ever seen at Highbury.
18th March 1978. Arsenal 4, Bristol City 1

Alan Sunderland fires home the third goal.

"Bristol had no answer to the languid left foot magic of Liam Brady, the fastidious passing of Alan Hudson, who looks like he is back to stay and the fierce drive of the fair-haired David Price," wrote Alan Hoby of the Sunday Express.

Where Arsenal under Neill Peaked. *1ˢᵗ April, 1978.*
Arsenal 3, Manchester United 1.

Liam Brady and Malcolm Macdonald celebrate as Arsenal put United to the sword.

"Arsenal played the most superb football that I've seen this season," wrote David Miller of the Daily Express. "The left-sided penetration of Liam Brady, Graham Rix and Malcolm Macdonald with support from Frank Stapleton, David Price and Alan Hudson was as good as anything I've seen. It was so fluent, that it even drew spontaneous applause from the main bevy of United supporters."

The Erratic Genius. *15ᵗʰ April, 1978.*
Arsenal 2, Newcastle United 1

"Alan Hudson's ambling control always threatened to turn this low-key game and he sent in a beautifully floated cross from the right with all the nonchalance of flicking a speck of dust off his lapel, for David Price to ram home the winner," wrote James Lawton of the Daily Express

Firing Blanks. *6ᵗʰ May, 1978.*
The F.A Cup Final. Ipswich Town 1, Arsenal 0.

*Arsenal's swashbuckling centre-forward Malcolm Macdonald was
carrying a knee injury and only managed a single shot on target. A few
days later he would undergo a cartilage operation, but the reality of it
was, is that this would be one of his last ever games.*

Lightning Source UK Ltd.
Milton Keynes UK
UKOW04f0608051017
310455UK00001B/52/P